Orange Blossom Days

ALSO BY PATRICIA SCANLAN

Apartment 3B

Finishing Touches

Foreign Affairs

Promises, Promises

Mirror Mirror

Francesca's Party

Two for Joy

Double Wedding

Divided Loyalties

Coming Home

With All My Love

A Time for Friends

TRILOGIES

City Girl

City Lives

City Woman

Forgive and Forget

Happy Ever After

Love and Marriage

Orange Blossom Days

A Novel

Patricia Scanlan

ATRIA PAPERBACK

NEW YORK   LONDON   TORONTO   SYDNEY   NEW DELHI

ATRIA
PAPERBACK

An Imprint of Simon & Schuster, Inc.
1230 Avenue of the Americas
New York, NY 10020

Originally published in Great Britain in 2017 by Simon & Schuster
UK Ltd.

First Atria Paperback edition March 2018

ATRIA PAPERBACK and colophon are trademarks of
Simon & Schuster, Inc.

For information about special discounts for bulk purchases, please
contact Simon & Schuster Special Sales at 1-866-506-1949 or
business@simonandschuster.com.

The Simon & Schuster Speakers Bureau can bring authors to your
live event. For more information, or to book an event, contact the
Simon & Schuster Speakers Bureau at 1-866-248-3049 or visit our
website at www.simonspeakers.com.

Interior design by Kyoko Watanabe

Manufactured in the United States of America

10 9 8 7 6 5 4 3 2 1

Library of Congress Cataloging-in-Publication Data has been
applied for.

ISBN 978-1-5011-8103-0
ISBN 978-1-5011-8104-7 (ebook)

It was such a treat to set *Orange Blossom Days* in the south of Spain, where I've had great holidays and made some dear friends over the years.

He pasado algunos de mis momentos más felices en El Capricho, Calahonda, donde he degustado comida maravillosa y he llegado a conocer al fantástico personal, los mejores de la costa. Salvador, ir a tu chiringuito es como volver a casa. Me hace muy feliz dedicaros este libro a ti, Svetlana, Maurizio, Pedro, Juan, Antonio, Alberto, Antonio, Paco y Sylvia. Gracias por los abrazos, las cálidas bienvenidas, y los muchos Baileys, en la casa.

(I've spent some of my happiest times in **El Capricho, Calahonda**, where I've eaten wonderful food and got to know the fantastic staff, who are the best on the Costa. Salvador, coming to your *chiringuito* is like coming home: I am so happy to dedicate my book to you and Svetlana, Maurizio, Pedro, Juan, Antonio, Alberto, Antonio, Paco, and Sylvia. Thanks for the hugs and warm welcomes and the many Baileys, on the house.)

To Monir Alina, John and Sylvia Roots, and Sinead, Alannah and Oliver, great neighbors.

And to Emma and Brendan of **Be Clean**, who looked after and maintained our apartment as if it was their own, and who have become great friends.

And huge thanks to Aurora Garcia and Carlos, who worked so hard to make Mi Capricho a little piece of paradise, and who were always extremely helpful. And of course Tommy and Fabiana also, who run a fantastic Pool Bar and always give us a great reception when we come back.

And to new friends Jason and Luis, owners of **Atlantis Prop-**

erty Management and Real Estate SL: thanks for taking us all under your wings.

And to the staff of **The Hotel Petit Palace Santa Cruz,** Seville: thank you for delightful stays in your lovely hotel. Looking forward to coming back for many more.

Muchas gracias queridos amigos.

La Joya de Andalucía

The Jewel of Andalucía

Prologue

Anna

The AGM was in uproar. The clique from Madrid was protesting loudly at the attack on *El Presidente*.

"Standards are dropping," roared a French owner from Block 3.

"Pets were not allowed in the original constitution. And it should be kept like that. I am not prepared to pay maintenance fees to be kept awake by yapping pom-poms and have the smell of their turds wafting across my balcony! Just because he"—a German owner whose visage was the color of a crushed plum pointed a shaking finger at *El Presidente*—"because he wants his dog coming on holidays with him. Probably too mean to pay kennel fees," he added irately, wiping his dripping brow with a freshly laundered handkerchief.

"I want to know if *El Presidente* is prepared to pay, out of his *own* pocket, the money the community has been forced to pay, so he could appoint his smarmy little friend Facundo as a new concierge. How much of a backhand did he get for *that*?" Moira Anderson's indignant Scottish burr rang out over the hum of the air-conditioning. The *madrileños*, led by *El Presidente*'s cousin, erupted in furious denial at this scurrilous accusation.

"Well said, madam, well said!" an Englishman from Block 1 applauded. "Answer the question, Mr. President. Or, even better, resign!"

Anna MacDonald felt the throb of a headache begin over her left eye and temple. The ruckus would put the Barbary macaques in Gibraltar to shame, she thought wearily as the noisy yakking increased in tempo.

She and her husband, Austen, had holidayed in the south of Spain since their three children were toddlers. Taking charter holidays with JWT, which they'd saved hard for in the credit union. She'd always loved when the holiday brochures came out every January, and paid particular attention to the complexes that offered children's clubs.

As they became more affluent and their three children got older, they'd camped in France, explored Tuscany, and golfed in Portugal, but Andalucía's charms—the Moorish cities and towns, the food, the hospitality and friendliness of the Spanish people— lured them back many times over the years, and when she and Austen had first bought their penthouse apartment in La Joya de Andalucía, they'd been over the moon with delight. They'd taken early retirement to enjoy their sixties and they'd envisaged spending the long, dark winter months in their idyllic paradise. Now, several years down the road, life had changed to one she'd never imagined. And community politics, a recession, and bad behavior had turned life in La Joya sour. "The Jewel of Andalucía" had lost its sparkle for sure.

This carry-on just affirmed that she'd made the right decision. Anna noted *El Presidente*'s cold, stern, and forbidding gaze. *I've had enough of you, you little dictator,* she thought as she glared back at him, knowing that despite the uproar he would most likely be reelected, because most of the owners couldn't bear the hassle of taking on the responsibility the position entailed. And many wouldn't travel to attend the AGM in August, due to the oppressive heat. The Spanish clique would have their way once again and

El Presidente would be king of his own little fiefdom. As autocratic as a Saudi despot. Yapping dogs were a new lowering of standards, maintenance fees would rise, and *El Presidente* would sit on his balcony, monarch of all he surveyed, while his subjects grumbled among themselves at the poolside bar, plotting his overthrow at the *next* AGM.

Would she want to sit here in this hotel, in the small town of San Antonio del Mar, this time next year and listen to the same sort of carry-on? *Nope,* Anna decided. The Spanish dream was over. It was time to face up to reality, mend fences with her family, and go home. She'd run away for long enough.

Sally-Ann

Sally-Ann Connolly Cooper watched the shenanigans at the AGM, amused in spite of herself. This annual event was always so entertaining. At other AGMs she'd attended, she would meet up afterwards with her Spanish lover and tell him all the news. After their lusty lovemaking they would laugh and chat as they always did, sipping champagne, before he would leave her. This year, though, everything was *very* different. Her lover was getting married, and circumstances had changed radically in her own life. At the wrong side of thirty, it was time she settled down, Sally-Ann thought in amusement.

Who would have thought things would turn out the way they had? She would be going home to Texas with her twin daughters, to a very different setup. A better, more positive situation for *all* of them. And she wouldn't be saying good-bye to La Joya. She wouldn't have to saddle up and move on from her Andalucían paradise.

From the moment she'd stood on the wide wraparound balcony of the penthouse and looked, in awe, across the shimmering sea to the mysterious, magical High Atlas mountains on the continent of Africa, and seen the Pillars of Hercules stand guard over the narrow strait that separated the Atlantic Ocean from the Mediterranean, she'd known that Andalucía was special. It had been her first visit to Spain. A business trip with her husband, Cal, who owned a successful holiday rental company in the States. Branching out in Europe was a relatively new development for Cooper Enterprises, but it was paying dividends in more ways than one.

Sally-Ann sipped her complimentary prosecco, surprised at how relieved she was at the decision she'd made about her relationship with Cal. A relationship that had brought moments of grief and joy in equal measure, and a family unit that had survived because she hadn't let bitterness ruin her life.

Eduardo

Eduardo De La Fuente strove to keep his composure while he listened to the many complaints being hurled in his direction. What was wrong with these *imbécils*? Could they not see the improvements he'd brought to La Joya de Andalucía? The changes he'd wrought under his presidency had brought order and ease to the ungrateful owners' lives.

It was imperative that he be elected to continue his raft of improvements. But he knew too that he could not face being deposed in front of Beatriz, the woman who had reared him after his family had moved to New York. Her immense pride in his elevation to the position of president of the community had been heartwarming. At last he'd truly achieved something, in her eyes. Not even his position as a notary had given him this much satisfaction, Eduardo admitted ruefully.

And very soon he would be exchanging his third-floor apartment for the much-sought-after penthouse apartment he'd long desired, from the moment he'd set foot in the luxurious apartment complex. The closing of his property purchase was occurring in the next hour, in a notary's office in Marbella. *That* acquisition would be his crowning glory. Beatriz would not be able to tell him ever again that "second best is not good enough." For the first time in his life he'd taken a risk and it would be worth it.

He hoped his wife, Consuela, would be pleased. Since she'd started her *menopausia* she'd become more forceful, less pliant to his needs and wishes. Sometimes she was uncharacteristically stubborn. And as for all this New Age stuff she'd got into with her cousin, this so-called Renewal of Divine Feminine Energy she was embracing—such nonsense!

Eduardo refrained from rolling his eyes in derision. Consuela was seated in the audience, looking into the far distance, a million miles away in spirit, from the AGM and him!

How he looked forward to moving into his new abode. His aerie, from which he would be able to overlook everything and everyone in the community. Knowing that the owner who was selling up was a fierce opponent of his and would never have sold to him, Eduardo had bought the penthouse through a third party. A sly move but necessary. A faint flush tinged his sallow cheeks as a memory surfaced. This was not the time or place to think of her or *that*!

Eduardo turned his attention back to the business at hand, noticing the Irishwoman who had been elected to the position of secretary at the first AGM was glaring at him. She was very friendly with Constanza Torres, the concierge, another thorn in his side. He stared back coldly at Anna. Soon he too would be a *penthouse* owner and she could keep her glares to herself, as could the rest of the plebs with whom he was not in favor. He had his loyal supporters and today they would keep him—*por favor, Dios*—in his post as *El Presidente* of La Joya de Andalucía, a position in which he rightfully belonged.

Consuela

Consuela De La Fuente prayed fervently that her husband, Eduardo, would be reelected to the position of president of the management committee so she wouldn't have to live with his gloom and ire if he was rejected. Who would have thought Eduardo would turn this heavenly place into a . . . a . . . combat zone, she thought irritably. It was her own fault. She'd always adored the south and the sea. Coming down to the Costa reminded her of childhood days when her dear papa would drive the family from Madrid to spend a month with his brother and family in a house with blue shutters and a shaded, cobbled courtyard two minutes from the sea, in La Cala, further up the coast. Eduardo had had no such treats. A week in a village in the Pyrenees with Beatriz's cousin had been his annual childhood holiday. The highlight of which was a trip to Girona.

When Consuela had introduced him to the delights of La Cala and Andalucía, Eduardo had taken to it immediately, and from the first year they were married, he'd always spent most of August playing golf, enjoying the reviving sea breezes and laid-back lifestyle and escaping the scorching heat of the capital. It had always been a relaxing holiday, until they'd bought their own apartment. Or rather *he* had bought the apartment without telling her . . . to "surprise" her!

Sometimes, especially at AGM time, Consuela wondered if it was more trouble than it was worth.

Jutta

Jutta knew her window of opportunity was limited. She had to stay calm and make the most of the AGM at La Joya that was, very fortuitously for her, taking place right now, giving her some leeway to get on with her business. She felt sick. Nerves, she supposed disconsolately. She still couldn't believe all that had happened in the space of six weeks to turn her life upside down.

Her phone rang. It was Felipe, her husband.

"Did you get the tickets?" he asked.

"Yes," she said coolly. "I printed them out."

"OK, good, see you soon." He hung up.

Jutta sighed. Felipe, the love of her life. And this was what he'd brought them to. Perhaps her father had been right about him. Her papa had always had his reservations about his son-in-law.

A tear coursed down Jutta's cheek. Angrily she wiped it away. She didn't have time for tears or regrets. She had work to do. She glanced at her watch. The AGM was well under way. Would Eduardo De La Fuente be reelected? He was a very complex man, very power hungry. It would be a huge disappointment for him if he wasn't voted back in.

Jutta always enjoyed getting the gossip from Constanza. What would the concierge and Anna, Sally-Ann, and all her other clients say about her when they heard the news? To think she'd once dreamed about buying a penthouse in La Joya and becoming neighbors with the people she worked for. And it could have happened. In her mid-thirties now, she'd achieved far more than she'd ever expected out of life and been well on track to realize her dreams, she thought bitterly.

"Oh, just stop feeling sorry for yourself and get going," Jutta muttered irritably. She had to feed her young daughter as well as everything else because her au pair had left her in the lurch. What did she care about the owners in La Joya de Andalucía and their drama-filled AGMs? She'd enough drama in her own life.

PART I

Times of Our Lives

April 2006

OPENING WEEK

Señora Constanza Torres, the community manager for the newly completed apartment complex, La Joya de Andalucía, logged on to her computer, arranged her pen and notepad tidily on her desk, and placed the stack of acceptance forms containing the names and addresses of the new owners into a clear plastic folder that was neatly labeled. Constanza was nothing if not organized.

Today, after months of preparation, the apartments were ready for occupancy. The immaculate grounds were superbly landscaped. Lush flowering waterfalls of pink and purple bougainvillea cascaded over walls and balconies. The two swimming pools seemed in the early morning sun as though the universe had cast handfuls of glittering diamonds into their still, azure water. A hint of a breeze whispered through the drooping green fronds of the palm trees dotted around the lawns, and the scents of mimosa and lavender added to the luxurious ambiance of the gated frontline complex, which was so aptly named. The Jewel of Andalucía was her pride and joy and today, and in the weeks to come, Constanza would welcome the new owners and help them to settle into their holiday homes on Spain's southern coast.

The setting was unrivaled anywhere else on the Costa, Constanza thought proudly. Within sight of the majestic, imposing Rock of Gibraltar to their right; mysterious Africa looming in awe-inspiring grandeur on the horizon; and, to the left of them along the curving coastline, Estepona and Puerto Banús, playgrounds of the wealthy, international jet set. Behind the impressive development, the high Reales de Sierra Bermeja with their jagged-edged peaks was Constanza's favorite view, especially when the setting sun slipped gently down behind them, burnishing the sky with a kaleidoscope of pinks, purples, and gold banners.

She'd spoken to many of the new owners on the phone over the past months: soon, she would finally get to meet them in person. This new community would house a wide variety of residents from all over Europe and beyond. Most of them had been friendly, polite, excited, but a few had ruffled her feathers, most notably a dour Belgian lady who insisted she be allowed to bring her pet poodle, Poirot. Patiently but firmly, Constanza had explained there was a no-pet policy, enshrined in the Articles of Association, which were part of the terms and conditions of purchase. After many vexatious phone calls, Constanza was not looking forward to meeting *that* particular owner.

A rather serious and intense man from Madrid, Eduardo De La Fuente, was extremely insistent that all business be conducted through his secretary, and under no circumstances was any post to be sent, or phone calls made, to his private residence. Constanza wondered if he was buying his apartment as a love nest for his mistress. The secretary, a brisk, bossy, decidedly unchatty lady, always spoke of her boss in hushed tones as though he were God and, of course, conveyed the air of superiority common to the *madrileños*. Constanza was extremely interested to meet *him*.

The complex was unnaturally still. No builders, gardeners, plumbers, or electricians. It would never be this silent again, never be totally hers again as it had been all these past months.

She sat absorbing the silence, preparing for the busy days that lay ahead. The bell on the intercom rang. Her first clients. Constanza patted her hair, sat up straight, and pressed the entry key, watching as the gate opened smoothly to permit a taxi to enter.

As graciously as though she were inviting guests into her home, Constanza stood, hand extended, and smiled a welcome as a middle-aged, smartly dressed couple came through her office door.

"Welcome to La Joya de Andalucía. I am Señora Constanza Torres, your community manager," she introduced herself, both in Spanish and English, as she would to many new proprietors during the following days.

Chapter One

Anna / Austen

"Mr. and Mrs. MacDonald, these are your keys and gate fob. This one is for the entrance to your building, the community gates, and the garage. This one is your door key. My name is Señora Constanza Torres. I am the community manager. If you have any problems please don't hesitate to contact me. Let me take you to your new penthouse." The petite, middle-aged Spanish woman with flashing brown-black eyes and henna-hued, neatly bobbed hair smiled at Anna and her husband, Austen, as she handed them the keys to their new holiday home. Her English, though heavily accented, was perfect.

"*Por favor,*" a slim, handsome Spanish man in a navy suit who was standing in the doorway interrupted brusquely, and began speaking in rapid-fire Spanish that Anna, with her schoolgirl Spanish, could not follow.

Constanza Torres held up her hand authoritatively. "*Un momento por favor, Señor—*"

"*¿Cuánto tiempo llevará esto?*"

He was asking how long this would take, Anna translated, guessing that he was a new owner also. Imperious, arrogant, and a tad rude were her first impressions of the Spaniard, and she hoped that he wouldn't be their immediate neighbor.

"Be seated, if you please. I'll come to you when it is your time. There are others before you." Señora Torres spoke in English, unimpressed with her fellow countryman's officious impatience. She gave a dismissive wave towards the cane lounging chairs dotted around the tiled terrace at the entrance to the building, where another couple, a tall redhead and an equally tall dark-haired American man, waited to be given their keys. The community manager turned her attention back to the MacDonalds, a hint of exasperation flickering in her expressive brown eyes.

Anna suppressed a smile. It was clear the other man was not used to being so summarily dismissed and ignored. His mouth opened in astonishment at the manager's impertinence. He turned on his heel and marched over to a chair, glowering at them once he was seated, his fingers drumming a tattoo on the armrest.

"Let me show you to your apartment building," Señora Torres offered, disregarding him.

"Thank you, Señora." Austen stood back politely to let her precede him.

Constanza bowed graciously and led the way across the terrace and down the steps to the pathway that led through the verdant gardens towards their whitewashed building with its Moorish arches and mosaic-tiled finishes, which faced the sea.

"Oh, Austen, I'm so excited." Anna took her husband's hand and he squeezed hers back. "Isn't it something else that we own a place in Spain and can come out whenever we want? It will be great for the family to come over and join us now and again."

"Now and again," he warned. "Conor won't be interested, Tara will come to flop, but you know what Chloe's like . . . She'll want to bring all her pals out to party. We'll be lucky to get a look in!"

"She's just very sociable," Anna defended their youngest daughter.

"Too sociable for me," Austen retorted. "This is *our* haven, Anna."

"I know," she agreed lightly. "I can't quite believe it."

"Me neither. Imagine spending our winters out here away from freezing winds and non-stop rain. Imagine playing golf every single day!" Austen grinned at her, his tanned face flushed with pride at the rewards their hard work over the years had now brought them. A penthouse apartment in a plush seafront complex on Spain's southern coast. Who would have thought they would ever be able to afford such a luxury, he reflected, remembering that at the beginning of their marriage, all those years ago, he and Anna hadn't had two pennies to rub together.

"We deserve this, and how!" he declared, inhaling the scents of the flowering shrubs that wafted by on the balmy, salty sea breeze. "I was dreading retirement, but not now."

Anna laughed. "You mean you were dreading spending all that time with *me*. Sure, I'll probably see even less of you now than I did before, if you're going to be spending *every* day on the golf course."

"Well, not *every* day and not *all* the time. Think of what we can do for siesta in our little love nest," Austen murmured, winking and jangling the keys to their new abode.

Señora Torres opened the door to the first block of apartments that faced the sea and led them through a cool, marble-tiled entrance hall painted in shades of cream and duck-egg blue towards a lift. "Each floor has two apartments, but the penthouse does not share a landing; it is most private," she explained as the doors slid open. She jabbed the button for the fifth floor and they glided smoothly upwards. Anna couldn't contain her excitement when she stepped into the tiled hall and saw the white-painted door facing her with the number 9 in gleaming brass, just above the equally shiny brass doorknob.

The concierge smiled proudly at Austen as though she were personally gifting them their new home. "You may open." She indicated his keys. "Enjoy your new penthouse. I'll be in the office if you have any queries," she said before reentering the lift, smiling at them as the door closed and the lift began its descent.

Anna's first impressions were of bright lemony light as sunbeams spilled in through the floor-to-ceiling windows onto the honey-tinted tones of the marble floor. The smell of new wood and fresh paint was intoxicating and she stood in the center of the lounge breathing in the scents, remembering, unexpectedly, her exhilaration when she and Austen had got the keys to their three-bed semi in a newly built estate in Swords over thirty-two years ago.

Where had those years gone? How was it possible that she had two daughters, twenty-eight and twenty-three, and a son of twenty-five? How was it possible that in four years time she would be sixty? Sometimes the notion shocked her to her core!

Don't think about it, enjoy this new chapter in your life, she told herself briskly, gazing around at her surroundings. She would paint the lounge a buttery cream, she decided, with light blue accessories: this was going to be fun with a capital *F*.

Standing on the terrace looking out over the sapphire Mediterranean, a molten silky sheath with hardly a ripple on its gilded waters, Anna wondered if she would wake up and discover it was a dream. Austen was going to retire from his position as senior account manager with an international advertising agency, and she was going to hand over the reins of the cleaning company she'd built up—from a two-person operation to a company employing forty—to her manager.

It was going to be a massive change, she admitted, handing over control of the company she'd birthed, grown, fretted over, and run, with time-consuming passion, for so much of her married life. Would she adjust to a life not controlled by the demands of business? Even now, on holidays in Spain, she was edgy, constantly restraining herself from checking emails on her phone, expecting calls about some crisis or other. Austen had warned her to stay off her mobile. His was turned off. He'd no problem disconnecting, or retiring.

"I want to enjoy life while I'm still able to, before sinking into decrepitude. It's not all about work and material things, Anna, and I want to enjoy time with you. It's our time." Austen was surprisingly firm about it. And he was right, she admitted with some relief. She was exhausted, burnt-out, and flying on fumes. Being a full-time wife, mother, and MD was getting harder to juggle as she aged. In her thirties and forties she'd had boundless energy, but not anymore. She lived with a permanent weariness, chasing her free time like a miser chasing gold.

Her husband was right: they had worked damn hard for decades. He was sixty-two, she was fifty-six; their three children were reared and two had flown the nest. From now on it was all about reaping the rewards of their endeavors.

She couldn't wait to start decorating and buying furniture. They were going to employ the services of a German woman—a friend of theirs had suggested employing her—who operated from Marbella and was an expert at fitting out new apartments . . . fast.

Anna and Austen wanted to be able to use the penthouse as soon as they possibly could, without the hassle of waiting for furniture and drapes and kitchenware to be delivered. This Jutta Sauer person came highly recommended. She would supervise all deliveries and have the apartment cleaned and ready for occupation the next time they came out to Spain. They were meeting her later for an initial consultation and then the following morning to start furniture shopping immediately.

They were staying at a friend's apartment further up the coast, and though it was gorgeous, and they'd always enjoyed visiting, now that their own was handed over to them, they were longing to move in.

"Oh, Austen, look!" Anna exclaimed, noticing the bottle of champagne in an ice bucket, and two champagne flutes on the kitchen counter. "What a classy touch," she remarked, reading the welcome card from the sales firm who had sold them the penthouse.

"Let's crack it open! That's the joy of taking taxis. You can imbibe at any time of the day." Austen expertly uncorked the bottle. He poured the sparkling golden liquid into the glasses, handed her one, and raised his to hers. "I'm so glad we've done this, Anna. I know you weren't too sure at first when I showed you the brochure, but right this minute I couldn't think of anything better to do with my lump sum. It's an investment that's going to give us a *lot* of pleasure. To retirement—to us!" he toasted, his eyes glinting with anticipation.

"Yes, Austen, to us," Anna clinked back, feeling a surge of love for her husband. "We've done our bit, now it's *all* about us!"

◆

Austen tucked into a feast of perfectly cooked mussels in his favorite *chiringuito* on the southern coast of Spain: El Capricho. Anna was relishing every mouthful of her crispy lemon whitebait. "I love this place, I love the staff, I love the food, and I love the views," his wife said, taking a sip of chilled white wine and offering him one of her fish.

"Me too. There's some fine restaurants in San Antonio del Mar, and the *chiringuito* on the beach is good, but El Capricho has something that brings you back time and again, doesn't it?" Austen shucked some of his mussels onto her plate.

"I always feel completely relaxed the minute I sit down and order a G&T here. I love that Svetlana and Maurizio always know our drinks order every time we come back." The waiting staff of the popular restaurant were consummately professional but great fun, and there was always a lot of good-humored banter between them and the diners. Eating there had become a much-enjoyed ritual of their annual holidays.

It was coming to stay regularly with his golfing friends over the years that had persuaded Austen to consider buying a property on the coast. When he'd seen a glossy brochure for La Joya in the golf club in Marbella, he'd shown it to Anna and persuaded her that they should buy. She'd demurred at first, and he knew that part of her reluctance was because of their "children," as she persisted in calling them, to his mild irritation. She spent too much time running around after them. They were adults now, he pointed out, perfectly capable of running their own lives without their parents by their sides. She was only using them as an excuse, he'd insisted. His wife had got defensive, and told him he was talking rubbish and gone into one of her snits, but he'd stuck to his guns and told her she'd need to make a decision quickly, as the apartments were getting snapped up. He'd bulldozed her, he admitted privately, but she'd come around to his way of thinking and had given the joint purchase her blessing.

Now that they owned a property abroad, and he was retiring, he intended spending long chunks of time with Anna, exploring the cities and diverse regions of Spain at their leisure.

Leisure . . . what a delightful concept, Austen thought contentedly, sitting back in his chair, replete, signaling Maurizio to refill their glasses. Anna might have difficulty letting go of work; he would have none. After years of conscientious hard graft, Austen was looking forward to a work-free, "child"-free retirement immensely.

Chapter Two

Sally-Ann / Cal

"Well, what do you think?" Callahan Cooper closed the door behind the concierge and stood with his arms folded, looking around the clinically white lounge of the penthouse with its breathtaking views of the Mediterranean, the distant coastline and mysterious mountains of Morocco, and the massive slab of limestone rock that was Gibraltar.

"Awesome, Cal, truly awesome," his wife, Sally-Ann, enthused, gazing at the vista before stepping outside through the floor-to-ceiling sliding doors onto the large wraparound terracotta-tiled balcony. "And that breeze is to die for," she sighed, running her fingers through her mane of auburn hair.

They explored their new business acquisition, admiring the size of the rooms, their views, and the high-end finish, which was certainly on a par with many of Cal's other properties stateside. Buying rentals in Europe had increased his property portfolio enormously and added another dimension to his company. In spite of all that had happened between them, Sally-Ann couldn't help but admire his business acumen.

He opened closet doors, running an expert eye over their

layout. "This is just fine," he approved. "An excellent finish." His cell phone rang and she saw him glance at the number and slide it back into his chinos pocket.

"Take it," she said coolly. "It must be important, this is the third time it's rung in the last hour."

"It's cool. I'll catch them later," her husband said, shrugging, walking along the hallway towards the third bedroom. Sally-Ann's lips tightened. This latest bimbo was persistent, for sure. There was something different about this one. She couldn't put her finger on it. Cal was edgy, preoccupied. Perhaps this was "the One" that would finally lead to their divorce. Sally-Ann felt a knot tie up her gut. It had always been on the cards that this day would come. She wandered out to the balcony again, enjoying the way the breeze lifted her hair from her forehead, caressing her skin with its welcome, feathery touch.

After she'd found out for the first time several years ago that Cal had been unfaithful to her, and once the initial shock, anger, and grief had lessened somewhat, she'd decided for the sake of the children not to sue for divorce until they were older. Privately, she and Cal had agreed to go their separate ways. They could each see whomsoever they wanted to see, but her bottom line was no children with other partners unless they were divorced; and if either of them met someone they felt they could make a future with, then they would divorce as amicably as possible.

It had worked out reasonably well once she'd turned her back on her emotional longing for her husband and faced what had to be faced in her usual pragmatic way. But sometimes she felt she was being cowardly, using her girls as an excuse not to face the trauma and upheaval of divorce. Perhaps that dreaded time was now imminent, Sally-Ann surmised wearily.

"I'm tired. I'd like to go back to the hotel; it's been a long day." She walked back into the lounge, the stiletto heels of her Manolos echoing in the empty space.

"Sure thing," Cal agreed. "I'm going to play a round in Estepona. You have a siesta and we'll have dinner at the hotel. I'll book a table for eight." Sally-Ann saw the look of relief flash across her husband's face.

Couldn't wait to get away and ring his lady friend, she thought sourly as he closed and locked the door before following her across the entrance hall to the elevator.

They sat in silence while he drove along the winding coastal road that led from the apartments to the exclusive spa hotel in the charming town of San Antonio del Mar, west of Estepona. The whitewashed villas with their riotous abundance of colorful hanging baskets and the busy restaurants and tapas bars with their jaunty bright awnings soothed her irritation a little as she stared out through the car window and thought how gloriously vibrant Andalucía was.

One of the perks of being married to the owner and CEO of a holiday let firm was the opportunity to travel. Cal had branched out into European properties in the last few years and Sally-Ann had very much enjoyed her trips abroad. European culture and the fascinating histories and traditions of the countries she visited were such a contrast to her native Texas, and she soaked it all up eagerly and felt, sometimes, that she'd been born on the wrong continent.

"Go have a massage or a manicure and pedicure or whatever," Cal suggested, pulling up to the pillared portico of their hotel, where a doorman stood ready to open the car door for her.

"Perhaps I will. Enjoy your golf, and ring your lady friend and put her out of her misery." Sally-Ann slanted a cool glance at him.

Cal couldn't meet her eye. "You've had your flings," he muttered sullenly.

"Only after you had yours first. See y'all." She nodded at the doorman and he opened the passenger door with a polite smile. Sally-Ann swung her long, tanned legs out of the car and made a graceful exit. Head up, her face a mask of bland disinterest, she didn't look back.

◆

Cal sighed a force ten sigh as he watched his wife stride purposefully into the hotel. Women were the bane of his life, he scowled, revving the car engine and pulling away from the curb. Maybe he wouldn't go and play golf; maybe he'd just go and tie one on and give himself some Dutch courage for what was to come.

His cell rang again and connected to the Bluetooth. Four phone calls in less than two hours. Lenora could take lessons from his wife in how to behave in a cool manner.

"Yup?" he growled, taking the call.

"Have you said anything yet?" His mistress's voice was as clear as a bell. Hard to believe she was in a suite in the Ritz in Paris, nearly two thousand kilometers away.

"Nope!"

"Cal!" she exclaimed exasperatedly.

"Tonight, babe, tonight, I told ya that. Now, quit buggin' me or I won't say anything."

"Aw, hon," she sighed.

"It's OK, calm down, sugar doll. Why don't you go and de-stress with a massage or a manicure and pedicure," Cal suggested to a woman for the second time that day. "Put it on the tab."

"OK. I miss you, sweetie," Lenora said dolefully.

"I miss you too, darlin'. I'll see you when I see you. Bye, now." He didn't give her time to respond but clicked off the phone vowing to take no more calls this day.

He headed towards Estepona, enjoying the fast drive on the coastal autoroute. Spanish drivers were less civilized than their French counterparts, he acknowledged, listening to a cacophony of horns beeping at an unfortunate tourist who'd got his lanes confused. European driving didn't faze him, he was used to driving on the left. If he had the choice, he'd drive straight to Málaga Airport, fly to Paris, collect Lenora, and take the first flight out of Charles de Gaulle to Houston, but he couldn't leave Sally-Ann high and dry. He had to tell her that everything was going to change. She was his wife. She played her role with grace and panache and always had. That had to count for something, he thought grimly.

◆

Sally-Ann sat in her beautifully appointed air-conditioned suite and wondered why she had bothered to come with Cal on this business trip to Europe and, even more to the point, why he had asked her, this time. Things were not good between them. He was spending increasing lengths of time traveling, and he was short-tempered and stressed.

She was a thirty-nine-year-old woman with twin daughters on the cusp of their teens and a twenty-year-old marriage that had hit the skids. She needed to cut loose and start living, she thought gloomily, sprawling on the bed to flick through the TV channels. She should get up and go and lie by the pool, or have a massage as her husband had suggested, but she felt weary and lonely. She could ring her best friend, Grace, she supposed, but rejected the idea. Talking on the phone wasn't the same as lounging around the pool at home with her, necking a Bud and venting. Grace, pragmatic as always, would only tell her to stay put.

"Ya got a rich husband, a house to die for, home help for the kids, opportunities to travel . . . Sweetie, go find your kicks if ya need to but don't throw that lifestyle away." Grace was married to a successful orthodontist and she was still crazy about him, as he was about her. She and Sally-Ann had been friends since high school.

Sally-Ann's eyelids drooped and she drifted off to sleep, the rhythmic *whoosh, whoosh* of the sea and the breeze whispering through the white muslin curtains soothing her frazzled spirit.

Chapter Three

Eduardo / Consuela

Eduardo De La Fuente seethed with anger as he watched the community manager speaking animatedly on the phone to someone, with much gesticulation and eye rolling. If his secretary conducted herself like that he would sack her, Eduardo reflected, thinking of how demure and calm Luciana was, always knowing what he needed almost before he knew himself.

Finally the irritating woman put the phone down and looked across the desk at him. "My name is Señora Constanza Torres. I am the community manager, and you are . . . ?" She arched an eyebrow at him. She wore too much eyeliner for her age, he noted dourly. No class. His wife, Consuela, wore the minimum amount of makeup and certainly not eyeliner.

"I am Señor Eduardo De La Fuente, the owner of apartment number twenty-eight. I would like my keys *immediately*, please. It's ridiculous how long I've had to wait."

"It has been a busy day. Many new owners," the community manager said coldly. "Sign here, please, to say you have received your keys." She slid the keys and a sheet of paper across her desk towards him.

Eduardo signed with a flourish and added "Notary" beside his name. Señora Torres should know with whom she was dealing, he thought pompously. He was a person of some standing, not some mere tourist who was buying a pad in Spain to bring his golfing buddies to for debauched weekends. Eduardo's nostrils on his fine aquiline nose flared slightly as he took his keys from the *vaca mandona* in front of him. He was almost tempted to privately call her *una perra*, but he normally recoiled from using bad language; it was very uncouth, as his *Tía* Beatriz had drummed into him growing up. But if he couldn't think of Señora Torres as a bitch, he could most certainly think of her as a bossy cow!

"If you have any problems, please don't hesitate to contact me. Follow me to your building please," Señora Torres said briskly, as though he were some schoolboy and not a highly respected notary with his own successful firm in Madrid. She took off at a smart clip and he followed her, disgruntled that his day of pride was being marred by yet another domineering female. No wonder he disliked the species. She and Beatriz would get on like a house on fire, or perhaps they would boss each other around. It would be interesting to see what his aunt made of this community manager. Consuela, his wife, was such a gentle soul, she would get on with the devil himself, Eduardo thought fondly, his stern features softening when he thought of his beloved.

How he wanted to surprise Consuela. She had not even seen the plans. She'd never been to San Antonio del Mar. This would be his anniversary gift to her. And how he wanted his aunt to be delighted with his purchase, and proud of *him*. *Tía* Beatriz was not easily impressed, but surely this achievement would evoke some words of praise and pleasure. A beautiful apartment in a frontline complex, with the sea practically at their door. A haven to retreat to during the scorching summer months, like many of his business acquaintances who owned properties on the coast. Ah, yes, he'd dragged himself up the ladder of success and now he was reaping the rewards.

He looked up to his left and noticed the Irish couple—he'd heard the woman say *Irlandesa* before he'd interrupted their conversation with the community manager—walking around their wraparound balcony and felt a stab of envy. Eduardo would have liked very much to purchase a penthouse, but he was not willing to risk getting into debt. He was a conservative man; he prided himself on his financial rectitude. He had not gone over the top when affluence came, like some of his colleagues, who were taking out mortgages for villas with their own pools that would take years to pay off. And something else, Eduardo thought smugly. The property market in Spain was unsustainable. The bubble would burst eventually, but nobody wanted to admit it. And when it did, *then* he would buy his penthouse, he daydreamed as the community manager led him into the third block of apartments in the complex. They rode the lift to the third floor in frosty silence.

"*Aquí,*" Señora Torres indicated the door to her right. Eduardo knew that his cousin would be his neighbor across the hall. He was glad it was someone he knew. When he'd mentioned, in confidence, to Gabriel that he was thinking of purchasing an apartment on the Costa, his cousin had asked to see the plans. Gabriel, an architect, had been impressed. They had often discussed buying a holiday home, and now that Eduardo was taking the plunge, Gabriel decided he too would buy. They had taken the early morning AVE from Puerta de Atocha to Málaga, where they were met by a member of the sales team and driven to the prospective site, admired the view and the picturesque town, and then gone to look at the plans in the sales office in Marbella.

The sales rep, a sharp-suited Frenchwoman, had done her best to sell them each a penthouse, of which only three remained; but Eduardo had kept true to his borrowing principles, although he would very much have liked to purchase one. The south-facing beachfront apartments had all been snapped up, the Frenchwoman said proudly, and the upper-story west-facing apartments were sold too. So, because they didn't wish to be on the ground floor or the first floor, they had taken two adjoining third-floor apartments facing south—a bonus, but nevertheless with some of their sea view obstructed by the frontline blocks. Certainly not the best apartments in the complex. Nevertheless, there was a smaller pool than the main one facing the beach, and another beautiful garden. Eduardo reasoned it would be quieter and more private in the high season. They had put a deposit on their respective apartments and taken the fast train back to Madrid that evening.

He'd not said a word about his purchase to his wife.

Soon Consuela would know that she now had a summer home by the sea and could leave Madrid during the intense heat of high summer. His aunt would stay no longer than a week, ten days at the most—Eduardo knew that for sure. Beatriz was too rigid, too bound up in her routine to abandon it for the more relaxed lifestyle on the coast. He would not try and persuade her to stay longer than she wished. Of that his aunt need have no fear.

He opened the door to the apartment. "I have no further need of you. *Gracias,*" he said dismissively to the community manager.

Constanza Torres gave him a haughty stare. "*Nada,*" she replied, turning on her heel before he closed the door behind her.

Hopefully he wouldn't have to deal with the woman again. She was employed by the builders. Once the complex was handed over to the residents, they would employ their own concierge.

Eduardo dismissed her from his thoughts as he walked out to the balcony and was soothed by the rhythmic lilt of the sea. How refreshing! How soothing to the soul. This would truly be a place of rest and relaxation, he promised himself, taking deep breaths of sea air.

Eduardo felt a frisson of uncharacteristic excitement exploring his new abode, walking around the big, bright empty rooms, admiring the excellent finishes in the bathrooms and bedrooms. Seeing the glasses and champagne in the kitchen, he smiled. His aunt and wife could drink that; he would treat himself to a small snifter of brandy, his only indulgence, apart from the odd glass of dry sherry.

Today was a good day, Eduardo decided. They were few and far between.

He locked up, took the lift to the ground floor, and made sure to close the door of the building firmly behind him. Driving towards the impressive, high wrought-iron gates, he saw the community manager gesticulating to one of the gardeners who was working on the planters at the entrance. Bossing him around, no doubt. Her reign would be short-lived, Eduardo thought grimly, pressing his newly acquired fob to open the gates, which slid smoothly open at his touch.

Chapter Four

Jutta / Felipe

Jutta Sauer Perez studied her reflection critically in the gilt-edged cheval mirror she'd rescued from a skip some years ago. It was one of her most cherished possessions. In that mirror Jutta could see, every morning, how far she'd come in life. Her ruler-straight, expertly highlighted blond hair was shining. Her makeup, subtle but skillfully applied, accentuated her high cheekbones and green, gold-flecked eyes. The discreet pearl earrings and single strand around her slender neck were perfect for the look she wanted to present to her clients.

Today she wanted to be particularly *soignée*. The apartments at La Joya de Andalucía were being presented to their new owners and she'd three commissions for fit-outs already. Invariably, Jutta found that more would come her way from word-of-mouth endorsements. She'd never been so busy. It was just how she liked it to be.

Her husband, Felipe, had left at six a.m. to drive to Murcia to view some land his development company was interested in purchasing. Felipe and his partners were buying swaths of land on the Costas, several of which were already in development. He also had a portfolio of rental properties between Fuengirola and Marbella, which she managed.

"You should consider opening an office in Murcia or Alicante; you'd be swamped with work, Jutta. People are buying two and three apartments at a time; the Irish and British are mad for buy-to-let. The market is crazy up there. You should take advantage of it" was his constant refrain. "And they're generally not as expensive and deluxe as down here; you wouldn't have to be looking for all that designer stuff," he'd said to her this morning, before leaning down to kiss her good-bye.

"I like finding designer stuff, as you call it," Jutta insisted, wishing he would stop putting her under pressure. She was building up her own company at a slow and steady pace and that was how she liked it. She'd made excellent contacts in several furniture shops along the Costa del Sol, and she got first-rate commissions.

"But it's too time-consuming," Felipe argued. "You could fit out all your kitchens in Carrefour and—"

"Felipe, you concentrate on your business and I'll concentrate on mine," she'd interrupted calmly, and he'd shrugged and laughed and called her his little German tortoise.

"You have to think big like me, *querida*," he'd said this morning when she'd asked him if he did not think he was taking on too much. "See you tonight for dinner with the Americans."

"You'll be tired after all that driving." She leaned up on her elbow and yawned.

"You know me: I like driving, letting my baby purr along the motorway. I'll be there in four and a half hours, view the land, and have lunch with my partners, and back by six at the latest." He blew her a kiss and strode down the marble hall whistling.

Jutta shook her head. Her husband's stamina left her exhausted sometimes. It was madness doing that round trip and scheduling in a dinner with his American business partner. Callahan Cooper was from somewhere in Texas: Jutta wondered if he would wear a Stetson.

When she was barely a teenager and living in a quiet rural village near Dornburg in central Germany, she'd begun to watch reruns of *Dallas* with her mother, who had been a fan of the TV series since its inception. How she'd adored the fashion and the big shoulder pads and especially the notion that these glamorous women were successful in business—even if they were a disaster in the bedroom. How she longed to escape from the stultifying boredom of life in rural Germany. Jutta most emphatically did not wish to end up like her mother, a dutiful hausfrau helping her husband work the farm, addicted to American soaps, and whose highlight of the month was her visit to her sister in the city of Limburg to the south of them.

Strange, Jutta mused, that the university city of Koblenz where she'd studied computer sciences was twinned with Austin, Texas. She must mention that in conversation tonight. Jutta liked to map out topics of mutual interest before meeting clients.

How her life had changed when she'd left home to study in Koblenz. Her father had been so proud of her going to the brand-new university. When he'd seen the enormous library with the floor-to-ceiling windows and serried rows of book stacks that overlooked the campus, he'd said earnestly, "Study hard, daughter. You've been given a great opportunity: Grasp it with both hands."

Studying had been the last thing on Jutta's mind. She wanted to party and throw off the shackles of her old, constrained existence. Until university her social life had consisted of cycling to the neighboring village of Thalheim to see her best friends Agathe and Lise, or walking her dog, Spock, along the banks of the Grundbach, hoping against hope that she might meet Gunter Neumann, who had snogged her once, in the forest near her home one Saturday afternoon when she'd taken Spock for his walk. She would never forget that deep-mouthed kiss and his hands on her small budding breasts or the wild strange longing that had flooded her as he gave a breathless groan and buried his face in her hair before jumping to his feet and looking down at her, saying, "Don't tell anyone I kissed you, you're only a kid and my friends would make fun of me."

"I'm nearly fourteen," she protested.

"Still a kid, and a swotty one who wears glasses and has spots. Not cool. I like your hair, though," he'd said patronizingly, loping off between the slender saplings crowned by sun-dappled foliage.

She'd gone home, looked at herself in the mirror, seen what seemed to her to be pus-filled volcanic craters on her cheeks and chin, and thrown herself on her bed and sobbed her heart out. When Gunther had pointedly ignored her the following Monday at school, her heart had shattered into a million pieces and she'd thought herself the ugliest girl in the world.

Jutta grimaced, remembering the heartaches her teenage self had endured. How she would love to meet Gunther Neumann now and let him see her blemish-free skin and glossy straight hair. Lise had told her that Gunther, having failed his accountancy exams, was working in a pub in Berlin and had turned into a bit of a pothead.

She, on the other hand, ran her own company, Jutta thought smugly, stretching languorously in the big queen-sized bed she shared with her husband. And she could expand it if she so wished. In theory her husband's suggestion was good. Felipe was right, the Costa Blanca could be an ideal area to open a branch of Jutta Sauer Apartment Fit-Out and Letting Specialists, if she wanted to go down that route. But furnishing and servicing buy-to-let egg boxes was not what her company, in its present incarnation, was about.

Perhaps she would consider it in the future. Nerja and Almeria, east of Málaga, were more upmarket than the east coast and would suit her better. Quality was Jutta's mind-set; quantity, her husband's—and that was the difference in their business plans. Nevertheless her German common sense and his Spanish exuberance had got them this far. Two thriving businesses. An elegant apartment with sea views, in Elviria, close to Marbella.

Two Mercs—granted, hers was ten years old, but image was everything—and a lifestyle that was utterly different from the one she'd lived growing up in Germany all those years ago.

Her father, Oskar, had come to spend a holiday with them the previous year and had been astonished at her and Felipe's apparent affluence. "And you own all this?" He'd waved his hand at the spacious third-floor apartment as they sat on the balcony sipping his gift of schnapps after their meal in the Don Carlos hotel, which was in walking distance of their home.

"No, Papa, we rent it." Jutta wondered wearily why she'd invited him. He kept asking about the price of this and that and questioning where they got their money. She'd forgotten how nosey he was.

"And why would you not buy a property, since you are both in the business?" Oskar queried, his gnarled, liver-spotted hands shaking slightly as he raised his glass to his mouth. For the first time, Jutta conceded that her father was becoming somewhat frail. She didn't want to think about it, nor the consequences if he became unable to look after himself.

"It works out cheaper to rent, Oskar," Felipe interjected smoothly. "We pay our rent and our utilities, but we don't pay property taxes, maintenance fees, and so on. Those are our landlord's responsibility, and although they're reflected in the rent, it's still cheaper for us."

"I see." His father-in-law nodded. "I suppose that makes sense. But there is security in having a roof over your head that belongs to you."

"If you lived in a city at home you would have to rent, the property prices are so high," Jutta pointed out.

"Well, I don't. My house is my own. God rest your mother, I remember the day we got the deeds as though it were yesterday." He launched into the same story he'd told on numerous occasions, and Jutta yet again privately gave thanks that she'd left home a long time ago and did not have frequent contact with her widowed father, who held set, conservative views and who had never approved of Felipe.

"*Ein Schelm*,"—a rogue—Jutta had overheard him say to her mother after she'd finally introduced her family to the man she'd left them, her college, and her home for.

There had been ructions when she'd come home from a working holiday in Ibiza to tell her parents that she was leaving college to go to southern Spain with her new boyfriend. She couldn't quite believe it herself and had wondered once or twice if she was living in a fantasy.

Oskar had been most put out in her second year of university when she'd spent a mere two weeks of her long summer break in Dornburg. "I'm going to Spain with Lise for the rest of the summer. We're getting work there and I'm going to practice my Spanish and—"

"But what about us? I have work for you to do here," Oskar demanded angrily.

"I'm sorry, Papa. I spent all last summer at home. I need a holiday and to spread my wings a little—"

"Nonsense. This is not what I'm paying for you to go to university for, to fritter your time away in Spain. Speak to her, Klara," he instructed his wife.

"I think Jutta is right," declared Klara, much to her husband's dismay. "If I had the chances young women have today, I would take them," she continued, brushing paste onto the roll of new paper for the walls of the dining room, which Jutta was helping her to decorate.

Jutta couldn't hide her pleasure in her mother's words, remembering how pleased Klara had been for her when she'd got her place at university—the first member of her family to do so. Her mother had told Jutta to use the opportunity to see the world and have a life before settling down and getting married. Marriage, she informed her daughter, should not be the holy grail in her life, because sometimes it was simply another form of servitude.

With her mother's words ringing in her ears, and her father's disapproval preventing him from wishing her well, Jutta had taken the train to Frankfurt am Main, where she had met up with Lise, and escaped to Ibiza.

She'd been waitressing in a restaurant on the seafront when Felipe and some friends had taken a table on the terrace. She stood patiently waiting for them to choose their food, wishing her shift were over so she could go for a swim. A while later, as she reached over to give Felipe his beer, one of his friends placed his hands on her bottom and groped her. "Nice ass, Blondie," he leered.

Jutta straightened up, looked down at him, picked the jug of water from the table, and poured it over him. "*Arschloch!*" she said coldly, and walked away.

The Spaniard had jumped to his feet yelling, but Felipe had pushed him back in his chair and in rapid Spanish said something that shut him up.

Jutta had told her boss that she was not serving the Spanish pigs at table seven and he knew there was no point in arguing with her. She was a great worker—one of his best—but when she got stubborn, there was no changing her mind. He sent Domingo to serve them instead.

When the group was leaving, Felipe had come over to her, introduced himself, and apologized in English before handing her a large tip.

"No, thank you," she said coolly, refusing it. "But thank you for apologizing for your lowlife friend, seeing as he has not got the decency to do it himself."

The next morning, Felipe came to the restaurant, alone. "Coffee, *por favor*," he said, the expression in his brown eyes unashamedly sensual as he studied her languidly. How it happened, Jutta would never know, but a long-forgotten memory of her sexual awakening at Gunther's kiss enveloped her and a surge of desire throbbed between her legs, and she stared at the dark-haired, handsome man in front of her and almost gasped.

Felipe never took his eyes off her as she brought him his coffee, and she had to struggle hard not to let him see how thrown she was by his attention. When she handed him his bill on the little silver salver, his fingers lightly touched hers. "*Gracias,*" he said in his sexy voice.

He came every morning for a week and every morning she wore an air of studied detachment as she served him his coffee as though he were a mere tourist unworthy of her attention.

"What time do you finish work at?" he asked later that week in his broken English when she'd brought his bill as usual.

"Different times," she said offhandedly, wishing she felt as cool as she sounded.

"Let me bring you for a drink tonight. It's my last night on the island," he invited, his brown eyes—as dark as the coffee she'd served him—softly seductive.

How she *longed* to say yes. How she *longed* to say, in a wildly spontaneous moment of madness, "Forget the drink, just bring me to bed." For a moment she hesitated, but her pride came to her rescue. She wasn't *that* easy. Last night on the island, a drink and a shag—even though it would probably be the shag of her life—and then good-bye. No, thank you. "*Gracias.* I'm busy after work," she said coolly, and walked away without looking back.

The sun lost some of its sparkle in the following weeks, and Jutta veered between cursing herself and congratulating herself over her rejection of the sexy Spaniard. She partied with Lise after work and lay on a towel in a secluded cove she'd discovered after one of her cycling explorations of the island—toasting herself in the sun, her body turning golden, her hair becoming more blond from the sun's rays. She'd even slept with a younger, amusing Italian waiter she'd met at a club, but all the while her thoughts were on a dark-haired man with brown eyes who'd created a hotbed of desire in her with just one look.

Ten days before she left the island, as she was finishing her shift, he came back. Her heart thumped in her chest when she saw him sit at his favorite table. "A San Miguel, *por favor*," he said lazily, his eyes twinkling. She couldn't help the broad grin that crossed her face as they stared at each other.

"I came back for you," he said. "You haunt me."

Jutta laughed. "I think you are a practiced seducer. I'll not be a notch on your bedpost," she said lightly.

"I don't possess a bedpost, *Fraulein*." He studied her intently. "What time do you finish work?"

"Now," she said removing her white apron.

"Come with me."

"Tomorrow, meet me at Mateo's tapas bar at ten a.m. for coffee," Jutta threw over her shoulder, and walked back into the bar to get her bag and slip out through the kitchen entrance.

She would end up in his arms—she knew it—but she wasn't going to sleep with him tonight, reeking of food and alcohol and perspiration. She needed to wash her hair, shave her legs, manicure her nails, and moisturize her skin until it gleamed. She needed to know that she looked her absolute best. She needed to be in control.

She walked along the side of the building towards the archway that led to the cobbled side street where she lived.

"Jutta!" She heard her name and turned to see him striding towards her. Before she could stop him, he'd placed a hand on either side of her, trapping her against the wall. "I can't wait until ten a.m. tomorrow!" He stared into her eyes and she could hardly breathe.

"Jutta, Jutta, Jutta," he said huskily, lowering his mouth to hers, kissing her hungrily, then tenderly, pausing to look at her for a moment before kissing her again, his tongue igniting her to respond with equal passion.

"So?" he said, drawing away and smiling at her in the dark, with just the orange glow of a streetlamp pooling around them. "I can woo you and be a gentleman if that's what you want, or we can forget the wooing and go and make love right now, because I know you want to as much as I do."

That he'd come back from the mainland for her was wooing enough, Jutta decided there and then. "My apartment is down that street over there," she murmured. "But I want to shower; it's been a long day."

"That's allowed only if I'm permitted to assist." He took her hand and walked in the direction she'd indicated. Jutta swallowed hard. The idea of Felipe in the shower with her was so erotic, she was almost ready to come right there on the spot.

With shaking hands she opened the heavy wooden door to the compact apartment she shared with Lise, who, fortunately, had taken a trip to Majorca for the weekend. Felipe slipped his hands around her waist and up under her blouse, cupping her breasts as he kicked the door shut behind them. They never made it up the stairs. Pulling the clothes off each other, they sank into one another's embrace, leaning up against the door and moaning their pleasure as they came in hot, wet, shuddering spasms. They rested against each other silently, spent. Then he took her to the shower and they ravished each other all over again.

Jutta sighed remembering the passion of those early days. It had been nirvana. Taking the biggest leap of faith of her life, she'd abandoned her university degree in Germany to go and live with Felipe on the Costa del Sol, and never regretted it for a moment.

"Have you lost your mind as well as your morals?" Oskar had yelled, incandescent that the daughter he'd had the highest hopes for had betrayed him for a Spanish lothario. It didn't matter to him that Felipe was a college graduate with a business degree and had his own property development company.

"Stop that, Oskar," Klara ordered with a look that silenced her husband. "If you must go and live with this man, make sure you are protected and make sure you always have a bank account of your own" was all she said, but it was enough for Jutta. She'd left Dornburg with her mother's advice ringing in her ears and her father's back turned firmly against her.

But she'd flourished in her new homeland. The constant sunshine and heat, the relaxed ambiance of her environs, the cosmo-politan set that Felipe ran with, all eager to grab life by the throat and get rich with this venture or that, eased what little guilt she felt about leaving Germany, and within a year she'd earned enough to pay back her father for the college fees he'd spent on her now-defunct education. It had given her some amount of satisfaction to lodge that money in his bank account secure in the knowledge that she was, for the first time ever, independent, financially and in every other way.

When her mother had died suddenly during Jutta's second year in Spain, she'd been devastated, but relieved that she was no longer living at home. She'd gone back to Germany for the funeral and to stay awhile with her father, who in his grief had thawed towards her. She'd struggled against Oskar's desire for her to stay and become the woman of the house. He expected her to cook his meals as her mother had done, and even do his laundry and shop-ping. Her older sisters, Anka and Inga, with children of their own, would have been very happy for her to step into a housekeeping role had they been able to guilt-trip her into doing so. It was Felipe who had come to her rescue. He'd flown to Germany and booked return tickets for them both to Málaga, telling Oskar and the family that he and Jutta would eventually marry and that her place was at his side as they built up their business ventures together.

The two men had stared at each other, and it was Oskar who had dropped his gaze first, his shoulders drooping in disappoint-ment. When, a year later, she'd asked him if he wished to walk her up the aisle in a traditional church wedding, he'd told her it would be an act of hypocrisy to get married in a church when she'd been living with Felipe for years. That had suited Jutta fine; she hadn't wanted a church wedding and had only considered it for her fa-ther's sake. They had held a civil wedding in Marbella, with Lise and Agathe as her bridesmaids, and her sisters, her brother, and their families reluctant guests.

It had taken a long time for her father to become reconciled with what he saw as her "rejection and betrayal" of her family. Even now, she thought, looking at him sitting on her balcony, sipping his drink in the flamingo-hued sunset, he never lost a chance to make some pointed remark about how good her sisters were to him, how *dedicated* they were to his well-being. *Unlike you,* the words not spoken but very much implied.

When his holiday was over, she'd been glad to put Oskar on a plane to Frankfurt and return him to the bosom of her ever-disapproving family. She was no longer the daughter he remembered: she would never be that girl again.

Now, looking at the sophisticated image reflected back at her from her mirror, dressed in a superbly cut gray designer suit—one of three she called her "working" wardrobe—Jutta took a deep breath and lifted her chin. One day she and Felipe would indeed buy their luxury villa with their own pool and meticulously manicured grounds, or a penthouse in the likes of La Joya, and she would invite her father and brother and sisters and aunts to a housewarming party to show them what a *successful* man she'd married and how far she'd come from the reserved, gangly country girl they had known.

Today she would concentrate on her new clients, an Irish couple who had bought a penthouse in La Joya. She should call into the office, she supposed, but Christine and Olga, her assistants, would have a dozen queries for her, and long stories about clients who needed their community taxes paid or their air conditioners serviced, or would whinge about damage done by careless tenants or some such. Jutta hated that side of the job, and escaped from the office as much as she could. Perhaps today she would give it a miss. Once the new clients in La Joya were sorted, she would turn her attention to her office and spend an entire week there, she told herself, picking up her Chanel briefcase and setting off for work.

Chapter Five

Anna / Austen

Anna had watched the tall, blond, immaculately dressed woman stride across the foyer area of their new apartment complex the previous afternoon and known immediately that she was Jutta Sauer, who would be assisting her and Austen in the decorating of the penthouse. She'd found herself automatically tucking in her stomach and sitting straighter in her chair, relieved she'd only had the one glass of bubbly. She and Austen had agreed that he would come and look at the furniture with them the following day but that she would choose the kitchenware and other household necessities while he went to play golf.

The blond woman gazed around the seating area and Anna had stood up and given a wave. "Ms. Sauer?" she'd asked.

"Mrs. MacDonald?" the woman answered, walking over to her. Anna held out her hand. "Yes, I'm Anna and this is my husband, Austen."

"How do you do, please call me Jutta." She shook hands briskly and motioned for them to sit down.

Bossy, thought Anna, not sure if she quite liked her. *No small talk.*

Jutta had immediately got down to business. "Now, you have many choices where to shop to furnish your penthouse. I have the plans and have already seen one similar to yours with the same vista. You have been to Spain before?" She'd arched an eyebrow at them, her cool, green-eyed stare raking them up and down, studying them both.

"Yes, often," Anna affirmed.

"You know then, El Corte Inglés, La Cañada, Leroy Merlin? And of course in La Cañada we have Marks & Spencer and Habitat and, further up the coast, Dunnes"—she'd pronounced it "Dunnez"—"in Fuengirola, if you want an Irish homeware store. I also have a list of furniture shops with whom I do business. If you want an excellent choice of furniture, I'd recommend Mobile & Diseño, which is on the Autovía A-7, less than twenty minutes drive from here. It all really depends on what you are looking for, and how long you have to spend shopping. As you know, my fee is ten percent of whatever you purchase with me, and a hundred euros per day for my time. I would suggest drapes and furniture shopping first. Accessories and kitchenware after that."

"Sounds good to me," Austen remarked, stifling a yawn. "When do we start?"

"Tomorrow! I shall collect you at nine a.m. sharp in the foyer of the Don Carlos. I have many clients. My time is precious. I don't like to be kept waiting." Jutta picked up her briefcase, stood up, and held out her hand to Austen and then Anna. "It's very nice to meet you. Until tomorrow. Enjoy the rest of your day." She marched off towards her Merc without a backward glance.

"That's us told, then," Anna said drily, taken aback by Jutta's imperious manner. "I don't think I like her."

"She's businesslike. She knows her stuff. She doesn't hang around. That's fine with me." Austen wasn't perturbed. "Let's go and do as she suggests and enjoy our day." Lunch in El Capricho helped Anna put the bossy German to the back of her mind, but she made sure to set her alarm that night to be up and ready on time.

They'd taken a taxi to the plush hotel where Jutta wanted to meet and had enough time to sit and have coffee in the foyer before her arrival.

Anna glanced at her watch as she drained her cup. A minute to nine. She hoped that bossy-boots would be five minutes late. Childish, she knew, but it would take the wind out of Jutta's superior sails. On the stroke of the hour, the blonde strode into the foyer, immaculate, with not a hair out of place, looking like she'd stepped from the pages of *Vogue*.

"Good morning, Anna, Austen. Let's go and view some furniture and make a start. I'm parked in the car park; stay at the entrance and I'll pick you up," she commanded.

"I feel like a child of ten being bossed around by her," Anna grumbled, watching the younger woman walk purposefully out the door, a fuchsia pink Longchamps tote swinging from her shoulder.

"Look, if you really don't like her after today, we can go to someone else, but the Dalys said she's terrific at her job," Austen soothed. "Give her a chance."

"OK, OK," Anna said, scowling, and walked through the swing doors. Moments later Jutta's silver Merc cruised to a stop beside them. "You get in the front if you want; I'm sitting in the back," Anna muttered. The woman's attitude rankled. Her time was "precious" indeed. So was theirs, she thought indignantly.

"So," said Jutta crisply as Austen got in beside her, "I'll bring you to Mobile & Diseño first? It's very close by; that's why I suggested we meet here. It's what I generally do."

"Fine," Austen said authoritatively. "We're anxious to make a start. We want to have this all wrapped up ASAP."

"How long are you staying?" Jutta inquired, leaving the grounds and driving onto the slip road to join the A-7.

"Another four days, and then we'll be back in June for a month," Austen said chattily.

"Very nice to get that amount of time off." Jutta sat ramrod straight behind the wheel, unfazed by the impatience of the Spanish drivers who hooted and honked incessantly.

"Indeed," agreed Austen.

"What do you do?" Jutta asked.

"I'm just about to retire." Austen glanced back at his wife, who was uncharacteristically quiet.

"You look too young!" she remarked. With anyone else Anna would have suspected flattery. But Jutta was not the flattering type, she figured.

"Thank you." Austen smiled.

"And you? Do you work?" Jutta inquired, glancing at Anna in the rearview mirror.

"Yes." Anna decided she wasn't giving away any information about herself to the self-assured young woman.

"A lot of Irish women that I've met are just housewives," Jutta remarked derisively. "That would drive me mad. I *have* to work. My husband loves that I work." Jutta sped along the motorway towards another slip road.

"Whatever a woman's choice is, and they can afford it, is up to them," Anna retorted.

"Not my choice, for sure. Even if I ever have children." Jutta drove off the A-7 and minutes later swung into the car park of an elegant furniture showroom.

Poor kids; she'd be better off staying childless, thought Anna nastily, following Jutta and Austen up the gleaming marble steps to the upmarket furniture store.

"Look around, get an idea, see if there's anything you like. I'm going to look for the person I do business with. I've already let her know that we were on the way," Jutta ordered, giving an expansive wave around the store as though she owned it.

"Do we *really* need her?" Anna exclaimed in exasperation as Jutta's sharp footsteps clacked across the floor.

"She's brought us here. Without her we wouldn't have known about this place. She knows where everything is. And there's some classy-looking stuff on show. Didn't you say creamy lemon was a color you liked?" Austen said to distract her, pointing to a very attractive coffee table with a large terra-cotta and lemon lamp resting on it. Beside it, a long aubergine-colored sofa looked extremely comfortable.

"As long as she remembers *we're* employing *her*, not the other way around," Anna snapped. "And that sofa's the wrong color."

"Yes, but they do it in different colors; there's the selection." He pointed out the swatches that lay on the armrest.

"Oh!" said Anna, somewhat mollified, beginning to feel excited. "That lamp *is* rather fabulous."

"So is the price, but let's put good stuff in, because it will last," Austen counseled, walking over to look at some dining tables.

Four and a half hours later, Anna and Austen were exhausted but extremely satisfied when Jutta dropped them back at the hotel.

"I'll pick you up here again at nine a.m. tomorrow. Enjoy your evening." She still looked immaculate, with not a bead of perspiration or a hair out of place, Anna thought enviously, as a trickle of sweat ran down her cleavage. She couldn't wait to take her shoes off and have a shower. How the other woman walked in those high heels was a mystery to her.

"Thank you, Jutta. You played a blinder." Austen shook hands with her.

"A blinder?" She looked confused.

"You did a great job," he complimented.

"Ahhh, I see. Thank you. Yes, I am good at my job." Jutta smiled with no hint of false modesty. "*Buenas noches.*"

"That one is something else," Anna laughed as Austen took her hand and they walked into the cool air-conditioned foyer. " 'I am good at my job,' " she mimicked.

"She knows her stuff, though. We'd still be mooching around, trying to make up our minds. We'd never have found that place. I really like what we've chosen. Now let's have a quick drink here, go home and shower and change, and then have dinner in El Capricho and watch the sunset," Austen suggested.

"There'll be no argument from me." Anna yawned. "That sounds good. Imagine she has to go out to dinner with another client tonight, after the day she put in today. Rather her than me."

"The poor client." Austen grinned. "The worst of it is over for us. Once you have the stuff for the kitchen bought tomorrow, we can buy everything else in dribs and drabs when we're over in June. Are you sure you don't want me to come tomorrow?"

"No, you go play golf, honestly. As you say, the worst is over today. I wanted you to choose the furniture with me. I can do the rest," she said, sinking into a soft easy chair.

"Well, if you're sure."

"I am."

It suited Anna as much as it suited Austen. Her husband would have no interest whatsoever in crockery, cutlery, glassware, and the like. He'd end up getting irritated and she'd feel under pressure and she would be just as glad to leave him playing golf the following day so she could shop at her leisure.

"Today was another step nearer to our little piece of paradise," Austen observed later that night as they sat watching a full yellow moon shine a glistening gold ladder of light across the Mediterranean, all the way to Africa. They were sipping Baileys Irish Cream liqueur, compliments of Salvador, El Capricho's loquacious owner, following another delicious meal.

"I'll have to stop eating and drinking like this when we move in," Anna sighed happily. She invariably went home from Spain a half a stone heavier.

"Don't worry, we'll get into a fitness routine. We can walk on the boardwalk every morning and swim, and play tennis. We'll be grand," Austen said. "We won't know ourselves, Anna; we'll have the times of our lives here," he promised, raising his glass to hers.

Chapter Six

Eduardo / Consuela

Consuela De La Fuente sat on her lounger under an umbrella in the magnificent tropical gardens of the Don Carlos hotel and felt herself relax as the sea sang its peaceful song, quietly lapping the golden shore. *Tía* Beatriz had gone to her room to take a siesta. Eduardo had driven to a town near Estepona for a business meeting and had phoned her to tell her that he was delayed.

It was a rare treat to have this quiet time to herself without having to act as a buffer between the peevish, demanding elderly lady and Consuela's earnest, reserved husband.

Age and life's disappointments had turned Beatriz into a *cruz anciana*. And a cross old lady she certainly was, Consuela had to admit. She was a trial sometimes. But a trial Consuela had to endure. Beatriz had reared Eduardo and had shown him more love and care than his own parents ever had, and for that, Eduardo was in her thrall. Beatriz would be a constant and demanding presence in their lives for as long as she lived, and the way she was going, she might even outlive *them*, Consuela reflected humorously, dropping her book and settling in for a doze.

They always trained it down from Madrid to Málaga and hired

a car for the duration of their holiday. It was easier than subjecting his elderly aunt, who had stiff joints, to the long drive south.

The journey from Madrid through Castilla, La Mancha, and Andalucía was one of Beatriz's great pleasures in life. From the moment they rolled out of Puerta de Atocha until they rumbled along the narrow pass through the steep High Sierras and caught the first magical glimpses of the sea to reach María Zambrano station in Málaga, she would be as vivacious and excited as a child, commenting on everything that caught her eye. It was always a good start to their holiday.

Eduardo would bring her home after ten days and the return journey to Madrid was always subdued, as his aunt's holiday persona reverted to the rather stern, irascible individual they were more accustomed to.

"I'm sure you're glad to be rid of me," she would invariably say when Eduardo would make ready to leave, having settled her in her apartment and made her iced tea before returning to his office to work for a day or two, then taking the train back to the south to rejoin his wife.

"Do you know what she said?" he'd fume, repeating it to Consuela. "'I'm sure you're glad to be rid of me.' Did we not go out of our way to give her a pleasant holiday? She's so *utterly* ungrateful." Consuela would have to soothe and placate him until his ire had diminished and he could relax enough to enjoy what remained of their holiday.

This time was different, though. Eduardo, who always booked and arranged their holidays, had informed his wife and aunt that the apartment they usually stayed in would not be free for the first week and that he'd booked them into the Don Carlos hotel.

Beatriz was enjoying the experience immensely. So many people to observe, such exquisite food that she didn't have to prepare. Very different cuisine from the simple fare she permitted herself at home. And all because Eduardo was a successful notary and had his own firm, as Consuela had pointed out proudly when

Beatriz had exclaimed in delight at the size of her room and the views of the sea from her balcony.

Eduardo had permitted himself an uncharacteristic beam of pleasure at his wife's praise, especially when Beatriz had said with rare pride, "Yes, he has done very well, and worked hard."

This morning her husband had been positively giddy about his business meeting. "I'll be back at noon for lunch and after siesta we will take a drive along the coast," he told Consuela, kissing her on the cheek, as was his wont before leaving her. His good humor had not lasted, though. His call to say he would be delayed had been short, curt, and hardly informative. No doubt she'd know the reason why soon enough. Her eyelids eventually fluttered closed and the sound of the other hotel guests laughing and chatting drifted away.

Consuela gave a little snore that woke her up. She blinked, startled to see a large white sun umbrella above her before realizing where she was. She settled herself more comfortably on the lounger, knowing she could snooze uninterrupted for another while. Eduardo might be put out about the delay he was being caused. For his wife, it was a blessing in disguise.

◆

Beatriz Hernandez gave a sigh, stretched, and opened her eyes. Momentarily she was confused by her surroundings. A breeze crooned through the balcony door, and then she remembered. She was on holiday. Staying in a beautiful hotel, with Eduardo and Consuela. Not in her shaded bedroom in her apartment on Calle de Antonio López, in Madrid, with the trees, tall sentinels outside her wrought-iron balcony, limp and exhausted in the overwhelming heat of summer.

She lay listening to the sea, and a feeling of peace stole over her. This was heavenly indeed. She must make the most of every moment. The time would come when she would be too old and too infirm to accompany her relatives down south for their annual summer vacation. Beatriz lived in dread of advancing old age. She was eighty now and slowing down. Her siesta naps were becoming longer, and the walk to the Carrefour Express or down Calle Orgaz to reach her favorite spot on the Río Manzanares, and sit in the shade of the great trees that lined the riverbank, was getting more difficult. She dreaded becoming housebound.

She knew too that she was becoming more petulant and crotchety—well, more than normal, she admitted humorously. Even Consuela, who was customarily kind and gentle, could now show signs of exasperation. It didn't help, Beatriz supposed, that the younger woman was in the throes of *menopausia*.

She remembered her own menopause and the waves of rage and frustration that had come from nowhere, to imprison her in their unrelenting grip. Every feeling of sadness, regret, and desolation—and *Dios* knew she had many of them—had seemed even more pronounced and she'd thought she would go mad with despair.

Now in the winter of her life she had more equilibrium. But there was unfinished business that she still had to come to a decision about. Something she'd put off for many, many years. She could deal with it or let things be. It was hard to know what was for the best.

Beatriz lay drowsily against the pillows and her thoughts drifted back to a time long ago when she was happy and life held no hint of what was to come.

◆

"Beatriz and I have eaten lunch; why don't you have something on the terrace. I'll have a coffee with you," Consuela suggested to her husband, although she would have loved to continue lying under the shade of the white umbrella, relaxing in the late-afternoon sun. Eduardo was back from his business meeting and he'd phoned her and found where she was resting.

"I just want something light. We can eat dinner tonight. I want to go on our drive. After your coffee, will you check on Beatriz and see that she is up from her siesta?" Eduardo tried not to look at the blond beauty under an adjacent palm tree who was lying unashamedly topless, reading a magazine.

"Yes, *mi querido*," Consuela said, gathering her belongings and following her husband through the winding blossom-filled gardens to the terrace. Eduardo was in a strange humor; she'd never seen him so anxious to go on a drive while on holiday.

Eduardo scanned the menu impatiently and ordered a club sandwich and coffee for himself and coffee and a pastry for Consuela. He was hungry and ate the tasty sandwich with relish, all the time imagining the delight his surprise would bring to his wife and aunt. He devoured his meal swiftly and could see Consuela looking at him, perplexed. He usually ate every mouthful of food slowly, with mindful deliberation. "Go check on *Tía* Beatriz; I'll meet you in the foyer. Don't be too long," he urged, wiping mayonnaise from the side of his mouth with his napkin.

"Is anything wrong, *mi esposo*?" she asked, a little frown creasing her brow.

"Not a thing, *mi palomita*," he said using the endearment he always called her when he felt especially tender towards her. She was his little dove, his champion, and the apartment was very much his gift for her.

A smile crossed his wife's pleasant countenance. Consuela was not beautiful in the conventional way. Her features were too sturdy, her nose not quite straight, but her light-brown eyes splashed with tiny dots of hazel and ringed by long black lashes were invariably kind and her generous mouth could widen into a beautiful smile, showing her even, pearly white teeth with the merest hint of an overbite, which he found attractive. Eduardo wanted so much to tell her his momentous news. He felt a rare sense of boyish excitement as he watched her disappear inside the hotel.

"Where are you bringing us, Eduardo?" Beatriz asked, settling herself into the front seat of the hire car some twenty minutes later. (These days it took her longer to get dressed.) She always sat in the front seat when they were driving, feeling it was her due. Consuela was relegated to the back, much to her husband's chagrin. But that was the way of it and he was used to it now.

"To a delightful little town called San Antonio del Mar. It's just west of Estepona." Eduardo clipped on his aunt's seat belt and handed her the pearl-handled fan he'd bought her many years ago. She never traveled without it.

"Is that where our rental apartment is? I'll be sorry to leave the hotel." Beatriz flicked open her fan and settled back for the drive.

"Yes, but it won't be free to move into for a few more days." Eduardo drove towards the underpass to get to the far side of the A-7.

"Not like you to book an apartment that's not ready for our occupation," Beatriz remarked, giving an exaggerated gasp when Eduardo shot off the slip road into the heavy holiday traffic at speed. "Drive carefully, *sobrino*," she cautioned crossly. Eduardo sighed. She called him "nephew" when she was annoyed at him, which was frequently.

"This is a nice area," Consuela interjected smoothly. "Close to Marbella and the hospital. I'm sure property is expensive here."

"Indeed," agreed her husband. "And frontline properties all along this coast fetch a very high price, because there are so few sites left to build on the Costa," he added smugly, thinking of the frontline property he'd just purchased, a tribute to all his hard work and prudent financial management.

"Of course, corruption is rife along the Costa del Sol. Aren't mayors and government and council officials being investigated for bribery, fraud, and illegal planning decisions?" Beatriz sniffed, as though the *madrileños* would never descend to such levels of bad behavior.

The laissez-faire attitude of the southerners towards their business practices was looked upon with some contempt by the citizenry of the capital, and Beatriz and Eduardo both felt rather superior to their southern countrymen. The Costa del Sol was a very nice place to vacation but that was about it; Eduardo was extremely glad he didn't have to work there.

"Oh, Eduardo, this is very pretty," Consuela remarked when they drove around the square of San Antonio. The colorful flower baskets hanging from doors and windows, the bright awnings flapping in the sea breeze, and the multitude of pavement cafés and little shops against the backdrop of a sparkling azure sea was like something out of a holiday brochure.

"Yes, lovely, isn't it?" he agreed, taking a left turn that led them along a narrow road to large wrought-iron gates with white-washed planters of scarlet geraniums and purple petunias on either side. Purple bougainvillea tumbling over the walls gave great splashes of color against the white-painted background. Eduardo pressed the fob and the gates slid open.

"Is this where the apartment is?" Beatriz gazed around, noting the magnificent landscaped gardens.

"Indeed it is, Tía, indeed it is," Eduardo said jovially, swinging into his designated parking spot. There was no sign of that dreadful Torres woman at Reception, for which he was profoundly grateful.

"This is very, very nice," Consuela approved, "and so close to the sea. How wonderful. An excellent choice, Eduardo."

"I'm glad you think so." Her husband, smiled, helping his aunt out of the car. He led them to the arched entrance of the middle block, opened the door, and ushered them along the tiled hall to the lift.

"It smells of paint. Are these new apartments?" Beatriz asked, stepping into the lift with her characteristic sprightliness.

"Brand new." Eduardo followed Consuela in.

"Excuse me, are you going up?" A tall blond-haired woman in an expensive-looking suit click-clacked across the hall in her high heels and entered the lift behind them.

"We are. What floor?" Eduardo asked. He wondered if she was a new owner. A close neighbor, perhaps. He didn't want her introducing herself as an owner and asking if he was one and ruining his surprise.

"Second floor, please," she said coolly in excellent English. She looked Scandinavian, Eduardo mused as she stared straight ahead, her eyes hidden behind her large designer sunglasses. He pressed the requisite buttons and silence reigned as the lift glided silently upwards. The woman gave a slight nod of her head as she left the lift; the door closed on her retreating back and his secret was safe.

"Here we are, ladies," Eduardo said heartily when they reached the next floor. He placed his key into the lock of the door on the right.

"But it's empty," Beatriz declared, being the first to enter.

"That's because we have to furnish it," Eduardo explained, smiling at his wife.

"Furnish it? I don't understand. Do you mean . . . ?" Comprehension dawned. "Is it *ours*?" Consuela exclaimed, gazing around in astonishment.

"Yes, *mi querida*, this is our new holiday apartment. Happy anniversary, *mi amada esposa*."

"*Tsk*, Eduardo, that romantic talk doesn't suit you," Beatriz reproved. "Beloved wife" indeed. She might as well not be standing there, the way they were gazing at each other. She couldn't help the jealousy that flared inside. How *she'd* longed to be a beloved wife to a man who loved her, but it had never happened. Her nephew should keep his starry-eyed talk for when he was alone with Consuela and not be rubbing her nose in it, she thought crossly, stalking out to the balcony in high dudgeon.

Eduardo's face darkened with temper. Trust his aunt to ruin his grand moment. Surely she could have praised him for his achievement and offered him congratulations instead of mean-spirited reprimands.

Consuela, seeing his disappointment, placed a hand on his arm. "It's wonderful. I can't believe it," she exclaimed. "Our own place by the sea! And what *magnificent* views, Eduardo. We'll be very happy here," she said, reaching up to kiss his cheek.

"I hope so, Consuelo, I hope so," he said, squeezing her hand tightly and wishing heartily that his aunt Beatriz was ensconced in her apartment in Madrid and he could enjoy these once-in-a-lifetime moments alone with his wife.

◆

Beatriz stared out towards the Rock of Gibraltar before turning towards Estepona and the coastline beyond. What a beautiful place. What an outstanding view. Eduardo had done very well for himself. But a deep dread lodged in her stomach. He would want to spend a lot of time down here with Consuela and they wouldn't want to be bringing her all the time. She would get her summer holiday and then be abandoned in Madrid, she thought with rising panic. Christmas, Easter, alone—she could see it now. What she'd always dreaded was coming to pass. Tears brimmed in her eyes and she shook her head impatiently. They must not see her cry. She had her pride. She took several deep breaths and composed herself.

She could see other owners walking around their balconies, pointing, gesticulating, and laughing. Did they realize how blessed they were? How lucky they were? Beatriz thought enviously. What a delight it would be to spend the summer months in this idyllic place, listening to the sea and watching the light change over the Rock and the High Sierras behind them. She would have to take the crumbs that were offered to her and pretend to be grateful. It was the way of the elderly, she thought gloomily.

"Isn't it a beautiful view, *Tía*?" Consuela laid a gentle hand on her arm.

Beatriz's heart softened. Consuela was a great blessing in her life. She could not have asked for a kinder, more considerate and softhearted person to be Eduardo's wife. She knew that she was fortunate.

"Yes, Consuela, it is quite stunning," Beatriz agreed.

"What colors would you like in your bedroom, *Tía*? Something pastel and summery?" Consuela suggested lightly.

"I'm very fond of pale green," Beatriz admitted, hiding her pleasure. No one else but Consuela would even consider asking her what colors she would like.

"We will decorate your room together, so that you will feel at home in it," Consuela said thoughtfully, although Beatriz noted that Eduardo remained tight-lipped and stern looking. She should not have rebuked him as she had.

"You have done well, Eduardo. This is a fine achievement," Beatriz placated. "And perhaps one day you might be able to afford to buy a penthouse like those people over there," she added, just to let him know that he should never rest on his laurels. There was always something more to aspire to in this life, and, as she'd often told him, second best was *never* good enough.

Eduardo seethed silently as he watched his wife pander to the woman who had reared him longer than his own mother had. The woman whom, this very minute, he *detested*. His aunt did it *every* time. Ruined his happy moments, his moments of achievement, and made him feel less than nothing.

No accomplishment was ever good enough for Beatriz. Second best was never to be tolerated in her eyes. But, thought Eduardo bitterly, all through his life, that's what he'd been, second best. And nothing was going to change that.

Chapter Seven

Sally-Ann / Cal / Lenora

How she wished the evening was over. She wasn't in the mood for polite social chitchat. The German woman, Jutta, was hard going, Sally-Ann thought glumly, longing to glug her glass of red. Instead she sipped it genteelly and touched her napkin to the side of her mouth. The steak had been quite delicious but her appetite was poor tonight.

Felipe, the husband, Cal's new partner, was chatty, charming, all out to impress, a real salesman. Sally-Ann had met many of his ilk over the years. Felipe and Cal were discussing the property market in the UAE, and Sally-Ann listened to their discussions hoping that Cal wouldn't head out to the Persian Gulf, considering the decline in the market in the US. If Cal started going further afield, he could spread himself too thin, something she'd be advising him against later on in their post-dinner discussions.

"You know Fahd used to bring a massive entourage over from Saudi. Three jumbos on the tarmac at the airport . . ."

Fahd! You'd think Felipe knew the late Saudi king *personally*, Sally-Ann thought derisively.

". . . The yacht was so big, it had to refuel in Málaga, because

Marbella was too small. What a beauty, especially when the sails were up. It cost a hundred million green ones and had a hospital on board. One floor of the hospital here was kept open especially for him too," Felipe said chattily between mouthfuls of his rare steak.

"Pity he died last year," Jutta interjected. "His visits were worth millions to the local economy. El Corte Inglés closed to the public when he and the wives and entourage went shopping, and the florists made a fortune because whether anyone was staying in his palace or in the villas that they rented out, or not, the flowers got changed every day—"

"I think that's absolutely immoral. They're such hypocrites too, expecting their people to abide by strict Islamic codes while they break every religious law they're supposed to live by," Sally-Ann scoffed, surprised that her husband's colleague seemed so impressed by the Saudi royal family's excesses.

"And they certainly know how to break those laws," Felipe laughed. "They spend *millions* gambling in the casinos in Monte Carlo and London—"

"So much of that country's wealth is squandered on such dissolute behavior, and the Emirates are the same. So many people working there are treated appallingly . . . I'm talking about the foreign construction workers, the maids, and the like. How can they square treating folk like that with their appalling lifestyle and their religious beliefs?" Sally-Ann mused.

"What about the Mexicans and people of color in America who are on very low wages?" Jutta interjected coolly. "Who cleans *your* pool and minds *your* kids?"

"I take your point, Jutta. Although let me say that our nanny is from Brazil and gets well paid, with lots of perks, and while we do have a Mexican lady who deputizes when our nanny is on vacation, she can, like all American and Western women, vote, drive in public, and observe freely whatever religious practice, if any, that she so chooses. As well as dressing whatever way she wants to. Our culture—in theory, at least—maintains that women and men are equal. *Their* treatment of women is beyond *belief*, veils, long black cover-up garments. Public stonings for so-called adultery, while the man gets away with it. Jailed if they're raped! How appalling is that? And our governments continue to do business with them, and accommodate their excesses . . . sickening! Oh," she added, eyeballing Jutta, whom she decided that she did not care for, "our pool cleaners are two young gay guys from Lake Jackson who have set up a pool maintenance business in Houston, where we live, and are working their delightful little buns off so they can retire to Acapulco . . . in Mexico." Sally-Ann smiled sweetly, ignoring Cal's glare.

"And do *you* work?" Jutta asked, changing the subject, then raising her glass to her lips and studying Sally-Ann dispassionately.

"Well, of course I do. *This* is a working visit to Spain for Cal and me." She flashed a glance at her husband, who raised an eyebrow and frowned at her. She ignored his irritation, glad she'd made her point. A little passive-aggressively, to be sure—and she wasn't a fan of passive-aggressive behavior, preferring to shoot from the hip. "I own a company that creates and maintains travel websites for developers selling or letting deluxe properties. I designed Cal's company's website, actually. One of the reasons I came on this trip is to get background material and to organize videos and a photography shoot of La Joya and our other units up the coast. I've already done the same for the apartments in Biarritz, Antibes, Cap Ferrat, and Menton." Sally-Ann enjoyed the look of surprise that crossed the younger woman's face. Jutta had clearly taken her for a pampered socialite who spent her time getting her nails and hair done and lunching with the girls when she wasn't enjoying trips to foreign countries with her husband.

"We should get you to look at ours. It could do with a revamp. So could yours, Jutta," Felipe exclaimed expansively.

"Anytime," Sally-Ann said politely. "Y'all just let me know what y'all need doin'."

"Did Cal tell you we've discussed expanding our business to Morocco? Luxury villas." Felipe gazed at her with his melting brown eyes. *George Clooney has nothing on this guy,* Sally-Ann thought. The Spaniard was too smooth and smarmy for her liking.

"We haven't had that conversation yet." Cal motioned the wine waiter to order another bottle of the full-bodied Rioja they were drinking.

"So many conversations we have to have, sweetie," Sally-Ann said lightly to her husband, but her eyes were cold.

"So I believe you wish to have an input in the décor at La Joya, Sally-Ann?" Jutta got down to business.

"Indeed. I don't usually get involved in any aspect of the actual letting business, but I really like this area of Spain and I hope to spend a couple of weeks a year here, so I want to put my own stamp on this particular one," Sally-Ann said firmly.

"I have you scheduled in for the day after tomorrow," Jutta said crisply.

"Fine. I've already seen some furniture and fixtures and fittings that I like." Sally-Ann took another sip of wine.

"Oh!" Jutta looked a tad discommoded. "Where, may I ask?"

"Loft and Roomers."

"I see." The German woman was not best pleased.

Sally-Ann smiled. Jutta had her own stores to shop at, where, no doubt, she was well rewarded. But Sally-Ann knew her own mind and knew what she wanted, and if Jutta Sauer didn't like it, she could lump it.

◆

"Heck, Sally-Ann, did you have to be so argumentative tonight?" Cal demanded as they rode the elevator to their floor, having said their good-byes to the other couple.

"Oh, for goodness' sakes, Cal, he was way over the top and *she* sat there looking down her bony nose at us hick Texans. She was, like, so bloody superior. And I'd watch him, he's operating way too fast. And I'd steer clear of villas in Morocco too. Yanks aren't flavor of the month in that neck of the woods, and if there are any terrorist upheavals, they won't travel to North Africa to rent luxury villas. I'm not sayin' he's gonna go on the lam or anything but I bet he's wanting you to bankroll him. Don't! If you want my advice." Sally-Ann yawned.

"I hear what you're saying and I'm not a complete idiot. I see his game," her husband retorted. "Look, forget that. I'm not rushing into anything more with Felipe Perez. We need to talk," Cal said brusquely, swiping his card in the lock and opening the door to their two-bedroom suite before stepping back to let her go ahead of him.

"Cal, I'm tired. Do we *have* to talk tonight? It's been a very long day. I've had too much to drink and I just want to fall into bed," Sally-Ann groaned, kicking her Louboutins off and dropping her lilac pashmina on the back of a chair.

"Lenora is pregnant."

Sally-Ann wasn't *quite* sure what she'd heard. "Excuse me?" She turned to face her husband, who was standing in the lobby, arms folded, looking grim and weary.

"Lenora, the girl I've been seeing, is almost three months pregnant. I want you to hear it from me before anyone else blabs to you."

Sally-Ann stared at him. "You got a girl *pregnant*?"

"Yup. Look I—"

"What age is she?"

"Eh . . . twenty-four—"

"Oh, for God's sake, what on earth have you got in common with a chick of that age? You're nearly twice her age; how clichéd is that!" she derided, shocked at how much his announcement actually hurt. Cal couldn't look her in the eye as he moved past her to stare out the window.

"She's not a ditz; she's actually very intelligent," he snapped defensively. "She graduated summa cum laude—"

"Oh, yeah, in how to wiggle her pert little tush?" Sally-Ann jeered. "I don't care what she graduated in, Cal. We agreed. NO BABIES!" she yelled. "You've changed our family dynamic without a thought for me or the girls—"

"Listen to me. It changes *nothing.*" Cal jammed his thumbs in his waistband and stared at her. "It's not as though we're the couple of the year here. And we haven't been for quite some time. You can still see whom you want to see, I see who I want to see. You're still my wife, the mother of my kids—"

"Row back there, buster, we see other people because *you* started messing around after I lost our baby and the girls were little. At least, that's the first time I knew you were fucking other women. So *that* changed *everything.* But now you've moved the goalposts yet again and you've got a kid coming along. A stepbrother or -sister for our daughters. That changes a *hell* of a lot, mister," Sally-Ann exploded. "We had an agreement, Cal. Shame on YOU!"

"Calm down, y'all." Cal held up his hands as though to ward off her onslaught. "It wasn't planned."

"Not by you, you jackass, but I bet this Lenora chick knew *exactly* what she was doin'," she fumed, hands on her hips. "I suppose we better get a divorce. Well, it's gonna cost ya." Sally-Ann wanted to rake her nails down his tanned handsome face and kick him so hard in the *cojones,* he'd never recover.

"*Hell no!*" Cal looked horrified. "I'm not telling you this to look for a divorce. Look, I'm sorry. It wasn't my intention to have a child out of our marriage. I'll set Lenora and the kid up in an apartment in Galveston. I'll make sure she's well out of your hair—"

"Oh, sweet for her! Galveston by the sea! And what happens if *Lenora* has a son? You always wanted a son to leave the business to, just like your daddy left the business to you. Are the girls gonna be forgotten about?" Sally-Ann poked him hard in the chest.

"Don't *do* that!" he warned, swatting her hand away.

"You sicken me, Cal Cooper. I've put up with a lot from you, but this is beyond!" She turned away and walked to the bedroom.

"Listen, Sally-Ann. I'm not gonna divorce you. I don't want that and I know you don't. The girls are my priority. Life will just go on as before. You can have what you want and do what you want as always . . . within reason, of course," he added hastily.

"Is that so, *mister*? How magnanimous of you," she scoffed. "You might not be gonna divorce me, but I'm gonna divorce *you*!"

"No, no, let's talk," he urged, placing a hand on her arm.

She smacked it away. "There's nothing to talk about. So where is the little momma-to-be right now?"

"Paris," he muttered.

"Paris!"

"She's not been too well so she didn't want to be too far away from me," Cal sighed, loosening his tie.

"So that's why you flew in there? And the business in Paris y'all are heading for tomorrow is a cover for a rendezvous with your little *puta*," she sneered. "I knew somethin' was up this trip."

"Don't call her that," Cal growled.

"Do what ya like, Cal. I couldn't care less anymore. And from now on, take your business trips alone. I won't be entertaining any more of your smarmy business partners this side of the pond or at home. I'm done. Have fun in gay Paree! No need to say good-bye before ya go." She closed the bedroom door and leaned against it, drained.

She heard him move around and then the door to the other bedroom closed. At least she wouldn't have to see him again until they were both home in Texas.

She undressed, sat at the mirror in the sumptuous bathroom, and cold-creamed her face. Her stomach was in knots, and she felt like weeping. The one thing she'd been *adamant* about: no children with other partners while they were still married. He couldn't even abide by that for her. And he didn't want a divorce. He'd been resolute about that. It seemed that poor Lenora was going to be a single mother and not the second trophy wife of a successful, wealthy Texan businessman as she no doubt aspired to be.

And she, Sally-Ann Connolly Cooper, would remain the envied wife of the much-admired Callahan Cooper. Lucky, lucky her. Sally-Ann, staring at her reflection in the mirror, seeing the deadness in her eyes and the cobweb of fine lines that spun out from around them, and the droop of her pale lips, shook her head. *I'm a middle-aged mother of two; an ageing mare compared to the fresh little filly my darlin' husband is steppin' out with. Maybe I should be thankful he doesn't want a divorce,* she reflected, trying to get her head around the bombshell Cal had just dropped on her.

That's what Grace would be telling her. Stay put and take the affluent lifestyle and prestige that came with being Mrs. Cal Cooper. She could swallow her pride and keep the status quo or hightail it out of the marriage and take her chances on her own, and face the devastation divorce would cause their daughters. A daunting prospect, Sally-Ann conceded, dropping her used face wipes in the bin and switching off the light before slipping under the expensive sheets to toss and turn the night away.

◆

Cal poured himself a whiskey straight up and took a slug. It burned against the back of his throat and he waited until the heat warmed his belly before downing another mouthful. The ordeal was over. He'd told his wife about the child. To his surprise, Sally-Ann had taken the news much calmer than he'd expected. She'd ranted and raged—he'd expected that—but she'd run out of steam pretty quick. In the old days she would have clawed at him and slapped his face hard. She'd been a real spitfire when they were young.

He felt strangely sad. They'd been happy once, he and she. He'd met her at a barn dance, on his uncle's ranch, in their last year at high school. He was being groomed to take the reins of his father's company but he wanted one last summer of fun, and Sally-Ann

Connolly was very much the gal he wanted to share that fun with, much to the dismay of the many social-climbing matrons of Houston who had him earmarked for their respective daughters. The refreshing thing about being with Sally-Ann—who was the daughter of his uncle's neighbor, a cotton producer in Lubbock County, West Texas—was her lack of airs and graces. She couldn't give a hoot in hell that Cal was from a wealthy, successful family with half the young eligible and not-so-eligible women of the city after him. She was a straight-talking, no-nonsense, five-foot-ten, auburn-haired goddess and he fell for her . . . hard. It was a magical summer when the world was their oyster and nothing could go wrong. When she turned down Southwestern University in Georgetown and opted for Rice, in Houston, he couldn't have been happier.

Within a few short years they were married, with twins on the way eleven months after their honeymoon. But by the time Sally-Ann got pregnant with their third child, he'd felt completely lassoed.

She'd been real sick on that second pregnancy, hurling morning, noon, and night, as well as being up to her eyes setting up her own web design company. And then she'd lost the baby and had been utterly distraught. Her immense grief had been hard to deal with. He knew he couldn't emotionally sustain her. He tried, clumsily, to tell her that she needed to move on and take care of the two children who *were* alive—and take care of her own wounded spirit so that it would not be drowned by the weight of sorrow that she carried. She'd accused him of being cold and unfeeling. Going home from work became an ordeal and he stayed out longer and later, and that made things even worse between them.

Sex had gone out the window, understandably, and he'd strayed. He wasn't proud of himself, but he'd enjoyed the thrill of the chase and then the fleeting rewards. Once he'd done it the first time, it was easy to do it again. It took the edge off his despair at the way things were at home.

A well-meaning "friend," Susan Mosley, had ratted on him to Sally-Ann. Susan had made a drunken pass at him one night at a barbecue, about a year after Sally-Ann had lost their baby. He'd turned her down and she'd never forgiven him. Susan, with her high-pitched nasal whine and stringy blond hair and her surgically enhanced boobs, had never held any charms for him. Cal grinned, remembering how she'd called him a dirty, low-down skunk, too ladylike, even when she was drunk, to cuss.

Sally-Ann had laughed—a rare and unexpected pleasure—when he told her about Susan touching him up. "If I did that to her, it would be called sexual assault," he'd protested.

"If you did that to her, the whole of the South would know, she'd have got such a thrill," Sally-Ann had teased him, and he'd guffawed. They'd looked at each other, happy to have been unexpectedly "normal," and the spark was back and he'd thrown her on the bed and they'd had wild, raunchy sex and she'd laughed again afterwards when he told her they should invite Susan for a threesome.

Sally-Ann hadn't been laughing when Susan had taken her aside at the annual ladies' charity lunch for autistic children to tell her that her husband, Cal, was cheating on her, with Marcy Montgomery, and there had been more women before Marcy and all of *Texas* knew it and that Sally-Ann was being made a fool of and that she, Susan, didn't like to see that happening to a *dear* friend of hers.

Sally-Ann, showing the kind of spirit for which Cal loved her, had said cuttingly, "Well, thank *you*, Susan, good to know I have a 'friend' like you even if y'all groped Cal yourself, like the good ol' cowgirl y'all are, and would have ridden the flagpole if he hadn't turned you down," before walking away.

When Sally-Ann had told him, verbatim, what she'd said to chicken-legs Mosley, he'd never admired his wife so much. But it was too late for admiration. That episode had been the end of their marriage. "It felt," she told him in utter desolation, "like a double betrayal" when they had only just started to be intimate with each other again. She'd kicked him into a guest bedroom, behaved in public like a good wife should, gone out and got a young tennis coach to get it on with six months later—discreetly, of course—and they would probably have been fine if Lenora, whom he'd being seeing—discreetly, of course—for the past ten months hadn't got knocked up.

Frankly, Cal reflected, knocking back another whiskey, he was surprised by his wife's tame reaction to the news of Lenora's pregnancy. Perhaps she just didn't care enough anymore. *And why should she?* he supposed. She'd seemed more concerned about the girls than herself. He felt deflated to think that whatever residual affection she'd had for him was now completely dissipated. He'd meant it when he'd said he didn't want a divorce. He couldn't imagine a life without Sally-Ann there in the background. And he was *almost* sure she wouldn't want to leave the familiar security of what they had, to step out on her own.

She and the girls had a great lifestyle thanks to him. She was now going to be able to have vacations in Europe with the kids if she so wished. And she had a lot of social standing as his wife back in Houston, even though, at heart, she was a West Texan country gal rather than a city slicker.

The ping on his phone announced the arrival of a text. *It had to be Lenora*, he thought irritably.

Have you told her yet?

God, she'd plagued him for the past two days. He just couldn't face talking to her right now. It would be all "What did *she* say?" and "What did *you* say?" It had to be an age thing, this insecurity. Sally-Ann had not been impressed when she'd discovered how young Lenora was, and rightly so, Cal thought dolefully. His wife was right—he *was* a jackass—and now he was paying for it. And he sure as hell didn't want to marry Lenora, no matter how much she wanted to marry him. Once was enough to be married in a lifetime. Why be a glutton for punishment?

I was just fixin to text ya, he sent back.

Told her. Took it better than I expected. Too late to ring. Will phone ya tomorrow and see ya tomorrow around noon. Sleep tight Sweetie pie, XXX

He sent the text, turned off his phone, finished his whiskey, undressed, and got into bed.

It took Cal a long time to get to sleep. All he could think about was the look of contempt on Sally-Ann's face when she'd called him a jackass.

◆

If only he'd phoned her. Texting was *so* unsatisfactory, and he hadn't added his usual *love ya,* Lenora fretted, standing on the balcony of her hotel room and gazing at the illuminated majesty of the Eiffel Tower piercing the star-studded Parisian sky. She'd always wanted to go to Paris, France, and soon she would be reunited with her lover. The man of her dreams. The father of her unborn child.

It was a pity she was so exhausted. The pregnancy tiredness was *unreal!* Truth be told, she wasn't at all happy to be expecting a baby. But she'd begun to fear that Cal was cooling on her, and when she'd heard of his proposed European business trip with his wife, she'd known desperate measures were called for. She'd stopped taking her contraceptive pill, and although Cal hadn't realized it, she'd contrived to have more sex than usual when she was ovulating. Eleven weeks before the proposed business trip with Sally-Ann she'd discovered she was pregnant.

Lenora would never forget the look of shocked dismay in Cal's eyes when, over dinner in Le Bernardin, the famous French seafood restaurant in midtown Manhattan, she'd refused scallops, which she *adored,* and told him she couldn't eat them because she was pregnant. He was so stunned he'd lost his appetite, unheard-of for Cal. He'd recovered his equilibrium by dessert and stoically told her he would take care of her and get a place for her and the baby to live.

Although privately she was gutted at his initial reaction—because only a fool could persuade herself that Cal was happy to hear he was fathering another child—Lenora had kept her façade up and pretended to be over the moon at her impending motherhood. She'd hoped that the business trip at least would be canceled, but no. When she realized that Cal had every intention of going to the South of France and Spain with Sally-Ann, she'd played her "poorly, pregnant mother" card and insisted on going to Paris to be near him. Lenora *knew* in her heart of hearts Cal didn't want her traveling to Paris, but nevertheless he'd booked a room for her at the Ritz and paid for their flight tickets. They had traveled to Paris two days before Sally-Ann, who had flown direct to Nice.

Lenora had done a little sightseeing by herself when he'd left to join his wife, but it wasn't much fun on her own and she was lonely in the big strange city where she didn't understand the language.

What had Sally-Ann said when Cal had told her his news? Lenora wondered, stepping back into the bedroom and closing the French doors after reading his text. Had she been absolutely furious? Or did she care? The Connolly Coopers had an open marriage, according to Cal. Perhaps his wife wasn't put out. Sally-Ann had to be annoyed, surely? Lenora comforted herself. Her position would be untenable if Cal was planning on getting a place for Lenora and the baby. She sincerely hoped he would be living in it with *them* . . . his new family. Maybe Sally-Ann had demanded a divorce, wanting to get her mitts on her husband's wealth, and that was why Cal hadn't called. Lenora fervently hoped so. She was dying with curiosity as to what *exactly* had ensued. It was unnerving trying to second-guess what both Cal and Sally-Ann were really thinking about the situation.

It was unfortunate that her child would be born before she could marry its father, but Lenora reckoned that she'd a better chance of getting Cal up the aisle by having his child than not. It was a risk she'd taken, but hopefully it was a risk that would eventually pay off.

"Lenora Cooper . . . Mrs. Cal Cooper." She let the words float into the air, liking the sound of them. Or perhaps she'd give herself a double-barrel name like Sally-Ann had, thought Lenora, and include her maiden name. Lenora *Colton* Cooper!

How perfect. How absolutely perfect. She *loved* it. Lenora hummed "Under the Bridges of Paris," trying to keep her spirits up as she nibbled on a cracker and sipped Perrier water, too wound up to get undressed for bed.

Chapter Eight

Anna / Austen

"Isn't this bliss?" Anna raised her face to the sun while sipping her G&T, looking forward to her lunch. She was ravenous. She and Austen had spent the morning unpacking and washing the kitchenware, which had been delivered at ten a.m. Now her presses and drawers were filled with sparkling crystal, cutlery, and the gorgeous lemon-and-blue china she'd bought. Her fitted units now also housed a variety of pots and pans, and her kitchen counter was home to a coffee machine that had provided them with gallons of fresh coffee as they worked. She'd done a wash to test the new washing machine, and her and Austen's smalls, shirts, T-shirts, and trousers were drying in the breeze on a clothes dryer rack that had come with the kitchenware. The towels were gently tumbling in the dryer up in the penthouse.

"Just think of staying here for weeks on end—it's hard to imagine." Austen scoffed some olives and buttered a bread roll. They were at the beachside restaurant beside La Joya.

"I just can't wait to move in," Anna said, dipping a piece of bread into a ramekin of golden olive oil. "It's a pity the beds won't be delivered for a couple of weeks."

"The next time we come we'll be all sorted," Austen promised, leaning back in his chair to allow the waiters to place the dishes of red pepper salad, melon, and Serrano ham, freshly caught sardines straight off the grill, and the Caesar salad that they were sharing on the table.

They ate companionably, chatting occasionally or sometimes in silence, content in each other's company. The breeze, sweetly redolent of the sea, jasmine, and orange blossom, wafted around them, adding to their pleasure as they gazed across the Mediterranean to the coast of Africa and the High Atlas mountains.

"I think that's our immediate neighbor," Anna murmured, seeing a tall, willowy redhead striding along the narrow path that led from the gates of La Joya directly onto the beach.

"Great chassis. I won't mind looking at that view," Austen teased, winking at her.

"Is that so? Well, from what I saw of the hubby, *he* was quite a dish, so I don't give much for your chances," Anna countered, grinning.

"We seem to have quite a mix of neighbors, French, Spanish, English, American, Dutch, and Scandinavians so far," Austen observed.

"Very cosmopolitan. I met an Irishwoman in the Mercadona when you were playing golf yesterday, a widow; she's in the first penthouse in the next block. I've invited her for coffee when we're settled in. She spends the whole winter in Spain."

"Bit lonely, wouldn't it be, on your own?"

"She sounded as though she'd a large family at home and a wide circle of friends out here. You'll never be lonely with a penthouse in Spain," Anna laughed. "I'm getting texts from people I haven't spoken to in ages!"

"Only invite people you really want to see out here; there's nothing worse than visitors you can't relax with or have to 'host.'" Austen did air quotes.

"I know. I'm not going down that road. I'm not spending my

time worrying about guests. Whoever comes can muck in and look after themselves." Her phone dinged and she scrabbled in her bag for it.

"Would you put that bloody phone on silent," her husband remonstrated.

"Ah, I'm not doing too bad. I'm weaning myself off it," she retorted, grinning, finding it in the outside pocket.

"A text from Chloe, I think," she said, squinting at it while rooting for her glasses.

"Give it to me." Austen took the phone from her and opened the text. He had twenty-twenty vision still.

"Good God! What's this? What's she up to now?" he exclaimed, studying the screen as the phone began to chime.

"Let me see." She took the phone from him and studied the photo display before answering.

"What do you think, Mum? Will and I have just bought the ring. He had it designed especially for me! Isn't it awesome? We're engaged," her daughter squealed down the phone. "We're getting married next summer."

Anna and Austen stared at each other in dismay. A wedding—and no doubt, knowing Chloe, she'd want a big one—had not been on their agenda.

"That's wonderful, darling, I'm really happy for you both," Anna managed, heart sinking at the prospect of what lay ahead.

"We want to have an engagement party as soon as you and Dad get home. When will you be home?" her daughter burbled down the line.

"Tuesday . . . we'll be home late afternoon." Anna tried to keep her tone light.

"Brilliant, we'll have it on Saturday. So, should I ring the caterers?"

"Umm, that's not giving them much notice." Anna took a slug of red wine and made a face at Austen, who was listening in to the conversation. The whole of the restaurant could have heard. Chloe was so excited, she was practically yelling.

"Let me say hello to Dad," Chloe demanded.

Anna handed her husband the phone. "Hey, Dad, did you hear? What do you think? Isn't it brilliant?"

"Brilliant," agreed Austen, throwing his eyes up to heaven. "Congratulations to you and Will."

"Oh, I can't wait to see you both in black tie and top hats, and I can't wait to hear your speech. You'll have to say really sweet things about me," his daughter teased.

"I can't wait, either, love," Austen said with heavy irony, which sailed completely over Chloe's head as she babbled on excitedly about the most thrilling day of her life while her parents stared at each other in dismay at this unexpected and vaguely unwelcome development.

"That's put a spoke in our wheel for a bit," Austen remarked drily when Chloe had hung up. "We better put the brakes on the spending."

"I know. Oh, the thought of it. All that palaver for one day! And she'll want a big palaver." Anna moaned. "Black tie!"

"I draw the line at a top hat, I'm telling you that here and now, no matter what she says," Austen asserted.

Anna groaned silently. She could hear the rows between father and daughter already.

"Let's not think about it. We'll say nothing for the moment. Let her enjoy the excitement of it all and then we'll try and talk sense to her," Anna suggested. "Order another beer and a Baileys coffee for me. We might as well make the most of our last few days here."

Austen ordered their drinks and they sat in silence, trying to regain their previous joie de vivre, both wishing their daughter had saved her big news until they'd at least flown home.

Chapter Nine

Sally-Ann / Cal / Lenora

Sally-Ann tapped closed her emails and turned off her iPad. She'd completely focused on work for the last hour; now she was going to take a trip to the furniture shop Jutta Sauer had recommended. It was imperative to keep busy. It meant she didn't have to think about her marital problems.

She hadn't heard Cal leaving earlier. She'd fallen into an exhausted sleep in the early hours and it had been after nine when she'd woken. His luggage was gone and so was he. She'd ordered a room service breakfast—croissants and fresh fruit—and had eaten it on the balcony, deliberately emptying her mind of tumultuous emotions. Her thoughts had turned to her children and she'd felt a fierce longing to hold and cuddle them.

They would have to learn the truth at some stage, that they were going to have a new stepsister or brother. Savannah might be happy with the news, Sally-Ann thought ruefully. She was always asking Sally-Ann to have a baby. Madison would be gutted. She was her daddy's pet; she wouldn't want to share his affections with anyone.

Was Cal already in bed with his little filly? she wondered sourly.

What an asshole he was not to see a chick on the make. Sally-Ann simply could not bring herself to believe that this Lenora gal had got pregnant by mistake.

Cal's insistence that he did not want a divorce seemed real. Clearly he hadn't expected to become a father again. He'd be getting plenty of grief from his new woman when she found out that he wasn't divorcing Sally-Ann. Good enough for him, she scowled, running a brush through her hair and adding a slick of lipstick to her mouth.

She traveled down in the elevator to the basement car park and glanced at the directions Jutta had given her. The furniture shop was east of Marbella in the direction of Las Chapas, where Felipe Perez had built a block of apartments that Cal had bought into.

Felipe was a high flier for sure, Sally-Ann reflected. But unlike her savvy husband, she wasn't quite sure if the other man knew where his limit was. They were a strange couple, the Perezes. He was so lively and full of enthusiasm. She was so cool and reserved. They were still in love, though, she thought enviously, remembering the sideways glances and the way Felipe caressed his wife's arm as they sat side by side at the dinner table the previous night.

It was a while since she'd lain in a man's arms. She was lonely, and horny, Sally-Ann acknowledged glumly, gunning the engine of the hire car and taking the ramp at speed.

◆

"And did you ask her about getting a divorce, Cal?" Lenora probed anxiously, lying in a graceful pose on the enormous bed, waiting for her lover to get undressed.

"She wouldn't hear of it, Lenora. Under *no* circumstances does Sally-Ann want a divorce. I tried my best." Cal undid his belt and unzipped his jeans.

"And you *definitely* told her I was pregnant?" Lenora sat up in dismay, her cloud of chestnut hair tumbling around her shoulders.

"Yup!" Cal stepped out of his Calvin Klein Y-fronts. Lenora was momentarily distracted as she gazed at the impressive sight in front of her.

"So, what are we going to do?" she demanded as Cal pulled her into his arms.

"This," he said, bending his mouth to hers and silencing her with a kiss.

"But, Cal," she said a little while later when they parted to breathe, "you *have* to persuade her to agree. You *want* to be with me and the baby, don't you?"

"Of course I do, sweet honey pie. I'll keep asking. Now, forget about divorces and all that stuff and let's do what we do best," he murmured, sliding his hands down over her hips and pulling her in against him.

Later, as Cal lay beside her, asleep, Lenora stared at the ceiling. She'd not enjoyed their lovemaking as much as usual. Whoever said sex for women was all in the head was right, she admitted miserably. Her head was all over the place.

Was Cal lying to her?

Was he just using her for sex?

Had he really pressed Sally-Ann for a divorce?

What would Lenora do if he left her?

Was she going to end up a single mother?

Would it do any good for *her* to talk to Sally-Ann? Lenora wondered.

She'd have to get her hands on Sally-Ann's phone number. That shouldn't be too difficult over the next few days. She would ring Cal's wife and ask her why would she *want* to stay with a man who was clearly not in love with her anymore, and try and *shame* her into a divorce.

It might work. Nothing ventured, nothing gained, Lenora decided as a sudden wave of nausea washed over her and she had to breathe deeply to stop herself from being sick.

◆

Sally-Ann watched the young Spanish banker in his smart navy suit and crisp white shirt as he patiently explained a point for the third time to the retired English couple who were opening a euro account to receive their sterling pension payments from the UK.

He reminded her of a younger version of Cal, she decided, noticing his long, tanned fingers and the clean cut of his jawline. His hair, inky black, curled a little just to the collar of his shirt and for a moment she had an image of herself running her hands through it.

Hell and damnation! she thought, amused. *Y'all need a man for sure, Ms. Sally.* The banker caught her eye and her smile and gave her a tiny wink. Sally-Ann winked back, enjoying the brief flirtation.

The woman at the next desk became free and beckoned to her, to Sally-Ann's disappointment. Now that she'd made the connection with Señor Dishy, she would have liked to conduct her business with him.

Sally-Ann had her Spanish account set up and was ready to leave while the young woman's colleague was still explaining to his elderly clients about rates going down as well as up.

He gave her a broad smile when she passed his desk and she noted approvingly his gleaming white teeth, so attractive against his tan. She smiled back and nodded and felt a little more light-hearted.

Y'all still got something, she told herself, swinging her car keys and deciding to have a coffee at one of the pavement coffee bars that lined the street. She ordered a latte and a custard pastry and was licking the sticky goo off her finger when she heard a man say, "*Hola.*"

It was the young banker. Sally-Ann wiped her mouth with her napkin. "*Hola* yourself." She was taken aback.

"May I?" He indicated the other chair at her round white table.

"Of course." She nodded. "Are you on a lunch break?"

"No. We close the branch at two-thirty today." He sat and stretched out his long legs and waved at a waiter.

"Nice, short hours," Sally-Ann remarked, sipping her latte.

"This is *España*." He grinned. "And you are American?" His brown eyes glinted with good humor.

"Texan," she corrected, laughing.

"Is Texas not in the US?" He looked puzzled.

"It sure is, honey, but us Texas folk are proud of being from Texas."

"I see," he smiled. "Sebastian Mendoza." He held out his hand.

"Sally-Ann Connolly Cooper," she reciprocated, liking his firm handshake.

"Would you care for another coffee?" he asked politely when the waiter came to take his order.

"Why not? I'm not on a schedule," she agreed, enjoying the chance to have some human interaction, seeing as she'd been practically abandoned by Cal.

"So you are on holidays?" Sebastian sat back in his chair.

"No, not quite. It's a working vacation, sort of."

"And what do you work at?" he inquired, loosening his tie.

Sally-Ann gave him a brief outline of the reasons for her trip to Spain and they chatted easily about web design, holding accounts, and the cultural differences between Europe and America, and she was surprised to see that they had been talking for over half an hour.

"I must go. I have an appointment. So nice talking to you, Sebastian."

"*Gracias*, Sally-Ann, it was my pleasure also. Don't work too hard." He stood up and shook her hand.

"Don't worry, I won't." She smiled. A nice guy, she thought, and surprisingly easy to talk to. She figured he was in his late twenties. She could give him ten years at least. Cal wouldn't care if she had a fling with him, or anyone, she thought ruefully.

Her marriage was an empty, hollow sham of a thing. She was

married in name only and had been for a long time. It was time to face reality. Was this what she wanted in her life?

Sally-Ann weighed the pros and cons of keeping the status quo while she drove to La Joya. Did she *really* want the hassle of a divorce? Wasn't it easier to stay as she was? Easier for the girls too?

The gardener was waiting for her and they decided the best position for the pergola, Sally-Ann visualizing how the roof terrace would look with cane furniture and a patio table. It would be a tranquil haven.

She walked back outside when he'd left, enjoying the refreshing breeze. Her phone rang. She didn't recognize the number. It was an American cell. "Hello?"

"Is this Sally-Ann?" a female voice with a faint midwestern twang asked.

"It surely is. To whom am I speaking?" Sally-Ann would have expected a business caller to use her full name. She heard the young woman take a deep breath.

"Um, I'm Lenora. I know Cal has told you about me, and that I'm pregnant," the voice said, breathlessly, a touch nervously.

"Yes, my husband shot that scud missile at me yesterday," Sally-Ann said coldly. She was stunned. How *dare* Cal give his other woman her cell number? How damn dare he?

"Yes, er . . . well, I know he's asked you for a divorce and you've refused—"

"Excuse *me*?" Sally-Ann's voice rose a pitch.

"You've refused him a divorce even though I'm pregnant with his child." The hostility in Lenora's voice crackled down the line. "Why would you want to stay married to him?"

"Now y'all listen to me." Sally-Ann did not even try to disguise her fury. "Firstly I do *not* appreciate you having the goddamn cheek to ring me on my cell. I do *not* appreciate my husband giving you my number. I do *not* appreciate your attitude, missy. May I remind *you* that I am married to Cal and am the mother of his two legitimate children. And let me tell you in no uncertain terms,

Cal Cooper was the one who wouldn't hear of a divorce, not *me*. So, lady, you have a problem there, because I *will* be divorcin' that rattlesnake so quick it will make his eyes water. He's all yours, honey. You're both welcome to each other. And finally, under *no* circumstances do I *evah* want to *heah* ya little ho's voice again at the end of ma phone. Do y'all hear me?" Sally-Ann ranted, her southern accent becoming even more pronounced in her fury before she hung up.

How dare that little bitch ring her, and how dare Cal give her Sally-Ann's number and blatantly *lie* about the divorce. She dialed his number, roiling with fury.

"Yup, Sally-Ann, what's the problem?" Cal sounded surprisingly calm.

"I don't have a problem, mister . . . you do. How *dare* you give that little floozy of yours my cell numb—"

"Hey, whoa there! I didn't give anyone your cell number—"

"So, what's she ringing me for, askin' *me* why *I* wouldn't divorce you when she's expectin' an' all?" Sally-Ann demanded.

"She did *what*?" The shock in his voice told her he wasn't lying. But it didn't matter anymore.

"Y'all heard, Cal. And let me tell ya, I've had enough of this sham. I'm done. Lawyer up, buddy, 'cause you and I are gettin' a divorce!"

She was damned if she was going to enable her husband's crappy behavior. Cal had some nerve telling that girl that she wouldn't divorce him when it was *he* that was adamantly opposed to divorcing. Ha! Well, let him weasel his way out of *that*, she thought sourly. Now that Lenora knew the truth, he had nowhere to run.

◆

"You had *no* damned business ringing my wife. You had *no* damned business sneaking through my phone to get her number." Cal was so angry, he wanted to throw his suitcase at the huge mirror and watch it smash into smithereens.

"You *lied* to me, Cal!" Lenora yelled. "You said *she* didn't want to divorce and all the time it was *you* that didn't want one. I'm gonna have your child and you told me you wanted us to be together."

"Look, hog-tyin' me is *not* the way to make me want to stay with you, Lenora. And sneaking behind my back isn't, either. Now pack up, we're leaving. I've had enough of Europe, and your tantrums aren't helping. I'm getting the concierge to get us the hell out of Paris on the first flight available—"

"But we were supposed to be having a romantic few days here," Lenora protested, horrified.

"Well, you damn well made sure that's not going to happen, didn't you, honey? Pack up your duds, we're going home." Cal picked up the phone and rang down to the concierge, turning his back on Lenora.

Reluctantly she went to the wardrobe and took out the designer suitcase, part of a travel set Cal had bought her. Did "going home" mean they were going to be together, or was he going to dump her?

Seeing the implacable set of his back against her, Lenora decided that right now keeping silent was the best policy.

"I'll ring you back shortly, Monsieur Cooper," the concierge said politely after Cal made his request for the earliest flight he could get from Charles de Gaulle to Houston, first-class and preferably nonstop.

He could *strangle* Lenora. She'd really landed him in a load of cow shit. He did not want a divorce. He did not want a second marriage, and with the possessive way she was behaving, right now he didn't want to spend eleven hours on a flight to the States with her, let alone the rest of his life.

Cal picked up his cell. He needed to make an appointment with his lawyer. Sally-Ann's tone had left him in no doubt that she was going for a divorce. He wanted to make sure she didn't take him to the cleaners. If a battle was what his wife wanted, a battle was what she would get.

◆

"Excuse me?" A tanned woman in a floral sundress stood in front of Sally-Ann, who had gone down to the beachside restaurant for a restorative coffee.

"Hi, can I help ya?" Sally-Ann asked politely, wondering wildly if this was another of Cal's women.

"My name is Anna MacDonald. I'm your next-door neighbor in La Joya and . . . erm . . . well, the thing is, I was on the balcony earlier and couldn't help overhearing your phone conversation, and I don't mean to intrude, but I was just wondering if you were OK?"

"*Oh!* Oh my gosh! I'm so sorry y'all had to hear that. I guess I had raised my voice an octave or two. I'm truly sorry." Sally-Ann was mortified.

"Don't worry about it in the slightest," said the other woman. "I'm not being nosey and I don't want to intrude in a private matter; I just wanted to make sure you were OK, if you're on your own."

"Well, I guess I'm stunned, to tell ya the truth," Sally-Ann replied. "And it's very kind of you to be concerned. Again, I apologize for interrupting the peace at La Joya with my marital difficulties." She gave a wry smile.

"Oh, not at all. I hope you don't think I'm—"

"Hello, ladies. Enjoying the sun? How nice to have the time to relax." Jutta Sauer walked briskly past their table with a tanned, well-dressed couple in tow.

"Hi, y'all," Sally-Ann said dispiritedly.

"Hello, Jutta." Anna nodded as the tall German woman swept past.

"More lambs to the slaughter," Sally-Ann murmured acerbically, and Anna laughed.

"Are you one of her clients too?"

"I am, though to be honest I sometimes feel she's telling me what *she* wants, rather than the other way around."

"Yup, she's bossy all right." Sally-Ann managed a smile.

"But she's good at what she does, I can't deny it. We got some lovely pieces of furniture. Um . . . do you fancy a glass of wine? My husband's playing golf and I've done as much as I can up in the apartment and I'm thirsty!" Anna confessed. "But if you'd prefer to be by yourself, I understand perfectly, of course," she added considerately.

Sally-Ann felt some of the tension flow out of her body. A glass of chilled wine would be delicious, and kind company—and Anna was a kind woman, she felt—would be welcome, even if it was the company of a stranger. It would stave off the moment she dreaded, contacting her lawyer and taking the first step in the combat ahead.

"A glass," she laughed. "Hell no, let's have a bottle. My name is Sally-Ann Connolly Cooper, soon to lose the 'Cooper,' and I'm delighted to meet you, if under somewhat embarrassing circumstances."

"Likewise, and forget the circumstances," Anna returned, signaling the waiter and sitting down opposite Sally-Ann with a grin.

I like her, thought Sally-Ann gratefully, glad that her new neighbor wasn't that prickly Spanish man she'd encountered a couple of times. This was the weirdest day of her life, for sure, and there was trouble ahead. But for now she would drink her wine and look at the sea while getting to know the woman who had overheard her tell her husband she was divorcing him. Anna was surprisingly easy to talk to, and Sally-Ann found herself confiding her troubles to her new and sympathetic neighbor. When Austen, Anna's husband, joined them and pressed her to have dinner with them later in their penthouse, she found herself agreeing. It was better than being on her own, she reflected back at her hotel, turning on her laptop to have a Skype session with her girls.

"Mom, Mom, Savannah is being, like, real mean and she cheeked Grandma," Madison's indignant face filled the screen.

"You are a dirty little liar, Madison Connolly Cooper," yelled her twin.

"No I'm not, you did; you told Grandma to—"

"Girls! Girls, stop it or I'm shutting down the computer right this minute," Sally-Ann said sternly. It was always the same when she was away from home, and tonight she wasn't in the humor to pacify them.

"Noooo, Mommmm, don't do that," whined Madison. "Did you get me the flamenco dress and castanets you promised?"

"Not yet, but I will."

"And did you get me—"

"Girls, listen to yourselves. I'm ashamed of you," Sally-Ann said sternly. "What have I told you both before about asking for presents?"

"Sorry, Mom." Savannah had the grace to look ashamed. "Is Daddy with you?"

"No, he's in Paris, sweetie," Sally-Ann sighed.

"When will you be home?" Madison elbowed her sister out of the way.

"Soon."

"Good, 'cause I miss you," Madison said forlornly.

"And I miss *you*, pumpkin pie," Sally-Ann echoed, feeling a lonesome tug at her heartstrings. They had no idea what was rolling down the tracks towards them. Divorce and a new baby. A half brother or sister. That was if she and Cal decided they should know about the interloper who was coming into their lives. There were so many decisions to be made, so much to talk about and work out what was in their children's best interests. Much as she wanted to kick Cal into kingdom come, she didn't want their divorce to be one where the children were pawns in a nasty game. The less impact divorce had on them, the better, and for that she would do her best to maintain some sort of a reasonably civil relationship with her low-down snake of a double-dealing husband.

She chatted to the children for a while longer before stepping into the shower to wash her hair and prepare for her night out with her new neighbors. She could smell delicious aromas coming from the beach, where the hotel's chef was barbecuing for the guests. Her stomach rumbled. Sally-Ann gave a wry smile as she applied her makeup, a crimson-slashed sky reflected in her bedroom mirror. Never in any trauma in her life had she lost her appetite. Impending divorce, stepmotherhood, and deep unhappiness wasn't going to change that, it seemed.

Her phone vibrated and she flipped it open to see a text from Cal.

At CDG, flying home tonight. Give me the name of your lawyer and let's get the show on the road. The sooner this is settled the better, if you really want a divorce.

Sally-Ann's lips tightened. She knew what Cal was up to. He felt she was bluffing and he was putting the pressure on, hoping she would back down.

She closed her phone, switched it to silent, and put it in her bag. She would respond to that text if and when she felt like it, and certainly not tonight. If her husband thought he was running the show, he could damn well think again. He was the one with a pregnant mistress. He was the one on the back foot. He could send all the texts he liked; nothing was going to change that.

Chapter Ten

Jutta

Jutta glanced impatiently at her watch. The Spanish girl who was due for an interview was late. Not a good first impression. She studied the list of potential applicants who had applied to join the cleaning and maintenance team. There were three new positions up for grabs and she'd chosen ten from a long list of forty.

Olga, her office manager, had allotted twenty minutes per interview. Jutta would be stuck in the office all morning. She should have hired the new staff before La Joya had opened, but there had been a slight cash-flow problem, because some of her existing clients had not paid their fees on time. She'd had to source temporary cleaning staff for the new apartments now on her books. She much preferred to have her own cleaners. They knew she expected work of the highest standards. Jutta always made that very clear from the start. The new business being generated by Felipe's collaboration with the Americans would kick in financially in the near future, but Jutta liked to keep a tight control on her budgets and line of credit—unlike her husband, who never worried about such "trivialities."

"There's another girl out in Reception who's early—"

Olga didn't get to finish her sentence.

"Bring her in," Jutta ordered. "Tell"—she looked at the list—"Sofia Manrique, *if* she turns up, that she'll have to go to the end of the queue. Not that I'm much inclined to employ her. If she can't be on time for her job interview, what will she be like coming to work?"

Three candidates stood out. A young English couple and a Polish girl who reminded Jutta of her younger self. Jutta had already decided to employ them before finally giving the late applicant two minutes of her precious time.

Sofia Manrique, with her nose and belly piercings and headphones hanging around her neck, had sprawled in front of Jutta, earning a cold stare. "Let me give you a word of advice for further job interviews you will be applying for, Señorita. Be there five minutes early. Ditch the piercings and the headphones. Sit up straight and *pretend* at least to be interested. Today you have wasted my time and yours. *Adiós.*"

The young woman's jaw dropped at Jutta's chilly dismissal. She sloped out to Reception, muttering "*perra*" as she went. Olga hid a smile. Jutta had been called much worse than a bitch, by her own staff sometimes. She was a hard taskmaster, but she paid well.

"OK, Olga, let's go with these three. Do you agree?" Jutta asked, showing her the list with the three marked names.

"Fine. I'll get Christine to show them the ropes. They can start in Jasmine Gardens and work as a unit. Christine can do the monthly inspections while she's at it."

"Let me know their schedule so I can inspect the work," Jutta instructed. "Anything else I need to attend to while I'm here?"

"Yes. You got an email from Sally-Ann Connolly Cooper's website design firm with contact details, and three suggested formats for our proposed new website." Olga tapped on her keyboard and opened up the email.

"That was quick." Jutta was impressed in spite of herself, noting the background of muted pastels that gave an impression of class and elegance. The Texan must have got her people on it right away.

She studied the three proposals and pointed her finger at the first one. "Tell them I like that and look forward to seeing how they develop it. OK, I'm off to La Joya to take some measurements and then to Cabopino to look at a renovation project. Tell Christine to set up the direct debits for our new clients."

"Will do . . . Aren't you going to have any lunch?"

"I've a table booked in Da Bruno later; I'm treating a couple of concierges to lunch. It's always good to keep in with them." Jutta opened her bag, took out her bronzing powder and lipstick, and refreshed her makeup. "I must introduce myself to the community manager in La Joya, although I won't invite her to lunch. No point. Once the builders hand over, she'll be gone and there'll be a new concierge installed." Jutta was nothing if not pragmatic and never wasted expenses unless she was sure of a return.

It was a nuisance that La Joya was a twenty-minute drive west of their office in Marbella, while her other appointments were to the east; but she was used to scorching up and down the A-7, and she wanted to check measurements and take photographs of the third apartment she was fitting out in the new complex.

She took advantage of a red light to join the traffic flow, wondering idly if she would bump into the American woman again. The husband was going to Paris on business, and Sally-Ann was going to visit Mobile & Diseño at Jutta's suggestion. They had agreed over dinner the previous evening that Jutta would shop for the kitchenware, bed linen, and the like. After all, it was primarily a rental apartment; there was no point in spending a fortune on fine bone china and branded silver flatware.

They were an interesting couple, the Coopers. Sophisticated, well educated, well traveled, but clearly unhappy together. There had been an unmistakable coolness, more on her part than his. But they worked well together as a team, just like she and Felipe did.

Twenty minutes later she pulled into the entrance to La Joya and pressed her fob. The complex was busy. Furniture vans, TV and broadband installation vans, and a garden center van whose driver was loading massive terra-cotta planters onto a trolley. She pulled into her client's parking space and glanced over towards the office to see if the community manager was there. She could collect her client's post while she was at it. The woman was there and Jutta, all businesslike, made her way over to the office.

"*Hola*, I'm working for several owners in the complex. My name is Jutta Sauer and I just wanted to introduce myself to you," she said, handing the other woman her card.

"And I am Señora Constanza Torres. It's nice to meet you, Señora Sauer."

"If I could just collect my client's post while I'm here. Block three, number twenty-six," Jutta said politely.

"I'm very sorry, Ms. Sauer, but I need written permission from the owner before I can let you take their post," the other woman said firmly.

"Oh! But I have their keys." Jutta produced a set of keys with the client's name on it.

"Nevertheless, I must insist on written permission. You must understand, I have a responsibility as community manager."

"Very well, I'll see to it. *Adiós*." Jutta tried to hide her exasperation. Keys were keys; what more authority did the woman need?

"*Gracias, adiós*," Señora Torres replied graciously with a regal incline of her head, and Jutta felt she'd been summarily dismissed.

She marched out of the office and walked quickly to block three. The deliveryman with the planters was maneuvering himself and his loaded trolley into the lift. "Sorry," he said apologetically. "I just have to deliver these to the third floor and we won't all fit."

"No problem. Will you send it back down to me?" Jutta instructed. It was always the same when you were in a hurry. She could take the stairs, but instead she checked her emails and text messages while waiting, and eventually the lift came back down.

As she took measurements for a fitted unit, Jutta could hear the planters being rolled along the balcony directly above. They were enormous. Even when empty they were heavy. She hoped the balcony was built strongly enough to support them when they were filled with soil.

Her phone rang and she saw Felipe's number flash up. "Hey, babe," he said cheerily. "The bank has given us the go-ahead to buy the land in Alicante. We're going to build exactly as we did in Jasmine Gardens, same plan, same design; that will save us a fortune on architects' fees."

"Yes, but will you get planning permission for them?" Jutta asked the most important question.

"Don't worry about that, *cariña*, all sorted."

"Felipe, don't tell me you bribed someone," Jutta groaned.

"Would I?" he chuckled. "Get your glad rags on tonight, I'm bringing you to El Lago to celebrate."

"You're really pushing the boat out, Felipe. Shouldn't we wait until the first stone is laid?" Jutta suggested. El Lago was one of the most exclusive restaurants in Marbella, and her husband's favorite.

"We can celebrate again when that happens. There's a full moon tonight; I'm going to make love to you like you've never been made love to before, somewhere dark and moonlit," he said huskily, and she felt desire flare. Her husband loved outdoor sex and so did she. It would be a wonderful night of celebration if only that little niggle of anxiety that everything wasn't aboveboard with Felipe's latest venture would melt away.

There had been a big crackdown on corruption in the past year. Mayors, town councillors, and others were being arrested and charged. Jutta liked everything done properly. But mostly she'd found that it was all about paying hard cash so taxes wouldn't have to be paid or for favors granted. So different from her homeland. Well, Felipe could run his own company whatever way he wanted. She would run hers as she saw fit and she was glad that financially they were completely separate entities.

She finished up and called the lift down from the third floor. The Spanish owner from the apartment above was inside it. He barely nodded in her direction. He was a most unfriendly man, Jutta reflected. Apparently he was from Madrid. He was the type who would pay his taxes, she thought, amused, as the lift glided to a halt and she swept out ahead of him as though she owned the place. Señora Torres gave her a polite smile when they passed each other on the terrace. Jutta was tempted to ignore her, but she allowed herself a nod. The community manager would be gone soon enough. Jutta would make sure to ingratiate herself with whomever took over. It was well known that the concierges were the most powerful people in any complex, with their fingers on the pulse of all activity. Somehow or another, Jutta felt whoever came to take over from Señora Torres in La Joya would have their work cut out for them, with the likes of the owner from Madrid laying down the law.

Chapter Eleven

Eduardo / Consuela

Eduardo stood in his apartment lobby, irritated at the length of time it was taking for the lift to come to his floor. He could hear sounds below, a clattering and banging, men's voices, muttered curses. It had been like this all morning and it was getting on his nerves. He pulled open the door to the stairwell and marched down to the second floor. Opening the door to the landing, he saw two men, the blond-haired woman he'd seen in the building several times before, and a sofa that seemed to be stuck in the lift.

"If you got it in, you must be able to get it out," the blond woman was saying.

"That's what my girlfriend said last night," the younger man said, smirking.

Eduardo gave him a withering stare, disgusted at his smutty talk. "What is going on here?" he demanded. "I'm trying to access the lift to my floor."

"I'm sorry, we're having some difficulty with the furniture." The woman shot him a look of irritation.

"That lift isn't made for a sofa that size," Eduardo pointed out crossly. "It's too big and too heavy. You're going to cause damage."

"It's fine," said the older man dismissively. "We do this all the time in apartments."

"I beg your pardon, it looks far from fine to me." Eduardo glared at the man in the green overalls who had had the temerity to dismiss his concerns.

"I'm sorry about this. We'll have it sorted *pronto*," the blond woman snapped.

"As I say, I have concerns for the lift; after all, it is communal property, for *all* our use," Eduardo reiterated. "You should have considered the size when you were buying it." He glanced in at the apartment, which was directly below his, and saw boxes and cardboard and bubble wrap strewn over the floor. Dramatic orange curtains blazed against the windows and white walls. The color made him wince. Clearly his new neighbor had flamboyant tastes.

"Señor, if you leave us to our work, we will be done very shortly," the deliveryman said confidently.

"I shall be inspecting the lift and will make a complaint to the office if there is any damage. This is not good enough," Eduardo said coldly, opening the stairwell door to walk down to the ground floor.

"May I remind you, Señor," the woman said tartly in her quite proficient Spanish, "you yourself delayed use of the lift when you had those extremely heavy planters brought up to your apartment recently. I might add that they are on the balcony that overhangs this one and I hope your balcony can sustain the weight of them. I may have to make an inquiry about it."

Eduardo took a sharp breath at her impertinence. "Let me assure you, Señora, that you need have no cause for concern in the slightest. I apologize for delaying the lift. Nevertheless, I must protest the size of that sofa and I'll be inspecting the lift for damage." He was furious at being put on the back foot by that insolent German woman. He knew she was German because he'd heard her on her phone jabbering away in that guttural language.

"*Hijo de puta*," he heard as the door closed behind him. Eduardo's lips thinned at the slur: How *dare* that *pequeño bastardo* call him a son of a bitch! He marched out of the building and saw a large furniture van taking up three spaces because it was parked sideways. Another irritation. He noted the name of the company. A complaint would be issued from his secretary forthwith, and Señora Torres also would be informed that as community manager she should ensure that the lifts were not in danger of being damaged by removal companies delivering furniture that was clearly oversized and needed to be hoisted into the apartments by a crane.

"I shall come and inspect and see if your complaint is valid," Señora Torres said coldly when Eduardo stood in her office making his protests in his most officious voice.

"Of course it's valid, Señora. Would I be here otherwise?" Eduardo couldn't hide his indignation.

"You have already complained about children using big swimming rings in the large pool, and about residents hanging their towels over the—"

"We are not a tenement; there are standards," he said sharply. "And I, as an owner, expect—"

"Señor, after the first management committee meeting these issues will all be ironed out. But this is the settling-in time; we must make allowances," Señora Torres interrupted him briskly. "I shall check the issue with your lift in five minutes; I have some business to conduct on the phone first. Take a seat on the terrace. Excuse me, please." The community manager dismissed him as though he were some irritating little schoolboy, and Eduardo was fit to burst. *That woman acts as though she owned the complex,* he bristled, sitting on one of the cane chairs to await her royal pleasure.

He was in bad form today. He and Consuela had had a rare tiff. They had hired a painter to paint his aunt's bedroom the apple green she desired. Eduardo had been grumpy about it, he admitted. "I'm not a fan of that color, and it *is* my apartment. She forgets that and thinks she's entitled to have her say and dictate, like she's always done," he'd grumbled.

"Eduardo, it was I who asked her what color she would like," Consuela reminded him.

"Well, you should have asked *me* first," Eduardo retorted petulantly.

"Fine, you paint and decorate *your* apartment as *you* see fit," Consuela retorted, in a rare show of spirit, before walking out of their hotel room with her book and sunglasses to go and sit and read in the hotel gardens. They were on the last few days of their own holiday. He'd taken Beatriz home the previous week. They had selected their furniture and fittings, which would be delivered once the painting was finished, and Eduardo had very much hoped to have one or two nights in the apartment before they returned home to Madrid.

He would have to apologize to his wife for his bad behavior, he supposed; that was another irritant to add to the many that were besetting him today.

"I am ready now," Señora Torres broke in on his musings, and he stood up to follow her as she led the way at a brisk pace to his apartment block. In silence they walked into the foyer and she reached out to press the lift button. Eduardo inhaled a deep breath. Now she would understand his worry, he thought self-righteously, although he heard no sounds from above. The door slid open.

"Oh!" he exclaimed, peeved that his complaint *seemed* unjustified.

"Nothing to worry about I see. *Buen día,* Señor," the community manager said snippily before turning on her heel to walk to the entrance door.

The day would come when that woman would no longer be a part of the complex. Once the builders handed over to the new management committee, she would be, thankfully, gone. Eduardo glared at her retreating back. He would make sure he was on that committee, and once he was, rules would be obeyed and La Joya de Andalucía would most certainly *not* become a common or garden holiday resort like so many others along the coast. Standards would be maintained to the highest order, and he, Eduardo, would make certain sure of *that*!

◆

Consuela tried to relax and read her thriller, but she simply could not concentrate. It was very breezy, and the pages of her book flapped irritatingly, adding to her annoyance. It also didn't help that she felt she was getting her period. She had the cramps and the bloat, but nothing was happening. A rock of grief lay heavy in her chest. She was in her *menopausia* and knew that the chances of her having a child were nearly gone. A Niagara of tears slid down her cheeks beneath her sunglasses, and Consuela grieved for the passing of her youth and reproached herself for a life timidly lived. But most of all she wept knowing that now she would never be a mother. How she'd *longed* for a baby all her married life. Having a child of her own would have fulfilled her like nothing else.

Sometimes she felt Eduardo was just as glad not to have become a parent. He liked that he was the center of her attention always. He would not go and be tested to see why she could not conceive. He would not allow her to be tested, either. "It is the will of God if we have a child or not, Consuela, and all the tests in the world won't change that."

"Well, then, could we not adopt?" she'd asked him once.

"No, not now. Not ever. I would always be reminded of the fact that my parents left me to be reared by my aunt every time I looked at the child. *That* I do not wish." He'd been so emphatic, she'd never brought up the subject again.

She'd always subjugated her wishes to those of her husband, dampening down the resentment, knowing that he loved her because she was gentle and kind, the complete antithesis to Beatriz.

But this past year in particular, Consuela had felt herself being submerged in waves of fury, resentment, and bitter self-recrimination. *Why* had she taken the path of least resistance? *Why* had she put Eduardo's feelings and desires before hers? Always! Was this how her life would forever be? *Why* was she so unable to speak her truth about what *she* wanted? Her husband did not see her as an equal in their marriage; he never had. Her role in the tapestry of her husband's life was to support, cherish, and nourish him at all times, and although he could not be kinder to her, it wasn't enough now.

When she'd turned fifty, three years ago, she'd suggested that they have a different type of holiday. Just the two of them. A river cruise, she'd proposed. The Rhine, the Douro, the Canal du Midi—anywhere, just for a change. She'd been holidaying in the south since she was a child. There was nothing new for her there. It would be a nice birthday treat.

He'd thrown up many excuses—What if they didn't like the people they were sharing the cruise with? It would be a chore having to dine with strangers at every meal and make polite conversation. If the weather was bad, they would be trapped on board the vessel and it could be very boring. What if *Tía* Beatriz took ill when they were out of the country—despite the fact that his aunt had the constitution of an ox then? Consuela had given up.

It was after that rejection of her wishes—which coincided with the beginning of her menopause—that all the emotional moods and sensations began to overwhelm her.

Consuela took some deep breaths, relieved that she was far enough away from other holidaymakers that they could not hear her smothered sobs. She'd read a magazine article recently that had said that if issues were not dealt with, they would rise up and manifest until notice was taken of them and they were faced. Often it was in menopause these unresolved issues came up, the article explained. She'd hoped that her issues were minor, if any. But Consuela knew she was fooling herself and wished she hadn't picked up that magazine to read disturbing material that shone a harsh spotlight on her failings.

Today, as well as feeling sadness, she was *furious*, with a white-hot anger that she'd only once before experienced when her younger brother had broken the little ballerina on a cherished jewellery box her grandmother had given her for Christmas. It was an accident, her mother said, trying to soothe her heartbroken wails, but Consuela knew it was no accident. Juan Luis was jealous because she was their grandmother's favorite, and had twisted the little dancer hard to stop her dancing, a look of triumph on his face as he held the box away from her.

Never again until now had she felt such scorching anger. Eduardo had declared authoritatively that she should have *sought* his permission first before asking Beatriz what color she would like her bedroom painted. He'd called it *his* apartment. She'd only been trying to pacify his bloody aunt and make his life less stressful—as she always did, Consuela raged silently. And that was the thanks she got.

When he came back from whatever he was doing in the new apartment, he'd be cold and unapproachable, and she'd have to ingratiate herself back into his good books because she'd thrown a strop and called him on his offensive behavior. There would be frosty silence on his part until he was ready to thaw. Well, she wasn't having the last few days of her holiday ruined, Consuela decided with uncharacteristic determination. It was time she started making her own tapestry and doing what *she* wanted to do for a change. She lifted up her phone from her beach bag and dialed a number and held a short conversation with the woman at the other end. Five minutes later she gathered her book, bag, sunglasses, and sunscreen and hurried up to their room. Quickly, neatly, she packed her case, wrote a short note to her husband, freshened up her makeup, and closed the door behind her. Her heart was racing while she waited for the taxi the concierge had ordered for her to arrive.

Eduardo would be *astonished*, Consuela acknowledged when she saw the taxi pull up. Her actions were unprecedented in their marriage. Let him be astonished; let him be furious. For once in her life she was putting herself first, and if her husband wasn't careful she would go on a holiday cruise by *herself* next year, she decided recklessly, settling into the car and giving the driver the address of her destination. It had taken fifty-three years of giving and doing for others. *Not anymore*, Consuela thought as rebellion burned within her.

She settled back in her seat, watching the urbanizations along the coast flash by, interspersed with glimpses of shimmering blue sea and thickets of emerald forestry. *A time for me*, she reflected with a rueful smile, wondering how long she would be able to keep up her unexpected mutiny.

◆

Eduardo was weary when he arrived back at the Don Carlos. When the painter had left, he had washed all the floors and the tiles in the bathrooms and then swept and washed the terra-cotta tiles on the balcony. He'd rather enjoyed the uncommon physical labor, gaining a pleasing sense of satisfaction when he'd seen the gleaming surfaces and inhaled the mixture of scents—fresh paint and Don Limpio cleaning sprays—redolent of newness, cleanliness, and the promise of days of brandy and roses to come. The furniture was scheduled to arrive the following day. Perhaps they might even spend the night there, Eduardo thought, taking a bottle of cold Perrier from the minibar. He would have a short siesta on the bed and then go and look for his wife, who was no doubt lying under a palm tree, immersed in one of the gory thrillers she so favored.

He hoped her uncharacteristic huff had waned and that she was sorry for her ungracious behavior. He would forgive her, magnanimously, after her apology and then they would enjoy the last few days of their holiday before returning to the scorching heat of Madrid and the pressure of their day-to-day life. He drank thirstily and lay down on the bed, feeling the tiredness ebb from his body.

Eduardo awoke, unsure of where he was, then, remembering, glanced at the clock on his bedside locker. It was almost five-thirty and the afternoon was drifting into evening. He'd shower and change and go in search of Consuela, he decided, his gaze alighting on a white envelope propped up against the mirror. His name was written on it, in his wife's elegant cursive.

A feeling of unease overcame him as he stiffly rose off the bed. Why would Consuela be writing him a note? Had she gone somewhere, with a friend, perhaps—made an arrangement out of the blue? Why hadn't she phoned him? Or had she come into the room and not wanted to waken him? That was it, Eduardo decided. That was exactly it. Consuela was nothing if not thoughtful and always ever considerate of his needs. He yawned as he opened the envelope and removed the note written on the hotel's headed notepaper. He read it, and reread it, brow furrowed, a look of dismay and incomprehension crossing his sallow features.

> *Eduardo, today you went too far. I am hurt and offended by your behavior. I wish to have these last few days of holidays in peace without having to endure any of your moods. I'll meet you at María Zambrano station for our return to Madrid. Enjoy your apartment.*
> *Consuela.*

"*Oh, Madre de Dios!*" Eduardo threw his eyes heavenward towards the Holy Mother he'd just invoked. What was going on with his wife? Just when he needed her support and assistance. She was hurt, offended by his behavior! Just because he'd called it *his* apartment instead of theirs. How childish it was to get into a mood over a silly remark like that! He picked up his mobile phone and dialed her number. This was nonsense and she knew it. It rang out and the message minder came on. He took a deep breath. "Consuela, ring me please. This is silliness. I am sorry if you are offended. The furniture is coming tomorrow and I need you here with me to arrange it and make up the beds. I shall book dinner for eight p.m. this evening." He hung up, unable to think of anything else to say.

He waited with mounting impatience for his wife to call him back. But the call never came.

He rang her cousin and best friend, Catalina, but the call rang out.

He rang Consuela again and this time a text came.

Never call me silly again, Eduardo. I need some peace for a few days. I'll meet you at the station. I'll be keeping my phone off. C.

Eduardo read and reread her message. What was wrong with his wife? Was she ill? A brain tumor, perhaps, or the beginning of dementia? There was no logical reason for her to behave like this. True, she was a little more impatient and sometimes edgy these days, but that was that menopause event women went through, he presumed. It was something he didn't care to discuss with her. That was women's stuff. And besides, Consuela was not in the habit of discussing such matters with *anyone*.

Unable to face dinner alone in the restaurant, he called up a room service meal and picked at his pan-fried bream with lackluster appetite. In these last couple of days the purchase of the apartment, which had given him such immense pleasure to buy, was causing nothing but stress, he thought woefully. And all because of women. Ungracious women—his aunt; bossy women—Constanza Torres; and now an irrational woman—his wife, the one woman who had always been a comfort and joy to him.

Was the moon full? he wondered with dry humor, trying Consuela's number again.

"My heart is very heavy, Consuela. I bought the apartment as a surprise for you and this is how you reward me," he said. "Please call me in the morning. I am very worried about you. This is not normal behavior for you."

He undressed and got into bed. But sleep would not come, and he tossed and turned until dawn kissed the night sky in the east and the sun rose splendidly on the horizon.

◆

Consuela slept soundly in the double bed in her cousin's guest room in La Cala. The room in which she'd spent many nights on holidays as a child. The old familiar scents of lavender and wax furniture polish brought her instantly back to those happy days. A miraculous peace seemed to have descended on her as soon as she arrived to Catalina's warm embrace. Catalina, as close as a sister. They had no secrets from each other.

"Stay as long as you like; rest, relax, enjoy," the other woman invited kindly, offering her a dry sherry. Catalina didn't pry into the reasons Consuela had come to stay. She knew she would be told in good time.

Sitting in the shaded, high-walled courtyard, trailing bougain-villea and orange blossom in a glorious profusion of color, with the breeze blowing her hair away from her face and the soothing trickle of the water fountain—a comforting and familiar back-drop—Consuela felt the tension seep out of her body and knew she had, for the first time that she could remember, made a wise decision to put herself and her needs first.

◆

So it finally happened. She's had enough of Eduardo and his controlling ways, thought Catalina, busying herself preparing a tapas supper. *I never expected it would take so long.* She turned her phone to silent, knowing that, undoubtedly, Eduardo would ring her once he'd discovered Consuela's departure. It was one phone call that she would not be taking. Catalina smiled, and chopped and diced and drizzled olive oil on her ingredients while her dear cousin sipped her pre-supper sherry, enjoying her unaccustomed solitude.

Chapter Twelve

Constanza

Constanza Torres closed down her computer, arranged her papers neatly, and placed a thank-you card and a box of chocolates in her large shoulder bag. A grateful owner had left them for her and the kind gesture cheered her up enormously.

She was tired. It had been a long and eventful week. It was always the same when a new complex opened. Exhilarating and exhausting in equal measure.

Constanza picked up the letter that had been addressed to her and read it again, although she already knew it by heart. The builders' representative had spoken to an ad hoc committee of the new owners and it seemed as though they were very interested in asking her to take up the position as concierge.

She folded the letter neatly, replaced it in the envelope, and placed it in her bag. She turned off the lights and locked the office door. It was late, after ten p.m. She'd come back to La Joya to deliver an oven rack she'd purchased for one of the owners, who had found theirs to be missing. Above and beyond the call of duty, she knew, but she took pride in her job and was excellent at it. This was not conceit on Constanza's part. She'd worked on many new complexes on the Costa. She had a great reputation. Builders and developers vied for her services and expertise.

But she was somewhat weary of it now. Acting as a concierge would be a wind-down from the stress of new builds. She walked slowly around the gardens, enjoying the peace with only the crickets chirruping and the gentle hush of the sea. The gardens and pools illuminated with soft tinted lights looked magical in the velvet darkness, and the reflection of the full moon shimmered gold and silver on the gently rippling sea. This was one of the nicest apartment complexes she'd ever worked in. It was small compared to most. Exclusive. She'd loved it from the moment she'd first set foot in it.

Most of the owners were very pleasant, apart from one or two. But that was always the way. Constanza smiled to herself, remembering that she'd wondered if Eduardo De La Fuente was buying his apartment as a love nest. Who would have an affair with him? He was most officious and prim. It was a wonder he even had a wife! He would be a troublemaker, and the Belgian woman too. But she could deal with them. She had years of experience of dealing with the likes of them.

The idea of being in the one place, not having to move from new build to new build, was very attractive. If a formal offer of a position were made, she would take it, Constanza decided, looking out over the lights of Gibraltar and Africa.

Under her steady and experienced management the complex would indeed be *La Joya de Andalucía*. Constanza let herself out through the narrow gate that led to the beach. A glass of fruity red wine and a tapas supper awaited her in the beachside restaurant. And much deserved it was too, Constanza approved proudly, extremely pleased that the first week was, at last, over and the new owners were settling in.

PART II

Time for Change

Chapter Thirteen

NOVEMBER

Sally-Ann / Cal / Lenora

"So, what did she have?"

"A boy, eight pounds, eight ounces." Cal's voice held a note of pride that cut her to the quick.

"Well, ya always wanted a son and now y'all got one! Congratulations." Sally-Ann was pleased with how measured she sounded, when all she wanted to do was cuss her husband and his trashy girlfriend—and their new baby—the hell out of Texas.

"Thanks," he said awkwardly.

"Now, Cal, it's like this, you asked me to give y'all time to get things sorted with Lenora and to wait until the baby was born before telling the girls and your parents that we're divorcin'. I'm giving you two more weeks and then you and I are gonna sit down with the girls and have the 'talk.' And while I'm at it, you can tell that sneaky little asshole lawyer to have the good manners to respond promptly to my lawyer's requests. Yours might be a blow-in from New York, but manners maketh the man, and he should learn some good ol' southern etiquette."

"Anything else?" her husband inquired sarcastically.

"Yes, actually. I plan on heading over to Europe in early summer next year and I want to book a week in La Joya as well, so get your PA to email me a list of your planned out-of-town dates, 'cause you're gonna be minding the girls. You can introduce them to their new brother. And we need to talk about Thanksgiving and Christmas. I don't think I could fake another happy family occasion, so perhaps you and Lenora might step in and I'll take myself off somewhere sunny and quiet and pretend it's not happening."

"Aw, come on, now, Sally-Ann, there's no need to be like that," Cal retorted.

"So, what are y'all proposin'? That you and I pretend nothing's wrong and pretend like we're the Waltons? No. Not anymore. I'm done, Cal. I'm not continuing this charade any longer, and anyway, won't Lenora want you to be with her and your son for Thanksgivings and Christmases? I bet your damn hide she will."

"We haven't spoken about it. She just wanted to have the baby and get over the birth an' all. I don't think she's given any thought to Thanksgiving or Christmas." She could hear the exasperation in her husband's voice and that annoyed her even more. How *dare* he be exasperated with her? She wasn't the one ringing him up, telling him she'd just had a baby who wasn't his.

"Frankly, Cal, I don't give a rat's ass what you and Lenora do for Thanksgiving and Christmas. I'm just not doing happy families this year, so talk to your girlfriend and tell her that, as well as a new son, she now has two potential stepdaughters. Bye." Sally-Ann restrained herself from slamming the receiver into the cradle. Cal had called her on their house phone, having got no answer from her cell.

She caught a glance at herself in the antique triangular Tiffany mirror that hung in the hall and grimaced. She'd want to stop comfort eating; she was getting fatter than the pigs in the butcher hold. She'd put on half a stone since she'd found out about Lenora's pregnancy. She could see it on her ass and waistline and she didn't like it. She glanced at her watch, no time for a jog; she needed to get going to pick up the girls from school. Luiza, their au pair, was on a day off and Sally-Ann was working from home. She grabbed her purse and keys, slicked some coral lipstick on her lips, and hurried out to the car.

Fall's caress had tinged the trees with gold and russet, she noted absentmindedly. November was upon them, and no matter how much Cal wanted to put things off, it was time to tell their daughters and their families that the marriage was over and Cal was in a new setup. He was spending half the week down in Galveston in the beachfront apartment he'd bought for Lenora, and the other half of it with her and the girls. They were so used to him being away on business, they didn't much notice his absences.

Sally-Ann, to her immense shame, on impulse one day had driven onto I-45 South from Lamar Street and Allen Parkway and hit Galveston in just over an hour. She knew where the apartments were; they were part of Cal's property portfolio. Ocean View Cove was in a prime location on Seawall Boulevard.

She and the girls had spent a week in one of the apartments a few years back when it was vacant after being refurbished, and while Savannah and Madison had enjoyed building their sand castles and swimming in the Gulf, Sally-Ann had found it somewhat boring and hated the busy highway that snaked along the seafront.

She wondered how long Lenora would like the laid-back life on the Gulf Coast. Still, a two-bedroom, two-bathroom apartment with all mod cons, a balcony with ocean views, pool, gym, tennis court, and outdoor barbecue area was not to be sneezed at when you were used to a lot less.

She'd sat like a stalker for half an hour, parked across from the gated complex, watching cars driving in and out, wondering if she would see Cal's SUV or a pregnant brunette strolling out to cross to the beach.

"Jackass," she'd cursed herself. "What are you like?" *The Bold and the Beautiful* had nothing on her, she thought wryly, looking at three blond middle-aged women all looking vaguely surprised, heavily made up, jangling with bangles and dangly earrings, designer-label bags hanging from their arms, chattering animatedly as they made their way towards a beachside restaurant for lunch. No, she would die with boredom if she were stuck down here with a baby, Sally-Ann admitted.

Hunger drove her from the car to walk along the shore, with the wind whipping her hair into her eyes. She headed to Benno's, where she'd ordered a platter of shrimp, oysters, and crabmeat balls with coleslaw and potatoes, washed down with a beer, before heading home, disgusted with herself for driving to Galveston in the first place and, even worse, for pigging out.

In the weeks following her stalking trip, she'd tried not to think about the impending birth, which would add a whole new dimension to their family setup; but now, finally, Lenora's baby was born and she had to face it. Her daughters had a half brother and Cal was father to a child who had nothing to do with her and with whom she wanted to have no relationship.

How weird it all seemed, Sally-Ann mused, sliding in behind the wheel of her Buick Enclave and driving out of her tree-lined drive. Cal could tell the girls; it was all his doing. She wasn't going to make life easy on him. Why should she? she thought angrily, surprised at how upset she was. She'd felt as the months progressed that she'd come to terms with Lenora's pregnancy. Now that the child had actually been born, everything had changed. This new male would impact all their lives no matter how much in denial she was about it.

Should she keep it a secret from the twins? Or should they know about their new half brother? She'd argued the pros and cons of it with herself for weeks now. The news of the birth would emerge around town; scuttlebutt would make sure of that. What with social media and the never-ending tentacles of bitchy gossip that pervaded her social scene, it was a wonder anything was kept private anymore. It was a miracle that Cal hadn't been spotted already down in his hidey-hole in Galveston. No, it had to be faced and dealt with, and Cal would be doing *all* the talking; Sally-Ann was adamant as she called up her lawyer's name on Bluetooth to tell him the news.

"Great ammo for more alimony, darlin'. Don't you go gettin' knocked up until you have your divorce papers signed, sealed, an' delivered," her lawyer drawled, pragmatic as always, and she'd laughed.

"Not gonna happen, even if George Clooney *begs* me to have his child."

"*Especially* if George Clooney begs you to have his child," he chuckled, and hung up.

The traffic was heavy and she was lucky to find a space outside the school. It lifted her spirits to see her twin daughters chattering happily to their friends, Madison's ponytail swinging back and forth while she talked animatedly to her two besties on either side of her.

"Mom, can you go and have a coffee so we can hang out at the mall, pleeezzze?" Savannah begged, throwing her schoolbag into the back of the car with a clatter.

"I have to work, Savannah, and I don't like you hangin' in malls, and you know that," Sally-Ann said firmly.

"But, Mom, lots of the girls in our class go to the mall after school," Savannah whinged.

"Don't whine, please, Savannah."

"Aw, Mom, just this once," wheedled Madison. "You don't have to work twenty-four–seven." Sally-Ann hid her amusement. How many times had she said that to Cal during their marriage? Little ears had picked it up clearly.

"Come on, then," she agreed. The girls might as well have an hour of fun. She could have a latte and work on her iPad. She was very strict about letting the girls hang out in the local mall. Fortunately they were still biddable and hadn't got to the truly truculent stage of teenhood that some of her friends' children had. Sally-Ann was determined that Savannah and Madison would not become spoiled, sulky mall rats with the sense of entitlement that seemed to be the norm these days.

"You are a very good mother, Mom," Madison said earnestly, planting an unexpected kiss on Sally-Ann's cheek.

"Am I, Maddy? That's a nice thing to say." Sally-Ann was touched.

"Yup. You can be a bit strict—stricter than Dad, but you have a kind heart too."

"Well, thank you, darlin'. I suppose you'd like your allowance early."

"See? That's your kind heart part, Mom." Her daughter grinned.

"Do you think certain mall rats could be seen having a soda and a cookie with their mom before they go hangin', or would that be just too uncool for words?" Sally-Ann teased.

"We could go to Dunkin' Donuts, 'cause the girls don't go to that end of the mall," Savannah suggested, surreptitiously sliding a slick of nude lipstick across her lips.

"Nope, too many additives. How about Maracon?" Sally-Ann suggested, rather fancying one of their Irish-blend Kusmi iced teas and a raspberry white chocolate cupcake. She'd start her diet tomorrow, she promised herself.

"Cool," agreed Savannah.

"We have to bring Dad home a key lime mini; they're his favorite," Madison said loyally.

"And a Monarch for Luiza," reminded Savannah.

"Absolutely," agreed Sally-Ann, swinging into the McDuffie Street entrance to River Oaks. The girls still had generosity of spirit, she thought gratefully. It was a trait she would do her very best to nurture through the rocky road of growing up that lay ahead. She watched them walk across the car park towards the mall in excited anticipation and remembered how she and her friends would gather at Slim's Diner after school for soda and a cookie, flirtin' with the boys. It was a safer world then than the one her daughters inhabited, and watching other young teens gather in giddy groups, unsupervised, she knew there would be battles ahead when her daughters got older and wanted more freedom.

Motherhood wasn't easy, as Lenora would find to her cost, Sally-Ann thought, not feeling one bit sorry for the younger woman.

◆

"Hey, Dad, we bought you a key lime mini." Madison flung herself at Cal when he walked into the house the following evening.

"You are the kindest gals in the whole of Texas." Cal enveloped her in a bear hug and held out his arms to Savannah.

"Only Texas?" pouted his other daughter.

"Excuse me, ma'am," he teased. "The universe is what I meant to say. Do I get a Coke as well as a pie? I got a thirst on me that a waterin' hole wouldn't satisfy."

"Come on, Daddy. I'll get it for you." Madison led the way into the kitchen, where Sally-Ann was stacking the dishwasher after their supper.

"Hi," she said with faux cordiality, having heard his key in the door and the girls' conversation with him. "There's chicken popover pie, or mac and cheese if you're hungry." She kept her back to him.

"I already ate, thanks, but I'll have the key lime the girls bought me," he said, sitting on a barstool at the kitchen counter. "How y'all doin'?"

"Fine, jest fine," she said calmly, wanting to stick the steak knife she had in her hand into his ribs and give it a good twist as she did so.

"Here you go, Daddy." Madison presented him with his cake

and Savannah poured his Coke into a glass she'd filled with ice cubes.

"I'm a lucky man," Cal smiled, taking a swig of his drink. Sally-Ann swung around and eyeballed him. She had an inexplicable urge to smack him one in the chops. The twins were going to be shattered by what would soon be unfolding in their lives. She wanted to get it over and done with. This fake-happy family malarkey was doing her head in. Sally-Ann was so tempted to say "And now Daddy has something to tell you . . ." while they were all there in the kitchen.

Cal studied her warily and realized what she was feeling and an expression of alarm crossed his face. Watching her daughters' happy, innocent faces, she just could not bring herself to ruin their unconditional love for their father simply because she was feeling bitter and twisted and full of resentment. Tears came to her eyes and she struggled to maintain her composure.

Why was she so emotional? Her marriage was a marriage in name only, all for the sake of the girls, and had been for a long time. She and Cal had gone their separate ways. She'd had lovers after his betrayal of her. What was her problem? Why all of a sudden did it matter again? The questions raced around as the twins cuddled up to Cal, oblivious to their mother's turmoil.

Cal shook his head ever so slightly, wordlessly pleading for her silence as he stared at her in apprehension.

She lowered her gaze and saw his shoulders slump in relief. "I need to phone a colleague, Excuse me," she said flatly, fearing that she would blurt out some snide remark the longer she was in the room with him, and then the energy would change and a fight would start and the girls would become tense and watchful, and she didn't want that for them. She closed the dishwasher door and walked from the kitchen as casually as she could.

"Fuck you, Cal Cooper," she muttered, hurrying up the stairs, "and that manipulating little gold digger who got her claws into you and stitched you up, you dumbass *jerk*."

Cal watched her go and his heart rate slowed down. He knew the time was coming when he'd have to tell his beloved daughters that all was not as it seemed. But thankfully not right now. Sally-Ann had given him a bit of leeway.

The reveal had been postponed. He would not fall from his daughters' good graces today because of the good graces of his wife, he thought with immense relief, and some amount of uncomfortable shame.

◆

"And what about me? I want an end to this charade. I want the divorce over and done with so that I can move forward and get my life together. I hate living in this limbo you expect me to live in." Sally-Ann kept her voice low as she and Cal stood in the kitchen with the door closed, facing each other over the counter bar. The girls were doing their homework.

"I know, I know, and thanks for not sayin' anything earlier. I felt you wanted to." Her husband ran his hand wearily over his stubbly jaw and tried not to yawn.

"Are you going back to Galveston now?" she demanded, making a peanut butter and jelly sandwich for herself. She'd only picked at the pie for dinner; now her anger was making her hungry.

"No, I wasn't planning to." Cal thrust his hands into the hip pockets of his jeans.

"Lord Almighty, your girlfriend's just had a baby; you should be down there." Sally-Ann couldn't hide her disgust.

"She needs to sleep. I spent the afternoon with them—"

"More time than you ever spent with me when I had the girls," Sally-Ann retorted, slugging a mouthful of milk from her glass.

"First you ask me why I'm not there, then you say I didn't spend enough time with you. Do you want to have a row? Is that what you're gunnin' for?" Her husband glared at her.

"You bet I want to have a row with you, mister," she snapped. "I look at how happy our girls are and I *dread* what hearing about your new son is going to do to them."

"It doesn't mean I love them any the less," he protested.

"They're kids, Cal, they see that their mom and dad are splitting up, and that their dad's got a new family, and they're going to be devastated and feel rejected no matter how much you love them. Face up to it and stop running away from it and sticking your head in the sand. Deal with it, because we all have to." She was so angry she almost choked on her sandwich.

"Ah, quit naggin', woman," he muttered defensively.

"See, that's your answer—always has been. You don't want to hear the truth when things get rough. Cal, you need to grow up." They glowered at each other.

"When do you want to do it, then?" He grimaced.

"Eh . . . hello . . . I'm not doing it . . . you are," she said indignantly.

"On my own?" His jaw dropped. "Aw, come on. Sally-Ann—"

"Come on nothing, Cal. It's all your doing."

"So you want me to tell them we're divorcing and they have a new baby brother and you're not even going to be there? That's a bit callous. There's no need to rub my nose in it. I know you're mad at me, but it would make it easier on them if you were there to back me up when I tell them it's got nothing to do with them and I still love them."

"Easier on who? You?" she said truculently.

"All of us," he said quietly.

"I suppose so," she conceded. "Let's not drag it out. We'll do it at the weekend. What are you calling the baby?"

"Jake Wyatt, after her pa and my granddaddy," he said, somewhat abashed.

"Nice, congratulations," Sally-Ann managed. Hearing the child's name made her feel a mixture of sadness, rage, and misery.

"He's a fine little guy, with a full head of black hair," Cal said awkwardly.

"You better take some photos in case the girls want to see them," Sally-Ann said. "Excuse me, I'm going to see if they need any help with their homework." With her head held high she swept past him through the swing doors into the hall, wiping away the tears he hadn't seen as she walked upstairs to assist their daughters.

Cal swallowed hard as he watched his wife leave the room. He'd never felt so miserable in his entire life. His phone pinged. Reluctantly he flipped it open.

Don't stay away too long, your son and I are missing you! We love you, Lenora had texted. *Bad timing, darlin',* he thought grimly, because right this minute he was as angry with Lenora as much as he was with himself. Getting pregnant should be a joint decision. Having a child so early in their relationship had not been in *his* game plan. Now he was being *forced* to break up his family against his will, and right this moment resentment and anger, not love and tenderness, were the predominant emotions he was feeling towards his lover, the mother of his son.

He remembered the moment Jake had been placed in his arms. His son had stared at him, studying him intently before he'd given a tiny yawn and closed his eyes, his little fists crossed over his chest. Cal had been rocked to his core by the sudden, shocking, overwhelming wave of love he'd felt for this tiny being. His daughters had been born prematurely and whisked off to the ICU without him having a chance to hold them. Their early birth had been traumatic for Sally-Ann, and his energies had gone into comforting and supporting her rather than marveling at the perfection of their babies. That had come later. His heart softened as he thought of his son.

Sleep well both of u. Rest and take it easy. See u tomorrow. XXX, he texted back, hoping that would be enough. He knew he should say *I love you* back, but for tonight the kisses would have to suffice. He wasn't going to be emotionally blackmailed into saying *I love you* when he didn't feel it.

Can you call me? I'm lonely for u, came the plaintive response. *Not now. With the girls. Doing their schoolwork,* he fibbed. He wanted to remind Lenora he already had two children and they were entitled to his time too.

Cal turned off his phone. Lenora would be texting back and forth until he rang her, and he wasn't in the mood for it. He wasn't going to be at anyone's beck and call tonight. He needed to gather his reserves for what was to come.

◆

Lenora felt a boiling rage race through her like molten-hot lava when she read and reread the text in front of her.

Was Cal Cooper for *real*? She'd just endured the most horrific twenty-four hours of her life, after nine months of puking, and heartburn, and aching hips, and sciatica, and pelvic pain, and getting as fat as a walrus, and having her boobs dripping with milk, and drenching her panties in a drugstore line in front of half a dozen strangers when her waters broke, before delivering his son, after being prodded and poked and told to push by absolute strangers, with her nether regions bared to the world. And he had the absolute nerve to tell her he couldn't call because he was doing *schoolwork* with his girls.

> I need ur support, Cal. I've just given birth to ur . . . OUR SON!
> I *need* u to ring me.

She pressed "send" and waited. And waited . . . and waited. Incensed, she checked to see if the text had been read. It hadn't even been delivered. Fuming, she rang Cal's number and got his voice mail. The bastard had turned off his phone.

"How can you turn off your phone, Cal?" she demanded. "Aren't you at all concerned for me after what I went through? I could develop an infection or a clot or any number of things. Don't you CARE?" Her voice got higher and higher and she burst into tears before hanging up. She was sobbing into her pillow when the nurse arrived with that dreaded instrument of torture, the breast pump. Her beautiful pert breasts that Cal had so enjoyed were bursting, sore, blue-veined, stretch-marked globes that she couldn't bear to look at. When the midwife had asked if she was breast-feeding, Lenora had given an emphatic "*No!*" The idea of it made her shudder. Hell, she didn't even want to *bottle-feed*. She just wanted to hand over that squawking little bundle that was making strange snuffling little noises to a nurse, take a painkiller that would numb the soreness where she was stitched, and sleep and then wake up and find out that it had all been a nightmare and she was not a mother and her life was entirely her own again. Tears slid down her cheeks.

"Aw, is poor little Momma overwrought? It's natural, honey: Your hormones are all over the place. Now let's pump some of that milk out of you. Then you can change and feed baby and settle down for the night," the nurse soothed. Lenora felt a wave of dismay. Change a diaper! Give a bottle! *Oh, God! OH, MY GOOD GOD!* Lenora thought in horror. This was no nightmare. This was for *real*!

Chapter Fourteen

Sally-Ann / Cal / Lenora

"I hardly slept a wink; he won't stop crying and they're making me feed him and bathe him and all that stuff and I'm exhausted and you aren't even here. I bet you didn't abandon Sally-Ann when she had her kids," Lenora wailed down the phone at Cal.

"I haven't abandoned you, Lenora. I'll be with you tonight. I've meetings to go to, I have responsibilities to the twins, and you know all that. I can't be sitting at your bedside *all* day. Don't you want your friends to come visit? Your parents? You've just become a mother. Don't you want to show off your new baby?" Cal couldn't hide his bewilderment.

"Are you crazy, Cal? Mom will be moaning about her latest ailment; Dad will use it as an excuse to go and get tanked. I'll never get rid of them out of the apartment, and as for seeing my friends, haven't you seen how I look? Miss Piggy looks like a twig compared to me," she wept. "I don't want to be looking at them and remembering that I looked like they do, once."

"You'll get your figure back. You can use the gym, walk, swim. I'll get a nanny for you." Cal tried his best to be positive and encouraging when all he wanted to do was to tell Lenora to stop her silly nonsense and get on with it. He could hardly believe that the feisty, fun, competent young woman he'd fallen for could turn into this needy, weepy female who seemed unable to deal with becoming a first-time mother. And a last-time one, if they stayed together, he vowed silently.

"I think I've got postnatal depression," Lenora sobbed.

"Well, then, let's get you checked out by the doctors. Look, you're just feeling overwhelmed by it all. I'll be back down tonight and I can feed the baby and diaper him and you can have a rest," he promised.

"OK," Lenora whimpered as Jake began to cry in the background.

"What's wrong with him now? He's only just been fed," Lenora sniffed irritably.

"Perhaps he's got gas," Cal suggested patiently, wishing he was down in Galveston to pick up his little son and cuddle him, seeing it was clear he wouldn't be getting too many of those from his mother. "I'll be down as soon as I can. See ya," he said, and hung up, feeling even more heavyhearted than when he'd first picked up the phone.

This was one of the worst times of his life, bar none, he thought grimly, looking out his office window at Wells Fargo Plaza opposite. The early morning sun was flashing on the windows of the tall, all-glass building. Normally it was a view he never tired of, but he was completely distracted by the dramas in his private life. He couldn't run away from it anymore. Sally-Ann was right, the girls would have to be told about the baby, because he was going to have to spend more time than he'd planned in Galveston, for the first few months of Jake's life, until Lenora got on an even keel again. His wife was right too about Thanksgiving and Christmas. Lenora would expect him to be at her side.

If only she hadn't gone and got pregnant. That was unforeseen and unexpected. Had Lenora stitched him up like Sally-Ann claimed? He'd made it very clear to the younger woman when they began their relationship that his children were his priority and he wouldn't be getting a divorce for the foreseeable future. Lenora had totally accepted it, as far as he could see. In fact, not long before she got pregnant, he'd felt the relationship was drifting towards splitsville. Her pregnancy had changed everything.

All the lives that were being impacted because Lenora had possibly lied to him, Cal thought ruefully. No wonder he wasn't feeling very loving towards her right now. He'd been clear—very, very clear—that either she or he should use protection, and she'd assured him she'd take care of it. He'd trusted her to keep her word.

"It was one of those things," she'd said nonchalantly when he'd asked how she could have gotten pregnant. Sally-Ann didn't seem to think it was an accident, but whether it was or it wasn't, they were in the situation they were in, a situation he'd never envisaged.

Up until now he and Sally-Ann had managed their separation in a manner that gave them both freedom and still kept the family unit whole. It had suited him very well, and he felt his wife had been OK with it too. And the girls were none the wiser that anything untoward was up. No wonder Sally-Ann was furious with him. He was pissed off with himself.

He walked over to his desk and sat on his leather chair. His gaze alighted on a card Madison had given to him for Father's Day.

To the best daddy in the whole wide world. I love you to the sun and back, she'd written beneath a picture of a noble black stallion against a backdrop of Guadalupe Peak that she'd painted for him. She was talented at art, whereas Savannah excelled in science subjects.

He was going to have to tell his two precious girls that he was breaking up their family and he felt sick to his stomach. He flipped open his phone and texted his wife.

I'll be in G for a couple of days, L not doing too good. If u want me to tell the girls next weekend let me know what day is best for u. C

He took a deep breath and pressed "send" and had never felt so sad in his life.

◆

Sally-Ann read her husband's text and burst into tears, blinding her from her computer screen, where she was working on a presentation. Fortunately she was alone in her office, her PA having left five minutes previously to buy coffee and bagels for their coffee break. Now that the time had come—even though she'd pressed for it to happen—it all seemed very final and she knew things would change radically for her daughters. Real life would have an impact for the first time in their relatively sheltered lives. Their carefree existence would be shaken. They'd have to face issues that hadn't ever troubled them up to now, and she would be in the middle trying to balance their hurt, dismay, anger, and grief. If only that calculating little bitch hadn't got pregnant, their family unit would have survived intact for another few years, leaving the twins free to negotiate the difficulties of teen years without the added burden of the breakup of their parents' marriage.

Sally-Ann wiped her eyes and stared at Cal's text. She wondered what was up with Lenora. Panic, she thought wryly. Panic was the chief emotion she remembered in those early days when the twins had come home from their snug incubators and she'd felt quite overwhelmed at the constant and never-ending attention they required. Panic was Lenora's and Cal's problem, not hers. She had her own burdens to carry. "Not my circus," she muttered angrily.

What she needed to focus on was making sure the girls knew that they were still loved and cherished by Cal. He was a good father. She couldn't take that from him. It was important that Savannah and Madison recognized that when he broke his news to them. She didn't want the bombshell delivered in their home, she decided. But where could they go for the denouement? A hotel would be too public; so would a restaurant. A brain wave struck.

They could go camping! Up to Lake Conroe. It would take

just under an hour if they took I-45 North. If things went badly belly-up, they could get home easily and Cal could carry on to Galveston. Her mind raced, working out a plan that would make hearing the news easier on the girls.

How about we take a cottage up at Bishop's Landing on Conroe? It means we don't have to break the news at home. They can see that we can still do "family stuff" together and if things get too rough we can split and u can carry on down to G.

Two minutes later an answering text came back.

Perfect plan. Book it. Fri afternoon to Sunday. We can tell 'em Sunday morning.

Sally-Ann was sorely tempted to write back, *YOU can tell them and YOU book it, I'm busy at WORK,* but she refrained. There was no point in being petty. The cooler and calmer she and her husband were, the better for all of them.

◆

"Shhhh, there's a good little boy," Cal murmured, gently rubbing Jake's back and being rewarded with a burp. "Good fella. There's a great boy," he approved. "Isn't he amazing?" He glanced over at Lenora, who was flicking through the latest copy of *Vanity Fair.*

"Wonderful," she sighed with a degree of apathy that concerned him.

"He *is*, Lenora," he said firmly. "He's strong, hardy, a good grubber, and he sleeps well. We should be grateful for all those things. There are babies down there in ICU that are in pretty bad shape."

"I suppose," she shrugged, barely looking at him.

"I'm telling the twins about Jake, and that Sally-Ann and I are divorcing, this weekend." He sat on the side of the bed with the baby in his arms.

Lenora sat bolt upright. Although she would never agree, he thought she looked at her most beautiful with no makeup on her pretty face, and her full breasts with their marks of motherhood spilling out from her nightie, her chestnut hair tousled, tumbling over her shoulders.

"What does Sally-Ann think, or does she know you're gonna do it?" she demanded.

"She was the one who was pushing for it," Cal said carefully. Just because he was divorcing his wife, he had no intention of rushing into another marriage.

"Oh! Has she got someone else?" Lenora's eyes brightened. This was music to her ears.

"Not that I know of. It's because of Jake. She feels the girls should get to know their half brother."

"Really? So she wants us all to play happy families?" Lenora drawled, unimpressed at this piece of news. She didn't want to have anything to do with Cal's other children.

"She just wants everything out in the open. I guess she's right. We're taking the twins camping up to Conroe at the weekend and—"

"For the *whole* weekend? I'm going to be home from the hospital with a new baby and you're going to be gone for the *whole* weekend?" she ranted.

"It won't be for the *whole* weekend; I'll be back Sunday afternoon. Ask your sister to come and stay. Or I'll hire a nurse," he retorted. "Look, I can't just waltz in and say to my kids, 'Dad and Mom are divorcin', I love ya, see ya, bye.' I have to play fair with them and with Sally-Ann too."

"Well, your timing's crap, Cal," Lenora exclaimed heatedly.

"There is no good time to break that kind of news, Lenora. Trust me," he snapped. "And the sooner I do it, the sooner we can sort out our times together."

"What do you mean 'our times together'? Aren't you going to live with me now that you're getting a divorce?"

"Not for a while. I expect the girls will need a bit of time to get over the news and adjust to the idea of their mother and I being divorced before I go introducing them to you. And then we're going to have to work out custody arrangements and all of that. And, Lenora, before this goes any further, you knew I was married and had kids when you started dating me and I've always told you that they're a big part of my life. Just as this little guy is now," he added, kissing his son's downy little head, which was nestled against his shoulder.

"I suppose," Lenora said sulkily. "I just expected you to be around more after he was born."

"I'm here, aren't I? Why don't you try and go to sleep. I'm gonna take him for a walk so you can rest." Cal stood up and took a blanket out of Jake's cot and wrapped it tenderly around the now sleeping infant.

"Can't get away from me quick enough," Lenora said bitterly.

"Lenora, I'm trying to give you a break. Stop being like that." Cal glared at her.

"Whatever," she retorted, turning her back on him.

"Your momma is one contrary woman, Jake," Cal muttered, closing the door behind him and heading for the ground-floor café to drown his sorrows in a cappuccino while his new son slept in his arms.

◆

"Mom, I can't go camping next weekend, it's Elsa-May's birthday party on Saturday," Savannah informed her mother loftily when Sally-Ann told the twins that they were going on a camping weekend up at Lake Conroe the following Friday.

"Now hold on, missy: Did you not specifically tell me that you were *not* invited to Elsa-May's party? And were you not very upset about it? How come you've been invited at such short notice?" Sally-Ann handed her daughter a glass of fresh orange juice to have with her breakfast.

"Yeah, well, at first I wasn't invited, and neither was Lola, but yesterday after school Elsa-May came over to us and said we could go 'cause she'd a fight with Céline Wade and Bailey Farmington and they're not coming." Savannah poured maple syrup over her oatmeal.

"Honey's better for you than maple syrup," Sally-Ann said, as she did every morning.

"So I'm sorry, I just can't come." Savannah eyed her mother sternly.

"Is that so? And you're happy to be a second-best invitee because Elsa-May Jackson had a fight with two other girls and wants to use you and Lola to make them feel bad? And is inviting you to this party just to *use* you?"

"Mom, it's not like that," her daughter said indignantly.

"Isn't it? Have we not had this discussion before about Elsa-May and her not-very-nice habit of using you and Lola when it suits her?" Sally-Ann buttered her toast and took a gulp of hot coffee.

"This is the thing, Mom: she's the coolest girl in the class. *Everybody* wants to be invited to her party. And if I don't go, everyone will think I'm plumb loco." Savannah leaned her elbows on the table and stared earnestly at her mother.

"She's not a cool girl, darlin', she's a *mean* girl. And have we not had the discussion about self-respect and not worrying about what other people think? For all you know, Elsa-May will make it up with those two other girls and you will be dropped like a hot potato again, because that's the way she operates. You can't allow yourself to be dangled this way and that just to suit someone else."

"Mom, I just can't go camping and that's all," Savannah said stubbornly.

"I'm sorry, Savannah, but your dad and I have made an arrangement and booked a cabin for us to be together as a family, and that's the way it is. I had nothing penciled up on the board for you and Madison next weekend. You need to update me on your social diary. I've told you that before," Sally-Ann said firmly.

"Well, *my* self-respect says to stand up for myself and do what *I* want to do for *myself*, and I *want* to go to that party," Savannah raged. "I can't allow myself to be dangled this way and that just to suit you and Dad," she retorted triumphantly.

Madison paused from eating her oatmeal, spoon held in mid-air, eyes like saucers, as she studied her mother with interest to see what her response to Savannah's latest challenge would be.

Oh, crap, now what do I say? thought Sally-Ann, hoisted as she often was on her own petard, particularly in regards to Savannah, who would argue the hind legs off a donkey.

"Your father and I do not dangle you this way and that, Savannah. There's no need to be sassy. Now, you tell Elsa-May very politely that you have other plans made—and let her see that you aren't waiting on *her* to dangle *you* around," she added slyly. "And again, I remind you to let me know well in advance so I can put it up on the board if you have social events to go to." Sally-Ann did her best to sound as authoritative as possible.

"But, Mom—"

"I'm not arguing, Savannah—"

"You're not respecting *me*! I don't *want* to go camping," her daughter shouted.

"Don't shout, Savannah, I'm not deaf," Sally-Ann said mildly, sidetracking the "respect" issue. What was her defiant daughter going to be like when she heard about her parents' impending divorce? If she had Cal by her side, she'd give him such an earful.

"I'm *so* not going," Savannah retorted, jumping up from the table and running out of the room.

"You can discuss it with your father!" Sally-Ann shouted up the stairs after her, at her wits' end. "And get down here and stack your dishes."

"Are you OK, Mom?" Madison came and put her arms around her.

"I'm fine, darlin'. It's just your sister can be so pigheaded sometimes and she's very foolish to think that Elsa-May Jackson is a cool girl."

"She's just a bioch really, Mom, and I told Savannah that, and she told me to—oh, well, it doesn't matter." Madison suddenly realized that she'd nearly snitched on her twin for using the F-word, which was totally not allowed by their parents.

"Well, we all have to learn the lesson about being used, and some of us learn it the hard way. Come on, sweetie, finish your breakfast or you'll be late for school." Sally-Ann drained her now cold coffee and finished her toast.

"It's been ages since Dad's been anywhere with us. Are we having barbecue?" Madison asked, placing her and her twin's dishes neatly in the dishwasher. She was such a loyal little person, Sally-Ann thought affectionately.

"Of course, and a canoeing trip and a picnic like we always do."

"I'd much prefer that than going to a silly old party," said her daughter, who was a real outdoor, sporty child compared to her sibling, who preferred makeup and fashion and other girly things.

Sally-Ann felt a knot in her stomach. Poor Maddy. She knew the split would hit her hardest of all. She felt like she was betraying her daughter's anticipatory excitement. Perhaps the weekend away wasn't the best plan. But what *was* the right way to break the news, and where was the right place to do it? Nowhere, really. Sally-Ann sighed, clearing away her own dishes and wondering how she would survive the week ahead, trying to keep her mouth shut with Savannah, and trying not to murder Cal.

Chapter Fifteen

Sally-Ann / Cal / Lenora

Sally-Ann sat at the dressing table in a nightshirt, cold-creaming her face. In the mirror she could see Cal standing by the bed, unbuttoning his shirt, and she quickly averted her gaze. Her husband—or, rather, soon-to-be-*ex*-husband, she corrected herself—was still a very sexy man. She couldn't deny that, and she couldn't deny, either, that she was feeling PMS horniness, and the sight of that narrow line of dark hair snaking down his flat lean stomach, disappearing into his Calvin Kleins, made her groan inwardly.

In her haste to get the divorce talk over and done with, she hadn't thought out the implications of renting a log cabin with one king-sized bed and bunks when she'd booked. Smaller cabins were all that were left at such short notice.

The girls had swallowed the story of Cal sleeping in the other room at home because of his early starts or late arrivals with no questions all those years ago, and now it was just normal that their parents shared a room only when they were all away together. She hadn't slept in a bed with her husband in over a year. It was going to be beyond awkward, she thought gloomily.

"Savannah's attitude was a real bummer on the way down," Cal remarked, unbuckling his leather belt and unzipping his jeans. Their daughter had merely grunted replies to questions and eye-rolled her way to Lake Conroe, despite Cal doing his best to engage her in conversation.

"Yep, I get it all the time lately," Sally-Ann retorted. "She's testing the boundaries. I suppose we all did it."

"I guess. You were pretty good at it. Remember you were grounded for a week after you told your paw you could hold your liquor better than he could when he caught you drinking at the Wesleys' Labor Day party, many moons ago?" He grinned.

Sally-Ann laughed. "He was fit to be tied, and so was Momma when she heard I was caught drinking beer and what I'd said."

"And you told him to go to the barber and get his ears lowered when he grounded you for staying out past curfew with me. You were a mighty sassy teen."

"Paw was pretty strict; I just *had* to rebel!" She laughed again, remembering the battles she'd had with her poor father.

"I guess we'll just have to remind ourselves of those entertaining episodes when our pair start having their rebellions." Cal yawned, diving under the comforter.

"I'd say we'll be having a lot of 'episodes,' as you call them, when you tell them what's coming down the tracks," Sally-Ann sighed.

"And you've *really* thought this out? You definitely want a divorce?" Cal said somberly. She turned to look at him, surprised by his tone.

"Yeah, I do. Don't you?"

He shrugged. "I thought we were managing fine with our little arrangement, if you really want to know."

"We were, but things have changed. You moved the goalposts when you decided to have another child, Cal," she said, annoyed that he would think she'd just decided out of the blue to ask for a divorce.

"Let's get one thing clear here, Sally-Ann, *I* didn't decide to have another child. She told me she was protected. The *last* thing I want is another child, believe me," Cal said emphatically.

"That's neither here nor there now, I guess. Whether any of us like it or not, there's a little boy out there and he's going to need you as much as the girls do. He's entitled to be parented by you too, so it's time we sorted our situation and deal with what's happened." She turned back to the mirror and rooted in her bag for her hairbrush.

"You're very fair-minded." He was subdued.

"Our mess has nothing to do with him. And that's why we've got to keep things civil between us, for the girls. It's got to be about them now, not about our rancor and bitterness," she said, letting her hair down from its topknot, glad he couldn't see her face.

"And *do* you feel rancor and bitterness?" he asked hesitantly.

"Oh, I do, believe me, I do, Cal." She grimaced. "It comes in waves. I was doing OK until I heard about the pregnancy. And the day the baby was born, I hated you, because I knew what it's going to do to the girls. If it was just me, I could cope with it," she said flatly.

"I've never hated you." Sally-Ann had never seen him look so sad.

"You haven't got my alimony demands yet," she said with an attempt at humor.

"Ha!" She could see him smiling at her while she brushed her hair in firm broad strokes until it crackled with electricity. Cal lay against the pillows with his hands behind his head, looking at her the way he used to in the old days, and she thought how surreal and, it had to be said, how *agreeable* it was, to be having this entirely calm and reasonable conversation at bedtime, just like a normal husband and wife, and not a couple who were hours away from announcing their divorce.

"It's strange, but this is nice. You, the girls, and me," he ventured, catching the vibe.

"Don't go there, Cal. The only reason we're here *en famille* is to tell our children we're divorcing, don't forget," she said sharply.

"I just don't want us to rush into anything." He turned on his side to look at her.

"Oh, for God's sake, Cal, our marriage has been over for years. It's about time we acknowledged it. Surely Lenora's been putting pressure on you to divorce me?" She swung around and arched an eyebrow at him.

"Of course she has," Cal said irritably. "But let's be clear, just because you and I are getting a divorce doesn't mean I'm goin' rushin' up the aisle with *her*."

"That's *your* business, Cal. I just want my end of it sorted now that this baby has arrived. I don't want to be living in a limbo anymore. And I think it would be much easier on the girls to get to know their half brother as a baby. You can't fight with a baby," she added wryly.

"And you *definitely* think they should get to know him?"

"Don't you?"

"It would be good, I suppose," he agreed slowly. "Especially when they're all older and the resentments will have faded. Nothing worse than finding out when the will's being read," he joked halfheartedly.

"*Exactly!*" She turned back to her ablutions, rubbing hand cream onto her elbows and hands. Eventually she could put the moment off no longer and walked over to her side of the bed. She popped a pill into her mouth and drank some water to wash it down and slid her eye mask out from under the pillow, where she'd placed it earlier.

"What'cha poppin'?" Cal asked.

"A sleeper. I don't want to be awake all night. I haven't been able to sleep all week worrying," she told him, slipping under the plump comforter. The other reason she'd taken a sleeping pill was because she didn't want to be lying beside him, twisting and turning and longing for sex. She wasn't going to tell *him* that, of course.

"I'm sticking in earplugs so I won't hear you if you say anything to me," she said coolly, switching off her side lamp and pulling the mask down over her eyes. "Night, Cal."

"Night, Sally-Ann," he said forlornly from his side of the bed, and she jammed her earplugs in and lay very still in her dark cocoon, thankful that the bed was wide and there was no physical contact, waiting for her sleeper to take effect. She was as taut as a wire but eventually the silent, black void worked its magic and, assisted by the sleeping tablet, she fell into a deep sleep, oblivious to her husband, who tossed and turned for hours, listening to her even breathing before finally falling into an unsettled slumber.

◆

Sally-Ann was still dead to the world ten hours later when Madison shook her by the shoulder to tell her that Cal had cooked breakfast and it was nearly ready to be served. "An' we're eating outside, Mom; wear a sweatshirt," Madison advised, looking as fresh as a daisy in her denim shorts and white Gap T-shirt. The aroma of sizzling bacon and freshly brewed coffee wafted through the bedroom door, and her stomach growled. She couldn't believe she'd slept right through and had the best sleep she'd had since Cal's baby was born.

"You slept well, and you snored," Cal teased when she emerged onto the veranda, where he'd ordered the girls to set the big wooden picnic table.

"I did *not* snore," Sally-Ann retorted indignantly, yawning and tying her hair up with a scrunchie. She'd pulled on a sweatshirt, but once she stepped out of the shade, the sun was warm on her face and the temperature gauge on the deck indicated 70.

"Yup, ya did." He handed her a plate loaded with crispy bacon and scrambled eggs, and pointed to a stack of pancakes drizzled with maple syrup. "Savannah and I cooked the pancakes." He gave the smallest wink.

"Thanks, honey, they look lovely." Sally-Ann smiled at her

daughter, who was sitting, with her hair straightened, makeup expertly applied, waiting to be told to take it off.

Sally-Ann ignored the makeup. She wasn't going to start a fight. Cal had clearly appeased Savannah enough for her to cooperate with making breakfast. That would do for today.

"So, what's our plan today?" Madison poured fresh orange juice for everyone. She always liked to have her day mapped out.

"How about we take a canoe trip along the lake, find a place to tie up, go on a hike, and then have a picnic? Come back and do some fishing and have barbecue for supper?" Cal suggested easily, forking eggs and bacon into his mouth.

"Cool," agreed Madison, who couldn't wait to get into the canoe.

"Aw, can we not go to Papa's on the Lake?" Savannah protested.

"It'll be packed; it always is." Cal made a face. "I like coming here to get *away* from crowds and city life."

"We're not gonna meet anybody hiking," Savannah pouted.

"Who do you want to meet?" He eyed her quizzically.

"*Dad* . . . boys . . . duh!" She rolled her eyes so dramatically, Sally-Ann almost spluttered her orange juice in amusement. It was good for her husband to get a taste of what she was enduring almost daily now from the teen queen.

"Oh! I was wondering why you were wearing that stuff on your face." He shook his head. "Savannah, don't be in a rush to grow up," he advised. "It's not all it's cracked up to be. Trust me."

"Why don't we forget the picnic; we can have a late lunch in Papa's after our hike, go fishing later in the afternoon, and still have barbecue here," Sally-Ann suggested.

"But I'll be all hot and sweaty after hikin' and my hair will go frizzy, Mom," Savannah pointed out irately.

"Oh! Right! OK, then, how about we have brunch at Papa's tomorrow, before we go home, and you can dress up to the nines and be all nice and fresh?" she suggested.

"OK, cool, thanks," Savannah, realizing this was a better option, agreed.

"Let's hope she'll have an appetite for brunch after what she's going to hear. At least she'll have her makeup on," Cal murmured, filling the dishwasher with the dirty breakfast dishes while she took the cold cuts and deli provisions out of the fridge for their picnic.

"Cal," she remonstrated, laughing in spite of herself. "When do you want to tell them?" she asked, buttering crusty bread.

"I guess tomorrow morning," he sighed. "Let them sleep well tonight."

"Sure," she agreed sadly.

He came to the table and stood behind her and put his arms around her. "I'm sorry," he murmured, turning her to face him so he could hug her.

She rested her head on his shoulder, inhaling the familiar scent of him, a lump the size of a melon lodged in her throat.

"Me too, Cal. Now you'd better let me go or I'm going to lose it and howl." She swallowed hard.

"OK," he said reluctantly, and walked out of the kitchen to finish clearing the table, leaving her with tears streaming silently down her cheeks.

You big stupid asshole, Cal. It shouldn't have ended up like this, she thought as anger and sadness and a host of mixed emotions hit her. Sally-Ann tried to compose herself for the day ahead, afraid one of the girls might walk in and see her crying.

◆

She would never hear the *phee-bee* call of the phoebe, echoing through the trees, without remembering the Sunday morning Cal told their daughters that their lives were about to change. Sally-Ann could barely swallow the coffee he'd brewed. Her throat was completely constricted. Even the heat of the sun on her back couldn't warm her. She felt cold deep in the pit of her stomach. She was sitting beside her husband at the picnic table on the veranda, opposite the girls, who were tucking into the French toast he'd made for them to keep them going until they had their brunch later at Papa's on the Lake. They were laughing and teasing each other, blissfully oblivious to what was about to unfold.

She picked at a fruit cup he'd prepared for her, but her stomach was so knotted, she thought she would puke if she ate any more.

"Come on, Maddy, let me straighten your hair," Savannah offered her sister, shoving the last piece of toast into her mouth. "Let me turn you into a sophisticated city gal!"

"I don't want to be sophisticated. I prefer the outdoor look," Madison demurred. She hated anyone fiddling at her hair and was perfectly happy to tie it up in a ponytail.

Cal cleared his throat. "Er . . . before you go, girls, we . . ." He glanced at Sally-Ann, who was pale with tension. "Erm, that is, *I* have something I need to tell you."

The twins, hearing the timber of his voice, looked at each other, perplexed. "Aw, Dad, don't say we're moving to Miami," Savannah groaned. Madison looked startled at this notion.

"No, no, we're not moving," he assured them. "At least, you're not," he amended.

"Are you, Daddy?" Madison—always the more intuitive of the twins—catching the nuance in his sentence, looked suddenly apprehensive.

Cal took a deep breath, and in spite of herself Sally-Ann felt a frisson of sympathy. Almost of its own volition her hand reached out to cover his. He gave her a grateful glance and, anxious to get it out as quickly as possible, blurted, "Girls, I need to tell you something. You have a new half brother. His name is Jake. He was born a few days ago. Your mom and I are going to divorce. But, *honestly*, nothing will change about the way we feel about you," he told them earnestly. "We *both* want you to know—"

"Dad! *No!*" shouted Savannah, jumping to her feet.

Madison looked from Cal to Sally-Ann, desperation in her eyes, as though searching to see if this was some weird prank. Observing the gravity of her parents' expressions, her face crumpled and she let out a low, animal-like wail. In an instant Sally-Ann was out of her seat to rush to her side, holding her, comforting her. "It's OK, darlin', everything's going to be OK," she promised bleakly.

"No!" Madison sobbed into her mother's shoulder. "Don't get a divorce, please, *please* don't get a divorce," she begged.

"I *hate* you, Dad," Savannah shouted. "I don't want any baby brother called Jake. Why did you have sex with someone else and make a baby?" She glared at her father before turning to Sally-Ann. "Would you not have sex with him? Is that why he went to someone else? That's why Magnolia Taylor's dad left her mom, 'cause she wouldn't do sex. It's *your* fault, Mom," she accused viciously.

"*No!* Savannah," Cal said sternly. "That has nothing to do with it. It's *my* fault, not your mother's. Your mother has been a great wife and she's a fantastic mother and you know that. Don't you blame her for this. Do you hear me? I won't allow it. Now apologize."

Savannah remained stubbornly mute, glowering at her father with all the hate she could muster. "Savannah, do you hear me? Apologize to your mother, right now," Cal ordered.

"Don't tell me what to do you . . . you . . . low-down, two-timin' snake, you and that big fuckin' fat ho of yours . . . that . . . that you're screwing," Savannah roared, red-faced.

Cal jumped to his feet, eyes glittering black. "Don't you evah, *evah* speak to me like that again, Savannah Connolly Cooper. Don't *evah* let me hear that vile language outta—"

"It's OK, Cal," Sally-Ann said firmly, raising her palm to him and moving to Savannah's side. She went to put her arm around her.

"Just leave me alone, Mom. I hate the two of you," her daughter shouted, pushing her away aggressively before running inside, crying.

"Please don't divorce. Please, Mom, *please*, Daddy," Madison implored, ghost-white with shock, stunned by her father's pronouncement and her twin's hysterical and cuss-laden outburst.

"I'm sorry, darlin', it's for the best." Sally-Ann was almost in tears herself. Should she have just put up with things and waited until they were older to save her daughters from this turmoil? Had she made a huge mistake? She wished now that nothing had been said. The fallout wasn't worth it.

Cal was grim-faced. "Maddy, it won't make any difference to how I feel about you and your sister. I love you. I always will. We'll *always* be a family."

"No we won't, Daddy, 'cause you'll be with that other baby and Mom will be on her own with us so we *won't* be a family, so don't say we *will*," she protested before pulling away from Sally-Ann and following her twin inside.

"That went well." Cal shook his head. "Did you hear that mouthful out of Savannah? I couldn't believe my ears. Where did she hear language like that?"

"Oh, Cal, get real! All the kids are full of it. Y'all don't know the half of it. They all know what blow jobs are, and who's goin' down on who, and who's gettin' licked out or fingered," Sally-Ann said wearily.

"Jesus wept," he swore. "But they're only thirteen!"

"And?" she drawled sarcastically. "Remember y'all at fourteen and the reputation y'all had for making out behind the Lowells' hay barn?"

"That was different," he growled, horrified that his young daughters knew such things.

"Nothing's different, really. Dianne Bennett got knocked up by Beau Sawyer and she was only thirteen and a half even though she looked about sixteen."

"Jeez, yeah, I remember: she was sent to stay with her aunt over in El Paso." Cal shook his head and inhaled deeply.

Sally-Ann sat back down and took a swig of cold coffee. She was shaking. "Let them calm down for a while and absorb it." She put her head in her hands, massaging her temples, which were beginning to throb.

"Here, how about if I make us fresh coffee?" he asked, desperate to be doing something. Grabbing the coffee percolator he disappeared into the kitchen.

Sally-Ann sat alone, face raised to the sun. It was done. The words had been said. And everything had changed utterly. Maddy was right: now she was no longer part of a marriage. To all intents and purposes she was a woman on her own.

◆

The trip to Papa's on the Lake was canceled. No one wanted brunch; in fact, Sally-Ann wondered if she'd ever want to eat again. The girls packed their bags in stony silence and marched out to Cal's SUV without a backward glance. Cal and Sally-Ann locked up between them. "Say nothing; let them start a conversation if they want to," Sally-Ann suggested as Cal double-checked the door to make sure it was locked.

"I need to head down to Galveston this afternoon," he said apologetically.

"Thanks," she snapped. "You fire your ballistic missile and then piss off, leaving me to handle the fallout."

"I'll be with you for a couple of hours. We'll be home by one. I'll stay until around four," he offered lamely.

"We'll see how it goes. You might be better just dropping us off," she retorted, walking ahead of him down the steps of the deck.

"Sally-Ann, thanks for your support. I appreciate it." He caught her by the arm and turned her to face him. She glanced across at the car, where their daughters were watching them from the backseat.

"I'm going to kiss you on the cheek," she said. "The girls are looking. It might ease their pain if they can see us behaving in an *affectionate* manner."

"OK," he agreed, bending his head. She kissed his cheek, feeling the hard plane of his jaw against hers, and his arms tightened around her and she felt his breath against her ear as his lips touched her skin. She leaned against him for a moment before taking a deep breath and drawing away.

"OK. Let's hit the road and see what happens—"

"Sally-Ann, I think I still love—"

"Don't say it, Cal, don't *dare* say that to me," Sally-Ann hissed. "We are *done*."

She walked down the path ahead of him trying not to show her fury. To bring them to this point and then tell her he thought he still might love her—was it because it was true, or was it because Lenora was proving to be more of a handful than he'd expected and he wanted out and she and the girls were the perfect excuse for him to back off? No way, she decided. Cal could go to hell in a handbasket. She was finished. From now on it would be all about her and the girls. She climbed into the SUV and turned to her daughters.

"Girls, we're all in this together as a family. We can sink or swim. It all depends on our attitude. And I don't know about you, but I intend to swim. Just letting y'all know."

They drove back to Houston in silence, broken only by the sounds of Madison's quiet sobs as she huddled up in the backseat beside her sister, who was listening to Beyoncé on her iPod.

"Why don't you just head on down to your baby boy?" Sally-Ann suggested coolly when they pulled up outside the house an hour later.

"Let me help unpack and I'll have a sandwich and then I'll head off. Unless the girls want me to stay for a while . . ." He looked over his shoulder at his daughters.

Savannah ignored him and jumped out of the car as though he hadn't spoken.

"I'll make your sandwich, Daddy," Madison gulped, and Sally-Ann saw tears glitter in his eyes and almost cried herself.

He ate the crab sandwich Madison prepared for him, drank a cup of coffee, and stood up. "I'll call tomorrow," he said.

"OK, bye. Drive safe," Sally-Ann said for Maddy's benefit. He could end up in the creek for all she cared right now.

"Bye, sweetheart." He held out his arms and Madison ran into them and hugged him tightly. "Thank you for the sandwich. It was a lifesaver. And it was kind of you to make it, because I know you're upset and a bit mad with me. Call me on my cell if you want to talk," he murmured into her ear, squeezing her in a bear hug. "Don't forget I'm your daddy and I love you and I'm always here for you."

"I love you too, Daddy." There was a break in her voice and he could feel her tears against his neck. He hugged her again and drew away. "Savannah, I'm going," he called up the stairs.

There was no response. He took the stairs two at a time and knocked on her bedroom door. "Please come to the door and talk to me before I leave," he said.

"Go away!" she yelled.

"If you need to talk to me, call me on my cell. I'll see you later in the week." Silence greeted this pronouncement. Sighing, Cal walked down the stairs and glanced at Sally-Ann. She gave a shrug.

"She'll come around eventually. It may take time; you know what she's like."

"OK, I'll talk to you tomorrow. Bye." He looked so downbeat, she couldn't help but feel sorry for him, and that irritated her again.

She walked back into the kitchen and heard him open the front door.

"Take care, Maddy. I love you," he said, and his loyal daughter stood at the door waving while her mother and twin cried silent tears and the old grandfather clock in the hall chimed out the hour that Cal Cooper's life changed irrevocably.

As the electronic gates opened and he drove past them, he remembered how he'd felt so tied down and oppressed driving between them morning after morning when the girls were little; and now that the ties that bound him were finally loosened, he realized that right now freedom wasn't what he wanted at all.

Freedom was where he was driving from. Lenora and his new son were at the other end of the journey, and if she had her way, there'd be no freedom for him in Galveston. He'd set himself a tough row to hoe, and he only had himself to blame.

◆

Lying propped up against her pillows, alone in her king-sized marital bed, Sally-Ann scrolled through her emails halfheartedly.

She saw an email that she was cc'd on from Jutta Sauer with details of her monthly inspection of La Joya. The penthouse was currently leased out on a six-month rental until the spring, and all seemed well. The tenant was keeping the property in good shape, reported the German woman.

A longing to run away to Andalucía, far from the trials ahead, swept over her. She flicked through her computer diary for the following year. The girls were scheduled to spend a week in Disney World with their aunt and cousins in early summer. She was going to book La Joya for herself for that week, come hell or high water, she decided. A glint lit up her eyes. She'd book a meeting with her sexy banker too. Knowing that she had a week in paradise to look forward to would keep her afloat in the choppy seas ahead.

The sound of sobbing caught at her heart and she flung back the comforter to hurry to Maddy's room.

"Don't cry, sweetie," she urged. "Everything will be OK, I promise." She sat on the side of the bed rubbing Madison's hunched-up form under the bedclothes. A movement at the door caught her eye.

"Is Maddy OK?" Savannah looked young and vulnerable with her hair tossed over her shoulders, all traces of the sullen teenager evaporated in drowsy weariness.

"She's sad, like we all are, darlin'. Why don't I make us all some hot chocolate and we'll all have it in my bed and sleep there tonight?" she suggested.

"Thanks, Mom," hiccupped Maddy, emerging from under her covers.

"And you know what? Let's bunk off work and school tomorrow and have a girls' movie day in our pj's. It's gonna be raining—first time in weeks. Perfect for a day at home." Sally-Ann linked arms with her two daughters as they walked across the landing to her bedroom.

"Can we have hot dogs and popcorn?" Savannah inquired, always one to wring every advantage from a situation.

"Sure, sweetie," Sally-Ann agreed, trying to banish the thought that she was a bad mother for allowing her kids to skip school and comfort-eat junk food as an antidote to life's hardships. She'd need to watch out for the comfort-eating jag, otherwise she'd waddle over to Europe and no man, let alone her sexy banker, would find her attractive, and she'd be alone for the rest of her life. On that gloomy note, Sally-Ann tucked her daughters into her bed and went downstairs to make hot chocolate.

Chapter Sixteen

Anna / Austen

"Look, Dad, if you and Mum are giving us money as a gift, we should be able to spend it as *we* wish!" Chloe MacDonald said heatedly, glaring at her father over the rim of her coffee mug.

"Twenty-five thousand euros is a lot of hard-earned money, Chloe; I don't want to see it all wasted on one day—"

"It's our *wedding* day!" Chloe shouted, green eyes flashing with indignation.

"I *know* that, madam. No need to shout. I'm just saying the wedding day is only one day in a lifetime of marriage. After that, real life begins and it's good to have some sort of safety net beneath you, if you get a chance of it, instead of frittering it all away on a day out to impress your friends."

"I'm not trying to impress my friends, Dad. This is going to be *the* most important day of my life. I want it to be really special and you're *ruining* it already," Chloe raged, marching out of the kitchen in high dudgeon.

"For crying out loud, that one is beyond reasoning with," Austen exploded.

"Austen, will you calm down. You're going at this like a bull in a china shop," Anna said wearily.

"If our parents had given us that amount of money, we'd have been able to buy two friggin' houses."

"It's all relative—"

"Relative my arse, Anna. Ten thousand of that at least should go towards putting a deposit on a house."

"Don't be rude; I was just pointing out that when we got married, the amount our parents gave us would be the equivalent in today's money, so don't make comparisons, because it's meaningless and getting us nowhere."

"But, Anna, she's spending crazy money on *nonsense.*" Her husband couldn't hide his irritation. "How can you spend three thousand euros on a dress you're only going to wear once? And why does she need *four* bridesmaids?"

"I know," Anna sighed. "I've tried to point all of this out to her—in a *diplomatic* way," she added pointedly. "She's set on having a big wedding and there's no getting around it."

"Right, then, if that's what she wants, let her do what she wants, but she needn't come running to me when things get tight. If she wants to fritter away the money we gave her, fine; she won't be getting any more—"

"OK, give it a rest. I've heard it all before." Anna stood up from the table and took the cups over to the sink. She felt like crying. If it was like this now, what was it going to be like in the weeks leading up to the wedding?

"Will we nip over to Spain for a couple of days and spend some of their inheritance?" Austen came over to her and put his arms around her. She rested her head on his chest, loving the sound of his steady heartbeat at her ear. Austen was so solid—in every way—she'd always felt the worries of the world drift away when she was in the circle of his arms.

"That sounds like heaven," she murmured, "but it's only six weeks to Christmas and I've done nothing—"

"We could do our Christmas shopping in the market."

"Ha, you mean *I* could do our Christmas shopping in the market while you play golf!"

"Well, let's not quibble about minor considerations," he teased. "Will I go online and book us a flight and let's just take off? That's one of the reasons we bought the apartment . . . to be spontaneous!" He grinned at her, his eyes glinting in challenge and amusement.

"OK, then," Anna agreed impulsively. "Let's be 'spontaneous' for once in our lives."

"That's my girl." Austen's eyes lit up and he headed for the computer to make the bookings.

◆

"You're going to Spain *again*?" Chloe exclaimed later that evening while she pressed her Victoria Beckham jeans to go out on the town with her fiancé. "When are we going to sit down and do the guest list? And you said you'd get your friend to make the cake; have you organized that yet? And you said you'd sort the flowers. We need to get going on stuff, Mum. I want those little mini trees at the entrance and a red carpet. I really think I should hire a wedding planner."

"And how much will that cost?" Anna said drily. "I've spoken to Aideen about the cake—"

"Five tiers, including red velvet and biscuit cake layers," demanded her daughter.

"Yes. And Malone's will—"

"*Malone's!* They're so old-fashioned. I want a florist with a cutting edge and something out of the ordinary!" exclaimed Chloe.

"Chloe, will you *listen* to yourself! I suppose you'll be telling me next you want *Hello!* or *VIP* to cover it. Your dad is right about frittering away money. You'll be in the church for an hour and a half max—the most you've ever spent in it in years," she observed. "And what will you do with your cutting-edge flower arrangements then? They'll wilt and be thrown out and that's hundreds of euros down the tube. Be sensible about some of it, love," Anna urged.

"But, Mum, I want something different. I don't want boring old flower arrangements, I want the *ooooh* factor," Chloe said earnestly.

"I understand that." Anna tried not to show her exasperation. "But think of all the lovely things you could buy for the house . . ."

"We'll get all that on the wedding list." Chloe dismissed that notion airily. "Look, you know all the weddings we've been to, and they're all very samey; Will and I don't want that, and you and Dad are being wet blankets and making us feel bad."

"Well, that's the last thing we want to do, Chloe, but we're just trying to point out that twenty-five thousand euros is a *huge* amount of money and it shouldn't all go on one day," Anna said firmly. "It's far from cutting-edge florists you were reared on—don't forget that—and there's more to marriage than the wedding day."

"Yeah, well, it's far from pads in Spain *you* and Dad were reared on, and look at you hopping back and forth there," Chloe said sulkily.

"True," Anna said calmly. "The difference is your dad and I *worked* our asses off for that luxury—and investment, I may add—in our retirement years. Which, I might also point out, will be part of your fairly substantial inheritance, unless we blow every penny—and, believe, me we're very tempted to. If you and Will can do as well as your dad and I have done for ourselves and our family, you will be doing very well indeed," Anna snapped, furious at her daughter's selfish attitude.

"I suppose," her daughter grudgingly admitted. "Can we please just stop talking about it now, because it's depressing me and taking all the good out of my plans."

Anna looked at her daughter's dejected expression and wondered where had she gone wrong in rearing her. Such a sense of entitlement—and it was not just her, it was endemic with her daughter's generation. Chloe was indeed a child of the Celtic Tiger, the boom years when the economy soared, and lack or prudence was *not* in her vocabulary. All she and most of her generation had known was the privilege of affluence. She would never understand where her parents were coming from, and Anna didn't know if that was a good or a bad thing.

◆

"I just don't get it, Will. Mum and Dad are supposed to be paying for the wedding and now they're banging on about not spending all of the money they're giving us on it. I mean, we'll be buying a house ourselves. We'll get our own mortgage without having to ask *them* for anything, so what's the big deal about spending the dosh on our wedding?" Chloe moaned, nibbling on the strawberry that garnished her daiquiri. They were having cocktails in the Clarence before meeting up with a few friends for a meal later on. "Don't they realize that you won't get a decent wedding for anything less?"

"It's a parent thing," her fiancé pacified her, wondering how long this new irritation would last.

"The way Mum was going on, you'd think the economy was going to collapse and we were all going to be *paupers*. I don't see any signs of a downturn." Chloe sipped her cocktail through its colorful straw and felt some of her tension drift away.

"Well, there is a lot of talk about us not being able to sustain our spending and lifestyle. David McWilliams, that economist, is always going on about it."

"Yes, well, our readership is up and there's lots of money being spent out there. We're doing a feature on mobile homes for the yummy mummy set, on a very exclusive site in Wicklow, where the mobiles can cost anything up to a hundred K." Chloe was an assistant editor on a glossy magazine.

"That's mad! Imagine spending a hundred thousand on a caravan," Will teased.

"They're a bit more than caravans," Chloe laughed, nestling in against him. Will was right, it *was* a parent thing. Her folks would calm down eventually and she would have the wedding she'd set her heart on.

Chapter Seventeen

JANUARY 2007

Anna / Austen

"This is the best thing we ever did, Anna. I'm really enjoying playing golf out here and I'm looking forward to the lads coming over next week." Austen raised his glass of San Miguel.

"I know. Can you believe it's only *five* weeks since we were here last? Christmas is done and dusted. Yippee! They're having gale-force storms at home and it's seventy degrees down here on the Costa," Anna agreed smugly, stretching out her tanned legs, sipping her wine.

They'd ordered tapas, having enjoyed a communal lunch earlier with several of the other owners who had attended the first AGM for the management of La Joya. It had been a convivial affair and Anna had put her name forward to act as secretary for the first year, and had been proposed, seconded, and elected.

She and Austen were beginning to get to know some of the other residents. A couple of introductory drinks and barbecues, organized by the couple who ran the poolside tapas bar in the complex, had been a huge success, and there was a friendly, relaxed holiday vibe about the place that added to the owners' enjoyment of their luxurious beachfront abodes.

"Well done for putting your name forward for secretary." Austen smiled at her.

"Well, I figure the first year or two will be the easiest, because Constanza Torres has *everything* under control, so I don't expect my duties to be too onerous, and then I'll have done my stint and made my contribution." Anna raised her face to the sun. "I'm glad your gang are coming out for a visit to play golf. I can't wait to get the girls over later in the year."

"Great, isn't it? A real win-win; I get to play golf with the lads out here, and when you're over with the women, I get to play more golf at home. Could life get any better?" he teased.

"We could always go up to the apartment and make wild, passionate, unbridled love." Anna slanted a glance at him, eyes sparkling.

Austen grinned across the table at his wife. "Are we living the dream or what?"

"We are. Now drink up and take me to bed and ride me ragged, I'm having a time-of-life hormone surge!" Anna declared, wanting to make the most of the only good thing about the whole feckin' unwanted menopausal experience.

"God, I love when you talk dirty and I *love* those hormone surges," Austen laughed, and drained his glass. He signaled the waiter for the bill and grabbed his wife's hand. "Come on, Jezebel MacDonald, and have your wicked hormonal way with me. I'm all yours."

She'd so dreaded her fifties, Anna reflected, walking hand in hand with her husband across the beach to La Joya, but right now she was happier and more relaxed than she'd ever been in her entire life. All the stresses of rearing the girls and running a business and a home had taken their toll over the years. Sometimes she and Austen had been like ships that passed in the night. Now they had precious time to spend with each other. It was almost like the early days of their marriage when all they had wanted to do was to be together.

Thank you. She sent a silent prayer of gratitude, feeling the firm, strong clasp of her husband's hand in hers and feeling deliciously aroused at the thoughts of what those long fingers would soon be doing to her.

They had just walked into the bedroom and were turning to kiss each other when the phone rang. Anna paused from opening the zip on her sundress.

"Leave it," urged Austen, cupping her breasts and bending to kiss the nape of her neck.

Once she would have been unable to relax until she'd seen who was calling, but the new, retired Anna only hesitated for a moment before ignoring the demanding shrill of her phone, to press herself wantonly against her husband, moaning with pleasure as his caresses feathered lightly across her nipples and she could feel his hardness against her.

Later, sated and lying drowsily in his arms, she murmured, "I wonder who was ringing me."

"You'll find out soon enough," Austen said, entwining his fingers in hers. She forgot about the call until she heard her phone ring again, in the distant depths of her bag. They were sitting on the balcony, watching the sky turn a flaming orange, the dipping sun setting the sea alight. "I'll get it for you," said her long-suffering husband.

"Ah, you're a pet," she said gratefully when he handed it to her and she saw she'd missed two calls from Tara.

"Hello, what's happening?" she said when her daughter answered her phone.

"Mam, I'm pregnant! We're going to have a baby. You're going to be grandparents," her eldest announced excitedly. "I was going to wait until you got home to tell you, but I just can't. I was bursting to tell you. We found out two days ago."

"Tara, that's *wonderful* news! I'm so excited," Anna exclaimed. "When are you due?"

"November," Tara bubbled.

"Here, let me pass you on to your father so you can tell him." Anna handed Austen the phone.

"What's happening in November that's got your mother so excited?" he asked.

"You're going to be a granddaddy," Tara said proudly.

"Ah, Tara, I'm so pleased for you. Not too happy with the G-word though. I'm too young for that and it won't do my street cred any good," he teased. "But that's fantastic. I'll put you back on to your mother: she's practically grabbing the phone off me. Bye, pet. Take care of yourself."

"I will, Dad," his daughter said affectionately, and he gave the phone back to Anna and went into the kitchen to refresh their drinks. A grandfather! Him! It was a bit of a jolt when he heard Tara tell him he would be a granddaddy. Another thought struck him. If the baby was due in November, Anna would want to be at home. They would have to come out earlier in the autumn. That was a bit of a pain in the ass, but he'd better not say anything about it; it would be selfish. And he *was* happy for Tara and James. He poured cava into his wife's glass and cracked open another bottle of beer for himself.

"I can't believe it," Anna said, beaming when he handed her the glass of bubbly. "Just as well I didn't know earlier, it might have put a dampener on my surges, knowing I was riding a granddad," she grinned.

"Yes, Granny," he countered. "Two can play at that game."

"OMG! Granny! *Never.* I'm not going to be called *that*!" protested Anna.

"Well, whatever you want to call yourself, we are now officially on the road to old age. We're going to be grandparents."

"It's all happening, isn't it? Retirement, a wedding, and now a new baby. We'll be up to our eyes."

"All the more reason to relax out here as often as we can," Austen said, knowing his wife was going to be caught up with family stuff and the following year would see them at home a lot more than he'd anticipated. *So much for having a luxury penthouse abroad,* he thought, trying not to feel resentful.

Chapter Eighteen

Eduardo / Consuela

"I would advise that your aunt not be left alone for the first few days of her recuperation; we will be discharging her tomorrow. She'll make a full recovery; nevertheless, the bronchitis and pneumonia have weakened her and I would recommend plenty of rest and good nourishment." The consultant gave a polite smile, held out his hand for a brief handshake, and was gone, striding down the hospital corridor to his next patient, hardly waiting to hear Eduardo's clipped words of thanks.

Frowning, Eduardo dialed his wife's number. *Tía* Beatriz's forthcoming discharge was most inconvenient. He'd planned to take the train to Málaga later on with his cousin, to be in attendance at tomorrow's inaugural meeting of the residents of La Joya and to form their new management committee for the urbanization.

Eduardo was most anxious to put his name forward for the position of *El Presidente*. Or, failing in his bid for that post, the secretary's position would be advantageous. He would know *everything* that was going on. Standards needed to be raised, a firm hand on the tiller was necessary, and he *wanted* a role on the new committee. He was not content to be on the sidelines like so many of the residents, taking no part in the running of their community.

"*Sí*, Eduardo?" Consuela's voice in his ear brought him back to reality.

"Beatriz is being discharged tomorrow. She's not to be left alone for the next few days, which of course means we should have her to stay with us," he said glumly.

"Very well, I'll freshen up the guest room and make sure the electric blanket is switched on when you bring her home," his wife said calmly.

"I don't suppose . . . eh . . . erm"—Eduardo felt uncharacteristically hesitant—"that *you* would collect her and bring her home, Consuela? You know I had planned to go to that meeting down in La Joya with Gabriel—"

"You know Beatriz wouldn't be happy with that," Consuela interrupted him. "She'd get in a huff and say she was being a nuisance to me and that she was putting me out, and insist on going home to her own apartment in a taxi."

"But that's ridiculous!" Eduardo couldn't hide his exasperation.

"I know. But you know what she's like. I'm sorry, you'll either have to postpone her discharge or cancel the trip to La Joya. I don't want to have to have an argument with her at the hospital."

"But it's a very *important* meeting, Consuela. I *want* to be on that management committee."

"You could get Gabriel to propose you and vote for you as well. Proxies are allowed," his wife pointed out, irritatingly unaware of how crucial the meeting was to him.

"Consuela, I feel as though you don't realize just how—" To his immense chagrin his wife interrupted him yet again.

"I have to go, Eduardo, it's time for a class. *Adiós.*"

Like his aunt's consultant, Consuela didn't bother waiting for his farewells, either, Eduardo fumed, slipping his phone into his pocket. His wife had recently started giving cookery and knitting classes at a center for disadvantaged mothers, and was rarely at home in the mornings now. Since their disastrous holiday the previous summer, Consuela seemed like another person.

"I am doing what *I* want, for a change," she'd said coldly when she'd told him on their return to Madrid that she was going to do some form of charity work in the mornings, and he'd asked if this was absolutely necessary.

At least she was at home, with their evening meal in preparation, when he returned each day from work. Eduardo supposed he should be thankful for small mercies. But she was no longer as soft and compliant as she used to be, and was much more argumentative. That bloody *menopausia* was a curse on men, and him in particular, Eduardo mused miserably as his heretofore gentle and accommodating wife was, as the months progressed, turning into someone he didn't recognize.

"I'm having a pause from men and a life that is no longer fulfilling me," she'd told him smartly when he'd tentatively broached the subject of her menopausal irritability and other symptoms, and asked her whether she should see a doctor.

A pause from men! Eduardo couldn't believe his ears that his wife could even think in those terms. What a nonsensical utterance to spout. The kind of tripe so-called feminist types came out with. When he'd first become a notary, it was rare to have a female colleague. Now they were ten a penny and perfume was as prevalent as male cologne on the office floor. Not to his liking at all. It was bad enough enduring such behavior at work without having to come home to it.

Until the row that had changed everything the previous year, Consuela had never refused him sex; now she often said she didn't feel like it, and made no apologies for her refusals, either. Another unwelcome development in their marriage.

Taking a deep breath, Eduardo knocked on the door of the room his aunt shared with two other patients. Beatriz was resting against her pillows, her white hair plaited in a severe braid rather than its usual topknot. Her bifocal glasses were perched on the end of her nose and she was reading *El Mundo* with deep interest. Beatriz had all her wits about her and kept up with current affairs better than he did, Eduardo acknowledged, wishing he'd had time to have a coffee and read *his* newspaper.

"Discharged tomorrow—what good news," he said with faux cheeriness, sitting on the chair beside her bed. "And of course you will come and stay with us for a few days?"

"I would rather go home." His aunt lowered her glasses.

And I would rather you went home too, Eduardo thought. "I know that, but your consultant thinks it's best that you not be on your own for a few days. You've been in hospital for more than two weeks and you'll be weaker than you think."

"Very well, you may take me back to your apartment. I'll recuperate for a week." Beatriz spoke as though she were doing *him* the favor. "Now I want you to get me three boxes of LuXocolat chocolate strawberries and three gift cards, for the staff and dinner ladies, and bring them with you when you come to collect me."

"Of course." He scribbled a note in the slim notepad he carried in his inside pocket and stood up. "I have meetings to attend. I must go." He leaned down and kissed his aunt's soft, unlined cheek. He was so tempted to say that he must also ring Gabriel and cancel his trip down south because of her, but he restrained himself.

"*Gracias,*" she murmured, picking up her paper again, and once again he felt ignored, and furious that she'd not acknowledged that he'd taken time off work to come and meet with her consultant.

And does she think that I don't work, and that I have time to go shopping for chocolates as well as spending half the morning waiting to talk to her specialist? he seethed, paying his parking charges and striding along the rows of cars until he came to his own black BMW. The traffic was heavy and that made him even more irritable.

His BlackBerry beeped, indicating he had a text, while he was sitting idling at traffic lights. He clicked on it and was sorry that he had.

Eduardo, do you think there is any need for me to fly over to see Beatriz? Is her illness serious? She assures me it isn't but I'm concerned. Mama X

Eduardo's lips thinned. He'd no wish to have his mother flying over to Madrid from the States to see her sister. It would mean he'd have to offer to put her up and he'd have to spend time with her. *That* was something he had no desire to do. His relationship with his mother was strained at the best of times. He sat drumming his fingers on the steering wheel, waiting for the lights to change. A child, a young boy of about seven, gamboled across the street ahead of his mother, who was pushing a buggy. Carefree, lively, he chatted animatedly to the young woman, who smiled at his capers.

He'd been like that young fellow once, Eduardo thought sadly. Until he'd been abandoned by his parents to the care of *Tía* Beatriz.

"Don't go there," he muttered. "The past is the past." He began texting.

No need to travel, Madre—he never called his mother *Mamá*—*Beatriz is recovering very well. If I feel it is necessary for you to come I'll let you know. Gracias.*

Polite but to the point, and he was subtly letting his mother know that *he* was in control of when she would be allowed to visit her sister and abandoned son. The lights changed and he drove off, averting his eyes from the young mother, who was ruffling her little boy's hair affectionately.

By the time Eduardo arrived at his office, his mother was banished to the back of his mind, where he preferred her to reside, leaving him undisturbed.

"Luciana, would you organize to have three boxes of these

chocolates and three gift cards bought for me for tomorrow, please. This is the brand name." He dropped his scribbled note onto his secretary's desk. "Who have we next?"

"The Chavez Janssen apartment sale. All parties are in room four."

"Ah, yes, the Dutch couple buying in Chamberi." He took the file and flicked through it. Everything was in order. And the bank draft was made out to the sellers. Not that he would give any indication that this was so. Eduardo liked keeping the clients and their representatives on edge until the last moment.

He straightened his shoulders, flicked some imaginary dust off his lapel, and prepared to make his entrance. This was his favorite moment in his working day. He strode down the corridor and stepped briskly into room 4. The polite chitchat between the buyers, the sellers, and their brokers stopped and an expectant hush descended on the people sitting at the long rectangular table. Eduardo savored this energy change, this unspoken acknowledgment that someone important had entered the room. He, the notary, without whom neither side could either sell nor buy. *He* held the power of yea or nay. Eduardo reveled in the formality of it all. He also enjoyed seeing clients in his splendid oak-furnished office, watching their reactions to his somber, measured tones as he literally laid down the law.

"*Hola.*" Eduardo bowed slightly and took his place at the top of the table, relishing the familiar surge of authority which comforted him that, in his career, at least, he was in control and all was satisfactory and as it should be.

◆

Why am I so consumed with anger and resentment? Why are all these unwelcome emotions swirling around me? I feel as though I'm in a washing machine being spun and tossed, completely out of control . . . I have never been so unsettled in my life . . . and yet . . . there are times I am exhilarated.

Consuela paused and lifted her head from the red embossed notebook in which she'd taken to writing a daily journal. It was late and she was tired but she was reluctant to join her husband in their large mahogany bed. They had rowed yet again after dinner. Eduardo had been cold and stern as they sat together eating the *cocido madrileño* she'd prepared for their meal.

She'd not been inclined to instigate conversation or to try and coax him out of his bad humor, as she would once have done. *Why should I have to pander to him?* she'd thought indignantly, pushing some chickpeas and pork belly around her plate, her appetite waning as her resentment increased.

"*Madre* sent me a text. She wanted to know should she come and visit Beatriz." Eduardo dipped some crusty bread into his gravy and ate it absentmindedly.

Ah! thought his wife. No wonder he was annoyed. Contact with his mother *and* a missed trip to La Joya explained his extra-sour visage. "What did you say?" Consuela kept her tone neutral.

"I told her there was no need. I told her that *I* would let her know if *I* felt it was necessary for her to visit."

"Perhaps you should consult with Beatriz. She might *like* to see her sister. She did have a nasty dose and she isn't getting any younger," Consuela pointed out.

"There's no need. She's on the road to recovery." Her husband glared at her and resumed eating.

"Suit yourself," she said and noted the look of surprise that crossed Eduardo's face at her unaccustomed riposte. The meal had dragged on in strained silence. "Will you be collecting Beatriz before or after lunch tomorrow?" she asked finally, planning the next day's evening meal in her head. She would cook *escudella barrejada*. *Tía* Beatriz was particularly partial to the pasta-and-soup dish.

"I've not decided yet." Eduardo wiped his lips primly with his napkin.

"I'd like to be able to plan my day." Consuela pushed her plate away.

"We all make plans and God laughs! *I* was supposed to be on my way to Málaga right now," he retorted petulantly.

"Oh, for heaven's sake, Eduardo! Stop trying to make me feel guilty about not collecting *Tía* Beatriz. She's *your* aunt, not mine. And I explained my reasons to you. You can be so *unreasonable* at times. I'm *sick* of it!" It had erupted out of her, a surging, unstoppable outburst. She'd felt like a bloody naughty schoolgirl sitting in silence at the table. Her resentment was like bile in her throat.

"And *I'm* sick of you and *your* moods. You never used to be like this. That cousin of yours is a bad influence on you, with her weird ideas and outlandish practices. She has you under her spell. You were always a supportive wife. Now you're . . . you're . . . *una musaraña irracional.*" He'd flung his napkin on the table and stormed out of the room.

Consuela chewed her pen, remembering her husband's bitter words. He'd never insulted her before, never called her names. Was she the irrational shrew he'd accused her of being? And as for her being influenced by her cousin Catalina . . . well, that she could not deny, especially in this last year, when they had grown even closer than ever before.

Consuela flipped through the pages of the diary her cousin had encouraged her to keep.

To beautiful Consuela.

A transformational journal of evolving, to find the Goddess within, Catalina had written in her elegant cursive on the flyleaf of the richly embossed red notebook she'd gifted Consuela with at Christmas.

"What does *that* mean?" Eduardo had sneered after he'd picked the book up from the side table where she'd laid it and read the inscription. " 'Goddess within'—such drivel that Catalina comes out with. No wonder her husband left her."

"*She* actually left *him*, Eduardo, because he did not respect *her,* or her beliefs, or her right to become her own person. And I would ask *you* in the future to respect what is *mine* and to ask my permission to read personal things that have nothing to do with *you!*" Consuela had felt a now-familiar blaze of fury at her husband's condescension and snatched the diary from his hands, much to his astonishment.

She gave a sardonic smile at the memory. If Eduardo thought the goddess within was nonsense, wait until he heard she was going to attend a seminar in Seville with her cousin on "The Emergence of the Divine Feminine and the Letting Go of the Patriarchy."

A thought struck her. "How interesting," she murmured, taking down a dictionary and flipping the pages to find the definition of "patriarchy":

Patriarchy is a social system in which males hold primary power, predominate in roles of political leadership, moral authority, social privilege, and control of property; in the domain of the family, fathers or father-figures hold authority over women and children.

Eduardo, her husband, the man she'd left her father's house for, was the very *essence* of the patriarchy, as had been her father. Both carrying an energy from which she was now choosing to break free. No wonder Eduardo was tetchy and calling her names. Their relationship was evolving from an authority-based one, with him holding the power, to one of equality, where she, after years of playing the subservient wife—which Consuela had to admit had been her choice—was finally emerging into her own power to become his equal. Catalina had told her that in many unequal partnerships the strain of unwelcome change often brought the relationship to a breaking point, as had happened with Catalina's own marriage.

Consuela's dark eyes gleamed with anticipation and she picked up her pen.

In spite of the whirlpool of emotions that rage within me, I am excited by this new knowledge that is coming my way. My world has opened up immeasurably. The books I am reading, the conversations I am having with enlightened women, resonate deeply with my spirit. I look forward to releasing the past and all the old ways that no longer serve me or who I am. I look forward to emerging into my own power and finding and being my true self at last. I am remembering!

Consuela could understand her husband's discomfiture. She must try hard not to make this evolution of hers a battle between them, she decided, switching off the light and heading for the bedroom. She undressed in their en-suite and padded silently to her side of the bed. She knew Eduardo was awake.

"*Buenas noches, mi querido,*" she murmured as she always did. She felt her husband tense, knew he was struggling with himself to accept her olive branch. If he didn't, it was not her fault, it was his choice, she reminded herself.

"*Buenas noches,*" Eduardo muttered, not very graciously, Consuela had to admit. There was no endearment, but still, it was better than frigid silence. He was a good husband, as good as he knew how. If this "personality change" of hers was an unanticipated and unexpected roller coaster for her, no wonder he was unsettled. If it were the other way around, and the roles were reversed, she would be just as thrown, she reasoned.

She slid her fingers into Eduardo's and was glad his own tightened around hers, and they lay together in a silence that was no longer hostile until both of them drifted off to sleep.

Chapter Nineteen

Jutta

"Slow down, daughter," Oskar Sauer urged as he limped and puffed his way from Terminal 1 at Frankfurt Airport to the S-Bahn.

"Sorry, Papa." Jutta stopped and let her father catch his breath. There was a train departing from Platform 4 to Frankfurt Main in five minutes and she wanted to be on it so they would be in plenty of time to make their homeward-bound connection. She'd suggested a wheelchair at the airport but her father wouldn't hear of it. "I'm not getting in one of those. I'm not an invalid yet!" he'd puffed and wheezed, and she'd thought he was going to expire there and then. *That's what you think,* she'd thought crossly as they'd made slow progress from Terminal 3 in Málaga to the security check-in.

Oskar had spent the three weeks since Christmas with her and Felipe, and she was spending a week in Germany to settle her father back home after his travels. She felt very sorry for herself. Her sisters, Anka and Inga, had told her in no uncertain terms that she had to share in the minding of their father and give them some respite. *They* had decided that she would take him for three weeks every January and three weeks in June. Her brother, Friedrich, visited from Strasbourg once every six weeks or so and seemed to think that that was his duty done.

Jutta understood why her sisters would need a complete break from Oskar. He was a demanding father, with old-fashioned views of family and the place of women in society. He felt *entitled* to their care. The fact that they had lives of their own to live was not a consideration for him.

"Anyway, January is a good time for him to go to Spain. It's much warmer than Germany down south; it will be good for his arthritis," Anka had remarked on the phone to her when she'd called to tell Jutta that their father had been delivered to the Frankfurt Airport and checked in and would be with her in five hours' time.

"I won't be able to spend all day with him while he's here. I work; you realize that. I have a business," Jutta explained.

"January must be very quiet. It's not the holiday season." Anka was dismissive.

"Actually it's very busy, with Germans and Scandinavians escaping winter weather. All the apartments on our books are let, Anka." Jutta tried to keep the sharpness out of her tone. Anka was a stay-at-home wife and mother, and she and her husband and three teenage children were going skiing in the French Alps the following day and had another trip planned in March. Felipe and Jutta hadn't had a holiday in almost a year and had no plans for one in the foreseeable future.

"Well, at least you don't have kids. You're a free agent," Anka sniffed. "I'd better go. We have to pack. Don't forget to give Papa his water tablets in the morning; if he takes them too late, he will be up and down peeing all night and won't sleep, and that will make him cranky."

"Crankier than normal, you mean," Jutta muttered, and Anka laughed. "Bear up, you only have him for two months a year. Inga and I have him the rest of the time." Anka was not at all sorry for her, and Jutta supposed that if she were in her sister's shoes, she wouldn't be, either.

The problem was that she didn't *like* her father very much. She didn't like his racist views, his right-wing politics, and his authoritarian attitude. Oskar was of a generation and a mind-set that was utterly foreign to hers. Spain was the furthest he'd traveled, and as far as he was concerned, the Costa del Sol was a haven for criminals, drug lords, and shady characters from Africa and the Middle East.

"Don't waste your time arguing with him," Felipe had advised when she'd rowed with Oskar over his rudeness to a young Moroccan who was selling his wares at one of the beach restaurants where they were having dinner.

"Get the hell away from here, you layabout, with your fake Rolex watches, and go and pay taxes like the rest of us have to, to keep ourselves and our nations out of debt," he'd muttered irritably in German, waving him away.

"Papa, that's very rude! You can't talk like—"

"I can speak to whom I like, and I don't want any of those *hoojiii hoojiii* sellers annoying me when I'm eating my meal. They shouldn't be allowed to bother diners." Oskar glared at her.

Fortunately the young man did not understand German, and good-naturedly smiled at Jutta before moving to the next table. Felipe had had to hide his amusement behind his napkin. "*Hoojiii hoojiiis*—I love it," he whispered that night when they were in bed and he was sliding his hand up under her nightshirt.

Jutta hated making love knowing that her father was in the next bedroom, although fortunately his deafness prevented him from hearing her muffled groans. His rumbling snores echoed along the hallway. He would tell her the following morning, as he did most days, that he'd "hardly slept a wink."

He would wake up early, long before the winter sunrise, and she would feel obliged to leave the comfort of her bed and her husband's warm body and make Oskar coffee and serve him croissants and a selection of ham and cheese for his breakfast.

But later, when she came home to check on him in the afternoon, and saw him napping on the balcony with his face raised to the sun, as was his custom, Jutta would soften and chide herself for her meanness of spirit. He'd provided well for his family. Now it was time for his family to step up to the plate and take care of him in his declining years.

As the January days turned into weeks, Jutta had struggled to maintain her equilibrium. Having someone else in the apartment was stressful; having her aged parent doubly so. She couldn't walk around in her underwear, or nightwear, and lie with her head in Felipe's lap watching TV in the evening. She couldn't curse or be impatient and irritable with her PMS, and she seemed to be constantly serving coffee and cookies. She had to resort to keeping a bottle of wine in the bedroom, because Oskar didn't like to see her drink more than a glass with her evening meal and would lecture her if she had a refill. She felt she was fifteen years old again.

The morning of his departure from Spain finally arrived, and Jutta had breathed a deep sigh of relief when the door of the Lufthansa Airbus had been shut and the aircraft had rolled away from the terminal building on the first stage of their journey home.

Only a week more to go, she comforted herself several hours later, having negotiated the concourse at Frankfurt Airport and helped Oskar onto the commuter train that would take about eleven minutes to Frankfurt Main. She'd booked the ICE fast train to Limburg Süd, and after another change Anka would be at Frickhofen station to meet them. Oskar had dozed as the countryside flashed by and Jutta would like to have dozed herself, exhausted from the stress of traveling with him. The next time she journeyed with him, her father *would* use a wheelchair. She would insist on it and to hell with his pride.

No! The next time she would *not* travel back to Germany; she would put him on the plane and tell Friedrich to collect him from the airport and bring him home. Her lazy lump of a brother got away with murder. Jutta scowled, rooting in her purse to buy two cups of coffee from the snack trolley. It was a short journey and she hoped the coffee would restore her.

"It's nice to come home on a day when the weather is good—although I'll miss the heat." Oskar had perked up, drinking his beverage and demolishing the biscuits she gave him in two mouthfuls. The fields were dusted with powdery snow. The sky was clear and piercingly blue, and the dark green fir trees in the forests that covered the slopes of the hills were so different from the prickly green pine trees of her adoptive country. She'd shivered walking from the warmth of the Airbus into the air bridge and wrapped her scarf up around her neck and ears. They had left 70 degrees in Málaga and arrived to below freezing in Frankfurt.

"Back to the cold and civilization," Oskar remarked, but his eyes held a glimmer of amusement, and she laughed.

"I hope you enjoyed your holiday, Papa," she'd said, welcoming the warmth of the train.

"I did, daughter. It was a change and the heat was good for me, and good for my bones but it's nice to be home. I want to visit Klara's grave. And I'm sure you'll be glad to have the apartment to yourself again."

"I never said that, Papa," she said defensively.

"No, you didn't, and you were kind, you didn't make me feel like a nuisance the way the other two do." Oskar's rheumy blue eyes looked sad and she felt an uncharacteristic pang of sympathy for him.

"Don't say that, Papa," she murmured.

"Well, they do," he said grumpily. "I know they have children and busy lives, but I was a good father too, and I looked after *my* parents without complaining."

Your parents both died in their early seventies and didn't need much minding, she was tempted to say tartly.

"You look very well, Papa, tanned and healthy," Anka declared when they walked down the platform to greet them at

Frickhofen. She didn't embrace her father. She hefted Oskar's case into her Volvo station wagon. "You should go to Spain more often."

"Jutta and Felipe looked after me very well—and made me feel *most* welcome," Oskar added pointedly.

"I should hope so," Anka remarked, proffering her cheek for Jutta to kiss. "Love the highlights, or is that from the sun?" She studied her younger sister critically.

"Thanks. Both. I got it styled and highlighted at Christmas." Jutta helped her father into the front seat of the car.

"You probably need highlights now. I thought you'd gone quite mousy the last time I saw you," Anka remarked, putting the key into the ignition and waiting for Oskar to fasten his seat belt.

"Well, I suppose mousy is better than outright gray the way you went," Jutta riposted smartly. Her oldest sister could be quite the bitch. She'd be in a bad humor now because their father was back home and her freedom was curtailed.

She should stop letting them make her feel guilty, Jutta reflected as they drove towards Dornburg in the deepening dusk. They had made their choices and she had made hers; her sisters could just deal with it.

In fairness, Anka had the log fire burning and their father's house was warm and welcoming when the weary travelers finally put the key in the door. The fridge was full, and a big casserole of *Tüffel un Plum*, his favorite stew of smoked ham, prunes, and potatoes, was simmering in the oven. The familiar scent of cloves and bay leaves made Jutta's mouth water, and she realized she was starving after all the traveling.

Anka served them their meal and left them to eat, with hasty promises to see them the following day. Jutta thought of Felipe's family and how warmly they were always welcomed when they went to visit.

"She didn't stay long," Oskar said, holding his plate out for another helping of casserole.

"I suppose when you have children you have a lot of chores." Jutta tried to take the sting out of it.

"Ummmm." Oskar wasn't impressed.

Inga phoned while they were finishing off their meal with semolina dumplings and ice cream. "Hi, *Süßling*, welcome home," she said cheerily. Well, at least she'd called her "sweetie" just like she had when they were young. Jutta smiled.

"Hi, Inga, great to hear you. When am I going to see you and my lovely nieces?"

"Um . . . well, I'm a little tied up, so it'll probably be Thursday," her middle sister demurred.

"Oh!" Jutta couldn't hide her disappointment. Clearly Inga was going to string out her freedom for another few days. Jutta felt utterly fed up. She'd given Inga and her family the use of an apartment for ten days the previous summer, and had wined them and dined them and driven them all around Andalucía while they were on holiday, and Inga couldn't even be arsed to come and see her, let alone come and welcome home her dad, whom she hadn't seen for almost a month.

"OK, I'll put you on to Papa to say hello. I'll see you when I see you, then," she said flatly, handing the phone to Oskar. When he went to hand it back to her, after a brief conversation, Jutta shook her head. She wouldn't be so accommodating the next time Inga wanted a freebie holiday on the Costa del Sol.

"They can all go to hell, Felipe, and book their own apartments from now on," she grumbled to her husband later, when she'd cleaned up after their meal and made hot chocolate for Oskar. She'd phoned him from her old bedroom, lying on the single bed, covered by the patchwork quilt that her mother had made. The cozy room in the eaves, with the window opposite her bed facing towards the twinkling lights of the village in the distance, remained as it had been since her student days. A faded poster of U2 taped with yellowing Sellotape still hung on the side of the pine wardrobe. Her old pink teddy lay against the pillows.

The pale lemon moonlight illuminated the fields in their frosty filigree, a beam stealing in through the window to be reflected in the oval mirror of the dressing table, with its collection of half-empty bottles of perfume. The picturesque moonlit tapestry soothed her wounded feelings.

"Aw, my poor little *cariña*. Don't mind them; I'll make a big fuss of you when you get home. Let's fly up to Barcelona and stay with my cousin for a weekend and have some fun when you get back."

"Can we afford to?" she asked, wishing Felipe was with her right now.

"Of course we can."

"OK. I love you."

"I love you too, Jutta. I'll call you tomorrow."

Jutta switched off the light and snuggled into the warm hollow of the bed. She hadn't slept in flannelette sheets since she'd last been home, and she felt a sudden sharp ache of sadness for her mother. The house was so different without her mother's solid, comforting presence. Klara had been the glue that had held the Sauer family together. Now there was no cohesion, no real focal point like there had been when she was alive. They all lived their own lives, immersed in their own family setups with little reference to each other; their only thing in common now was their father. When Oskar passed away she wasn't even sure if she'd particularly want to see her siblings anymore. *How lonely and awful is that?* Jutta thought glumly.

Maybe it was time she and Felipe thought about having children, having a family unit of their own. And she'd be able to use her children as an excuse, as her sisters had, when trying to avoid taking on more responsibility for Oskar. He could live well into his nineties.

Could they afford a child, though? Felipe had been caught unexpectedly for unpaid property taxes, and the payment had made a huge dent in their savings. She was scrupulous in her business practices; she paid every penny she was obliged to. Felipe was much more casual, always trying—like many of his colleagues in the property development and rental business—to evade his taxes.

She snuggled under the quilt and closed her eyes, listening to the unfamiliar creaks and moans of the house as it settled down for the night. Gradually her body relaxed and drowsiness overcame her, and Jutta eventually fell asleep in her room under the eaves.

◆

Felipe gazed out at the moonlit shimmering sea. He hated sleeping on his own, hated not feeling Jutta's supple, toned body against his. He'd told her that they could afford to fly to Barcelona, and for now they could, but there was a problem in Alicante that was going to cost him dear. His partner in one of the property development deals had gone bankrupt, and his other partner was getting cold feet. He wasn't going to say anything to Jutta yet. He'd see how things unfolded. If he could get someone else to invest, it could all be salvaged. He might give Cal Cooper a call.

Felipe poured himself another beer and went back inside. The evenings were chilly, although the temperatures rose much higher during the day. The only good thing was that his father-in-law was gone. Three weeks in the sour Hun's company was three weeks too much. But he loved his wife, and for her he'd endured Oskar's dour personality with as good a grace as he could muster. Hell, he might even have another couple of beers, he thought. After two, Oskar had looked disapprovingly at him as though he, Felipe, was someone who had alcohol problems.

He kicked off his shoes, loosened his tie, sprawled on the sofa, and surfed the TV channels until he found a football match. He was king of his own home again, but for how much longer could they afford to rent a frontline apartment? Felipe sighed. He'd skated on thin ice for the last six months, unbeknownst to Jutta. Now the cracks were beginning to show.

◆

Oskar kissed his dead wife's photograph and replaced it on his bed-side locker. "Good night, Klara," he murmured. It was his bedtime ritual. He turned off the lamp and lay in his familiar bed with the big bolster pillow and the gold-and-chocolate-brown patchwork quilt that Klara had made when they were first married. The year before she'd died, she'd reworked it, replacing worn patches and bias binding, which she'd sewn to the front and whipstitched by hand all around the back, in the traditional way, eschewing the use of the sewing machine. He'd always enjoyed when she was quilting. They would sit opposite each other at the stove while he read his paper and she stitched. He would read out items of interest and they would discuss them or sometimes just sit in companionable silence.

The void in his life since she'd left it was immense, and his loneliness knew no bounds. But he kept those feelings to himself for the most part. Only with Jutta could he lower his guard a little. She was the kindest of his children, perhaps because she was the youngest and her mother's favorite. Her little dumpling, Klara had called her.

Exhaustion swept over him. It had been a long and tiring day. He hoped very much that he would sleep well in his own bed. There were nights in Spain when he hadn't slept a wink.

It was good too to have Jutta staying with him for the next week. Comforting to have someone else in the house, especially at night. Oskar yawned and pulled the quilt up under his chin, wondering if the dull ache of Klara's loss would ever leave him. He lay sleepily listening to the wind whispering through the fir trees and thinking it was just like the sound of the sea shushing against the shore in Andalucía.

Chapter Twenty

Jutta

"Jutta, I'm sorry to have to bother you, but something happened in La Joya, in the Vissers' apartment. Veronique was carrying a bucket of bleach out to the balcony and she tripped over the Hoover, and the bleach splattered over the rug in the lounge—"

"*Oh, Christus!* Is there much damage? Can we get it cleaned?" Jutta's heart sank.

"I've looked at it. I even asked Constanza Torres could she recommend anyone—she runs her own cleaning team in the complex. But no luck, Jutta, it's impossible to get the bleach marks out because it's splattered all over. Even the crayon tip we googled up wouldn't do it. We'd done a pre-arrival shop and that was being delivered, and Veronique was going out to the balcony to clean the table and chairs when it happened. We'll just have to tell them. I don't mind doing it, but you know how fussy Mrs. Visser is. Even if we managed to lighten some of the stains, she'd spot them. You know what she's like," Jutta's maintenance manager said morosely.

"I know." Merel and Jan Visser were one of Jutta's least favorite clients. They were demanding, tight with money, arguing over every item on the apartment maintenance and laundry bill. Shopping with them to furnish the apartment had been a nightmare. The rug in question had not been purchased under Jutta's auspices, so she couldn't even try and get a replacement in twenty-four hours.

"I'll phone her myself, Christine. Knowing her, she'd demand to speak to me anyway. Anything else to report?"

"Umm, that cranky Spanish guy, Eduardo, above the Hoffmanns complained to Constanza that people who were staying in the Hoffmanns' were hanging their towels on the balcony—"

"*Oh, por el amor de Dios!*" Jutta shook her head. "Anything else that's *serious*?"

Christine laughed. "Not really. The Cullens in Mi Capricho have a broken pane of glass; that's sorted, and the repainting of the bedroom in the villa in La Cala is almost finished."

"OK, thanks, Christine. I'll ring the Vissers immediately and get back to you. And tell Veronique to try and be more careful."

"Will do. *Adiós.*"

"*Adiós*, Christine." Jutta poured herself another cup of coffee and absentmindedly nibbled on a slice of Edam that was on the cheese board on the breakfast table.

"Could you not even have breakfast without being on that phone? You're all addicted to your phones. It's not civilized," Oskar remonstrated from the top of the table, frowning as she scrolled through her messages.

"Papa, I have a business to run and things happen. When it's your own business, you have to deal with stuff immediately."

"Well, surely you can have breakfast without having your head stuck in it? Is it too much to ask for you to chat to your old papa during mealtimes?"

"Sorry about that, Papa." Jutta swallowed down her irritation and put her phone down. She'd ring her client from the privacy of her bedroom.

"Ach, I'm just an old nuisance to you all, you'd be better off without me," her father went off on his familiar refrain.

"No you're not; don't be saying that," Jutta chided.

"That other pair haven't put in an appearance since you arrived. Don't think I don't know what's going on," he grumbled, buttering his croissant. "They're staying away because you're here; they only come because they feel they have to, to do my shopping and feed me. I'm telling you, Jutta, I'm nothing more than a nuisance and I hate being dependent on them."

"You know, Papa, you could be much more independent if you wished," Jutta said firmly.

"How so? My arthritis is getting worse and so are my gallstones. I need a knee replacement. Who is going to look after me when I have that?" he groused.

"Why don't you hire a housekeeper to come in for a few hours every day to cook and clean—"

"Are you mad, daughter? I don't have that kind of money," Oskar interrupted, glaring at her.

"Yes you do, Papa. You aren't a pauper by any means. You have a good pension. You still save. Use your money to make yourself independent and then when Inga and Anka come to visit, they can sit and talk to you and not have to worry about cooking your meals and doing your housework," Jutta said firmly.

"I need my money in case I have to go to a nursing home. You seem to think I'm some sort of millionaire," he scoffed.

"I'm merely pointing out options, Papa."

"Were you talking to the others about this?" He cocked a wary eye at her. "Making plans behind my back. I won't have it—"

"Have I seen the others since I arrived?" Jutta shot back indignantly.

"You could have been talking to them on the phone," he observed.

"I wasn't. No one is making any plans behind your back, Papa. I was just suggesting something that might make *you* feel more independent and empowered. I was thinking about *you*!"

"I don't want strangers in my house." Oskar's tone was sulky, and Jutta bit back her retort. Losing his independence slowly but surely as he aged must be a tremendous blow, she acknowledged. The old saying "Once a man, twice a child" was now proving very true in Oskar's case. It was hard to believe that her once strong, commanding, seemingly invincible father was now becoming as petulant and dependent and in need of assistance as a child.

"Think about it, that's all I'm saying. Now I have to make a call to a client and I'll tidy up after the breakfast when I'm finished. Excuse me." Jutta stood up and took her phone from the table.

She trudged up the narrow stairs to her bedroom and sat on the bed, heavyhearted. She'd had enough of listening to all their moans. All she wanted to do was go back home to Spain. And what was more, she decided, Oskar could go to a rehab hospital after his knee operation because she wasn't coming back to Germany for a week in the high season, which was when his operation was scheduled for.

It was raining outside, great sheets of molten grayness obliterating the view of Dornburg and the fields. She'd forgotten how miserable and grim it was here when it rained and how hemmed in it always made her feel. Jutta missed the wide expanse of her sea view. Being landlocked again was slightly claustrophobic.

She propped herself up against her pillows, scrolling down her client list until she found the Vissers' number.

Merel answered. Just her luck, thought Jutta. Jan was easier to deal with. "Mrs. Visser, how are you? Good, I hope. I'm afraid one of my cleaners spilled some bleach on your drawing room rug. We will, of course, replace it," she said briskly, deciding it was better, with Merel Visser, to get to the point straightaway.

"My Berber rug? My very *expensive* Berber rug?" The Dutch woman's voice rose an octave.

"I'm afraid so."

"I'm . . . I'm . . . this is not good. It took me a long time to get the perfect rug for that room. How damaged is it?"

"I haven't seen it myself. I'm in Germany at the moment, but my office manager tells me it's quite stained." Jutta kept her tone cool and crisp.

"I'll see what it's like tomorrow when I arrive. I'm not happy about this at all, Frau Sauer. I particularly like the colors and . . . and . . . the ethnic resonance of that rug."

"I could try some of the markets and look for something similar," Jutta offered.

"I don't want *rubbish* from the markets. I bought it in a carpet shop in Tangier, and that is where I'll be going to replace it, at your expense, *mijn goede vrouw. Goede dag.*"

"Good day to you too, my good woman," Jutta muttered to the disconnected phone. She felt like a five-year-old after their frosty encounter. She fired off a text to Christine.

> Spoke to Madam Visser. Not impressed. Offer her a day trip
> to Tangier from Málaga, and tell her we will give her €400
> MAX for a replacement rug. Tell her to make a claim to her
> insurance company. And make one to ours. Thanks! J.

Thank goodness she had efficient staff, Jutta thought, taking a deep breath before going downstairs to try and be a patient and understanding daughter.

◆

"And furthermore, you need to encourage Papa to either get a stairlift or move his bed downstairs until his op is over and he's completely mobile again. He's having difficulty getting up the stairs. Organize whatever he needs doing," Jutta spoke firmly to her brother the following morning, having just finished packing her case.

"Can't the girls do that?" blustered Friedrich.

"He won't listen to any of us. He might listen to you. You *are* the son and heir, and besides, they do more than enough for him. They're constantly at his beck and call," Jutta retorted sharply.

"It's all right for you flying up from Spain once a year and putting your spoke in; *we're* there all the time," her brother snapped.

"Excuse me, but from what I've heard, you make an appearance twice a month for a quick visit. If you can look after Helga's mother, you can spare a bit more time for your own parent."

"That's uncalled-for—"

"Eh . . . I don't think so, Friedrich—you get away very lightly—but Papa is getting older and more dependent and he's going to need more of all our help, so get over it and start pulling your weight. Bye." Jutta didn't give him time to respond and hung up.

Her brother could get into a snit if he wanted to, but she'd said her piece and put it up to him. She could do no more.

She took one last glance around her bedroom. It had been her haven once again, as it had been when she was a teenager dreaming of escaping her boring, mundane, village life.

She took the case off her bed and straightened the quilt where it was creased. "I miss you, Mama," she murmured before closing the door behind her.

"It will be lonely for me now that you're going, daughter." Oskar looked at her despondently and she felt her heart soften as she saw the dejected stoop of his shoulders and the sadness in his tired blue eyes.

"I might try and get back for a quick visit when you go to have your knee done. I'll wait until you're out of hospital and in rehab and then I can walk with you," Jutta heard herself say, despite vowing to herself that she was not coming back home to Germany in the high season.

"And maybe you could stay with me for a few days when I get home?" Oscar asked, brightening up. Jutta's heart sank. Typical of her father, give him an inch and he'd take a mile.

"We'll see," she demurred. "It's a very busy time of the year for me."

"Ah, sure, I'm only an old nuisance," Oskar muttered.

"Stop that, Papa, it's not fair to keep saying that. We're all doing our best for you," she said sharply.

"I suppose you are," Oskar admitted reluctantly.

"And think about what I said to you about getting someone in to do housekeeping. You'd be very independent and you could tell us all to get lost," she teased.

Oskar laughed. "Now. that's an idea. Safe journey, daughter. I see Anka's outside in the car. I'll miss you. I'll be at their tender mercies now that you're gone," he jested, making a face.

She put her arms around him and gave him a swift hug, dismayed at how diminished he was from the strong, vibrant father she remembered in her youth. "I'll phone you tonight," she promised him as his own arms tightened around her and a fleeting, most uncharacteristic wave of love enveloped her. She'd always respected and admired her father, but until now she'd never felt love for him. After all these years it was his frailty that evoked that emotion, she thought, surprised.

"Take care, Papa, and I'll miss you too," she murmured.

"Will you, Jutta?" He looked her in the eye.

"Yes, Papa, I will. Our time together was . . . was precious." She smiled at him and was happy to see the way his faded blue eyes lit up at her words.

A sharp toot on the horn reminded her that time was of the essence. "Talk tonight," she promised, and couldn't help the lump that rose to her throat when she turned to wave and saw him standing alone in the doorway.

"You're not crying, are you?" Anka was astonished as she crunched along the gravel drive and Oskar stood waving stoically.

"Mad, isn't it?" sniffed Jutta, rooting for a tissue in her bag.

"I thought you'd be delighted to get away."

"I am . . . and I'm not," she sniffled. "It's just when I see him on his own without Mama, and see how he's getting old, it makes me sad."

"Feel free to come home *anytime*," her sister replied, swinging the Volvo onto the main road and out of sight of the farmhouse.

"Maybe I'm not *that* sad." Jutta composed herself, but even hours later, flying over Madrid and south towards Málaga and her husband's loving arms, the memory of her father's hug caused her a pang, and she knew she would fly back to Germany in the summer no matter how busy she was in Andalucía.

◆

"I'm not happy having to do a day trip to Tangiers. It's a very long day; I'd prefer to stay overnight," Merel Visser said crossly.

"You know the insurance will cover it, Mevrouw Visser. The offer of the day trip was a gesture of goodwill." Jutta was polite but firm. She was not spending another cent of company money on a damned rug.

"I'll think about it. Perhaps it's time to change my maintenance company," the other woman said, her little chipmunk eyes glinting slyly, staring hard at Jutta.

"That's entirely a matter for yourself, Mevrouw Visser. Let me know as soon as you make a decision. *Goede dag*." She strode out of the apartment, back straight, head up. Merel Visser could go to hell if she thought Jutta was going to grovel to her to keep her business.

She was marching towards Constanza's office when she heard brisk footsteps behind her.

"*Discúlpame, por favor.*" The voice was cold, authoritative. The "Excuse me, please" was not uttered in a friendly tenor. Jutta felt her hackles rise. Now what? She turned to find Eduardo De La Fuente studying her, black eyes stony and aloof.

"*Sí?*" she answered back in Spanish.

"I've seen you in the grounds this past year. You rent out apartments, is that correct?"

"Furnish, maintain, and rent, yes. And you are?" she asked coolly. She wasn't going to be interrogated by that little Spanish upstart. He was the bane of poor Constanza's life. She'd become friendly with the concierge after their initial froideur, and always enjoyed stopping for a chat when she visited the complex.

"Eduardo De La Fuente. I'm an owner in the urbanization and as such I have a strong interest in keeping standards up. I notice in some apartments people are putting towels over the balconies. I would be obliged if you would tell your clients that this is not permitted."

"Any clients I rent an apartment to are given a list of the rules of the community, Señor."

"Yes, well, the people in the apartment below me have ignored those rules, and that is one of your apartments if I'm not mistaken," Eduardo interrupted.

"It was an apartment I furnished and, yes, I maintain it. However, I do not provide a rental service to those particular owners. They rent it out themselves. You may speak to *them* of your concerns. *Adiós.*" She turned her back on him and lengthened her stride, fuming at his cheek. Did he think he *owned* La Joya?

This time two days ago she'd been snoozing on the sofa in front of a blazing stove while her father napped in his armchair. And to think she couldn't *wait* to get back to Spain. All she'd had since her return was hassle. And her sisters thought she led a carefree life of sun and sangria.

Sliding behind the wheel of her Merc, Jutta grimaced. Felipe had driven to Alicante that morning to try and salvage a deal that was threatening to go belly-up. She was irritated with him. Why couldn't he take it slowly and not dive in over his head with his development deals? Sometimes her husband could be overimpulsive and not think about the consequences of his behavior. She hated the way business was done in Spain, all the under-the-counter stuff. Eduardo De La Fuente had little to worry him if a few towels hanging over balconies was his prime concern.

She pressed her fob and waited for the wrought-iron gates to open. She had client taxes to pay in Ayuntamiento de Mijas in La Cala and then she was meeting a new client for lunch in Marbella. She sincerely hoped the queues in La Cala's town hall wouldn't be too long, but from previous experience she knew that was a forlorn hope. She waved at Constanza, who was chatting to the security guard, and drove through the gates, annoyed with herself for not appreciating her relatively stress-free week at home in Germany.

Chapter Twenty-One

MAY

Anna

Anna gave the champagne flutes one last shine and placed them alongside the platter of smoked salmon and brown bread. Dishes of stuffed olives, hummus, and pâté covered the rectangular coffee table and the smell of cooking wafted out of the open-plan kitchen at the other end of the room.

She was so looking forward to a long weekend in Spain with "the Girls" as Austen teasingly called them, although it was a long time since they'd left their girlhood behind them. Three of her oldest and best friends, Mary, Yvonne, and Breda, were coming to supper and to stay the night. They had to be at the airport at five a.m. the following morning, to catch the seven a.m. flight to Málaga. It was their first visit to the penthouse and she was dying to show it to them and spend time in their company. Trying to get a date that suited all of them had been well nigh impossible.

The doorbell chimed and she hurried to greet her friends. "Hiya, girls, come in, dump your luggage in your room, change into your jim-jams if you want," she invited the two women who stood on her doorstep laden with cases, carrier bags, and handbags.

"That's exactly what I'm going to do. I was wearing friggin' heels all day, because I had a load of meetings, and my feet are killing me." Yvonne hugged her warmly.

"Me too. I've had my shower and washed my hair, and, as you can see, I'm not wearing makeup, so I'm ready for bed after we've had this." Mary, Yvonne's sister-in-law, handed Anna a bottle of chilled Moët. "From Yvonnie and me, to toast the new pad and to celebrate us all *finally* getting away together again. Where's Breda? Do we have to wait until she comes to start? It's nine o'clock already . . ." Mary glanced at her watch.

"She texted; she's on her way. She got delayed at work. Thanks *so* much for this. Prosecco would have done fine. I've got champers in the fridge too." Anna ushered her guests to the kitchen.

"Don't be daft! It had to be champers. This is a big deal. Not even an apartment, but a *penthouse* no less. How posh will we be? And besides, how often do we get to do this? No kids, no husbands, just us and books? *That* deserves champers. Let's get the party going, then." Mary opened her case, pulled out a nightshirt, and hurried upstairs to change.

"I'm going to do the same." Yvonne rooted for her cotton pj's and toilet bag and followed her sister-in-law upstairs. Anna lit some candles around the family room. Even though it was mid-May the nights were still chilly and she'd lit the stove, which blazed away, making the room snug and inviting.

Mary had just uncorked the champagne when the doorbell pealed again and Yvonne, on her way downstairs, detoured to open the door. A tall, blond-haired woman stood there looking slightly frazzled. "Sorry I'm late, last-minute hiccup at work and then I couldn't find—"

"Don't worry, it's all fine now, Breda. Calm down and get your ass in here," Yvonne grinned, taking her case from her.

"Did you take a taxi?" Anna came out from the kitchen and hugged her friend.

"No, hubby gave me a lift," Breda said, divesting herself of her scarf and jacket.

"Why didn't you ask him in, for goodness' sake?" Anna took them from her and hung them on the hallstand.

"It's a *girls'* night, Anna," Breda retorted. "Where's Austen?"

"He knew better than to hang around, so he told me he'd give us some 'space.' He went over to a friend's to look at a car that's giving trouble, and then they're going for a pint. Do you want to change?"

"No, I want to eat. Whatever you're cooking smells delicious. I haven't eaten all day."

"Sit yourself down, then." Mary appeared, handing Breda a champagne flute full of chilled sparkling golden bubbly.

"Oh, I *so* need this! Thanks, Mary. It was *mad* at work. I've brought a bottle too. The least I can bring for having four blissful nights in Spain." Breda sank into an armchair and kicked off her shoes.

"God, we'll be pissed if we drink three bottles," Anna remarked, taking a slug from her own glass.

"We could leave one for when we come home," Yvonne suggested, handing around the starters.

"Good thinking," Mary agreed, spreading a cracker lightly with pâté. "And then we can book into rehab!"

They laughed and began to relax, falling into easy banter and talking as only old and dear friends can.

They weren't laughing too much sitting in Austen's car en route to Dublin Airport at quarter to five the following morning, and plenty of yawning could be heard as they cruised along a deserted Collins Avenue.

"Just think, we'll be snoozing on the balcony after lunch and we'll get the dying rays until sunset," Anna reminded them, rooting frantically in her bag for her phone.

"What *are* you looking for?" Her husband glanced over at her. He was used to his wife excavating one of her many cavernous bags. She was invariably looking for her keys, phone, or glasses.

"Ring me, will you?" she ordered irritably. "Honest to God, I drive myself mad."

"Us too," murmured Mary sotto voce.

"I heard that, madam," Anna retorted as Austen clicked on her number on the Bluetooth and her phone tinkled in the depths of her bag.

"Have you got your boarding card and glasses?" Austen got in lane for the airport as they sped along the M1.

"Yep."

"I brought two pairs of magnifiers in case anyone loses theirs," Yvonne said helpfully.

"What are we like?" groaned Mary. "This middle-age stuff is driving me nuts."

" 'We'! Speak for yourself. And 'we' are not talking about middle age or that horrible M-word this weekend," retorted Breda, who was discreetly checking her bag to locate her passport.

"I'll remind you of that when you start flapping your hands around your face because you're 'too warm,' " Mary said smugly as Austen drove up to Terminal 2. They were still laughing as they clambered out of the car at the set-down area.

"Have a great trip, ladies," said Austen chuckling, then hugging Anna tightly before kissing her as they all stood at the curb with their cases.

"Don't worry, Austen, we will," Mary declared. "We may never come back."

◆

Eight hours later the quartet were sitting on a terrace at the beachside restaurant sipping postprandial Baileys, having enjoyed a tasty lunch of freshly caught fish accompanied by delicious sauces, side salads, and a crisp, chilled white wine. They were *completely* relaxed.

Anna gazed at the molten silver sea gently lapping the shore of the curving, sandy beach, just yards away. She couldn't ever remember being so relaxed and contented. Although she and Austen had worried about retiring from work and discussed it endlessly, having finally taken the leap—and what a leap, buying the penthouse as well—she knew they had made the right choice. Seeing the stress and tiredness in her friends' faces reminded her of the exhaustion that came with juggling home and career. For the first couple of months of her retirement she'd been like a cat on a griddle, unable to relax, but gradually she'd adjusted and allowed herself to slow down and enjoy her new circumstances.

It had given her enormous pleasure to see her friends' delight when they explored the penthouse and balcony, soaking in the views of the coast and the exquisite gardens, admiring her décor, and knowing that this little jaunt would hopefully be the first of many and that they too could share in her good fortune. They had deposited their luggage into their rooms, freshened up, and headed straight down to the restaurant for a much-anticipated pre-lunch G&T. Now, replete and relaxed, the holiday feeling was really kicking in.

"Anna! Darlin'," a familiar Texas drawl exclaimed, and Anna turned to see Sally-Ann beaming at her, tanned and glowing in a pale green and white sundress.

"Fancy y'all being here the same time as me," she exclaimed, bending down to give Anna a kiss.

"I thought you'd be over in July or August?" Anna returned her kiss warmly.

Sally-Ann made a face. "Anna, after the last few months that I've put in, I couldn't wait until summer. I need to chill. And how!"

"Oh, right, of course you do!" Anna patted her hand sympathetically. She'd get Sally-Ann on her own at some stage to catch up on all the news. They'd kept up by email and text since their first long, boozy lunch, when they'd hit it off so well.

"Girls, this is our neighbor, Sally-Ann Connolly Cooper."

Anna made the introductions. "We came out this morning on the seven a.m. flight. We're slightly shattered, to say the least. Are you here on your own?"

"Yup, I sure am, honey. And in about twenty minutes you'll see the reason why. Will y'all have another drink? Let me order us one."

"No, you have one with us. Let me get it," Anna insisted as an attentive waiter arrived at their table.

"Well, if y'all don't mind. I don't want to be butting in on your conversation," Sally-Ann demurred.

"Conversation," laughed Yvonne. "We'll all be snoring in a minute."

"I'll have another Baileys for the road, with Sally-Ann," Mary said breezily.

"She's the youngest of us; she's still able to hold her drink," Anna teased as Sally-Ann sat down at the table and the waiter went to get their order. They chatted easily among themselves, and then Sally-Ann nudged Anna. "That's my reason for coming to lunch," she murmured, indicating a tall, exceedingly handsome Spanish man wearing a smart gray suit who was striding along the boardwalk.

"*Dishyyyy,*" murmured Anna.

"Isn't he hot?" Sally-Ann grinned. "He has the most delicious buns evah!"

"Is he your husband?" Yvonne asked innocently.

Sally-Ann gave a peal of laughter. "I wish, honey, I wish. He's my Spanish banker, Sebastian, and I'm hopin' he's gonna be a little bit more, if y'all know what I mean." She winked.

"Oh! Sorry!" Yvonne said, flustered.

"No apologies necessary, darlin'," the other woman laughed.

"'*Ride, Sally, ride,*'" Mary sang and Anna spluttered into her glass as the others hooted with laughter while Mary explained what a ride meant in the Irish vernacular.

"I *love* it," the leggy Texan exclaimed, guffawing. "I'll see y'all, and I'll do my best to keep the hollerin' to a minimum." Sally-Ann took her leave of them and went to greet the young man, leading him to a reserved table for two in the shade of a magnificent flowering orange blossom.

"She can holler all she likes, I won't hear 'cause I'm gonna sleep, y'all." Mary grinned, yawning.

Anna finished her Baileys and felt deliciously woozy. "I'm slightly pissed," she remarked giddily.

"You're singing to the choir, sister." Yvonne waved at the waiter for the bill.

"OK, let's do the kitty while we're at it." Mary hauled up her bag and took out a red purse. She was always in charge of the kitty when they went on one of their jaunts. She put in a hundred euros and they all extracted crisp new notes from their wallets and handed them to her, to go into the battered red purse that had traveled far and wide with them.

This was why she loved going away with her three friends, Anna mused as the bill came, and glasses went on to study it and calculate the tip. Everything was divided equally, there was no hassle about money, they were utterly at ease in each other's company, and they knew everything about each other and could depend on each other in their hours of need. What more could you want from friendship?

They only had to walk a couple of yards to the wrought-iron gate that opened onto the grounds of La Joya, and, giggling and teasing each other about their various states of inebriation, they made their way through the sumptuous gardens to the apartment block. Twenty minutes later, slathered in sun cream, with sunglasses on and the big green-and-cream-striped awning shading their faces, the four of them lay on their sun loungers, books at the ready.

"How decadent is this? Tiddly at three o'clock in the afternoon. Basking in the sun and able to read for as long as we want. Bliss." Mary wriggled her toes and picked up her thriller.

"Sally-Ann might need her earplugs in," Yvonne remarked, settling herself comfortably.

"Why?" murmured Breda, who was half-asleep already.

"Because when we all start snoring, her hollerin' is going to be well and truly drowned out."

They all guffawed and were snoozing long before Sally-Ann put the key in her front door.

◆

"Oh, look at those rugs. I'd love one for the dining room!" Mary exclaimed, detouring to a stall that had a colorful selection hanging from display racks. "That terra-cotta and gold one would be perfect."

"And how *exactly* are you going to get it home . . . fly it?" Yvonne deadpanned.

"Ha ha! Smarty-pants," Mary retorted good-humoredly. "We'll say nothing about the giant ceramic turtle we had to lug home for *you* the last time we were away." Yvonne loved ceramic turtles and had quite the collection from their jaunts abroad.

Anna giggled. It was market day in San Antonio on the third day of their mini-break and they were thoroughly enjoying browsing among the stalls. They had got up early, eaten breakfast on the balcony, and had headed out in high spirits.

"Let's have a coffee in that lovely shaded café under the archway," Breda suggested a little later as the sun rose higher and more people began to crowd into the market.

The peace and shade of the neat Moorish-style square that was entered through a stone archway that led off a narrow cobbled side street was a welcome contrast to the noisy hustle and bustle of the market. An ornate fountain poured a soothing waterfall and the birds sang in the green trailing ivy that covered the walls of the buildings. Orange blossoms perfumed the air and the aroma of freshly brewed coffee and croissants straight out of the oven mingled with the floral scents.

"Oh, this *is* the life." Anna dropped her shopping bags and stretched her legs under the round table that stood in the shade of the old courtyard walls. They gave their order to the waiter and sat enjoying the peaceful ambiance of their surroundings.

They were finishing a second cup of coffee when Anna's phone tinkled and she scrolled through her messages and made a face.

"Who's annoying you?" Yvonne asked lazily, eating the last crumb of a flaked almond croissant.

"It's a text from Jeananne Mangan."

A universal groan greeted that news. Jeananne "We Have a Villa in Antibes" Mangan was a real pain in the butt.

"What does she want?" Mary made a face. "Posting up a photo of her new Jimmy Choo shoes, or her Tom Ford blusher! Or her sea views in Antibes, no doubt. Here, let me take a photo of my M&S loafers and impress the hell out of her." She waved her baby-blue summer-shod feet in the air.

The others laughed.

"'Hi, Anna, long time no see,'" Anna read out, squinting to see the message on her screen. "'I heard you've bought an apartment on the Costa del Sol. We're going to our villa in Antibes for a month next week. If you're over, Roger and I could drive down and stay a couple of days and catch up—'"

"OMG! Sneery Hole Mangan and Jeananne! Imagine being stuck in close quarters with them for a few days. A fate worse than death!" Mary wrinkled her nose.

"She is just *such* an opportunist," Breda remarked as Anna snapped her phone shut and put it in her bag.

"And they're so mean! I've never met such a miserly couple," Yvonne added.

"I know. Austen would go mad if they came down here. Did you ever see Sneery Hole's tweets? He's so pompous and superior and such a know-it-all. He just LOVES Twitter. And it's perfect for him, the little notice box," Anna grimaced.

"She's as bad! And does she love to show off, posting on Facebook about her never-ending social life!"

"Not to mention her prizewinning garden—"

"And the villa in Antibes—"

"*And* the designer shoes and handbags—"

"And, my God, she is so attached to that selfie stick thing."

"Talk about *posing*! Looking ever so 'surprised' with those big doe eyes and the tattooed eyebrows and Botoxed this and fillered that," they bitched and then hooted, laughing long and loudly.

"Oh, God, we're right wagons." Anna wiped the tears from her eyes.

"Yeah, real bitches." Yvonne laughed.

"Huh! With the likes of Roger and Jeananne, you couldn't possibly *not* be bitchy!" Mary jeered.

"It's only because we're on holliers. What goes on in Spain stays in Spain." Breda poured them all more coffee.

"We'll probably have to ask them to the wedding, though," Anna sighed.

"Don't put Sneery Hole sitting beside me, because he might get a kick *up* his hole." Yvonne scowled, remembering a barbecue of theirs he'd crashed, and, after eating his fill and in his cups, had said condescendingly, "What am I doing, sitting in a boring back garden, drinking cheap red wine, when I could be in Antibes?" She was particularly incensed because he'd drunk a full bottle of Bin 555—certainly *not* a cheap red—and then gone rooting in their drinks cupboard and helped himself to a treble brandy.

"Why do you have to ask *them*?" Breda was aghast.

"Well, you know the way Chloe socializes with their two—"

"Mine socialize with them as well but that pair will *not* be coming to any weddings that we have," Yvonne retorted. "I think you're *mad*. And they get nasty when they're drunk, the pair of them. Dissing everyone around them."

Anna groaned. She'd been trying not to think of the wedding while she was away, but it was looming on the horizon and decisions were going to have to be made about who was coming.

"I do feel for you, Anna, you're the first of us to have a wedding on her hands," Mary said sympathetically. "Frankly I've always thought Gretna Green was a great idea!"

"It's the utter *waste* of money," Anna exclaimed exasperatedly. "Limos, chocolate fountains, three-day hen parties, favors! Don't get me going."

"They really get on my nerves. Favors!" snorted Mary. "It's far from favors they were reared. I thought the bride and groom *got* wedding presents from the guests, not the other way around."

"Chloe wants a big bash. Her father and I are giving them a generous lump sum, but we'd much prefer them to use some of it towards a deposit for a house and scale down the wedding. There's no talking to her. This generation is all about entitlement and show and 'me, me, me.' I ask myself: Was it the way I reared her—"

"Don't beat yourself up, Anna. We all gave all our kids things we never had or aspired to have. They're the Celtic Tiger generation. They never faced what we did in the eighties, emigration, unemployment, and the like; but when the property bubble bursts at home, and the economy starts to slide, it will be a different kettle of fish," Mary observed.

"*Exactly!* That's what worries me."

Anna's phone pinged again and she glanced at it. "Speak of the devil." She threw her eyes up to heaven and opened the text.

Can I have the Hen Party in La Joya, probs from Thurs to Sun? Is there a cheap hotel nearby for the rest of the gang? Can u suss it out for me while you're there? XXX

"Listen to this and don't laugh, she wants to have her hen party *here*. A long weekend. I've to suss out a cheap hotel nearby." Anna shook her head in disbelief. "What planet is she on? How much is *that* going to cost? If Austen hears that she's planning to go abroad for her hen party, he'll go ballistic. They're going to the Maldives for their honeymoon!"

"She won't get cheap flights to Málaga for a hen party. Ryanair are sometimes dearer than Aer Lingus. I've never got a real bargain flight in all the years I've been coming out here, because Málaga's one of the most lucrative runs," Mary pointed out.

"I've just decided she's not getting all that money into her hands. We'll pay for the wedding ourselves from our own account and then give the rest of it to her in dribs and drabs for necessities. I'm not having our hard-earned cash squandered on nonsense," Anna said with an angry glint in her eye as she responded.

Absolutely NOT, Chloe. And don't even mention that you are considering going abroad for a hen party to your father. We'll talk when I get home. This is all getting out of hand and you need to be realistic.

"She'll probably get in a huff now and not speak to me for a week," Anna scowled, pressing "send." "As if we haven't enough to worry about with Tara and the baby," she grumbled, taking a long gulp of her drink. "At least *she* doesn't want a big wedding. She's talking about a registry office marriage and a hand-fastening ceremony at the Hill of Tara, her namesake's ancient monument. You should have seen Austen's face when she came out with that one."

"That sounds fantastic," Yvonne enthused. "Really authentic for her, because she's so into nature and earth energy. And you won't have to spend a fortune on it, either."

"I was dubious when she first floated the idea, but it's beginning to look more appealing by the second."

"Look, don't think about any of it now, we came away to have a break from real life and all its stresses and strains. Let's go back to La Joya, have a read and a swim, and then have a glass of prosecco," Breda suggested.

"Prosecco, the answer to everything," Yvonne joked while Mary extracted the kitty purse from her bag and signaled for the bill.

I wish Prosecco was the answer to everything. And I wish this break would never end, Anna thought dejectedly a few hours later, reading a text from her eldest daughter to say that she was on a drip in the Rotunda Maternity hospital because she had a kidney infection and she was being kept in overnight because of dehydration.

You're in the best place, pet. I'll see you tomorrow. Come and stay with us for a night or two when you get out of hospital, she texted back, feeling a flutter of anxiety. Tara was not having the easiest pregnancy. Anna would be glad when it was all over and her first grandchild was safely delivered.

She said nothing to her companions about the latest MacDonald family drama as, refreshed from a swim, they lounged on the balcony reading and sipping the chilled golden drink from slender flutes, enjoying the balmy breeze that feathered across the sea from Africa to temper the afternoon heat.

Anna took a sip of her prosecco, trying to regain her earlier indolence. But the bubbly fizz failed to take the edge off her preoccupation. Tara had five more months to go, and if the last four were anything to go by, there was a rocky road ahead. And Anna knew that Austen and Chloe would continue to argue bitterly about the forthcoming wedding and she would be stuck right there in the middle, wishing she was back in Andalucía with her face raised to the sun, listening to the ever-calming serenade of the sea.

Chapter Twenty-Two

JULY

Cal / Lenora / Sally-Ann

"You want to stay another week? Hell, Lenora, you've been away from Jake for five days already." Cal tried to keep the exasperation out of his voice. He knew his girlfriend was struggling with motherhood; he didn't want to put pressure on her, but he'd given her a lot of leeway and this was pushing it.

"Look, it's OK for you, Cal, flitting down to Galveston when it suits you and then flitting back to your family, as well as making your business trips. I'm stuck in that backwater with a cranky baby. I want to be living my life somewhere exciting and vibrant. I'm too young to closet myself in an apartment in Galveston. I had a good life before I met you," Lenora snapped.

"Hey, hey, I don't 'flit' around," he snapped. "I have a business to run. I work damn hard. It's that hard work that provides the apartment that you were happy to move into when you were pregnant. You were happy enough as well to abandon your *life* to fly to Europe with me last year. Be a bit consistent here, Lenora, and own your decisions," Cal retorted.

"Yeah, well, things are different now. I feel trapped. I didn't know it was going to be like this when you got me pregnant—"

"Whoa, Lenora, let's backtrack there a bit. When *I* got you pregnant?"

"Yes," she said indignantly.

"Excuse me, but I *clearly* remember asking you if you were protected or did I need to use condoms when we started sleeping together, and you said you were on the pill, so don't lay that one on me, Lenora. Take *some* responsibility." Cal was furious at her attitude. "I asked you did you want a termination and you said no, you wanted to have the baby—"

"I didn't know it was going to be like this. I didn't realize how *entombed* I was going to be. I didn't realize how little time we'd be spending together!" she shouted.

"Oh, come on, Lenora, you're a savvy young woman, not some ditz. You knew what my lifestyle was like. You knew what you were getting into. I told you not to give up your job, but you said you wanted to be with me. And then you got pregnant without even asking me if I wanted another child. You knew I already had two daughters. I can't say I was thrilled when you told me you had a bun in the oven but I accepted it and got on with it. I'm providing for you and our child, I'm doing my best for us. You need to adapt to your new circumstances and make the most of them, just as I've had to."

"Listen, Cal, you led me to believe that your marriage was over and that you were going to divorce Sally-Ann. I thought we had a future together. I didn't think that future included ending up stuck in a retirement home for the elderly down in Galveston."

"My marriage *is* over, Lenora. It was over in all but name when we met, but you just couldn't wait, could you? You pushed and pushed and pushed instead of letting our relationship evolve—"

"Evolve," snorted Lenora. "You men are all the same, wanting your cake and eating it. Why don't you just admit it, I was your bit on the side—"

"No! You take that back, I wasn't cheating on Sally-Ann with you. You know that's not true, so cut the crap. I repeat, Sally-Ann and I had gone our separate ways in our marriage and you were aware of that, but I *do* have two daughters with her and I have a responsibility to them. I *never* led you to believe that I'd move from Houston. And you *didn't* object to the apartment when you first saw it. You actually told me you loved it. What *do* you want, exactly, Lenora?"

"Oh, Cal, stop being so mean to me," Lenora begged.

"Sorry, I'm just trying to be realistic here," Cal apologized, accepting that he'd been somewhat accusatory.

"Cal, let's move to New York." He could hear the excitement in her voice and wondered if anything he'd said had sunk in. "You travel there regularly," she continued eagerly. "Let's get a full-time nanny, and I can go back to work—"

"Do you realize that you haven't even asked me how Jake is? Don't you miss him at *all*?" Cal asked, flabbergasted that she could seriously imagine that he could just up sticks and move a thou-sand-plus miles away from his daughters and his business HQ.

Silence descended down the line between them. He could hear her sharp intake of breath as though she were right beside him.

"Not even a little bit?" he probed, appalled.

"I'm not mother material." Lenora burst into tears. "Cal, I can't help it. I'm irritated and resentful all the time. I'm exhausted look-ing after him. I haven't ever felt that wave of love everyone keeps going on about. I'm a failure at motherhood. I *hate* it. I just want to have my old life back. I want some freedom," she wept.

"You have a part-time nanny. You have some freedom, but you're a mother now, Lenora. Life changes when you become a parent. Someone is depending on *you*! Your *own child*." He could totally understand her shock at being tied—he'd experienced that himself when the twins were young: that trapped feeling had led him to be unfaithful to Sally-Ann—but he couldn't disguise his bewilderment at her almost total lack of interest in Jake.

"Well, I don't *want* a child depending on me. I don't want *anyone* depending on me. Why don't you care about what *I* want?" she shouted.

"I *do* care, I'm trying to do the best for *all* of us," he explained patiently.

"No, you're trying to do what's best for *you*! What sacrifices are you making? None. Your life hasn't changed. Mine has. I *have* no life, Cal, and I'm sick of it."

"Are you telling me you want out?"

He heard Lenora exhale in stunned surprise at his blunt question. She was silent for a moment.

"I don't know . . . I think so, Cal. I can't do this. I'm staying in New York for another week to think things over. And let me tell you something: you don't want a divorce—you never have—and I hate being with someone whose heart isn't in the relationship."

"It is," he protested lamely.

"It's not and you know it, Cal. You need to face up to the fact that you still have some sort of connection with Sally-Ann—and I'm not talking about your kids—and deal with it instead of being gutless, sitting on the fence as if it's all got nothing to do with you."

"Look, do you want to get married? I'll speed up the divorce," he growled, unwilling to admit the truth of her words.

"That says it all," she scorned. "Do *I* want to get married. I mean, what kind of a proposal is that?" she added sulkily.

"Oh, Lenora, grow up," Cal said wearily, at his wits' end with her.

"Go fuck yourself, Cal, it's not all about *you*," she shouted, slamming down the phone.

Cal stared at the receiver, shaking his head. How could he have got himself into such an unholy mess? If Lenora hadn't got pregnant, the relationship would have run its course and foundered a whole lot sooner, he admitted. It had been sliding as it was.

At least she'd turned down his reluctant offer of marriage. He wouldn't ask her again. He'd had a lucky escape and he knew it. Let Lenora have her freedom; he'd be damned careful to lay out the parameters of the relationship the next time he started dating a woman . . . *if* there was a next time.

Cal heard Jake whimper in his cot and walked over and lifted him into his arms. The infant snuggled in against him and flashed him a big toothless smile, knuckling his little fists into his dribbling mouth. He was teething and his cheeks were like two rosy cherries. Lenora had been scheduled to return from her five-day city break in a couple of hours. It was Sunday and the nanny had worked until Cal had arrived at the apartment at midday. He had a meeting scheduled in Miami the following morning. He would have to leave before six to get from Galveston to George Bush Intercontinental for his flight. The nanny had told him she was taking tomorrow off, after her five days of baby minding, in the expectation that Lenora would be back from New York.

He pulled open the fridge door and saw Jake's baby bottles neatly lined up and some pureed meals prepared. That was a relief, he thought glumly, staring down at his son, who was lying contentedly in his arms. Jake's face suddenly grew red and he scrunched up his eyes, making little grunting sounds. Moments later the familiar pong of a poopy diaper scented the kitchen.

Cal wrinkled his nostrils. "OK, mister! I better do something about that," he sighed, heading for the changing station. If Lenora were here, she'd be emitting gusty sighs and making faces at having to diaper her son. When she said she wasn't mother material, she wasn't exaggerating, Cal reflected, whisking off the baby's onesie with practiced ease. Had his expectations of her been too high? Was he constantly unconsciously comparing her to Sally-Ann, who seemed to have taken to babies with a natural ease, knuckling down to her maternal duties with a stoic acceptance that was in complete contrast to Lenora, who had struggled with her new responsibilities from the moment their son was born?

He'd suggested that she get herself checked out for postnatal depression, and she'd snapped that she didn't need a doctor to tell her that she was depressed. She *knew* she was depressed. Her depression disappeared when her friends flew down for the weekend and the nanny had complete charge of Jake. There'd been no sign of depression when they'd gone skiing in Aspen for three days after Christmas. She'd been her energetic vivacious self, racing down the slopes without a care in the world. It was only when she got back to their son that her mood had changed and discontent had set in again.

"How can she not want to be with you?" he murmured, tickling Jake's little fat belly, laughing as his little boy chuckled delightedly. "She doesn't know what she's missing."

He fed Jake a few spoonfuls of his puree, gave him a bottle, burped him, and laid him on his shoulder until his eyelids drooped and his long dark lashes fanned across his cheek. Cal laid him gently in his cot, covered him up snugly, and stood looking at him. He needed to make alternative arrangements for tomorrow, and until Lenora decided she was coming home.

He took a beer from the fridge, cracked it open, and sat with his leg over the side of the chair, trying to raise his courage to ring Sally-Ann. "All she can do is say no," he muttered, scrolling to her number.

She answered after a couple of rings.

"Yup?"

He tried to judge if she was cool but friendly or cool and antagonistic.

"It's me . . ." he said hesitantly.

"I know that, Cal, your name came up," she drawled, and he could imagine her rolling her eyes towards heaven. "What's wrong?" she asked, and he smiled. His wife was always as sharp as a tack.

"I'm in trouble and I need to ask a big favor of you."

"Shoot," she said, but he sensed unease in her.

"Lenora's just phoned. She says she's staying longer than planned in New York. The nanny's off until Tuesday and I have to be in Miami tomorrow morning—"

"And you want me to mind the baby," she finished for him.

"It's a big ask, I know. If it's too much, I'll ring Mom."

"Don't do that," Sally-Ann said slowly. "Your mom's too old to be looking after a very young baby. You better bring him here. The girls will be over the moon, not . . . so don't expect too much from them," she added drily.

"Are you *sure* it's OK with you?" he hedged. "If it's too much to ask, I'll ring Mom, honestly. Or I might even cancel the meetings. It's typical. We're at a crucial juncture in financing a new development. Look, sorry, Sally-Ann, I shouldn't have asked. Forget it."

"Well, you did ask, and I've said yes," she said in a crisp matter-of-fact voice that made him smile. He'd forgotten how decisive and no-nonsense his wife could be.

"I thought you'd tell me to get lost," Cal admitted.

"I'm not *that* much of a bitch, Cal."

"You're not a bitch at all, Sally-Ann," he said quietly.

"I am, trust me," she retorted, but he sensed there was a smile behind her words.

"Will I leave now, or would you prefer if I came in the morning? It will be around seven a.m. when I land on your doorstep, if it's tomorrow," he warned.

"Oh, come on now, for goodness' sake. No point in making a drama out of it. By the time you get the baby sorted before traveling you'll be up before cock crow, if you wait until tomorrow," Sally-Ann instructed. "I'll freshen up the guest room for you. Bring a few changes of clothes for him, diapers, wipes, bottles, formula, a pacifier if he has one, and your travel cot. Our cot is in the attic somewhere."

"OK, I better get packing. This little guy has more gear than the king of Siam. Thanks, Sally-Ann, I really, *really* appreciate this, and—"

"OK, Cal, no need to grovel," his wife interjected. "See you when I see you. Bye." She hung up and he took another slug of his beer and reflected on what a stalwart woman Sally-Ann had proved herself to be since they'd announced the news of their divorce. If it was OK with her, he was going to ask if she'd mind if he got an apartment in Houston for himself, the baby, and a nanny—and Lenora, *if* she decided to come back. It was time to stop hiding from family and friends.

The news of Jake's birth was known only to his immediate family. His mother had been pretty pissed with him and had been full of sympathy for Sally-Ann and the girls until Sally-Ann had a chat with her and set her straight about the circumstances of Jake's conception, telling her that it was as much of a shock to Cal as it was to Sally-Ann. That had been more than decent of her.

His mom hadn't yet met her new grandson. It was time she did, Cal resolved. He was done with commuting to Galveston. He wanted to spend more time with his daughters to reassure them that he was as much their daddy as ever he'd been, divorce or no, and he wanted them to fall in love with their baby brother.

Maybe Lenora had done him a favor. Cal stood up, took a deep breath, and began the daunting task of packing for his son's first trip to Houston.

◆

Lenora poured herself a glass of red and took a swig. Her hand was shaking as she held the glass, and she moved over to the sofa and flopped down, staring unseeingly at the panoramic view of the Hell Gate Bridge, the East River, and Astoria Park from the big glass floor-to-ceiling window in the lounge of the small but perfectly appointed two-bed apartment rented by her older sister, Lana.

The thought of going back to Galveston and the baby had induced a deep wave of depression that had almost overwhelmed her. She just couldn't do it; not for a while anyway, if ever, she'd decided that morning when her sister had offered to drive her to

JFK. The relief of having made the phone call to Cal to tell him that she was postponing her return was indescribable. She felt she could breathe again.

In fairness he'd been a lot more reasonable than she'd expected about her non-return. Patience wasn't exactly a virtue of his. Cal was a hothead, inclined to explode, and she was sure he'd have let fly at her and made a scene. He really had no idea of how being here for the past few days had shown Lenora more than anything that motherhood was not her forte. It wasn't even the great social life out in clubs and bars—although she was thoroughly enjoying that aspect of her stay—that was soothing her fraught spirit; it was the absence of her baby and all his requirements—crying, needing to be fed, bathed, dressed, undressed, that went on 24-7—that was the true balm of her escape from Galveston.

Even Cal offering her marriage, something she'd longed for for months before she'd got pregnant—the reason she'd got pregnant in the first place—was not enough to make her want to be his wife.

Lenora took another gulp of wine. She'd made a real mess of her life. When she'd fallen for Cal, she'd thought marriage to him would be the ultimate result. He was sexy, fun, and wealthy. A wonderful catch. Or so she'd believed. He was also a father who loved his kids, a businessman who was immersed in his work, and the ten-year difference in their ages—when he would want to flop and eat in after a long day's work and she would want to get the hell out of the apartment after being stuck with the baby all day—was something she truly hadn't expected. She'd thought none of it through, except the notion of wearing his ring on her finger while they lived a high-flying social life. In her dream world their child was looked after by a nanny full-time.

She'd only discovered when she'd lived with her lover that Cal actually *liked* children and enjoyed doing family stuff. He'd wanted for her to eventually meet his daughters and for them to meet Jake. He'd told her he would be looking for shared custody. She would have to endure his girls living with them part-time.

She hadn't expected any of this to turn out as it had. If she could roll back the clock, she would never have stopped taking the pill.

"So, what did Cal say when you told him you were staying in New York for another few days?" Her sister, wrapped in a toweling robe, emerged from the bathroom, where she'd been indulging in a long soak and pamper session after a hard week's work and a long night of partying.

"He asked me if I want to get married." Lenora nibbled on some sushi. She'd prepared a light lunch for both of them, since neither of them had surfaced for breakfast, but her appetite had disappeared.

"Are you kidding me?" Lana's jaw dropped open.

"Nope!"

"Wow! But that's what you wanted. Why the long face?" Lana poured herself a glass of chilled chardonnay and topped up her sister's glass of red.

"Oh, come on, Lana, I'm not that stupid to think he's madly in love with me and wants nothing more than to make me his beloved wife. It was a duty call. 'Do you *want* to get married?' What kind of a proposal is that, for God's sake?"

"You could always get married and stick it out for a year or two and file for divorce and get a whacking big settlement," Lana pointed out pragmatically.

"I suppose so. I hung up on him, I was so ticked off." Lenora scowled.

"For goodness' sake, play your cards right. Use your head, forget your heart," Lana advised. "That's the best strategy with men."

"It hasn't worked out the way I thought it would. I'm getting the feeling that he doesn't want to be with me anymore. I deliberately got pregnant so that he'd marry me. Now he's asked me, but not the way I wanted. And I've got a baby that I've got no maternal feelings for and don't want to be with. *Imagine* a mother saying that about her own child. How horrible am I, Lana? I'm *unnatural*." Lenora burst into tears.

"You're not unnatural, Lenora." Lana sat down beside her and hugged her. "You're being honest. There are many, many women out there who've had children that they don't want and are afraid to admit it because it's sort of a taboo subject. At least you have the self-awareness and the guts to say it. Look at Mom. She's not maternal by any stretch of the imagination. She turned to the bottle when we were growing up because she felt trapped and couldn't admit it. How can you expect to be maternal when you never experienced what it was to be mothered?" Lana added bitterly.

"She did her best, I suppose," Lenora sniffled. "She's just not a kid hugger, and I guess I inherited that from her."

"Maybe time will change how you feel about your little boy," Lana said.

"Maybe. I don't know. I just know I can't go back there right now."

"That's OK. Stay here for another week and see how it goes."

"Thanks for being so understanding and not judging me," Lenora said gratefully.

"I don't believe in judging. We all choose our own paths, they say. I'm just glad I haven't chosen yours." Lana grinned, giving her sister another hug. "See if absence makes the heart grow fonder for the baby and Cal. Now, take that frown off your face and let's get dressed and hit the town. I've got tickets for Carolines on Broadway: fantastic cocktails and great stand-up comedy—just what you need to put a smile on your face."

"I'm not in the humor for comedy," Lenora protested.

"What do you want to do, go to a sad movie and sit there tearing up, or sit here feeling sorry for yourself? Not having it, sis. Shift your fabulous tush, get dressed, and come on. You choose your choice, now live with it," Lana ordered, before biting into a sushi roll with relish.

You choose your choice, now live with it. Her sister's words slithered back into her mind twelve hours later while Lenora lay in bed, a tad woozy after several potent cocktails. Perhaps another week in the city would result in her maternal gene kicking in. She might get a terrible longing to see Jake, she thought drowsily. Right now, though, she was very glad not to have to get up to attend to her son's needs. Cal could do that, and after a week without her there he might not be quite so enamored of second-time fatherhood. The thought gave her some comfort and she fell into a sound sleep, oblivious to the sirens of the ambulances racing along Crescent Street to the nearby cardiology hospital.

Chapter Twenty-Three

Sally-Ann

"Savannah, Madison, I need to speak to you both, please!" Sally-Ann yelled up the stairs after her conversation with Cal.

"I'm busy, Mom!" shouted Savannah.

Madison appeared on the landing, taking her earbuds out of her ears. "What's up, Mom?"

"Savannah, get down heah right this minute!" Sally-Ann roared. Since Cal had told his daughters about their parents' divorce, Savannah's transformation into a truculent, insolent teen had accelerated, and each day was becoming a wearisome battle in which it seemed to Sally-Ann that she was constantly suppressing her temper and pretending to be calm and reasonable or else yelling at her daughter, as she was now. Madison, during these times of confrontation, withdrew into the comfort of her iPod, distressed that the twin she loved and the mother she adored were in constant conflict.

Savannah stomped down the stairs, eyes flashing venom. "What? I told you I was busy."

"Watch the way you speak to me, missy. I've told ya before y'all are getting too damn big for your britches and I won't stand for it."

Sally-Ann, suffering a megadose of PMS, resisted the overpowering urge to smack her daughter and—in the moment that every parent on the planet experiences— suddenly realized she sounded just like her pop used to when he chastised her.

Savannah stared at her, slitty-eyed, arms folded.

"What do you need us for, Mom?" Madison asked.

"I need you both to be the best people you can be and the best and kindest daughters that I know you are." She eyeballed Savannah, who, hearing these unexpected words, looked disconcerted in spite of herself.

"What's going on, Mom?" Madison was suddenly wary.

"Your dad is stuck and asked a favor of me, and I said yes, and I want you both to support me—to support us, OK?"

"OK, Mom," Madison agreed instantly.

"Savannah?" Sally-Ann looked at her intently.

"I'd like to know first before I agree to anything," she said cheekily.

"Don't be mean, Sav," Madison chided her twin.

"OK," she agreed with bad grace.

"Great. Now the thing is, due to circumstances outside his control, Dad needs to leave the baby with us to—"

"No way, Mom. NO WAY!" Savannah shouted. "Why are you being nice to him after what he's done to us?"

"Sweetie, our divorce has nothing to do with that little baby."

"Yeah, but it's got somethin' to do with Dad's ho!"

"Savannah, don't call Lenora that. I won't allow it," Sally-Ann rebuked her sternly. "Let me tell you something, it wasn't Lenora that broke up our marriage. We had already gone our different ways a good while back. The problem with your dad and I was that we got married too young." She looked at the mutinous expression on Savannah's face, the pinched worry on Madison's, and her heart went out to them.

"Look, let's have some gal talk, heart to heart. No holds barred. It's a fine day, let's fire up the barbecue, sit out in the yard, and toast some s'mores and gab and not fight. Whaddya say?" She reached over and gave them each a hug.

"OK, Mom," Savannah agreed, relaxing into her mother's embrace, much to Sally-Ann's relief.

"Cool." Madison hugged her back.

"OK, let's have a couple of hot dogs while we're at it," Sally-Ann suggested. "Maddy, go get the cushions. Savannah, get the glasses and Coke. We have about two hours before your dad arrives with the baby."

Twenty minutes later, the hot dogs were on the grill and Savannah had set the table with the sauces, some paper napkins, and the drinks. Sally-Ann poured the Coke into glasses and raised hers. "Let's clink. My toast today is to mothers and daughters—and gal talk."

"And to sisters," Maddy clinked, smiling at her twin.

"And to . . . erm . . . I don't know." Savannah clinked unenthusiastically.

"OK, sit down, relax, and I'll try and explain what went wrong with Daddy and me," Sally-Ann invited, drawing her chair in to the table. "You know we started dating a few months before I went to college, and we fell madly in love—"

"Did you lose your virginity to him?" Savannah eyed her over her Coke glass, the bubbles tickling her nose.

"I did."

"After the third date?" Maddy inquired.

"No, not quite so soon. Things were different then. Girls didn't put out as much as they do now. You know what Great-grandma Connolly told me when I went on my first date with Cal?" She grinned at the girls.

"To save yourself for marriage." Savannah rolled her eyes up to heaven.

"Well, kinda. She said"—Sally-Ann cleared her throat and mimicked her great-grandmother's southern twang—"'Y'all don't go 'round relaxin' your morals, missy, and keep your bloomers up!'"

"Bloomers!" shrieked the girls, guffawing. "She called panties 'bloomers'?" Savannah sniggered.

"She sure did. Great-grandma Connolly was a hoot an' a half. But she had the right idea. Girls, you need to be careful out there. Don't let yourselves be touched up and fingered by boys you don't know. *Like* the boy . . . or girl . . . you're with. Don't be a sheeple and follow the herd, just because everyone else is. Think for yourselves. That's one of the most important pieces of advice I can give you. Reason things out for yourselves; make decisions because it's something that feels right for you, not because everyone else thinks it's cool."

"Diana Barton is gay; she told us last week. How do you know if you're gay?" Maddy asked.

"Well, you might prefer to be with girls; you might fancy them instead of boys. But don't fret about it, you are what you are and you'll know in time. I wouldn't even worry about it, Maddy. Your dad and I won't care what you are as long as you're both happy and have plenty of self-respect. And," she added firmly, "don't make the mistake your dad and I made of getting married too young. There's no rush. Just make sure you love who you're going to marry."

"Do you not love Dad anymore? Does he not love you?" Savannah eyeballed her.

"Let's say we're not 'in' love. There'll always be a bond because of our two lovely girls. If I didn't care about him, I wouldn't help him out of his dilemma now, would I?"

"I suppose not," she muttered.

"Might you meet someone new and get married to them?" Maddy ventured hesitantly.

"Well, if I do, it will be when you both have finished high school and are leaving home to go to college," Sally-Ann promised them, and saw both of them visibly relax.

"So, did Dad cheat on you many times?" Savannah probed.

"That's neither here nor there now, sweetie. We are where we are and we've all got to move forward," Sally-Ann said firmly. She wasn't, much as she'd like to, going to make Cal the fall guy even though he'd done the dirty on her. She didn't want her daughters disrespecting their father.

"Is that why he sleeps in the other room, and not because he gets up early to go to meetings?" Savannah asked.

"It is," agreed Sally-Ann, forking the hot dogs onto the buns.

"Don't you mind him having sex with that other lady?"

"Well, I did mind it at the beginning . . . It hurt, but that's life, and sometimes things happen to us that hurt us, but we can grow from it," she said lamely.

"Why? How are you growing?" Maddy slathered on ketchup and mustard and handed a hot dog wrapped in a napkin to her sister.

"Erm . . ." Sally-Ann wished with all her heart that the interrogation would stop. "I . . . ah . . . I'm trying to practice forgiveness. I'm trying not to hold on to bitterness and anger, because let me tell y'all, that's the worst thing you can do."

"Why?" Savannah demanded.

"Because when you're bitter and twisted, the only one who gets hurt is you. You can hang on to bad things and say, 'Poor me, this bad thing happened to me and I'm never going to get over it,' and you can hold that energy in you for the rest of your life, or else you can say, 'OK, a bad thing happened in my life, but I'm gonna move on and I'm not giving it any more energy.' That's one of the lessons in life we have to learn. The sooner we let go of stuff, the better. It makes room for better things to come into our lives."

"I get that," Savannah said slowly. "When Beth Ann Regan was bullying me last year, I was so mad, it was all I could think about. And then I decided I was going to forget about her and make other friends an' I did, and I never think of Beth Ann Regan now—"

"She started to bully Francine Lee." Maddy licked her fingers. "You should tell Francine what to do so she can get over it."

"Exactly. And I was very impressed by the way you dealt with that, Savannah. So moving on is the way to go. And now let's move on and toast some s'mores," Sally-Ann teased, and they laughed. "And, please, when Dad comes with that little baby, be kind," she added. "Don't forget that baby has nothing to do with any of our stuff. It's not his fault, OK?" She arched an eyebrow at them.

"OK," they agreed, Savannah more grudgingly than Maddy, and Sally-Ann gave an inward sigh of relief that she'd managed somehow to get things back on an even keel—for the time being, anyway.

◆

"Here he is!" Madison yelled, hurrying out from the front lounge, where she'd been keeping watch while doing her homework. Sally-Ann, who'd been scrolling through her emails in the kitchen, felt her stomach flip-flop. Now that the actual moment of seeing Cal's child by Lenora had arrived, she felt sick. She should have just refused his request, she thought, annoyed at herself and wishing she could practice some of the high-falutin advice she'd given the girls earlier. What a grand old hypocrite she was, she thought gloomily, wishing her heart would stop pounding. Madison had the door open before Cal had even unlocked the car door to lift out the baby carrier.

Sally-Ann watched from the hallway as Cal reached out and hugged his daughter tightly. Maddy was such a little peacemaker and always had been, Sally-Ann thought fondly, wishing she could be as openhearted.

"Hi, Sally-Ann," Cal called over as he lifted out the baby carrier. Maddy peeped in and Sally-Ann heard her say in disappointment, "Aw, he's asleep."

"Traveling in the car always knocks him out," her father explained, hoisting a baby bag over his shoulder and crossing over to the front door. Sally-Ann met his gaze and her lip wobbled. She swallowed hard and looked in at the little mite, wrapped in a onesie and cardigan with a little blue knitted cap on his head. His long black lashes brushed his rosy-red cheeks and she saw that he had Cal's chin with the Cooper cleft. Myriad emotions smote her. Grief, loneliness, envy, broodiness, but mostly heart-melting awe at his innocent loveliness.

"He's a fine little fella," she gulped. "Give him to me and get the rest of his stuff."

"Are you OK, Mom?" Madison asked anxiously, observing her mother's upset.

"Fine, sweetie." Sally-Ann made a supreme effort and smiled at her daughter. Cal looked at her and looked away, an expression of dismay crossing his rugged face.

"I'll get the rest of his things. Will you help me, Maddy?" he asked flatly.

"Sure, Dad," she agreed, casting another anxious glance at Sally-Ann.

"I'll take him into the lounge." Sally-Ann took the baby carrier from her husband.

"Where's Savannah?" he inquired.

"In her room," Sally-Ann said quietly, "and she says she's staying there, so let her be," she warned, before turning to walk into the lounge with the baby. She laid the carrier on the sofa and heard him give a little snuffle. His eyelashes flickered and then, all of a sudden, a pair of startling blue eyes stared intently at her and her breath caught in her throat. She couldn't explain it. It was as though they had always known each other. An "old soul," her great-grandma would have called him. Sally-Ann stared back at the blue-eyed son of Cal and another woman, and then the baby smiled at her—the widest, happiest, most joyful smile—and her heartbreak receded and she found herself smiling back at him and longing to cuddle him.

"Oh, Cal, he's adorable," she murmured when her husband entered the room laden down with baby gear.

"Yeah, he is, isn't he?" Cal came and stood beside her as they peered in at the beaming baby.

"It's strange, and you might think this is a weird thing to say, but I always thought the baby I lost was a son. It's like Jake's being here has healed a wound that was always there in the core of me," she confided.

"Aw, Sally-Ann, that's a great thing to hear, darlin'. Take him and cuddle him," Cal urged.

"He might not take to me," she demurred.

"Naw, he's a happy-go-lucky little dude," his father said, lifting him out of the carrier and handing him to her. Jake settled against her shoulder and gazed up at her and another smile illuminated his face as he gooed and gurgled as though trying to speak, his fists waving in the air before finding their way into his mouth, and she gazed at him in delight, loving the feel of him in her arms.

"Let me see, Mom, let me see," Madison said eagerly.

"Do you want to hold him?" Sally-Ann asked.

"Oh, can I?" Madison was excited.

"Sit down and I'll hand him to you," Sally-Ann instructed, laying the child into his half sister's embrace when she'd settled back on the sofa with her arms out for him.

"Oh, wow! Mom! Look, he's smiling at me." Madison was beyond thrilled and Sally-Ann gave a silent prayer of thanks that her instincts had been right, in Maddy's case, at least. Getting to know their half brother as a baby would be far easier than in years to come, when he was older. "Can I give him his bottle when it's feeding time?" she asked.

"Of course you can," Cal agreed, utterly thankful that Jake would have one sister who loved him, and more grateful to Sally-Ann than he'd ever been.

"Thank you," he murmured earnestly, his eyes probing hers with that blue-eyed intensity that in the old days would send delicious shivers down her spine. "Jake and I are in your debt."

"You are, he isn't, he gets a 'get out of jail free' pass," she remarked lightly, turning away from him to watch Madison cuddling her baby brother. She didn't want Cal getting any ideas that the divorce was no longer an option. Whether Lenora and he got back together or not was no longer her concern. Now that it had been broached to the girls, she wanted to draw a line under their relationship, and the sooner the better.

Stubborn to the last, Savannah stayed in her room until the following morning when she heard her father leave for the airport.

"Mom, will that baby be gone when we get home from school?" she demanded, appearing at Sally-Ann's bedroom door. Sally-Ann yawned and sat up to drink the cup of coffee Cal had brought her before he left.

"I don't think so. Dad has meetings in Miami and he won't be back until late afternoon. Why?"

"I was just wondering," she said grumpily.

"You don't have to see him if you don't want to," Sally-Ann assured her, "but Jake is a lovely little baby and your sister and I had a very nice time with him last night."

"Yeah, well, I'm not interested," Savannah replied, waiting for the backlash.

"Fine." Sally-Ann shrugged. "Your choice. Your decision."

"Oh!" Her daughter couldn't hide her surprise, but Sally-Ann ignored her, pretending to scroll through her phone instead, and Savannah, seeing she was getting no argument from her, wandered off to her room, but not before peeping into Cal's room, where Jake lay sleeping in his travel cot.

Sally-Ann was in the bathroom when she heard the baby wail.

"Mom!" shouted Savannah. "That baby is crying. Get him quick!"

"He'll be fine," she called back.

"Mom, you can't leave him!" Savannah yelled indignantly with a note of panic in her voice. "Pick him up."

"I can't!" she yelled. "I'm putting in a tampon. You go pick him up."

She heard Savannah stomp along the landing as the wails got louder and more heartrending and then silence descended.

Sally-Ann took her time finishing her ablutions before padding silently across the landing to see Jake being held by Savannah as a sleepy Madison peered over her sister's shoulder, entertaining him with his baby rattle.

"Good boy, don't cry," she heard Savannah say with a tender awkwardness that brought a lump to Sally-Ann's throat. "I bet you're hungry."

"He just guzzles his bottle, don't you, Jake?" Madison cooed.

"How do you know? Did they let you feed him?" Savannah jiggled Jake in her arms.

"Yeah, it was cool. He loves me; he kept smiling at me, didn't you, baby? Can I hold him?" she begged.

"In a minute. You got to feed him and hold him last night. It's my turn," Savannah declared.

"That was 'cause you didn't come down 'cause you were being a bioch," Madison protested. "Dad was pretty down about you staying in your room."

"So?" sniffed her sister. "He's not gonna get in *my* good books that easy. Sure he isn't, baby Jake?" She gazed down at her half brother, making baby noises. "OMG, Maddy, look, he's laughing. I'm making him laugh," she exclaimed delightedly.

Smiling, Sally-Ann slipped back to her own room. Her next battle today would be sorting out rows about whose turn it was to hold and feed Jake. She wanted *her* turn as well. Great-grandma Connolly had always maintained that good often came out of bad. Perhaps she was right, Sally-Ann reflected. Jake Cooper had come into their lives and in less than twenty-four hours had brought a healing of sorts to their family with just his big, wide, happy smiles and goo-gooing gorgeousness. She hoped against hope that it would last.

PART III

Time Marches On

Chapter Twenty-Four

NOVEMBER 2007

Constanza

Constanza Torres shivered, walking in the shade, where the sun was not yet high enough to brighten the façade of block 1 of La Joya. It was early November, and temperatures were in the sixties, far from the eighties that she liked.

On her rounds, she'd seen Austen MacDonald and another man doing laps of the big pool, slicing through the water at speed, circling around the little island up in the deep end—massed with daphne and vibrant pink geraniums—before racing each other back, and wondered how the Irishman and his friend were not frozen.

It always amused Constanza to see the hardy Irish and British out in their shorts and sundresses, making the most of the winter sun even in January, while she and her compatriots were wrapped up in their winter woollies.

Austen was on his own. His wife was staying at home to be near her pregnant daughter. He wasn't happy about it, Constanza could tell, but she refrained from comment. She always listened but rarely gave an opinion. Discretion and prudence was paramount in her job.

She'd become friendly with Anna MacDonald in those first early months after La Joya had opened its gates to the new owners. She and Anna had worked as a team when Anna had become secretary of the management committee, and Constanza had been very sorry to see her resign after her stint.

Constanza sighed, letting herself into her office, glad of the warmth provided by the electric heater. In previous years there'd been more owners and visitors staying during the winter. But many changes had taken place in La Joya in these past months, and not changes for the good, Constanza thought gloomily as she poured coffee from her percolator.

Other owners were experiencing the same type of problems as Anna and Austen. Minding grandchildren and taking care of elderly parents seemed to be on the increase as incomes dropped and the wings of freedom were clipped.

Gone too were the days of hopping on a flight to Spain for a long weekend. Several of the apartments were up for sale, with owners unable to pay their mortgages The carefree buzz of excitement and exuberance that had reigned in the early years had changed, and there was an underlying sense of anxiety as taxes and maintenance fees went up and services were cut.

The global downturn was having a disastrous effect on the Spanish economy. The property bubble had burst, half-finished developments littered the country, and unemployment was rampant. Walking along the promenade of San Antonio del Mar, it was easy to see the ravages the recession was wreaking on the local economy. Where once the cafés and restaurants would be full of ex-pats having breakfast or morning coffee, reading their papers, meeting up with friends, now bored waiters wiped empty tables that were already clean, and attended any customer who sat at one of the tables under the colorful awnings like royalty.

Constanza could see the effects of the slump in La Joya too. People were in arrears with their maintenance fees, with some owners owing thousands to the community. It was an enormous worry and the current community president, an affable Englishman whom she liked and got on with, was tearing his hair out and couldn't wait for his term of office to be over.

Constanza sipped her coffee and glanced at her emails. Her heart sank when she saw Eduardo De La Fuente's name among them. That horrible, arrogant *madrileño* was the bane of her life. From the moment he'd set foot in the complex, he'd behaved like he owned the place and was constantly finding fault with her and all the other employees.

She wasn't being aggressive enough chasing owners for fees.

People were hanging towels on balconies.

The cleaners weren't thorough when cleaning the common areas.

The gardeners weren't doing a good job.

The planting was haphazard.

Diego and Mateo, the caretakers, spent more time smoking than working.

His complaints were never-ending.

Once Eduardo had marched up to her office waving a paper cup and napkin he'd found on the lawn and torn a strip off the two men, in front of people she was dealing with, until she'd put her hand up and said sternly, "You bring your complaints to me and I'll investigate them."

"Señora, I am an owner here; I'll have my say," he retorted.

"And *I* am the concierge here, employed by the community, and *I'll* have *mine*, and *I* say you bring your many complaints to *me*," she'd said icily, and had glared at him until he'd looked away. *Madre de Dios*, but he would drive a saint to drink. All he desired was to become the president of the committee, and if and when he did, she would pay for her perceived impudence, Constanza knew.

Thus far, because he was unpopular with the Irish and British owners, De La Fuente had been thwarted from achieving his goal.

But this was the year he might actually achieve his dream. He'd proposed at the last AGM that the meeting be changed to August, when more owners were on-site than there were in January. The Madrid contingent would all be down, seeking sanctuary from the intense heat of summer, and they would support him.

Combined with the fact that the presidency had become a poisoned chalice because of the community debt, not to mention feuding among a few factions, and disagreements about the allowing of pets onto the complex, and about whether to allow an area to be set aside for children to play football in, the enthusiasm for the position was wearing off.

Would she even be here this time next year? Constanza reflected despondently. The AGM traditionally would have taken place on the third Saturday of January, and she would have had the relief of knowing that her job was safe for another year, but now it was unsettling to know that for the next nine months she would have this uncertainty hanging over her.

If the *madrileño* achieved his goal, her position would be very shaky indeed. She would have to depend on the loyalty of the other owners to maintain her status.

But she would fight De La Fuente every step of the way, Constanza vowed. She loved La Joya and, for the most part, she enjoyed her work. It was challenging and interesting. A prissy little jumped-up notary from the capital who had ideas above his station was not going to get the better of *her*.

Chapter Twenty-Five

Anna / Austen

She could hear a shrill ringing rousing her from the deepest depths of sleep. Beside her, Austen stirred. "Wha . . . what's that?" he slurred as Anna, realizing it was the phone and it was the early hours of the morning, shot up into a sitting position, reaching across her husband to grab the receiver.

"Hello," she said, trying to keep the anxiety out of her voice.

"Mrs. Mac, they've decided to do a caesarean on Tara. Her blood pressure's gone sky-high and they say it's the best option now because of the preeclampsia. I just phoned to let you know. I've to go and get gowned up."

"Oh! OK. James, will we come in?" Anna's stomach gave a sickening lurch.

"You probably won't be allowed in. You won't be in in time for the birth. They've done all the pre-op stuff and given her the epidural; they're doing it in the next few minutes, so I'll ring you as soon as I can." James sounded so flustered and anxious, Anna wanted to race into the maternity hospital and hold his and Tara's hands.

"All right, love. We're here the minute you need us. I'll turn my mobile on if you want to text," she said reassuringly, moving away from Austen to let him sit up. "It will be fine," she added, but she was talking to thin air. Her daughter's partner had turned off his phone and was hurrying down the corridor to the operating theater.

"What's happening?" Austen gazed bleary-eyed at Anna and yawned prodigiously.

"They're doing a caesarean on Tara." Anna's lip wobbled and she burst into tears as every primal motherly instinct she possessed made her want to get to the Rotunda as fast as she could to be by her child's side during her hour of greatest need.

"She'll be OK; sure they're very commonplace," Austen said gruffly, trying to hide his anxiety. He put his arm around Anna and she buried her face into the strong, tanned column of his neck. "At least she won't have to endure labor. Remember yours, with her? Twenty hours that seemed to go on and on," he reminded her.

"I know, but you only have caesareans if there's something up, and it takes much longer to get over it." Anna wiped her eyes with the back of her hand. "Will we have a cup of tea? I can't see myself going back to sleep."

"You stay there, I'll make it," Austen offered, flinging back the duvet.

"What time is it, anyway?" she asked, groaning when he switched on his bedside lamp, the light causing her to squint.

"Five-thirty—nearly time to get up." He smiled down at her. "Will I make you some toast?"

"I don't think I could eat. My stomach is tied up in knots."

"I'll make some anyway; you can try and nibble on it," he said kindly. "And I'll turn on the heating for a while, it's nippy." He pulled on his dressing gown and fished for his slippers under the bed.

"Thanks," Anna said gratefully, switching on her mobile phone.

It was chilly, and she could hear the rain battering a tattoo against the Velux window in the en-suite, and the faint jangle of a wind chime every so often when gusts of wind swirled around the apple trees. Snow was forecast. Winter's grip had taken a firm hold even though it was not yet mid-November. Anna pulled the duvet up under her chin and lay back against the pillows, wondering if her first grandchild was being born at that very moment. She hoped James would text once the baby was lifted out of Tara and checked over. That should be in the next twenty minutes or so, she figured. If he waited until she was wheeled into Recovery, it could be an hour.

What a pity for Tara of all people, who was so into natural health and well-being and who had longed to give birth naturally, even planning a home birth before her pregnancy had developed complications. Now she'd to undergo the birthing procedure she'd been dreading all along.

Chloe, on the other hand, would probably *demand* a caesarean, Anna thought wryly, musing that her daughters were chalk and cheese. At least the baby would be born in plenty of time for Tara to be able to undertake her chief bridesmaid duties at her sister's post-Christmas wedding.

The invitations had to be sent in the next few days. They sat in their baby-blue-and-cream boxes on her desk, in her home office, reproaching her daily. Miss Chloe could spend one evening this week stuffing them into envelopes and sticking the stamps on them.

A wedding on the day after St. Stephen's Day. Only Chloe could be oblivious to the utter hassle her chosen wedding date was causing her parents, who dreaded the thought of driving to a country house on a day that most people would be lolling around in pajamas, watching TV, scoffing chocolates, and eating turkey and stuffing sandwiches.

When the five-star hotel in Wicklow that Chloe had her heart set on was unavailable for the May wedding she'd originally wanted, she had been gutted. Anna and Austen had been secretly delighted. The opulent, Palladian-style pile had a minimum spend on food and drink that *didn't* include the venue hire. That *also* had a minimum spend. She'd seen her husband's eyebrows shoot to the top of his head and the grim set of his jaw when he'd heard *that* particular snippet of information, and only her sharp nudge in his ribs had kept him quiet, if silently fuming, as the venue's wedding planner explained the costs in detail.

"Is she *serious*, Anna? What bloody planet is she on? There's a credit crunch going on, the economy's on the slide, and she's behaving like we're bloody millionaires," he hissed while his daughter listened with rapt attention to the planner's description of the "On Terrace Welcome Reception," which would add *another* couple of thousand to the already substantial bill.

Very fortunately for them, the hotel was booked up for May and June, and Will was not able to take the chunk of leave from work for a wedding and two-week honeymoon in July. Chloe had had to go back to the drawing board, much to her chagrin. Flicking through some brochures at a wedding fair, a bride dressed in a medieval gown in a country house setting had caught her eye and excitement had taken hold again.

"Mum, we've decided we're going to have a winter wedding in a country house that has its own church on the estate. It's going to be gorgeous, lots of candles, and fairy lights, and holly wreaths and trailing ivy and a punch, eggnog, and champagne reception. And my dress is going to be pagan-style, edged with fur trim on the sleeves. It's going to be, like, so awesome and *so* different. And the brilliant thing is, it's actually available on the twenty-seventh of December—"

"The day after St. Stephen's Day," Anna had squawked in dismay.

"Yeah, they had a cancellation and they'll give us a discount if we take it," Chloe exclaimed excitedly. "It's *perfect*, and we'll have our honeymoon in the Maldives while you're all shivering in the winter chill," she said, grinning and dancing around the kitchen like a sprite. "*And*—this will cheer Dad up—it's all in. No minimum spend, and the room rates are very reasonable."

Anna, when she'd seen the venue herself, had been impressed with the total package, and had decided pragmatically that she should be grateful the wedding was taking place sooner than planned so she'd have less time to worry about it. Best of all, while Chloe and Will were basking in the sun in the Maldives, she and Austen would be flopping for a month in La Joya, knowing that, duty done in regards to Chloe's wedding, they would be free agents to *finally* do as they pleased for their retirement.

A month would be a long time not to see her new grandchild, she thought guiltily. Babies changed so quickly in those early months, and Tara might feel a bit isolated if both she and Chloe were away. She might have to rethink. Austen could have some of his golfing pals over the first week and she might stay that week at home. She wouldn't mention anything to her husband yet. He'd hoped to persuade her to travel to their penthouse as they had the previous year, in November, but she'd been reluctant to leave Tara, who had struggled in the last months of her pregnancy.

In the end she'd persuaded Austen to go golfing, but he'd been irritated that she wouldn't come with him and he'd been uncharacteristically cool with her, much to her annoyance.

Did he not see that she couldn't waltz off to Spain while her daughter needed her? Or was it guilt, perhaps, that he was swanning off, leaving her to hold the fort, that made him cantankerous?

Crotchety or not, Anna was glad he was home in time for their grandchild's birth. A mother's bond was stronger than any other—even that between husband and wife, she admitted, wishing with every fiber of her being that she was at her daughter's side right now to encourage, support, and share Tara's most elemental, powerful, spiritual moment.

Anna remembered as though the years had passed in the blink of an eye the moment she'd given birth to her firstborn. Exhausted after a long, painful labor, she'd somehow found the energy to summon a surge of unexpected force for that last final effort. A calmness—a grace, even, she reflected afterwards—had come upon her, and Austen, the midwife, and the nurses had faded from her ken as her focus lasered on the child emerging from her womb. She'd felt a wave of primordial power, reassurance, and immense love wash over her as she brought forth her daughter into the world.

Her mother had told Anna that she would discover reserves within herself for childbirth, when she'd confided her fears and apprehension to her. And it had happened just as her mother had promised, when Anna needed it most.

No doubt her mother was with Tara in spirit, Anna thought sadly, tears brimming in her eyes. It was nine years since Anna's beloved mother had passed, and while the overwhelming grief had lessened and become more manageable, as others who had endured the loss of a parent had promised her it would, she missed her greatly, especially at times like this. As she prayed a heartfelt prayer to her mother, a sense of peace washed over her and Anna just *knew* all would be well.

"Here you go, and for goodness' sake, stop crying. Tara will be fine." Austen strode into the bedroom and handed her a plate of toast dripping in butter and placed her mug of tea on her bedside table.

"I know she will." Anna gulped, taking a sip of the hot, welcome tea and a bite of toast, crunchy and oozing butter, the way she liked it. "Ooohhh, this is lovely. You make the best toast."

"I know," Austen said smugly, getting back into bed beside her and snaffling a slice for himself. They ate their early breakfast companionably, sitting up against their pillows; knees against knees, shoulders against shoulders and Anna thought how lucky she was to have such a strong, loving, and affectionate relationship with her husband even after all their years of marriage and the minutiae of everyday life. Some of the couples they socialized with had not been so lucky. Although she and Austen had been tested many times, they had come through with a deep appreciation of each other.

Her phone beeped and she nearly dropped her mug, all fingers and thumbs as she handed it to Austen to hold while she scrabbled to find her phone in the folds of the duvet and open the message.

"Awww, Austen, look, it's the baby. A photo." Her eyes welled with tears again as they gazed at the image of their first grandchild, a baby boy, wrapped snugly in a blanket with a little blue hat on his head.

All well. Tara is fine. Our new son. 8lbs 8 ounces we'll ring soon when she is in the recovery room.

"Can you believe it?" said Austen, handing her back her tea. "We're *grandparents*. It only seems like yesterday when I was holding Tara and you were eating your tea and toast after giving birth. Where did the years go?"

"I don't know . . . I just don't know." Anna gazed at the image of the peaceful little baby, who looked so calm and untroubled as he slept in his father's arms. *May he always be as peaceful. Thank you, Mam, for Tara's safe delivery and the gift of this new baby.* She offered up a silent prayer of immense gratitude, snuggling in against her husband as the tension of the last hour drained away, and she began to plan a batch cook to fill Tara's freezer for the busy but exciting days ahead.

◆

"Here's your first grandchild, Mum, Michael Austen Anthony Collins," Tara said happily, handing her precious baby to Anna with a look of utter pride. Despite the trauma of the caesarean and the lack of sleep, she looked radiant.

"Well done, darling, I'm so proud of you," Anna praised, taking the little bundle in her arms and gazing adoringly at the sleeping baby with his shock of black hair. He was a MacDonald all right, she thought, noting his determined little chin and straight nose, secretly thrilled that her grandchild favored *their* side of the family.

"He's a fine little chap." Austen stood at her shoulder gazing down at him in delight.

"How are you bearing up, James?" Anna turned to Tara's partner, leaning up to kiss him on his stubbly cheek, noting his gray pallor and the dark circles around his eyes.

"Grand, I'm grand," he said stoutly. "Sure Tara did all the work—"

"I'd never have managed without you, love. You were my rock," Tara said gratefully. "And I think you should go home and go to bed for a couple of hours."

"Why don't you come home with me? I'll cook you a fry-up and then you can go home and get your head down and Anna can stay here for a while with Tara," Austen suggested.

"Great idea, Dad," enthused his daughter. "James, you were awesome but you're bog-eyed with tiredness. Go with Dad."

"Are you sure? I'll stay if you want me to, no bother," James offered.

"Scoot!" Tara grinned. "I want to go asleep myself. The painkillers are making me drowsy."

"Off with the pair of you. And make the most of it, James. Your last hours of freedom." Anna gave him an affectionate hug.

"Listen to her, she speaks the truth. Come on, lad, while the going is good." Austen patted the younger man on the back before leaning down to kiss Tara good-bye.

"See you tomorrow." Her father smiled at her.

"See you later, babes." James kissed Tara and leaned in and kissed his son on his tiny snub nose before following Austen out the door.

"Well, how are you *really*? How did it go?" Anna sat in the chair beside her daughter's bed, grandchild asleep in her arms, the pale, wintry sun emerging from behind sullen clouds to stream down around them like rays from heaven.

"I was scared, petrified when they said they were going to do the caesarean, but once it started and James was holding my hand, the strangest thing . . . Mum, you probably think I was imagining it, but I *really* felt Nana was beside me. I had her medal around my neck and I could feel her so close."

"Of course she was there." Anna smiled at her with a sense of overpowering love. "I felt her too."

"He's gorgeous, isn't he?"

"He's beautiful. Here, you hold him for a while before we put him in his cot," Anna said, remembering how she'd wished her visitors would leave when her babies were born so she didn't have to share the cuddles with them.

"Thanks, Mum," Tara said, holding her arms out for her son. She lay back against the pillows, a perfect Madonna, thought Anna, taking a photo that she would frame to remember this most matchless moment.

◆

"They've just left the hospital," Anna informed her husband, who was setting a match to the firelighters in the stove.

"Perfect timing. Stick on the kettle and we'll have ten minutes to ourselves to watch the lunchtime news before pandemonium breaks out," Austen suggested. Tara, James, and the baby were going to stay with Anna and Austen for a week while Tara recovered from her caesarean. Anna was delighted that her daughter was coming home. Every new mother needed help, especially a first-time mum, and Anna couldn't wait to get her hands on her new grandson.

She made the tea and shucked a few chocolate biscuits onto a plate. She was doing her best to lose a few pounds for the wedding, but this was a day of celebration, she reasoned a tad guiltily, longing to dunk the biscuits in her tea and feel the chocolate melting on her tongue.

"Good God Almighty," she heard her husband exclaim as he shot up straight on the sofa where he'd sprawled to watch the news, in the family room that adjoined the kitchen.

"What?" she asked in alarm at his tone.

"Listen." He held up his hand and she heard the newsreader reporting the collapse of a company founded by an ex-Anglo banker. ISTC. What was it about ISTC? Anna tried to focus as she saw the dismay creasing her husband's face.

A dawning awareness made her mouth suddenly dry. They had invested one hundred thousand euros in that company just weeks ago, in mid-August, at the behest of their stockbroker who had assured them it was a "surefire bet." Fifty thousand each.

"Thank God we didn't take out a mortgage in Spain; at least we have that asset behind us," Austen said, gray-faced. "You know, Anna, there's going to be no soft landing for the economy no matter what those fools of politicians are saying. We're in for a hell of a depression. This is the start of it."

"Don't say that, Austen. Are you sure the money's gone? Can't we become creditors and get some of it back?" She handed him his mug of tea.

"I can tell you here and now, we're not going to get one *cent* back." Austen's jaw was taut with anger. "And we're only in the penny-halfpenny place. I know people who've invested a million and more in that bloody company."

"Who?"

"The Kingstons did. And Ed and Maura Reilly whacked five hundred K in. His lump sum."

"His *whole* lump sum?" Anna was aghast.

"Yeah. I told him to go easy, spread it out a bit. But he wouldn't listen to me. And of course the stockbrokers were egging him on, the greedy, corrupt bastards. I *bet* they knew it was on the slide when we bought in, listening to what's on the news. No wonder they were piling on the pressure. They got their big whack of commission."

"Look, let's meet the accountant next week and have a chat and see if we can salvage anything—"

"It's gone, Anna, one hundred thousand smackers of hard work down the drain." He exhaled. "Down the drain," he repeated incredulously.

"OK, let's park it for the time being. They'll be home soon with the baby. Let's not let this spoil our happiness in our new grandson," she urged, putting her arms around him, feeling sick to her stomach.

"Easier said than done," he retorted. "God, I feel such a fool. But it came so *highly* recommended." He shook his head in disbelief. "The caliber of the investors was impeccable. It was supposed to be a blue-chip company. What the hell went wrong?"

"Look, think of the positives. We own our own home and the property in Spain. We have bank shares. We have savings in bonds in the post office and we have your pension and an income from my business. We're doing more than OK."

"I suppose," he conceded. "But it's bloody hard to swallow that that amount of money has just gone nowhere."

"I know. Half of it was mine," she reminded him. "At least it wasn't a hundred thousand *each*!"

"Yeah, I suppose so," Austen said glumly. "OK, let's park it, as you say, and make a fuss of Tara and the baby." He slumped back on the sofa.

"And not a word to anyone."

"Yes, boss." Her husband managed a half smile and she took his face in her hands and kissed him tenderly, wishing she could get her hands on the bloody stockbroker who had urged them to invest in the "surefire" deal.

Just when they had been set to enjoy their retirement, this had to happen. There was always *something* to worry about, Anna thought ruefully, hoping Austen wouldn't dwell too much on their monetary loss and let it spoil the new joy that had come into their life.

◆

"Now, it's like this, Chloe, your mother and I have just suffered a big financial loss on our investments. One hundred thousand euros, to be precise," Austen said dourly. "And while we are delighted to pay for your wedding and give you some money towards a house, you have to cut back and be realistic. I know you're sending the invitations out this week. I want you and Will to go through everything with a fine-tooth comb and cut out silly frivolities or else pay for them out of your own pockets. We'll pay for the horse-drawn carriage and red carpet into the church and of course the drinks reception and the meal." Austen's tone brooked no argument.

Chloe gave a gasp of dismay. "You lost all that money in investments. OMG! How?"

"A company we had invested some of our pension in went belly-up. There's a big downturn worldwide, Chloe. There are property crashes and job losses in the cards. I'd think carefully about spending a fortune on one day, that's all I'm saying."

"What a bummer," she groaned.

"Indeed," agreed Anna, not sure if Chloe was referring to the loss of her parents' savings or having to cut back on the wedding. "Now, why don't we go through the invite list and pare it back to those you really *want* at the wedding, those we feel we *should* invite, or to whose family weddings we've been invited, and those whom you wanted to be at the wedding because you just wanted to show off a bit." She grinned at her daughter's indignant expression.

"I'll leave you women to it." Austen made his escape.

"I wasn't going to show off, Mum," Chloe said indignantly.

"Ah, go on. Why are you thinking of inviting Marianne Fitzgerald and her bloke? You don't particularly like her."

"Well, Johnny is nice, and we do hang around with them," Chloe said sulkily.

"They can come to the afters," Anna said firmly. "Come on, let's go through the list and get rid of some altogether, and demote the likes of Marianne and Johnny to the afters do. As Dad said, we're delighted to pay for the wedding, but things have changed and we don't have money to scatter about."

Subdued, Chloe sat down beside her to scale down the day she had dreamed of since she was a little girl.

Chapter Twenty-Six

DECEMBER

Anna / Austen

"You're the most beautiful bride I've ever seen," Austen said proudly, gazing with admiration at the vision before him.

Chloe, dressed in a sumptuous gold brocade and tulle gown, looked like a medieval princess. An A-line-style dress with fitted sleeves that grew wide at the bottom and were trimmed with white faux fur was accessorized with a rich crimson sash that fitted snugly around Chloe's tiny waist. The neckline, crimson and gold, adorned with glittering diamanté crystals, showed off the pearl-and-diamond-encrusted cross that Anna had worn on her own wedding day.

The veil falling from a diamanté barrette that held Chloe's upswept chignon gave her the ethereal look that she'd been striving for.

"Thanks, Daddy." Chloe beamed, thrilled with herself, and leaned up to kiss his cheek.

"Right, then. Conor and I'll head over to the church to join

Tara and the flower girls," Anna said, amused that her daughter hadn't a hint of nerves. This was her day and she was looking forward immensely to being the center of attention. But then, Chloe had always enjoyed being the center of attention, Anna thought fondly. It came with being the youngest, she supposed.

"Good luck, little sis, I'll be the one heckling when they ask is there any reason for the marriage not to go ahead. I'll be telling Will to run for his life." Conor, a strapping six foot two, towered over his youngest sister. He gave her a kiss, high-fived Austen, and laid an arm around his mother's shoulder.

"Do you want a piggyback?" he teased. "I don't know how you can walk in them things." He indicated her elegant cream high-heel slingbacks.

"I can manage fine, thank you." Anna grinned at him, delighted that he was home from Canada. In one way Chloe's unexpected Christmas wedding had worked out very well, as it was the first time the whole family had been together in over a year. Had she got married in the summer as planned, Conor might not have made it home.

"Thanks for everything, Mum and Dad. It's going to be the most beautiful wedding ever," Chloe said gratefully, tucking her arm into her father's. Austen looked exceedingly handsome in his charcoal-gray morning suit that emphasized his broad shoulders and lean midriff. His tan and tight haircut emphasized his rugged good looks, and Anna couldn't help but be proud of her beloved husband. She straightened his tie and looked at him admiringly.

"See ya later, ya sexy ride," she whispered in his ear, and he laughed and pinched her ass underneath her coat.

"I heard that. Get a room," groaned Conor.

"Couldn't think of anything I'd prefer to do more," Anna said smartly. "Come on before my hormones get the better of me."

"*Mum!*" chided Chloe, giggling. "That's so inappropriate in front of your kids."

"Do you hear them, Austen? Wait until they see us on the

dance floor. *Dirty Dancing* will have nothing on *us*." Anna winked at her husband as her son escorted her out of the room.

Sharp fingers of arctic air stung her ears and nose as they crunched along the frosty, curving gravel drive to the little chapel that lay on the grounds of the grand, ivy-clad country house that they had chosen to hold the wedding in.

Knots of guests were gathered outside, and a hum of chat and laughter lifted Anna's spirits. Now that it was all happening and everything was in place, she felt some of the tension she'd carried for the past few months ease away. The arched doorway, dressed in pine boughs laced with creamy winter jasmine, led into a red-and-cream-tiled narthex. A bank of scarlet poinsettias and flickering cream candles on a side table that held the marriage ceremony booklets gave a Christmassy air.

"Very, very classy, Anna, and you look *stunning*," Breda greeted her with a kiss as Mary hugged Conor and Yvonne took a photo of them.

"Thanks. It's a Maire Forkin design. I fell in love with the color," Anna said, doing a twirl in her beautifully fitted cerise dress with a simple boat neckline under the matching tailored coat.

"Very slimming too," Mary complimented.

"That's the Spanx. I swear to God, I nearly pulled a muscle in my back trying to get into the friggin' thing." Anna grinned. "Sorry for dragging you all the way here the day after St. Stephen's Day." She felt suddenly carefree. The girls were here, her wing-women. There was nothing more she could do now except enjoy herself.

Tara emerged from the church, a glorious goddess in her pagan-style bridesmaid's dress of rich emerald green with a gold sash at the waist and gold trim on the sleeves and neck. "I got the five-minutes warning, everybody, better get inside. The horse-drawn carriage has arrived up at the house," she announced to the assembled guests.

A frisson of anticipation rippled among them and they made

their way into the church, sliding into the gleaming, polished pews as the organist played "In the Bleak Midwinter."

"I'll stay with Tara until they arrive; you go in out of the cold and sit beside Granddad," Conor offered, flattening out a wrinkle in the red carpet that led down the step to where the bridal carriage would come to a halt.

"Right, see you in a minute," Anna agreed, turning to make her way up the holly-wreathed aisle to where her father sat with her brother and sister-in-law and a niece and nephew.

It had worked out rather nicely, thought Anna, waving at an aunt and uncle, and stopping to have a quick word with Will's parents. The church was just large enough to accommodate family and close friends, and the overflow of guests was ensconced in the ballroom in the main house, watching on a big screen.

She knew some people were miffed not to be in the church, but she didn't care. Small and intimate was much more desirable than the big palaver that would have taken place if Chloe had got the wedding she originally wanted. And crucially now, because of their financial debacle, the wedding had worked out less expensive than they'd feared.

She took her place in the pew beside her father and he squeezed her hand. "I remember the day I walked you up the aisle. It only seems like yesterday," he murmured.

"I know. And without half the fuss of what goes on today, and we turned out great." She smiled at him, wishing her mother was there to be at his side. "Mam would have liked this church. It's like the one you got married in."

"I was just thinking the same thing," her dad remarked as the organist began to play the wedding march and a rustle of expectancy shivered along the congregation.

Hearing the music swell to a thundering crescendo, Anna's throat constricted and two big tears plopped down her cheeks. She glanced across at Mary—who was Chloe's godmother—and Yvonne, knowing they'd be bawling too, and caught an answering tearstained wink from Mary while Yvonne delved into her bag for a tissue.

Chloe wafted past on Austen's arm, turning to smile at Anna, and she was glad that her daughter had got a wedding that would make her happy, knowing that her and Will's future would be rocky for the foreseeable future with all that chaos and uncertainty that was battering the economy. Her new son-in-law looked so proud and happy when Austen placed Chloe's hand in his, she couldn't help but be reassured that Chloe had found a fine young man to share her life with.

"You did great, and you look great," she whispered to Austen, slipping her hand into his when he sat down beside her, the first part of his duties accomplished.

"Right back at you, Anna. You look beautiful and the church looks fantastic," he complimented, squeezing her hand tightly as the priest invited them all to stand.

The words of the ceremony floated over her, bringing many memories to mind, and she had to struggle not to let her emotions get the better of her when the priest pronounced Chloe and Will man and wife. Knowing what she was feeling, Austen leaned down during the applause and murmured, "One down, two to go, yaaay!" and winked at her, making her laugh. If Chloe and Will were as happy as she and Austen were, they would be doing very well indeed.

◆

"Ohhhhh, were we not good enough for the church?" Jeananne Mangan chirruped, glass of champagne in her hand, as the guests mingled during the drinks reception.

"'Fraid not," said Anna lightly. "The hoi polloi had to watch it on the big screen."

"We had planned to go to the villa in Antibes for Christmas," the other woman remarked—decidedly unimpressed with that putdown—"but we felt it would be rude not to come to Chloe's wedding, she being such friends with our pair."

"Well, honestly, Jeananne, you should have gone. It wouldn't have bothered us in the slightest. You could have been enjoying lovely warm weather instead of this arctic chill," Anna retorted. She wasn't in the humor for the other woman's passive-aggressive snide comments.

"Oh, well, you put yourself out for friends, don't you? Even if we were relegated to the benches." Jeananne gave a saccharine smile.

"Excuse me a sec, Jeananne, I just want to make sure Dad has a drink." Anna could see the expressions on Yvonne's and Mary's faces when they heard the other woman's bad-mannered acerbity, and she thought she might laugh.

"*We* practically had front-row seats, lucky us, but then, we've been *friends* with Anna for a long time—like sisters, really," Yvonne chipped in airily, handing a glass of punch to Mary, who turned away to hide her amusement.

"How many of those have *you* had?" sniffed Jeananne derisively.

"Not as many as your Roger. He's sampling the eggnog, punch, *and* champers. He'll have a mighty hangover in the morning, Jeananne," Yvonne riposted and Mary had to walk away and giggle into her drink as Jeananne "We Have a Villa in Antibes" Mangan was rendered uncharacteristically speechless.

"You're so deliciously bitchy," Mary chuckled when Yvonne rejoined her.

"I wasn't letting that wagon get away with her impertinent rudeness. Who does she think she is?" Yvonne was unapologetic.

"Look at her tottering around on her Dolces. She'll be lucky she doesn't trip and break her ankle . . . or her neck."

"And the pantsuit is 'Stella,' I heard her telling someone earlier. Trust Jeananne to wear white to a wedding." Mary helped herself to a canapé.

"I bet you're giving out about Jeananne," Breda said, joining them. "Whatever she said to you, Yvonne, I thought you were going to pour your punch over her."

"Oh, don't tempt me," Yvonne laughed. "That would ruin the 'Stella' outfit."

"I just don't get Stella McCartney as a designer. None of her pants ever fit well. They're always really baggy around the crotch and they make you look huge. Mind you, Jeananne would need baggy pants around that pear-shaped arse of hers," Mary scorned as the other pair erupted into guffaws.

"What are you laughing at?" Anna came over and raised her glass to them.

"Mary was just being a bitch," explained Yvonne, grinning.

"Kettle and pots, madam; sure I'm only trottin' after you," laughed Mary, filling their friend in.

"She's a real boot, isn't she? I can tell you she won't be coming to any more MacDonald weddings, that's for sure," Anna declared. "I never met anyone more pass remarkable."

"Downright rude, I'd call it," retorted Breda, helping herself to another glass of champers. "Cheers, girls."

"I wish I could sit at your table. We'd have such a laugh," Anna sighed. "I better go and do my mother-of-the-bride duty. See you when I see you."

Several hours later, when the meal was over and the speeches delivered and while they were waiting for the dance floor to be set up, Anna, Austen, and Tara were sitting, having a quiet drink together, when Roger Mangan ambled over to them. Anna groaned when she saw him coming. As usual, their golfing acquaintance was three sheets to the wind, his ruddy visage and glassy little marble eyes a sure sign that he'd been overindulging.

"Good wedding, Austy. I was just saying to the Foleys over there what a clever move it was to host it in a small venue. Saving a fortune by having to cut down on the guest list to accommodate the space. No flies on you, boyo, although I heard you got hammered with ISTC. Just as well you saved a few thou on the wedding so," he slurred. "Let me give you a word of advice, stash your dough offshore, in Panama. Taib Carrell Investments. Safe as houses and no tax." He winked. "Don't say I don't help out my friends, even if we're not good enough to sit in the church."

"I'll bear that in mind, Roger, very kind of you," Austen said calmly, laying a restraining hand over Anna's. Her eyes were sparking with anger.

"Oh, here you are," exclaimed Jeananne shrilly. "I was wondering where you'd got to."

"Just giving Austen some financial advice," Roger bellowed.

"Oh, yes, I heard you made a bad investment," Jeananne said condescendingly. "And I heard the Kingstons got hit for a million. There won't be a peep out of her down in the golf club now, I'd say. She does love to go on and on about the place in Sandy Lane."

"And do you still have the villa in Antibes, Jeananne?" Tara asked demurely.

"Tara, how are you? We do indeed." Jeananne beamed, completely oblivious to the sarcasm. "I believe you had to have an emergency caesar. Now, I had an emergency caesar with Zach and it nearly *killed* me. I hope you weren't butchered like I was, the scar was hideous and—"

"Oh, don't start on about that," Roger griped. "That's women's talk; I'm going to the bar." He lurched away and Jeananne frowned. "I'd better go after him, he does like to indulge at weddings," she trilled, but behind the gay façade she was furious. It was always the same now when they went anywhere. Roger had turned into an obnoxious lush, and she was the one who had to take the flak for his bad behavior. It was just too mortifying for words.

"Of course he indulges, when it's free drink," Anna retorted, watching Jeananne totter after him. "God, he has some nerve. I wanted to give him a puck in the jaw."

"He's hammered; no point in talking to him," Austen said. "Forget it."

"I detest that man, and her as well," Tara fumed.

"Well, they won't be coming to your hand-fastening ceremony," Anna assured her.

Tara laughed. "You can say that again, my wedding will be a hell of a lot different to this one, I promise you."

"Music to my ears, my dear." Austen patted her arm. "Music to my ears."

◆

"After all the fuss and hassle, it's finally over. Well done, Anna. You did a magnificent job," Austen complimented his wife as they lay exhausted, snuggled together in the enormous four-poster bed in their tower room.

"So did you," she yawned. "It did all go really well, didn't it, apart from the Mangans and their antics. No class, either of them, for all their designer gear, big Merc, and villa in Antibes."

"Don't give them a second thought. They won't be coming to any other parties we give," Austen assured her.

"That's if we can afford to give parties," Anna said drily. "We don't have any dough stashed offshore."

"Let's not go there," Austen said drowsily as his arm tightened around her. "The wedding's over, the grandchild's thriving, it's our turn now. Let's get to Spain and enjoy our retirement like we'd always planned."

"Sounds good to me," Anna agreed, but her husband was already asleep.

Chapter Twenty-Seven

JANUARY 2008

Austen

Austen pressed his fob and waited for the gates to La Joya to open. Under a sapphire sky he could see the sea, incandescent in the morning sun. Geraniums, blossoming lantana, and passionflower filled the grounds with glorious bursts of color. Normally this welcome sight never failed to lift Austen's spirits, and it did to an extent, but it wasn't the same when Anna wasn't here to share it.

She'd insisted on staying in Dublin for a week so that Tara wouldn't feel too isolated, seeing as Chloe was away on her honeymoon. Baby Michael was poorly, running a temperature, and Tara, naturally, was worried about him. But that was part and parcel of motherhood, Austen thought irritably, parking the car and unloading his luggage. Anna's mother hadn't come running every time Tara had got temperatures when she was a baby. In those days you just got on with it. This generation was so *dependent*, he thought glumly, opening the door to his block.

Anna knew he was annoyed with her. He'd been curt when

he'd snapped, "For God's sake, Anna, they have to cut the apron strings at some stage in their lives. What's the point in having a place abroad if you're going to cancel trips every time someone sneezes?"

"Don't be mean, Austen. It's only for a week. I'll be with you for three more of them. Being a first-time mother is *hard* going," she'd protested heatedly.

"*You* had to get on with it. Your mother lived in Wicklow and couldn't come haring up to Dublin every time one of the kids got sick. Can't her mother-in-law muck in?"

"Austen, just stop. I'll be out on the tenth, and that's the end of it." Their good-byes had been cool when she'd dropped him to the airport. She'd proffered her cheek rather than her lips for his farewell kiss and he hadn't looked back to wave at her.

He'd been childish, he admitted, letting himself into the penthouse and heading straight to the fridge for a beer. Jutta's people had been in to do an arrival clean and the penthouse was sparkling, smelling of lavender. The fridge had been stocked with all the basics; he'd do a shop tomorrow.

Half an hour later he sat at their favorite table, under the orange blossom, in the restaurant that now felt so familiar. He'd been greeted warmly, presented with a glass of wine, a dish of olives, and a basket of bread rolls while he perused the menu.

He slid his phone out of his jeans pocket and scrolled for her number. "Hi, I'm in the restaurant," he said when she answered. "And I miss you and I'm sorry for being grumpy."

"I miss you too, Austen; I *wish* I was there with you, but I'm glad I stayed, because Tara had to bring the baby in to Temple Street and he's on an antibiotic drip."

"Is it serious?" he asked, alarmed, hot coals of guilt burning him.

"He has an ear and throat infection, the poor little dote, but he'll be all right," she assured him.

"Sorry, Anna."

"It's OK; I know you were looking forward to us going out together. You enjoy your golf and relax and then you can make a big fuss of me when I arrive." He could tell she was smiling.

"I love you," he murmured, lowering his voice, embarrassed that anyone might hear him.

"I love you too. Enjoy your lunch and afternoon nap."

"I will." He smiled.

"Bye, love," she said, and hung up. Austen put his phone away and absentmindedly nibbled on a piece of crusty bread. Much as he loved his children, they needed to realize that he and Anna had their own lives to lead, and his dear wife needed to recognize that too.

◆

"What's wrong with our poor little baba? My little darling, aren't you? I couldn't go off to Spain and leave you when you're not well," Anna crooned, rocking her grandson gently in her arms. She'd packed Tara and James off to bed the minute they'd arrived back home from their twelve-hour stint at the hospital and told them she'd keep the baby in her room for the night. They didn't need much persuading, and—looking at their pale, exhausted faces—she wondered how Austen had forgotten the sleepless nights and anxious days they had gone through with Tara.

Sometimes Austen was very black-and-white. "We paid our dues, we've done our bit, it's time for us. You're worn-out after that wedding," he'd argued impatiently when she'd told him she wasn't going with him for the first week of their holidays.

"It's a one-off," she'd snapped. "I wouldn't enjoy a second of it if I was there because I'd be worrying about them. God Almighty, Austen, you're getting hard in your old age."

"And you're getting soft in the head," he'd shot back before slamming the door as he went off to have a round of golf.

It was good that he'd phoned earlier. She smiled, kissing the baby's downy head. And his conscience must have been at him, because he'd told her he loved her. He was probably snoring now after his early start, limbs flung to the four winds in their big bed in La Joya.

Anna yawned and the baby stirred in her arms. "Shushhh," she murmured soothingly. If all went well, she'd be with her husband this time next week. They should make the most of it, little family dramas notwithstanding.

◆

The excruciating pain hit Anna that night like a bolt from the blue as she lay in bed twisting and turning, unable to sleep. She felt feverish and nauseous and the pain became more intense, moving from her chest like a knife in her back and shoulder blade.

Oh, Jesus, am I having a heart attack? she thought frantically, struggling into a sitting position and switching on the lamp in her daughter's guest room. She tried to breathe deeply, but the pain was so severe, she groaned. "Tara," she called out weakly as a wave of nausea overtook her. "Tara."

Her daughter appeared at the door, bleary-eyed, hair disheveled. "What is it, Mum?" she asked, her sleepiness turning to anxiety when she saw her mother's pinched white face. "God, you look awful," she exclaimed as Anna gave another groan.

James appeared, stubbly-faced and rubbing his eyes, his black hair sticking up over his head. "Mum's not well," Tara exclaimed, terrified as Anna doubled over in agony. "Ring an ambulance quick."

"Oh, no, not an ambulance, not the ER," Anna gasped. She'd prefer to have a heart attack than endure a night on a trolley in the emergency room. Tara placed some pillows behind her back and she lay against them, giving short, shallow breaths as she heard James talking to the emergency services, her anxiety mounting as the pain increased.

When the ambulance crew arrived, she relaxed somewhat, feeling safer knowing that they could assist her. Calmly, expertly, they carried out a cardiogram as she lay there, convinced that she was having a heart attack and feeling like death.

The paramedic studied the readout. "It seems normal, but let's get you into hospital and run an echocardiogram—"

"What's that?" she asked weakly. "Is that the balloon thing?"

"No, no," he reassured her, "that's an angioplasty. An echocardiogram is an ultrasound. Doesn't hurt a bit. Now we'll get you into the chair and have you in hospital in no time."

"Will I ring Dad?" Tara asked anxiously.

"Under no circumstances, Tara. Do you hear me?" Anna instructed. The last thing she needed was Austen flying home and doing a jig in the ER.

"OK, I'll get dressed and come with you."

"Please don't. Stay and mind Michael."

"He'll be fine for a couple of hours with James. I'm coming with you," Tara said firmly, hurrying to her bedroom to throw on some clothes.

Why did this have to happen? Anna fretted a couple of hours later, lying on a narrow, hard, uncomfortable trolley in a curtained-off cubicle in the emergency department. The ultrasound had confirmed that she wasn't having a heart attack, and when she'd heard that, she'd insisted that her daughter take a taxi home.

"Look, they've to do blood tests and more scans, so I'm going to be in until the morning at least. I'll ring you as soon as I know anything, and not a word to your father, or Chloe if she rings," Anna ordered, in as firm a tone as she could manage. There was no point in both of them having a sleepless night. "Don't worry"— she mustered a faint grin—"I'm not going to kick the bucket."

It was a long, painful, sleepless night before she saw, through a small window, the faint rays of daylight lighten up the eastern sky and heard the clatter of the breakfast trolleys and was utterly relieved that morning had finally dawned.

"Will I come in?" Yvonne, who had been alerted by Tara, asked Anna by phone a couple of hours later as she lay against her pillows with a drip in her arm feeding her fluids, having earlier been injected with intravenous antibiotics.

"No, you will not," Anna declared. "It's not my heart, it's my bloody gall bladder."

"Your *gall bladder*?"

"How friggin' middle-aged is that?" Anna made a face. "And so it begins . . . the slippery slope to decrepitude."

"Don't say that. I'm the same age as you."

"No more fry-ups or cheese, rich sauces. and oily foods, and I've to cut down on drinking."

"*Nooooooo!*"

"Yep. What a fantastic start to the year."

"Take lashings of bread soda," Yvonne advised.

"Yes, Doctor." Anna grinned. "Thank God I wouldn't let Tara ring Austen. Imagine if he'd flown home to find out it was only a gall bladder attack."

"It sounds as though it was pretty painful," Yvonne said.

"It was horrendous. I wouldn't wish it on my worst enemy. Or even Jeananne," she added with a touch of humor.

"Wow! That bad. You take it easy, missus, and let me know if I can bring you in anything," her friend said sympathetically.

"I will," promised Anna, holding out her arm as yet another phlebotomy technician came to take more blood.

◆

"Anna, I'll never forgive you for not letting Tara ring me," Austen admonished her, shocked when she'd told him what had happened to her the previous week. They were sitting in El Capricho, waiting for Svetlana to bring their drinks. A tonic water for her . . . no gin, much to the lovely Russian's dismay. "No drink? *Catastrophe!*" she had exclaimed, and Anna had laughed.

"Look, I'm fine; I just have to watch my diet," she reassured him. "It was bloody painful, but the antibiotics have cleared up the infection and here I am. If I get any pain I've to go to the ER here."

"It's stress—"

"It's middle age. What do they say? Fat, fair, and over forty, a prime candidate for gallstones," she deadpanned.

"You're not fat!" Austen protested.

"Well, curvy, then," she said lightly.

"Anna, it's time to start looking after yourself. If anything happened to you, I don't know what I'd do," Austen said seriously.

"Nothing's going to happen to me, so relax," Anna sighed, wishing she could indulge in a large G&T and a juicy steak with pepper sauce.

Chapter Twenty-Eight

AUGUST

Eduardo / Consuela

"Should I be elected to the office of president, my main focus will be to deal with the increasing debt to the community because of the unacceptable number of owners in arrears. I will propose to name and shame these owners. And with the cooperation of the governing board I'll work to regularize the debt and file legal claims if necessary." Eduardo paused and stared sternly over his bifocals at the audience in front of him. "It is imperative, ladies and gentlemen," he resumed, after letting his words sink in for a moment or two, "that we build up a *substantial* reserve fund. That too will be my aim.

"I'll also seek to upgrade the general maintenance of the urbanization, which in the past year has become unsatisfactory and slipshod"—a small dig at the outgoing president. "Thank you for your kind attention."

Eduardo gave a little bow to his audience, noting *Tía* Beatriz applauding him and looking uncharacteristically delighted. A barb of bitterness laced with anger lacerated his heart. Consuela should have been there to listen to his speech and to offer her support during the AGM. But no, he thought, indignantly. She preferred to be gadding off with Catalina somewhere in the north of the country, to listen to some ex-nun give a talk on Mary Magdalene and feminine energy or some such nonsense. Had Catalina actually mentioned "goddess energy" or had he been daydreaming? Consuela's cousin was for the birds and a *pagan* as well, with her outlandish beliefs. Eduardo scowled, slipping his cue cards into his jacket pocket and walking down to resume his seat beside Beatriz.

Every year at the AGM he'd stood up and put himself forward for the position he'd coveted from the beginning. This time he'd kept his list of proposals short. He hoped that his words would strike a chord and lead to his election.

"*Excelente discurso, Eduardo,*" murmured his aunt.

"*Gracias,*" he said, giving her a smile. Ever loyal Beatriz, giving him some rare words of praise. It was a balm of sorts for his wife's most hurtful act of indifference.

The moderator—a fellow Spaniard who was supportive of his campaign—thanked him and called upon the assembled owners to vote for each candidate. The proxies were already converted and Eduardo sat ruler straight, not touching the back of his chair, flicking a pink blossom from the sleeve of his immaculate cream linen suit. Only the muscle jerking in the side of his jaw gave any indication of how tense he was. Being rejected previously had been humiliating. An affront to his professional dignity. Hopefully this year the imbeciles would realize that a firm hand was needed on the tiller.

The first candidate, a Swede, Sven Olsson, received about two dozen votes, Eduardo calculated swiftly. Not nearly enough. He'd expected that.

Now it was either him or his implacable enemy Pablo Moralez. Eduardo's palms became damp as a forest of hands rose to support his opponent. The secretary counted row by row, and Eduardo felt the familiar sinking feeling of rejection. If Moralez became president, he might even sell up, he thought belligerently.

He felt the way he'd felt when he was a young boy at school and, having plucked up all the courage he could muster, he'd asked two other boys of his age if he could be their friend. "We have enough friends," the bigger of the two said cuttingly, and Eduardo had felt his heart shrivel and sting as if stung by a thousand wasps as he watched them walk away and tried hard not to cry.

"Your votes, please, for Señor Eduardo De La Fuente," called the secretary. A slew of hands were raised in the air. Most of his fellow *madrileños*, surprisingly several Dutch, and an Irish owner; his best ever result, he thought, heart racing. It would be the proxies that would determine the vote.

Would it be third time lucky? he wondered. If Consuela were there, she would be soothing his anxiety . . . or perhaps not, he thought gloomily. His wife had changed, become almost hard in her attitude, he would say. Just when he needed her most, she was not there for him. If he became president, he'd need to travel down to La Joya more often. Would he be able to depend on his wife to keep an eye on Beatriz in his absence? "She's your aunt, not mine"—Consuela had fired a warning shot across his bows in their most recent battle of wills. Because that was what their marriage was now, he conceded—a battle of wills—and, to his great disquiet, his wife was no longer happy to be swayed by his reasoned arguments. Most definitely not; in fact, she was beginning to gain the upper hand and do *exactly* as she pleased.

Yet again his life was in upheaval because of a woman's will. He remembered, reluctantly—not wishing to travel back to the most painful days of his childhood—Beatriz *begging* his mother not to take him to America. "All his friends are here, Isabella. His life is here; you cannot do that to him. Let him stay here in Spain with me until he is older, when he will be less shy and able to make

friends better." He'd been outside in the hall listening, drawn to
the parlor doorway by unaccustomed raised voices.

"But I can't do that to him. What do I say to him? He'll think I
abandoned him," Isabella exclaimed.

"No, no, I'll explain to him that you are doing this in his best
interests. Try it for six months. Go see if you like America. If you
think you will settle. Then we'll talk and make a decision," Beatriz
advised.

"Oh, Beatriz, I just want to do the best for us all," his mother
groaned.

"As do I, *querida*. As do I," his aunt affirmed.

Eduardo had hastened away, heart thumping. His parents were
going to America and thinking of leaving him with his aunt. *Tía*
Beatriz, who lived with them, was quite strict and not as affectionate as his mother, who gave very nice cuddles.

Eduardo was torn. He liked his home in Madrid, and he liked
his school. He would be going to a strange country, with a strange
language. *That* he would not like.

His mother had found him hiding in his fort, in his bedroom.
He loved his fort made of two plaid rugs laid over the back of a
chair and his brass bedstead.

"*Querido*," she said softly, crawling under his blankets and
putting her arm around him, "I have something to tell you. Papa
and I have to go away on a plane. Papa is going to work in a big
hospital and get more training. You are going to stay here with
Tía Beatriz, and when we are settled and if we like it, we will come
back for you."

"And will I go on a plane?"

"You will," she promised, squeezing him tight until he laughed.

He'd gone on a plane to visit his parents six months later. His
mother's belly was round and hard. She had a baby in it, she told
him. A brother or sister for him. *Tía* Beatriz had cried a lot. She
didn't like Chicago, Eduardo heard her tell Isabella. It was too cold
and much too windy. "And not a good place for Eduardo," she'd

said emphatically. "Especially now that you are pregnant. This isn't the time for him to stay. Have your baby first and get over the birth and then see."

His mother hadn't argued. She was tired and sick a lot of the time. Too tired and sick to find a new school for him and do all the things a mother had to do. Eduardo had returned to Madrid with his aunt with promises that when he had finished his year in school he would go to live in America.

His father, Santiago, an ambitious workaholic determined to climb the ladder of his cardiology career, had moved to New York less than a year after moving to Chicago. Their baby daughter, Eduardo's new sister, Victoria, was six months old when he met her. Isabella and Santiago had flown home to Madrid for Christmas and it had been a joyful reunion for the entire extended family, who were entranced with the new arrival.

Mostly what he remembered about that Christmas was his excitement on Epiphany Eve, leaving three glasses of cognac, with satsumas and walnuts, for the three kings, Melchior, Balthazar, and Gaspar. Putting his shoes under the Christmas tree to be filled with presents before going to bed, hoping against hope that he'd been good enough to get a gift and not some pieces of coal.

It was the happiest time of his life. Eduardo sighed, still remembering as though it were yesterday his utter joy on discovering the biggest train set he'd ever seen, waiting for him under the tree. A Hornby train set with a steam engine. His mother had been as excited as he was. "Do you like it, *querido*? Isn't it amazing?" she exclaimed, offering him a big slice of cream-filled *roscón*.

A train set, and cake for breakfast. What could be better than that?

He'd never gone to live in America. Santiago had moved the family yet again, to the West Coast—first to Seattle, then to LA—and it seemed easier for Eduardo to stay with Beatriz in Madrid, where at least there was continuity and stability of sorts in his life.

Santiago had ended up having an affair with the widow of one of his patients, and Isabella, distraught at her husband's betrayal, had secured herself a hefty settlement and divorced him. After the divorce, Eduardo never heard from his father again. Had Santiago been a presence in his life, it would have been devastating; as it was, it didn't impact him unduly until he was older and his father's rejection of him intensified his feelings of unworthiness.

Isabella had remarried—her second husband was a professor of law at Boston University—and after bearing him a son and a daughter had finally settled down to the stable family life that had always eluded her. By then Eduardo was focused on his own studies and career advancement, and his future was very firmly in the city of his birth.

A sharp nudge in his ribs drew Eduardo from his reverie. "The announcement of the result is being made," murmured his aunt, noticing that he was distracted.

The secretary took to the podium, having added the votes of the absent owners. He glanced in Eduardo's direction. "*Damas y caballeros*, ladies and gentlemen, our vote for the position is now concluded, and I am pleased to announce that Señor Eduardo De La Fuente will be our next president, winning by a margin of three votes. Thank you to the other candidates. We will now move on to the election of the governing board and administrator."

A polite smattering of applause greeted his announcement, although Eduardo thought he heard a groan coming from the far right of the audience. Beatriz was beaming at him proudly.

"*Bien hecho, mi hijo.*" She patted his hand. "Well done, my boy" was the highest praise his aunt ever gave him, and he smiled at her warmly, pleased that she felt this achievement warranted such commendation.

"*Gracias querida tía,*" he replied, the smile softening his stern features. "I've done it; at last I've done it. Now I will make La Joya the most desirable urbanization on the south coast." His mind began to race, making plans, before he stilled it and brought his focus back to his governing board. He needed board members he could mold to his way of thinking, preferably men, not strong-willed, argumentative women like that Irishwoman, Anna Mac-Donald, who'd been the secretary the first year. She'd been rather dismissive of him as the year wore on and had been extremely slow answering his emails. He didn't see her at the meeting, although her husband was in the middle row. The husband had voted for Moralez, he noted sourly. It didn't matter; Eduardo dismissed the thought. He was now *El Presidente*, and things were going to change.

Impulsively he took his phone out of his pocket to call his wife and tell her his great news. And then he remembered her immense disloyalty and thought, *No! She doesn't deserve to know. Let her stew.*

◆

"Although the decline of Mary of Magdala's reputation as an apostle and leader began after her death, it was Pope Gregory the First—or Saint Gregory the Great, as he is now known—while preaching in Rome in 1591, who completed her transformation to penitent prostitute, which subsequently has been reinforced in art and literature—"

"Excuse me," a woman in the row in front of Consuela raised her hand. "Is that the Pope Gregory who was in the *Heiros Gamos*, or Sacred Union, with Mathilda of Tuscany?"

"No, that was Pope Gregory the Seventh." The petite ash-blond woman who was giving the lecture smiled. "I think Mathilda might have given him a good telling off if he'd called the Magdalene a prostitute."

"I don't think you or I are in a *Heiros Gamos* relationship, tragically," whispered Catalina to Consuela, and Consuela giggled. She'd read about the *Hieros Gamos*, where two equals—twin souls—reunite through the Sacred Marriage, which was often not a marriage in the conventional sense but one of sacred partners who became as one and were transformed esoterically.

What she had with Eduardo was not a marriage of twin souls,

for sure. From the journey of self-discovery she'd undertaken, and with the mind-expanding knowledge she'd gained, she now knew that they had met and married to learn from each other. It was even possible they had covenanted to undertake this journey together before they had come back to earth, if some of the metaphysical books she read were to be believed. Whether they would stay married, she wasn't sure, Consuela thought ruefully.

Eduardo had been angry and put out when she told him that she wouldn't be at his side for this year's AGM. It coincided with a talk about the reemergence of the Magdalene Divine Feminine Energy that she very much wanted to attend. It was being held in Girona, and Catalina had suggested they spend a second day exploring the northern city before taking the AVE back down to Málaga via Madrid, where they would overnight.

Consuela had impulsively agreed, not realizing that it clashed with La Joya's AGM.

"But you *always* come to the AGM with me. I'm much more optimistic about winning the election this year," Eduardo exclaimed when she told him she wouldn't be attending with him. "You'll just have to cancel."

The way he went on about winning that position, you would think he was running for the White House, Consuela thought irritably, but she maintained her equanimity in the face of his wrathful disappointment.

"I'm sorry, Eduardo. This talk is something I very much wish to hear. I'll be gone for three days. Catalina and I are going to Girona for two days and spending a night—"

"Three days! Three *days!*" he interjected in disbelief. "I'm sorry. You simply cannot, Consuela! What about Beatriz? She'll be in La Joya with us that week." He shook his head vigorously to emphasize his point. "You'll have to tell Catalina that you can't go and that's just all there is to it," he ordered, his face resolute as he stared at her across the breakfast table a month before they were due to take their August break.

"I'm afraid, Eduardo, I'll do no such thing," Consuela said quietly.

"You're being most unreasonable, Consuela," Eduardo argued.

"I think not. It is *you* who are the unreasonable one. I have new interests in my life. I want to be able to enjoy them," she pointed out firmly before eating some toast.

"That's fine, enjoy your new interests, but it's *most* inconsiderate of you to book things during the holidays," he complained. His black eyes were flashing anger, and his mouth thinned as she calmly raised her cup to her lips and took a sip of coffee before answering him.

"I thought it *most* considerate of me, actually," she said mildly. "It means I'm not staying away from home when you're working, so that I can have your meals on the table and run errands for your aunt if need be. Be fair."

"I'll just have to tell Beatriz not to come until you are going to be there with her, then," Eduardo said sulkily, draining his coffee. He wiped his mouth with his linen napkin and stood up.

"Eduardo, Beatriz has made arrangements for her cat to be looked after, as she always does when she comes down to us on the coast. Don't go changing the dates on her. I'll only be gone three days—"

"Three days is just not *acceptable*, Consuela." He tried again to get her to see reason. "One night, perhaps, but three is being utterly selfish," he added snidely.

"It's like this, Eduardo. I'm extremely fond of Beatriz, but she's *your* aunt, not mine, and I have given her great care over the years. I am your *wife*, not your servant, nor your employee, nor your child. I find it *unacceptable* that you would tell me that going on a little trip is 'unacceptable.'" She did air quotes and glared at him.

"What's become of you? You're so argumentative now. Catalina has brainwashed you with her nonsense," Eduardo accused furiously before marching out into the hall to grab his briefcase and giving the door a good slam as he left.

Consuela gave a little sigh remembering that fraught exchange. She wondered if the presidential election had taken place yet. Perhaps she was a first lady, she thought with amusement, hoping for her husband's sake that this time he'd been elected. Perhaps she should hope for *her* sake too. Living with her husband for the weeks after his previous rejections had not been easy as he alternated between brooding silences and bile-filled rants about the owners who hadn't voted for him and their ill-considered "lack of foresight."

". . . The image of the fallen woman and repentant sinner is ingrained now in human consciousness, despite a recent change of attitude by the present-day Church. Now is the time to reveal the truth of who Mary Magdalene truly was and is. That is why we are here today. It's about taking a leap of faith," Consuela heard the speaker say, and guiltily focused on the discussion taking place. She'd come to learn and enjoy and not sit ruminating about her husband.

"If I had ignored my inner voice . . . and, I like to think, the voice of Mary Magdalene"—the speaker paused and smiled broadly—"I would have stayed a cloistered nun and never experienced the wondrous new journey I'm on. Bringing an awareness of the Magdalene energy has brought me all over the world," the ex-nun, in her elegant taupe pants suit and discreet gold jewellery, said joyfully.

"Listen to your inner voice, your gut, whatever moves you, and act upon it. Take leaps of faith!" she urged. "Otherwise you are sleepwalking through life."

Booking her place on the lecture had been her own leap of faith, Consuela reflected. Perhaps a small one, but a leap nevertheless.

Tomorrow she and Catalina were going to take a tour of the city's secret and mystical past, starting in the Rambla de la Llibertat, a bustling street in the heart of the Old Town, not far from the ancient Jewish Quarter known as the Call Jueu.

She was especially looking forward to visiting the Frenchwoman's Garden, which still had a buttress on the stone wall of the Torre Magdala, which had inspired the strange priest, Bérenger Saunière—who was devoted to Mary Magdalene and rumored to have found her grave—to replicate it in Rennes-le-Château in France.

Wait until Eduardo heard that she and Catalina were planning to visit France—where the Magdalene was revered—in the autumn. They were going to Cathar country, and to sites associated with her.

Her life was so much more interesting now that she had come to her senses and begun to seek self-knowledge, Consuela mused, enjoying her coffee during a break in the lecture. Thinking outside the box was stimulating mentally and spiritually.

Eduardo pooh-poohed the books she was reading and Catalina's "way out" beliefs, as he called them. Consuela permitted herself a broad smile. If he knew that she now believed in reincarnation and that she'd planned and chosen her current life path, including her marriage to him, before she had reincarnated into this life, he would think that she was completely loopers and advise her to see a psychiatrist.

Poor Eduardo, so straitlaced and trapped in his narrow, insular life and beliefs. No wonder becoming president of the management committee was so important to him. The position would give him a sense of control. To be in control of everything in his life was his way. Now, Consuela, who was practicing going with the flow of all that was new in her existence, felt a freedom she'd never experienced. She would never go back to being the compliant, unthinking woman she once was.

Eduardo had always paid her an allowance along with her housekeeping money, rather than have a joint account with her. She'd prudently saved over the years, and with the small inheritance she'd received from the sale of her parents' apartment after their deaths, she was very happy to spend it now, journeying, literally, on her new soul quest.

Eduardo wasn't interested in traveling, especially now that he had their apartment in La Joya. That was his choice and his decision. She wasn't prepared to be bound by her husband's preferences anymore. She was no longer sleepwalking! With that in mind, she refrained from switching on her mobile phone to see if there was any news of the presidential election from the Costa.

◆

Constanza Torres snapped closed her phone and took a deep breath. Her greatest fear had been realized. That bloody *madrileño* had won the presidency. He was now, to all intents and purposes, her boss.

She chewed the inside of her lip, tidying some papers on her desk. Her informant, an English widow with whom she was quite friendly, had tried to reassure her by telling her that his main focus was going to be reducing the arrears debt. Perhaps so, but Constanza knew what De La Fuente was like. She'd met his ilk before. He was the type to hold a grudge, and every perceived slight over the past few years would be held against her.

Although, she admitted ruefully, some of the slights had not been perceived, they'd been *actual* slights because he was an obnoxious, rude, pernickety man who liked nothing better than to order people around. Constanza was quite convinced that Eduardo looked down his haughty aristocratic nose at her. And not just her . . . *all* women . . . including his wife.

She might as well make the most of her freedom, Constanza thought disconsolately, dialing her husband's number to tell him the news. Once *El Presidente* was in residence, he'd be watching her like a hawk.

◆

Beatriz was glad to sit in the shade of the awning on the balcony sipping a glass of dry sherry. No one could serve her sherry like Eduardo. He always chilled the glasses first, before putting in the ice cubes, and then added an orange twist to the amber drink.

She ate a stuffed olive and took another sip of sherry. She was peckish. Consuela and Catalina had taken the AVE from Madrid, and Catalina was driving them from Málaga to La Joya. They all planned to go to a seafood restaurant in Cabopino for dinner. Tonight they would celebrate Eduardo's achievement. Finally getting the position of *El Presidente* was giving him as much satisfaction as when he got his law exams, Beatriz suspected.

There would be an edge at dinner. Eduardo was blaming Catalina for influencing his wife's new interest in, as he dramatically called it, "*lo oculto!*" There was nothing of the occult in Consuela's newfound interest in metaphysics, Beatriz realized. In fact, she'd read some of the books the younger woman was devouring and had enjoyed them. Especially the life-after-death ones. Now that she was getting nearer to her transition, she was interested to read what awaited her. Beatriz liked hearing about Consuela's metaphysical studies and she enjoyed their chats over lunch when the other woman came to visit.

Eduardo, of course, did not know that Beatriz supported his wife in her journey. She was always very careful to maintain her position of noninterference in their marriage, which, she admitted sadly, was going through a very rocky patch. Much as she felt sorry for Eduardo, who could not make head nor tail of Consuela's new desire to expand her life, beliefs, and vision, she was glad Consuela was being brave and sticking to her guns.

Braver than me, she thought with regret. Oh, such regrets she had that she'd stayed in her safe little boxed-up life, unwilling to risk having her heart broken after her first, and only, disastrous relationship.

Isabella had urged her to come and live in America with her but she'd refused. She'd cloistered herself like a nun, closed down every desire of her heart and body, and lived a safe and unexplored life of strict routine and duty. She'd smothered Eduardo, urging him to forget about girls and socializing and to study to get ahead in his life. For that she was sorry also.

Consuela had been living the safe life too, but now, like a butterfly emerging from her cocoon, she was taking a chance and spreading her wings. Still, Beatriz wouldn't hurt Eduardo's feelings by letting him see that she approved of his wife's transformation, which was having such a detrimental effect on their marriage.

If only he could emerge from his own cocoon, grow with Consuela, and shake off the shackles of work and duty and rigorous discipline that entrapped him. That would be a miracle indeed. If not, their future together could be rocky and poor Eduardo was going to find that being *El Presidente* might be all he had left in his life to give him the affirmation he constantly needed.

She'd withheld too much from him in an effort to turn his timidity into confident self-assurance. She hadn't wanted to mollycoddle him and turn him into a sissy, seeing as he had no male role model in his life. Santiago had done nothing for the boy. It had all been down to Isabella and her. Her brother-in-law was a restless, ambitious, impatient man. She'd said as much to Isabella, who didn't want to hear any criticism of her then soon-to-be husband.

Beatriz had met a young man like Santiago once, and fallen head over heels in love with him. But he'd left her without a backward glance, and she'd never given her heart to anyone again. The barriers had come up and stayed up. That was why she'd tried to warn her younger sister. She didn't want her precious Isabella to experience the heartbreak she had. Restless, ambitious, impatient men never stayed.

Eduardo had similar traits, but he also had a keen sense of duty and responsibility—instilled in him by her, Beatriz liked to think. Whether that was a saving grace or not remained to be seen. She'd tried her best to instill many good qualities in him, but she'd failed him too.

A tear slid down Beatriz's cheek and then another as she sat in the deepening dusk and watched the High Atlas mountains in Morocco darken behind a vibrant coral sky.

Chapter Twenty-Nine

Austen / Anna

"Eduardo De La Fuente got voted in as president." Austen gave his wife the news in his usual evening call, while he sat on the balcony sipping a beer as a slight breeze rose to temper the intense August heat.

"No!" Anna exclaimed in dismay.

"Yep, 'fraid so."

"Ah, feck it, it was bound to happen eventually. He's gone up for it every year. Was it a close vote?" Anna's voice was as clear as a bell. She could have been in the room next door rather than thousands of kilometers away in Dublin.

"Only three in it, unfortunately. There wasn't enough Irish or English here to make the difference. If they'd allowed their proxies to be used, it would have been another matter; but they didn't bother, so they needn't start complaining. Most of the Spaniards voted for him, apart from Pablo Moralez and his clique."

"Ah, sure they've been feuding from the time La Joya opened. Jostling for position, like two bloody tomcats marking their territory. The complaints they made about each other when I was secretary of the committee were unreal. Thank God I've done my spell; I'd hate to be on the new management board, with him in charge," Anna remarked. "Poor Constanza, he'll make her life hell. She's been dreading this all along."

"And maintenance fees are going up another hundred per annum. And they're going to name and shame the nonpayers and take them to court."

"At least we've paid up to date," Anna said. "Is it hot?"

"Scorching. You'd hate it."

"I know. I really can't handle the heat in August. But I miss you."

"Do you?" She knew he was smiling.

"Especially in bed at night. I may have to go and look for a toy boy," she teased.

"Ah, don't do that. I'll be home soon enough and you'll get fed up of me."

"I'm glad Tara and James are going out to you for a few days. It's the only holiday they'll get."

"I'm looking forward to them coming. I just hope you won't be knackered looking after Michael on your own. There's a lot of running around after him," Austen reminded her.

"Austen, I have a bit of news for you, and don't let on I've told you—"

"Good or bad?" he said warily.

"Well, surprising . . . but good, I suppose . . ." Anna hedged.

"Hit me with it," he sighed.

"Chloe's pregnant—"

"*What?* Is she mad? She's hardly six months married."

"At least she's married," Anna said humorously.

"Aw, Anna, could they not give themselves a chance to get on their feet?" Austen groaned.

"Well, at least they didn't buy a house and end up in negative equity, and they've rented a good-sized apartment. They're not doing too bad."

"When is it due?"

"January."

"That's our winter break scuppered so," he said irascibly.

"Sure you can go over and play golf," Anna placated.

"And what about you? It's not fair on you," he retorted.

"Austen, this is where we're at in our lives; we should be grateful to have such happy, healthy children. We're healthy ourselves. We'll have plenty of time in Spain. We'll be back out this September and October," she pointed out.

"Yeah, I suppose. Don't mind me. As long as they're happy, that's all that matters." He made an effort to show some positivity. "Was it planned?"

"Was what planned?"

"The pregnancy . . ."

"Erm . . . not by Will, I'd say, being honest. I know why Chloe got pregnant. Two of her good friends are expecting, and life is all talk about babies, and baby showers, and being yummy mummies and going for coffee mornings and so on, and you know what she's like! Can't bear to be left out. Has to keep up with her gang. It's a peer thing with half of them," his wife surmised astutely.

"It will be a different kettle of fish when they all have bawling babies," Austen drawled.

"Exactly. Talk later, love," Anna laughed.

"OK, bye." Austen hung up and went to the fridge and got himself a bottle of San Miguel. The ice-cold beer hit the back of his throat, and he gulped it thirstily. It was boiling outside and the constant air-conditioning was making his throat dry. He was hungry too. The AGM had taken forever.

He couldn't be bothered cooking, he decided, even though he'd salmon in the fridge and steak from the acclaimed Irish butcher in Calahonda. He strolled into the bedroom, pulled his T-shirt over his head, freshened up, put on a clean shirt, and made his way to the restaurant on the beach. He caught a waiter's attention and signaled for a beer. He'd have to nurse it so he wouldn't be over the limit, driving to the airport later.

Austen sighed, conscious of the empty seat opposite him. If Anna were here she'd have a G&T and stretch out her legs and say, "This is the life," and squeeze his hand before turning to watch a couple of small fishing boats landing their catch on the beach, or the yacht under sail that was drifting past towards Estepona or Puerto Banús.

He could understand that she didn't like to be here in August. It really was stinking hot, and even the sea breeze didn't make much difference; but late September was a lovely time to come, unless anything else went belly-up, he thought ruefully.

"You look very cross, Austen," he heard a voice say in familiar accented English.

"Ah, Jutta, it's yourself." He stood up politely to greet her.

"Sit down, sit down," she urged. "I've just come from doing an inspection before clients arrive tomorrow and I have to have a drink and some food before I face that highway from hell," she laughed. "Where is Anna?"

"She's at home; August is too hot for her. I came out for the AGM. Sit down," he invited politely, not sure if he wanted company or not.

"No, no," she demurred, "I don't want to invade your privacy."

"Nor I yours," he echoed, "but I've just ordered a beer and I can order you a drink, no problem."

"Perhaps I will, then, it's busy here now and I don't want to take up a table," Jutta sighed, running her fingers through her blond hair and sinking gracefully onto the chair opposite him.

"I hear Eduardo De La Fuente has been elected *El Presidente*. Poor Constanza," she remarked.

Jutta was an extremely elegant woman, always very well presented, Austen noted. Not a hair out of place, no damp red cheeks from the heat, makeup immaculate, smart in her white linen trousers and crisp red blouse.

"Funny you should say that, Anna said the same thing when I told her," he said, nodding his thanks to Domingo, the waiter, who had brought his beer. Austen raised an eyebrow at Jutta. "Wine, beer, spirits?"

"A dry white wine for me, thank you." Jutta smiled.

"And bring the menus, Domingo, *por favor*," Austen said.

"He likes to be in control, that man De La Fuente. He thinks Constanza should treat him the way his employees do, not as an equal," Jutta observed. "Unfortunately he is now in a position to tell her what to do. That's where the problem will lie."

"It will be an interesting year, for sure," Austen said, "Constanza is pretty feisty; he won't have it all his own way."

"Well, I can guarantee you, if he can't get her to resign, he will find some way to get rid of her. I wouldn't trust him as far as I'd throw him," Jutta said equably, and Austen laughed, as always entertained by her absolute sense of assurance that things would be as she predicted. Jutta was what his late mother would have called a "know-all," with something to say about everyone and everything. And a high moral authority that made her look down her nose at others, including the Irish, who, according to her, "couldn't grasp the concept of apartment maintenance fees because they were a race of house owners," "the Brits would die of hunger if they couldn't have their full English fry-up every day," and "the Spanish couldn't do a business deal without a bribe," in her view, despite the fact that her own husband was Spanish. He and Anna would listen to her proclamations in silent amusement when she took coffee with them each summer and presented her annual invoice.

Nevertheless, her business was growing and successful, and she was now expanding to add property sales to her services. She was good at her job, Austen conceded. "I believe you've gone into the sales area," he said as they raised glasses when her wine and the menus came. "Tell me, how badly has the property market been hit here?"

"Austen, it's a disaster," Jutta said calmly, perusing the menu. "There are wholesale repossessions in the buy-to-let sector. Of course, that doesn't apply to you—"

"Are we in negative equity, would you say?"

Jutta sat back and pursed her lips. "I think you won't *lose* money in urbanizations like La Joya, or the likes of Jasmine Gardens, or Mi Capricho, down the coast. High-end frontline properties won't make the mad money of a couple of years ago, but they won't lose their value. It's different with the huge housing developments, one on top of the other, with the shared pools and few amenities—up the hills in Mijas, say, where, if you haven't got a car, you're stuck. Or the Costa Blanca, where my husband has business interests. That's where the repossessions are. The banks are taking villas and apartments back at an enormous rate. You know if you miss two mortgage repayments, the bank comes after you immediately in Spain?"

"I'd heard that. I suppose it's a relief that at least we won't lose, should we ever have to sell, and hopefully the market will rise again." Austen drank the cold amber liquid in his glass, enjoying their conversation. Jutta knew her stuff and was interesting to talk to; it was better than sitting on his own while he waited to go and collect Tara and James when their flight got in around ten.

Chapter Thirty

Jutta

Jutta tucked into her crispy lemon whitebait with relish. She was pleased now with her decision to eat in the restaurant rather than go home. Her father was staying for a few weeks to recuperate from his knee replacement, and had been even more demanding than usual. She was at the end of her tether. Thank God she was flying back to Germany with him at the weekend. And this time, at least, she'd be pushing him in a wheelchair.

She liked Austen MacDonald. He was an interesting and intelligent man to converse with, and Jutta liked intelligent men. He was rather handsome too, she admitted, with his neatly cropped gray hair, intense eyes, and rugged good looks. A man who looked after himself. A man who kept his physique in good shape—unlike Felipe, who was beginning to thicken at the waist and develop jowls.

Her husband was drinking too much. She knew it was because of financial worry. He'd once come to her looking for money to pay his employees' wages That had shocked her, depressed her, and irritated her in equal measure. She'd given him the money he'd requested but had told him in no uncertain terms *never* to ask her again and to pay it back as soon as he could.

So, yes, it was pleasant indeed to sit outdoors and eat with this handsome, successful Irishman, whom she knew would pay for their meal and drinks, because that was what real men did and Austen MacDonald was a *real* man. In a million years she couldn't imagine *him* having to ask his wife for money to pay his employees' wages.

"Another glass of wine?" Austen asked.

"Why not, Austen, why not?" Jutta said gaily, raising her almost empty glass to him. She could always get a taxi home. She deserved some R & R, she decided.

◆

"It's not a good time to have a child. Business isn't good. There are way too many variables right now, Jutta," Felipe maintained as he sped along the A-7. He'd collected her from her flight back from Germany and his heart had sunk when, yet again, she'd brought up the subject of having a child.

"Felipe, we can't keep putting it off. I want a baby—"

"You want a baby so your sisters can stop emotionally blackmailing you to have your father stay with us more often," Felipe retorted.

"That too, certainly." Jutta didn't deny it. She'd come home from her latest sojourn with her father, and from confrontational sessions with her sisters and brother regarding his care, about who was doing this and who wasn't doing that, determined that her childless state would not be used against her anymore.

"That's no reason to have a child," her husband pointed out.

"It's only *part* of the reason. Your parents are always asking when are we going to present them with a grandchild. I don't want to be pregnant in my forties. I'm old enough now as it is, Felipe. The time has come. We've discussed it often enough over the last couple of years. We can't keep putting it off," she declared in her most firm and dictatorial tone. "I came off my pill in Germany," she added crisply.

Felipe laughed, amused at his wife, in spite of himself. "You always were a bossy little *Fräulein* with a mind of her own, and you are an even bossier *Frau*. What happens if *el buen Dios* doesn't bless us with a child?"

"We will adopt," she said determinedly. "But I think God *will* bless us, Felipe. The women in my family are very fertile."

"Perhaps *I* won't be."

"I think you will be," Jutta laughed, pleased that her husband hadn't argued too vehemently against her decision. The sooner she got pregnant, the better. She would hire an au pair immediately after the birth; Jutta didn't intend for motherhood to interfere with her work.

Her sisters would have one less salvo to fire her way, and by January, if all went well, she would tell her siblings that her father would have to stay at home and not make his annual winter pilgrimage to stay with her because of her pregnancy. Felipe might smarten up his act too, and start behaving responsibly in his business dealings, once he had a child to support.

It could be very much a win-win situation, Jutta mused, wondering why she'd left it so long.

NOVEMBER

"But you'll be past the dreadful tiredness and sickness of the first trimester. Surely you can take Papa for ten days so we can take our skiing holiday," Anka demanded furiously. "It's not as if we're asking you to take him for three weeks this time like you always do."

Jutta's lips thinned. "Anka, I'll ring you back. I'm with a client," she said irritably, and hung up. She'd lied—she wasn't with a client—but she didn't want to be bullied into a decision there and then about whether to take her father to stay in January.

She gazed out at the gunmetal sea roaring onto the shore. A howling gale raged outside and great banks of sullen clouds swept across the Mediterranean from Africa, with the threat of rain to come. A few hardy souls braved the strong winds and staggered along the beach, plastic ponchos flapping. It was unusually cold and wet on the Costa, and the tourists and owners who had flown to Spain for the winter were not getting much sun.

If the weather stayed the same in January, Oskar wouldn't even be able to sit out on the balcony as he liked to do, and they would all be cooped up together in the apartment. Could she bear it? Jutta thought wearily, burping because of rampant heartburn.

If she agreed to take him in January, though, she would be clear for the rest of the year. The baby was due in June. Under *no* circumstances would she be able to give her father his usual summer break. She would tell her sisters that if they wanted to come to Andalucía with Oskar in the summer, she would be *delighted* to find an apartment or villa for them all to rent.

That was what she would do, Jutta decided, taking back control. And if Anka and Inga didn't like it, that was their tough luck. Let them go and find another *piñata* to batter. She wasn't going to let them emotionally blackmail her anymore. She checked out her diary to see which dates suited her best and took a deep breath before dialing Anka back.

"*Hallo*, Jutta," her sister answered brusquely.

"Anka, I can take Dad from the fourth to the fourteenth of January. I won't be flying to Germany with him to bring him home. Tell Friedrich to get off his fat ass and bring him to Frankfurt Airport and put him on the plane to Málaga and to collect him when he comes home, if you or Inga don't want to do it. I can't stay talking any longer. I'm working. *Auf Wiedersehen.*"

She didn't wait for her sister to reply but hung up quickly. She'd had enough of family rows and resentment, enough of being treated with disrespect. From now on she was *definitely* stepping back, she told herself, although she said that every time. Soon her own family unit would be complete.

If her sisters were in any way nice to her, in any way appreciative of the fact that she *did* play her part in caring for their father, she wouldn't be so unbending. Jutta frowned, tapping her teeth with her pen, frustrated that she was yet again on the defensive. They were jealous bitches, and always had been. Just because she'd made a life for herself away from the tyrannies of home, she comforted herself—hating it when she was made to feel she was negligent in her familial duty by Anka and Inga.

Chapter Thirty-One

NOVEMBER

Sally-Ann / Cal / Lenora

"Look, let's see how it goes. It's just for an overnight. We owe it to Jake to work things out and give him a good family," Cal said patiently.

"I know, and I'm doing my best." Lenora pouted.

"And so am I," Cal reminded her. "I took you out of Galveston and got us a condo in Houston like you wanted. We have an au pair. You get to New York once a month. I think that's pretty fair."

"OK. OK," she snapped irritably. "Invite your girls if that's what you want—"

"I want you to want it too," Cal growled. "When the divorce is final, I'll have joint custody."

"I'm not used to teenagers," she said sulkily.

"It's a learning curve for all of us. Good night," he said exasperatedly, turning over on his side, away from her.

When, after she'd spent a month in New York without seeing their son, Cal had phoned Lenora to tell her he was renting an apartment in Houston and asked if they could try again for the sake of their little boy, Lenora had agreed. Now, months later, Cal knew in his heart it was never going to work. It had been a duty call, his sense of responsibility stronger than his desire to reunite with the mother of his son. Eva, the au pair, spent far more time with Jake than Lenora did. Sally-Ann and Jake's half sisters provided his cuddles while Cal plowed on, determined to do his best this time, seeing as he had failed his wife so abysmally all those years ago.

When the subject of Thanksgiving had come up again, he'd proposed that his daughters come to stay and finally be introduced to Lenora. "Savannah in particular loves makeup and girly stuff, and they both *adore* Jake," he'd informed her, wishing she'd make some kind of effort.

Sally-Ann had agreed to his suggestion. It was high time the twins met his new partner, she'd concurred, especially now that Jake had become so important to them. Blended families had to work things out, she'd told their daughters, urging them to agree to meet Lenora for their dad's sake and Jake's. She was going to spend Thanksgiving in West Texas with her parents.

Lenora had proposed a catered meal but Cal had nixed that. He'd cook the turkey himself with all the trimmings.

While he prepared and stuffed the bird, she slept in until he called her to feed their son, seeing as Eva was celebrating the day with her family. "And if y'all could set the table, that would be cool." He tried to keep the sarcasm out of his tone. He was nervous. If Savannah got into one of her moods, things could go belly-up very quickly. He'd offered to collect the girls, but Sally-Ann had said she'd drop them off on her way to the airport. Did that mean that she was going to come up to the condo? Cal wondered uneasily. Thus far she and Lenora had had no contact, and to her credit Sally-Ann had kept her thoughts about Lenora's extended hiatus—or nervous breakdown, as Lenora preferred to call it—in New York to herself. And when he brought Jake to visit, they never discussed her.

He'd much rather be in the middle of a stampede out on the plains than face what he had to face in a couple of hours, Cal thought ruefully, shoving a fistful of stuffing up the turkey.

◆

"Now, girls, be on your best behavior when you meet Lenora. Remember, your dad and I weren't a couple before he met her, so don't go holdin' any grudges. She's little Jake's momma, respect that," Sally-Ann reminded her daughters when they climbed into the car for the fifteen-minute journey across town to Cal's condo.

"I wish I was flying to see Grandma and Grandpa with you," Madison said glumly, clicking her seat belt into place.

"Look, y'all are gonna have a great time with Jake and your dad. He's bringing you to see a movie at the iPic tomorrow—premium seats too. Now, that's cool! Enjoy it, and I'll pick y'all up in the evening when I fly back," Sally-Ann advised.

"If you snore, I'll throw a book at you," Savannah warned her twin.

"Do not—do y'all hear me? DO NOT—disgrace the family by fighting," Sally-Ann warned, feeling utterly fraught. She could understand her daughters' angst. Hell, she was anxious herself about having to finally meet this woman Cal was living with and sharing parenthood with. She was just going to drop in for five minutes, pass the time of day, and make her excuses to leave.

She'd taken extra care with her appearance. New jeans that hugged her booty in a most flattering way, a black cashmere turtleneck jumper, and a Ralph Lauren quilted gilet. Cool but classy. High-heel ankle boots and a hot pink Gucci tote finished off her ensemble. Her auburn mane was swept up in a loose topknot with tendrils curling around her face, which she'd made up with extra care, assisted by Savannah, who was now an expert at contouring.

"You look like a model, Mom," her daughter approved loyally, and Sally-Ann hugged her and told her everything would work out just fine. It would tear the hearts out of the twins to see their father with this other woman, but they all had to bite the bullet and get on with it.

Cal was waiting for them at the entrance to the impressive new building just off Shady River Road and he directed her to a guest parking spot.

"Hey, girls." He greeted his daughters with bear hugs when they got out of the car, but his eyes were wary when he met Sally-Ann's. "I appreciate this," he said gruffly.

"It's cool," she said calmly, determined that he wouldn't know how rattled she was. There was an awkward silence in the elevator as it whooshed up to the tenth floor. "I can smell the turkey from here." Sally-Ann smiled when they exited to a tiled marble foyer where a striking young woman with a slender figure, flowing brown tresses, and huge, heavily made-up brown eyes in a heart-shaped face was standing waiting to greet them. She wore a figure-hugging red dress and skyscraper black Louboutins.

She's gorgeous looking, and so young! Sally-Ann felt like a crone as Lenora held out a delicate hand and gave her a limp handshake. "Hi, Sally-Ann," she said politely but not overly friendly.

"Nice to meet you, Lenora. Y'all have a beautiful little boy," Sally-Ann said graciously, taking the lead.

"Oh! Oh, thank you." The younger woman glanced over at Cal, who said proudly, "And these are my . . . er . . . our . . . daughters, Savannah and Madison. Girls, this is Lenora."

"Hi," said Madison awkwardly while Savannah muttered a "Hello."

"Come in, come in," Cal said expansively, ushering them into the bright glass-and-marble lounge, which seemed to rest on a canopy of trees below them.

"Nice view of the country club," Sally-Ann enthused, thinking how modern and minimalist the condo was, but not at all homely.

"*We* love it," Lenora said brightly, sliding her arm into Cal's as though signaling ownership. "It's beautiful to watch the sunset over drinks. It's our favorite thing."

"I'm sure." Sally-Ann smiled sweetly, enjoying Cal's discomfiture as he stood trapped beside Lenora.

"Where's Jake?" Madison asked eagerly.

"Having his nap, unfortunately," Cal replied, relieved at the change of subject. "Can I get y'all something to drink? Iced tea, coffee? Sally-Ann?" He moved away from Lenora, and beckoned to the girls to follow him into the kitchen.

"Not for me, Cal, thanks. I've a plane to catch; I'll pick up the girls tomorrow evening on the way back from the airport. Nice meeting you, Lenora. Happy Thanksgiving, y'all," she said, smoothly edging for the door.

"You too," the younger woman returned civilly if not over enthusiastically.

"Have fun, girls." Sally-Ann's heart went out to her daughters, who looked miserable and ill at ease. "See y'all tomorrow."

"Bye, Mom." Savannah threw her arms around her. "I love you."

"Me too," echoed Madison, hugging her tightly when Savannah let go.

"Give Jake a big kiss for me," she said softly, knowing if she didn't get away soon she'd burst into tears in front of them. "Bye, Cal."

She hurried into the lift and managed to keep her composure until the door of her car was safely closed behind her, when the floodgates opened. Sally-Ann cried all the way to the airport.

◆

"They don't like me, Cal," Lenora complained after she had shown the girls to their room and they were unpacking their overnight bag.

"Give them a chance; they're here less than thirty minutes. It's their first time to meet you. It's hard for them not having their mom around for Thanksgiving. It's a big deal for them. Put yourself in their shoes," Cal urged.

It was a stressful day, as Lenora and his daughters had struggled to find common ground. He knew the girls had tried hard to be polite. They were frankly astonished that Lenora took no part in the cooking process. Savannah had taken over the gravy making, while Madison had mashed and creamed the potatoes and he creamed the corn. He couldn't help but wish that he were in his old kitchen, with Sally-Ann directing operations, cooking Thanksgiving dinner together.

Lenora had stayed out of the kitchen, and sprawled on the sofa watching an old Bette Davis movie until Cal carried the bird to the table. She picked at the food, causing Savannah to comment with a saccharine smile, "That's why you're so *thin*, Lenora. I read that Victoria Beckham only eats steamed greens, and you're even thinner than *her*!"

"Yup, Mom calls those people 'clothes hangers,'" Madison supplied innocently, not realizing that her sister was being bitchy.

"Really?" Lenora retorted. "I think I'd prefer to be a clothes hanger than a fat hog." She glared at Savannah, who was shoveling creamed corn down her gob.

"Lenora!" Cal hissed.

"What?" she snapped. "I'm only telling your daughter what I think after she started making personal comments."

"At least I ain't a ho bag," Savannah muttered.

"Savannah, leave the table!" roared Cal, at the end of his tether, whereupon his two daughters burst into tears and vanished into their room.

It was that sort of day.

Chapter Thirty-Two

FEBRUARY 2009

Cal / Lenora

Cal was longing to see Jake. He'd been on a business trip to Miami for three days and by a stroke of good fortune had managed to get an earlier flight home than he'd planned, out of MIA. He hoped his little buddy hadn't gone for his walk with Eva, the au pair, who loved to power walk past the sumptuous mansions close to the country club, pushing Jake's buggy at a smart lick. He yawned as the elevator sped up to his floor. He wouldn't mind a nap himself.

The condo was empty. Lenora could be using the gym or taking a spinning class as she generally did in the mornings. He was about to make himself a coffee when a sound caught his attention, a woman laughing. Lenora must be on the phone in bed, he thought, rooting in his luggage for the elegant Fendi clutch he'd bought for her in the Design Center.

"Hi, babes, hope ya—" He stopped short at the sight that met his eyes. Lenora, naked, legs wrapped around a blond muscular young man as he carried her to the bed.

"Cal!" she shrieked, scrambling to cover herself up as the beef-cake dropped her onto the bed in dismay.

"Excuse me, I didn't know you were otherwise engaged," he said coldly. "Get dressed, sonny, and get outta here pronto. Lenora, we're done. Start packing."

Cal strode out of the bedroom back to the lounge. He had given it his best shot with the mother of his son. It was over. He was strangely unmoved at her betrayal. Lenora had made it easy for him to move on.

◆

Lenora finished arranging her dresses in the poky wardrobe of the egg box apartment Cal had rented for her in Jersey Village just north of downtown. The bedroom was tiny compared to the lavish boudoir she'd shared with Cal. She wouldn't be there for long, she thought confidently. Her lover, Boyd Garland, was loaded. Young-est son of a Texas oil baron, she'd met him at the Drake, a high-end lounge she often frequented with her girlfriends when Cal was out of town. Boyd had taken her to Next, one of the most exclusive clubs in the city. He'd bought her champagne, offered her coke, and treated her like royalty. She'd let him woo her for a month before they'd had a night of wild passion in his Piney Point Village mansion.

Cal Cooper was a pauper compared to Boyd Garland, and Boyd was single and mad about her. And best of all, she wouldn't have to endure those two little bitches, Savannah and Madison, any longer. Win-win, she thought smugly, daydreaming about scorching up to Cal's to visit Jake in a sexy new Porsche.

Because he'd caught her high on the hit of coke she and her lover had taken, he'd accused her of being an unfit mother and had warned her that her visits to their son would be supervised. That would change when she had the wealth of the Garlands behind her, Lenora vowed, her heart lifting when she saw Boyd's text to say he'd see her the following day if she was free.

Damn right she was free, in more ways than one, thought Le-nora gaily, her fingers flying over the screen.

Chapter Thirty-Three

Austen / Anna

"What a treat to have dinner with you, Dad." Tara sipped a glass of red and tucked into her crispy pork belly main. Chloe took a mouthful of her fish and nodded in agreement.

"My first decent lunch out since having the baby, I can't *believe* it! OMG, Tara, you should have warned me it would be this full on," the younger woman moaned, taking a welcome glug of white wine.

"I thought it would be nice to have time with my girls," Austen said easily, wondering if they would be so appreciative when his daughters heard what he had to say.

Anna was having an overnighter in a spa with Mary and Yvonne, a combined Christmas gift from Austen and her daughters, and he'd taken the opportunity to invite his girls to dinner at Picasso, in Clontarf.

"You still have a great tan, Dad. I believe it's very dodgy over there at the moment. A friend of mine is out in Marbella for her hen party and they're getting *drenched*," Chloe said.

"I didn't think any new bride would be able to afford a hen party abroad anymore," Austen remarked.

"Her mother gave her the money as a Christmas present. I'd love to have gone. If I hadn't been doing the odd commission at work, I'd have tried to swing it," Chloe said nonchalantly.

"And who would you have got to mind the baby? Will was telling me how hard it is for him to take leave now."

"Oh, I'm sure Mum wouldn't have minded. She'd have been glad for me to have a little break for myself after having a baby, and she *adores* Charlotte." Chloe was completely oblivious to her father's incredulity.

"But, Chloe, your mother's got to start taking things *easy*! She's had two gall bladder attacks since that first one, and stress brings them on. She's not as young as she used to be. Neither of us are. I want to give you both a bit of notice that I'm bringing her to Spain for four weeks, in April and May. I want to take her to Seville for a few days during orange blossom season. It's our anniversary and I want to surprise her. And in the autumn we want to go to Barcelona. I want us to spend time together just enjoying our retirement. She didn't come over after Christmas, and"—he paused and took a sip of beer—"you know that when we decided to buy an apartment in Spain, I envisaged that we would spend a large part of the winter months out there. That's not really happening at the moment."

He didn't say "because we have to mind our grandchildren"—he couldn't be that blunt—but he was determined that he and Anna were spending a chunk of time together this year no matter who was discommoded. "So you've got almost three months to make arrangements to get someone else to step in to mind the children. Plenty of time to get organized." He smiled at them, ignoring the looks of dismay that crossed both their faces.

"It's not that easy," Chloe groaned. "Will's mother is adamant that she's not doing baby minding. You know that. They have a mobile home in Brittas and they spend a lot of time down there."

"Is that so? Very nice for them," Austen said drily. Chloe's sulky face shaded a dull red.

"Why don't you use the money you'd have spent on the hen party to pay someone to mind Charlotte?" he suggested, knowing he was being somewhat churlish, but anxious that his daughter would start copping on and thinking of her mother for a change. Anna was taken far too much for granted and she was too soft to do anything about it. That was why he was stepping in.

"You've got to be careful who you get to mind your baby." Chloe pushed her plate away.

"I agree; that's why you have plenty of time to find someone by mid-April, and sure look, if you like them, perhaps they could take over permanently," Austen said cheerily. "What about you, Tara?" he asked, eyeing his elder daughter quizzically.

"I'll sort something, Dad," she said quietly. "Don't worry about it," and he did feel a tad guilty. Tara, he knew, appreciated more than her sister did all the child care Anna and he provided.

"Now, then, drink up and eat up," he urged, but he could see that his unexpected ultimatum had taken the edge off their appetites.

Austen sighed, spearing a crispy roast parsnip; this bloody recession had turned everyone's life upside down. Just his luck it coincided with his and Anna's retirement. As far as he could see, his kids were more dependent on them than ever.

◆

"I hope you didn't make them feel bad or that they were a nuisance, Austen." Anna tried to keep the exasperation out of her voice when her husband informed her of his lunchtime discussion with their daughters. Austen could be like a bull in a china shop sometimes, she agonized, wishing he'd kept his mouth shut. Tara in particular would feel the sting of his words. Chloe would, as always, think of herself.

"I didn't," he said crossly, thumping his pillow into shape. They had just got into bed and she was totally relaxed after her pampering sessions. Now there was the beginning of an atmosphere and he was getting huffy. Typical.

"No need to get ratty," she retorted irritably.

"*I'm* not getting ratty, *you're* the one who's getting ratty," he accused, his face sullen as he glared at her. "I simply explained that I wanted us to spend time together. What's so awful about that, Anna?" Austen demanded.

"Nothing," she sighed. "It's just not as easy as it used to be—"

"That's because you won't put your foot down. You let Chloe walk all over you," he exploded.

"Austen, I *don't*," she exclaimed indignantly, stung by his accusation.

"You do. You let her get away with murder. She's a grown woman, a mother. It's time she learned to stand on her own two feet. You need to start looking after yourself more."

"Look, when Tara had her baby, I . . . *we*," she corrected herself, "were there for her. I have to do the same for Chloe. Be fair. And it's hard going back to work and having to be separated from your baby, mister. Fathers don't *quite* get that," she added tartly.

"I've done my best for them. I've mucked in too," he snapped. "But I'm not going to mollycoddle them like you are and make myself ill from stress."

"Oh, fuck off, Austen, and don't be so dramatic," Anna snapped, switching off her bedside lamp and turning on her side away from him.

She lay fuming in the bed beside him, listening to him settle to read on his Kindle. The cheek of him, saying that she was mollycoddling the girls. She was helping them out like any mother would. Why did he not understand that she couldn't just *abandon* them?

As the recession had worsened, and the banks had been on the brink of collapse, she and Austen had discovered in horror that a large chunk of their savings had vanished into thin air when their bank shares had plummeted.

In the months following those dark days Austen had withdrawn into himself and become angry and bitter. "I worked hard for that bloody money; I didn't squander it and gamble it away like that fucker Sean Quinn. Do you know, Anna, he spent one hundred thousand euros on a cake that was flown over from New York for his daughter's wedding? That's two hundred and fifty euros a slice! And now we're paying for it and the millions he gambled to buy Anglo shares for which he gave his *personal* guarantee, which of course, he now maintains, doesn't apply to him the way a personal guarantee would apply to the rest of us gobshites who lie down and let those banking bastards walk all over us. And we'll be paying for the collapse of that bastard's insurance company on our car insurance for years to come. You mark my words. And he thinks it's OK to say he took a gamble that didn't pay off and that's it, we should feel *sorry* for him!"

His constant ranting and raving about it was doing her head in.

"Look, there's no point in being angry all the time; it's only affecting your health. Let it go, Austen!" she urged. "There's hundreds of thousands of us in the same boat and it's all relative anyway. There's billions of people would love our first-world problems," she'd said, trying to shut him up one day when, after watching the news, he'd started off on another tirade.

"Let it go, just like *that*?" He'd looked at her as if she were mad and shook his head. "How can you say that? Doesn't it bother you in the slightest? The corruption, the lying, the brazen disregard for law and order."

"Of course it does, Austen," she retorted, "but I'm not going to have that energy swirling around my brain, taking all the good out of life. It's happened—it's happening all over the world. A spotlight is being shone on all this darkness, and hopefully lessons will be learned and right-thinking people will come to prominence to lead us out of the mess we're in—"

"And if you believe that, you'll believe anything," he jeered.

"I lost money *too*. My business has been hit hard. Lots of our customers can't afford to have cleaning services now, so *my* income is dwindling, but I'm not going around whinging and moaning and wringing my hands, because we're very lucky we have a roof over our heads and food on the table, unlike millions of others!" she'd shouted, and he'd looked at her shocked, because Anna rarely shouted at him.

"You're right, sorry," he'd apologized brusquely, and she'd burst into tears and walked out to the garden to compose herself.

It had been a turning point of sorts. Her husband had been less vocal—in front of her, at any rate, with his rants at the TV when the news was on. He didn't mention their financial losses as often—but she knew it niggled away at him and understood on one level why. The hunter had lost what he'd gathered. The wiping out of their nest egg had emasculated Austen, who had always prided himself on his ability to support his family in a style to which they had never aspired in those early days of marriage, when they were living from payday to payday.

Anna understood more than he thought, but there was no point in living a life filled with resentment, anger, and regret. They could adapt and give thanks for all the assets they still had.

She understood too that it was only in Spain that Austen could put aside his bitterness. There was something about the easy, somnolent days in La Joya that induced a sense of well-being and distance from real life in Ireland. If her husband had his way, he would spend six months of the year out there.

She drifted off to sleep and woke around dawn to see the light lick along the top of the gold brocade curtains in their bedroom. She felt Austen move beside her and knew he was lying in his favorite position with his hand behind his head, staring up at the ceiling, ruminating on the day ahead.

"Morning," she murmured, offering the olive branch.

"Morning," he returned, but at least he sounded calm and approachable.

"Austen, please let's not fight." She turned over towards him and put her arm across him.

"I don't want to be fighting, Anna," he said, looking down at her. "But I have a point of view too and you're very dismissive of it."

"What?" She wasn't sure she'd heard him right.

"You're very dismissive of my viewpoint," he reiterated firmly.

"Well, I don't mean to be," she said slowly, shocked at what he'd just verbalized. "How? Just tell me," she invited, inwardly tensing at what might be coming.

"I . . . eh . . . well, the thing is, I always feel that you put the girls and their needs first and not mine. You take their side always—"

"Austen, I don't," she protested.

"You do it subconsciously. But you do, Anna. Constantly. Chloe's wedding, for instance. I had very little say about what *I* wanted, even though I was whacking a hell of a lot of money out on it," he pointed out, and she sensed a deep running anger, still, even though the wedding seemed so long ago and she'd forgotten about it. "You took her side in everything, and although we did manage to persuade her to bring the cost down, it was mostly her way or the highway no matter what I felt.

"This January I really wanted you to come out to La Joya and you wouldn't because of the babies. The same as last year. You tell me to go out on my own or go with my golfing buddies. That's not what I want. Say it was the other way around and I was constantly telling *you* to go out on your own or with the girls, how would you feel?" He looked intently at her, and in the brightening light of dawn she could see a hard, unfriendly glint in his eye that chilled her.

"Well?" he probed.

"I suppose . . . I suppose I'd feel . . . rejected," she admitted.

"Exactly, rejected, of no consequence, taken for granted, second fiddle, take your pick," he said, grim faced.

"I'm truly, truly sorry, Austen. I never meant to make you feel like that, I *promise* you," she said earnestly, horrified by his accusations.

"I know you don't mean it, but that's how I've felt in the last few years if you want to know the truth," he said flatly.

"But why didn't you *say* it to me?" She sat up and stared at him. "Why haven't you brought this up before now? Why have you kept it to yourself? That's not fair, Austen. You *always* do that. You won't tell me when things are bothering you, or talk to me about your feelings and emotional needs—"

"You do enough of that for the two of us," he quipped snarkily.

"Don't be mean," she said, hurt. "That was uncalled-for."

"Sorry," he apologized.

"How do you think I feel now, knowing this is how you've been feeling for ages?"

"This isn't about you, Anna," he sighed.

"It *is*, Austen! It bloody well is. It's about me in so far as it affects our relationship. It's about my failings as a *wife*. *Your* wife." She burst into tears, overwhelmed by his wounding accusations.

Austen's demeanor changed instantly.

"Anna, Anna, don't cry. I'm sorry I made you cry. I was harsh in what I said; I'm so sorry," he apologized, drawing her into his arms.

"But you said what you felt," she sobbed. "And you were right to say it, Austen. It's *I* who should apologize. I never meant to make you feel second best, *ever*. You're the most important person in my life." She gulped, her hair tousled, her face tear-streaked. "I love you with all my heart, Austen, I always have. Please, I beg you in future, tell me if . . . if you feel I'm neglecting you—"

"Aw, you don't neglect me," he groaned. "You're a great wife. I should have kept my big mouth shut."

"No, that's what's got us into a situation like this. Keeping your big mouth shut. You need to talk to me about stuff like this."

"I know. I'm sorry. I will in future," he promised.

"Ah, yeah, promises, promises," Anna replied, knowing that getting her husband to talk about his emotions was harder than pulling teeth.

"Do you know why I want you to come to Spain so badly in April?" He leaned on his elbow and studied her, running his finger gently along her cheek to wipe away her tears.

"Why?" she asked shakily.

"I want to bring you to Seville for our wedding anniversary."

"No!" she exclaimed, subdued, afraid she was going to cry again. "Really?"

"Really," he echoed. "And do you know why?"

Anna shook her head.

"Because I know you've always loved orange blossom. It was one of the first things I remember about you. We went for a walk in the Botanics when we were getting to know each other, and we walked past the orange blossoms and you stopped and inhaled the scent for ages, and you told me it was your favorite flower and I grabbed you and kissed you—"

"Oh, yes, I remember that," Anna exclaimed, absurdly pleased that he would remember that little romantic interlude. "How happy we were," she added, rubbing his arm and nuzzling in against his shoulder as the lump in her throat lessened and the pain of his wounding words eased.

"And then you carried orange blossoms in your wedding bouquet, and wore that spray at the side of your hair to hold your veil in place, and I wanted to bring you to Seville for orange blossom season because it's our wedding anniversary and we were very, very happy the day we were married, and in spite of what you might think, I *can* do the odd romantic thing," he said; and the old twinkle that she loved was back in his eyes and then they were kissing, and murmuring endearments, melting into each other's familiar nooks and crannies to make love with a passion they hadn't had lately.

Afterwards, when he'd gone down to make their tea and toast to bring back to bed, Anna lay snuggled against the pillows listening to the sound of distant traffic on the early morning commute and school run, thinking she could be lying in their bed in Spain, with the balcony doors open, listening to birdsong and the sound of the sea, and watching the morning sun rise in the eastern sky, across the Mediterranean.

She wished her husband understood that her longing to be there was as strong as his, but her bonds as a mother held her back from putting herself first. And, it seemed, from putting him first too.

She'd heard it said: If you can't love yourself, you can't love another. Just how did you get to the point of doing exactly what *you* wanted to do to nurture yourself, even if it meant discommoding others? she wondered.

And to do it *without* feeling guilty.

If she could learn that life lesson, she'd be on that plane to Málaga so fast, it would take her husband's breath away. Anna sighed, listening to Austen whistling in the kitchen while he made the tea.

Chapter Thirty-Four

APRIL

Anna / Austen

"I'm so glad we decided to come by train, Austen," Anna said, smiling at her husband as they wheeled their overnight travel cases through the plate-glass doors of the imposing entrance to María Zambrano train station. They were taking the nine fifteen AVE to Seville and had left themselves enough time to have breakfast in one of the restaurants on the sun-dappled concourse.

"It's a great idea. Well done for thinking of it. You're right, we'd have spent as much on petrol and parking as we would have on the tickets, and I believe Seville is a nightmare to drive in because the streets are so narrow. So ten out of ten, wife." Austen, looking tanned and healthy in his pale blue Lacoste short-sleeved shirt and cream chinos, flashed her a broad grin as he strode along beside her, hungry for his breakfast.

An hour later, relaxed and replete after their scrambled eggs and bacon, they laid their luggage on the security belt at the gate beside the sleek white dolphin-nosed train that would bring them to their destination.

"Impressive looking, isn't it?" Austen admired the AVE's flowing lines, gleaming where the sun shone on the white carriages embossed with the smart purple strip that emphasized its aerodynamic contours—hardly noticing the lithe blonde in the skimpy shorts and low-cut halter neck who had boarded just ahead of them, Anna thought in amusement.

She was excited, looking forward to the journey inland across the Spanish plains. "One thing about Renfe, they leave on the dot," Austen observed a couple of minutes later when the train began to glide out of the station, and a young couple who had reached the gate too late stood forlornly watching it leave the station. It snaked towards the Sierras, gathering speed as it whizzed past the airport and left the suburbs of Málaga behind it.

The passage through the tunnels and carved gorges of the jagged-edged mountains was breathtaking, and they sat entranced as each bend brought some new vista to be admired. The landscape changed as they left the coast and mountains behind them, opening out onto wide, fertile acres of vines spread on either side of the tracks. The sky, blue and white like speckled Delft pottery, seemed never-ending.

"You can see where the recession has hit the small towns, can't you?" Austen remarked as they raced past a station, weeds and brushwood growing unkempt and unchecked. An old redbrick factory building of intricately designed brickwork fallen into disrepair; houses boarded up and abandoned. It reminded Anna of something out of a spaghetti western.

An hour and eighteen minutes from when they left Málaga, precisely as advertised, the train slid smoothly into Córdoba Central.

"We should do a day trip here sometime. It has so much history, especially Roman history, which I love," Anna mused. "The two Senecas, the Younger and the Elder, came from here."

"I never knew that." Austen stretched his legs, hoping that no one would sit opposite them as passengers embarked while others disembarked onto the tiled platform. "When did the Moors come?" he inquired, glad that his wife always did her research before visiting anywhere. He hated sitting at computers.

"In 711 AD. But they were enlightened rulers and shared the Basilica of St. Vincent for their religious services until they erected a mosque, seemingly. It would be nice to see that sort of thing happening in today's strife-riven world."

"This is what I wanted for us, Anna." Austen reached over the table and took her hand. "To be able to go and meander around and soak up the history and the atmosphere of these spectacular cities and make the most of these years when we are fit and able and still fairly *compos mentis*."

"*Compos mentis*—speak for yourself," she laughed. "My marbles are gone with the wind. Three times this morning I put my glasses down and couldn't find them. And once they were on my head!"

"Well, *reasonably*, then," he teased as the train began to move backwards and changed tracks to loop back southeast to Seville.

They cruised into Santa Justa station, with its wide, modern concourse and impressive selection of shops, but it was the Plaza de Armas, the original station, its Neo-Mudéjar yellow-brick building, with the typical horseshoe arches and arabesque tiling outside, that had Anna snapping away with her camera, marveling at the magnificence of the clock tower.

"So you're liking your wedding anniversary present, then," Austen said smugly and she laughed, holding his hand in the taxi during the short trip to the hotel he'd chosen for them.

"Oh, it's *lovely*!" Anna exclaimed in delight when the taxi drove through the old Jewish quarter, with its narrow winding streets and pastel-painted buildings, to the elegant, yellow-bricked façade of their hotel, a pale vision in the light of the mid-morning sun. White-painted French windows opened onto ornate wrought-iron balconies. An elegant mansion with a slightly French ambiance, oozing character, the Petite Palace was a delightful choice for their few days in Seville.

The interior, all cool grays and marble arches, with a magnificent atrium, gave respite from the intensity of the midday heat. They checked in and were delighted with their cool, contemporary-designed room, the white muslin curtains fluttering in the welcome breeze when they opened the French doors.

"This hydromassage shower has so many controls, it looks like something from the bridge of the *Enterprise*," Austen informed her as he explored the bathroom, while Anna unpacked her case and hung up her clothes.

"Did I choose well?" He came back into the bedroom and put his arms around her. Austen had taken the advice of one of his golfing pals and chosen the hotel because it was within walking distance of the old town, where he knew Anna wanted to explore.

"We have to go to the Giralda. The Almohad minaret is one of only *three* left in the world," she'd informed him as she'd sat researching places of interest to visit on their trip. They'd view the magnificent cathedral, of course, but the place she was most longing to visit, the Royal Alcázar Palace and its stunning gardens, would be the highlight of their visit, she'd assured him.

"You did *great*. I *love* it. This is the best wedding anniversary present *ever*!"

"Here's something else you might need, with all that sun on your face." He opened his case and rooted under his shirts to hand her a gift box. "Tara wrapped it for me," he added, enjoying the look of surprise that brought a glow to her eyes.

"I was wondering. It's very posh with the ribbons and bows," she laughed, tearing off the paper to find a box with a selection of her favorite face creams and body lotions. "*Green Angel!* Oh, you're the best." She threw her arms around him, thrilled at his thoughtfulness. "The seaweed and collagen creams are *so* rich, and the body treatments are so pampery, I *love* what they do to my skin."

"Me too," he smiled, drawing her even closer.

"Do you like the camera I bought you?" She'd bought him a Leica X Vario. Conor, who shared his father's interest in photography, had given her advice on which one to choose. Anna was delighted to buy it for her beloved husband, wanting him to have a really good camera that she knew he wouldn't buy for himself.

"I love it almost as much as you," he teased, but he was chuffed with it and had protested that she'd spent far too much money on him when she'd given it to him at the start of their holiday.

Anna nestled in against him as his arms tightened around her and he lowered his mouth to hers in a long, slow, tender kiss that left her in no doubt that, despite their ups and downs, he loved her as much as he always had, and she loved him.

When she looked back on their trip to Seville, it was as though they'd been cocooned in a bubble where the trials and tribulations of real life didn't exist and they forgot about their family commitments, recessions, and financial losses.

A second honeymoon, Austen had called it, and, during the afternoon siestas—when the city shut down and people disappeared off the cobbled streets and a somnolent silence descended—in the cool of their shaded hotel room, they had made love, and laughed and teased each other like the young lovers they had once been, before snoozing until late afternoon, when it was as though a switch was flicked and the hum of chat and laughter and the clack-clack of heels on stone brought the city back to life again.

They had explored the splendor of the Royal Alcázar Palace, walking hand in hand through the glory of the verdant gardens with the sound of tinkling water flowing over marble fountains, and the heady scents of orange blossom, jasmine, and bougainvillea a backdrop to the awe-inspiring, intricate Moorish architecture. Austen had snapped away with his new camera, and his photographs of the Courtyard of the Maidens were as good as any professional would take, she'd told him proudly. Almost by accident, when they had sat down to take a breather on the steps near the Pool of Mercury, she'd noticed a recessed doorway. "Look at this, Austen," she exclaimed, leading him into a stunning, almost surreal arched chamber filled with golden light reflected in a long rectangular pool of water beneath the Gothic palace. "The Baths of Lady Maria Padilla," she read as her husband framed his view and photographed away to his heart's content.

"I think you should build me a bathing place like that," Anna giggled later at lunch, when she sipped from a glass of ice-cold bubbly prosecco and tucked into a feast of fat, juicy prawns.

"I'll excavate the garden for you, no problem. Conor can give me a hand with the arches," Austen said, offering her a taste of his scallops. "I got some great photographs today. It's a brilliant camera. I couldn't have asked for a better present from you."

"I'm glad," she said, reaching across the table to squeeze his hand. "You're always at the forefront of my mind, even if you don't think so sometimes."

"I know. I was having a male menopause moment when we had our row." He squeezed back.

"No, we need to let each other know how we feel. That row cleared the air, and look at us now, having the time of our life, and with so much to look forward to. We're doing OK, Austen," she smiled.

"Indeed we are."

That night they wandered around to the big square a couple of streets away and sat, having their evening meal, in one of the many tapas bars and restaurants that surrounded it. They drank in the atmosphere, loving the way families of all ages, from children to elderly grandparents, gathered to eat and enjoy each other's company as a peachy-pink dusk gave way to black velvet skies sprinkled with a handful of golden stars. The scent of the orange blossoms was intoxicating, and Anna wished she could bottle it and bring it with her to remind her of a time of bliss when she'd left all her responsibilities and worries behind her.

In the mornings, knowing that he hated shopping, Anna

would leave Austen nursing a coffee and reading a paper to shop in the myriad gift shops that lined the narrow streets leading to the square. One beautiful Aladdin's cave sold exquisite handmade jewelry at very reasonable prices, and she bought two stunning necklaces for her daughters and sneaked in a phone call to each of them, anxious to reassure herself that all was well with them and the children.

She'd promised Austen she would turn off her mobile and just phone home every third day. She envied him that he could shut off from the family so easily when he was away. She'd been so consumed with guilt at leaving them for an entire month, she'd given each of her daughters a couple of hundred euros to go towards their child-minding costs while she wasn't there to take up the slack.

Tara always put on a cheerful façade when she phoned, but Chloe would never lose an opportunity to have a moan and then say something like "Lucky you, gadding around Spain, in the sun." If Austen had heard her saying that, he would have lost it, and rightly so, Anna conceded, annoyed at her youngest daughter's emotional blackmail when she'd hung up after *that* particular phone call.

She put the thoughts of home out of her head and made her way back along Calle de Federico Rubio, which ran along the side of their hotel, enjoying the shade provided by the tall buildings on the narrow street before nipping into the Petite Palace to stow her shopping and refresh her hair and makeup. Austen, when she joined him at his favorite café across the road, ordered another coffee for himself and a cappuccino for her and announced that he'd booked a horse-drawn carriage to take them along the heady scented streets lined with orange blossom trees laden with their colorful bounty. The older he got, the more romantic he became, Anna thought happily, secretly delighted at this new treat.

On the last evening of their anniversary jaunt, they had gone to a flamenco night, and the wild Gypsy music and tapping of the castanets, and the passion of the dancers as they taunted and teased and challenged each other, had made her horny and she'd kissed Austen hungrily in the shadows of a narrow alley and whispered, "Let's go back to the hotel and ravish each other."

"And what age are you, now?" he teased, but he was as turned on as she was, and they'd hailed a taxi and snogged like teenagers in the backseat before finally falling onto the bed in a tangle of arms and legs and half-removed clothes to ride each other with a passion that left them breathless and laughing.

The memory of this night was a gift she would return to, she thought, smiling, lying sated and drowsy in his arms.

"What are you smiling at?" he asked.

"I'm just thinking this will be a night to remember when I have to use a walker and can't get my leg over you anymore," she grinned.

"Well, judging by tonight's performance, that's a long way away," Austen laughed, caressing her cheek with his forefinger. "Did you enjoy your wedding anniversary trip?"

"I did; it was the best ever. Did *you* enjoy it?"

"It was all I ever wanted," he murmured against her hair. "Next year we'll go to Cádiz."

"It's a date," Anna agreed, kissing him again, deliciously lethargic and ready for sleep.

Chapter Thirty-Five

JULY

Austen / Anna

Seville and their holiday in La Joya was like a dream, Austen mused glumly, washing up after his grandson's lunch of banana and Nutella sandwiches, and his granddaughter's mashed baby biscuits and pear.

The amount of work—the cleaning, tidying, and changing of clothes engendered by his charges—had initially astonished him when he'd started minding the children first. Now he was used to it. He hefted a load of soiled clothes and a detergent tab into the washing machine and turned it on. Anna was covering annual leave in her office and he was babysitting. She had to go back to work more often, since the company had had to let one of the office staff go. The recession had mucked up his wife's retirement plans too. Nothing was working out as they'd planned in those heady days when they'd driven through the gates of La Joya with nary a care in the world.

The sun was splitting the trees outside, and he'd decided to bring his grandchildren to the playground in the park, to see if he could exhaust them.

Getting them into their car seats and bringing their drinks and buggy would be another palaver. How he wished he was on the golf course in San Antonio del Mar, feeling the breeze feather his forehead as he sent his golf ball slicing crisply through the warm scented air to the verdant green in the far distance, with the sea glittering in the background.

Instead he was trapped in unwelcome domesticity, wondering if this was the way it would be for the school-going years: sitting in traffic jams day in day out, collecting his children's offspring from their various crèches and schools.

"Thank you, Granddad." Michael took a final draft of his milk and handed him the red baby cup to wash.

"Did you enjoy that?" he asked, loving the way the little boy, with his wide, hazel-flecked eyes, patted his hand affectionately.

"Yes, thank you." Michael wiped his mouth with his sleeve. "You make great samiches. Better than Gran," he said matter-of-factly.

"Do I?" Austen chuckled. Wait until he told Anna *that*.

"Yep, you put much more Nutella in them." Michael scooted off his chair and went to examine the washing machine, which fascinated him.

"Ahh, is that it?" Austen said, deciding perhaps he wouldn't tell his wife about his sandwich-making triumph for fear of getting a telling off about his over-generosity with the chocolaty treat.

"Go and get your coat," he instructed, wiping the egg off Charlotte's chin and wondering how she'd managed to get it in her hair. She wriggled against his ministrations, waving him away. "No, no," she protested.

"Give Granddad a kiss, you messy girl," Austen instructed, and his heart melted when her two little fat arms came around his neck and he was tightly hugged. How perfect it would be, if the time spent with his grandchildren were of his choosing, he thought guiltily. Was he abnormal for seeing his child-minding duties as an imposition and a chore?

He'd often heard Anna and her three comrades in arms bemoaning the lack of "me" time, and dismissed it—somewhat derisively, it must be said—as "women's talk." But now he was actually beginning to get it, he reflected with wry amusement, imagining what his wife and her friends would say if he suddenly announced he wanted "me" time.

Unlike Anna, he hadn't been worried about retiring. He hadn't wondered how he would fill his days. He didn't miss the cut and thrust of business in the slightest. That chapter was firmly ended and he'd moved on to the next without ever looking back. It felt like his mind and body had given a great sigh of relief that they didn't have to reach that intense point of drive and focus that had fired them for all those years.

Often now, though, it was his daughters and their children who made plans for him, and his "me" time was edging away from him before he'd had time to get used to it. And that was where his resentment lay.

After the row before their anniversary trip, and following his chat with his daughters, he'd hoped the child-minding issues had been settled; but when they had come home from Spain in mid-May after their month away, it was as though guilt propelled his wife to take up the reins again and once more the old resentments crept in—and this time he felt he couldn't say anything, because Anna would get stressed and her gallstones would act up and he didn't want to be contributing to that. He worried about her—a lot—but she pooh-poohed his concerns, which annoyed *him*. And then there was the constant reminder of the savings they'd lost. He knew it was pointless to dwell on it, but it *gnawed* at him, always there to put him in bad form if he let it, and today he did want to rage and lash out and take a flight to Málaga and to hell with the lot of them, Austen thought ruefully, hoisting his granddaughter out of her chair to bring her to her changing mat to change her nappy.

Perhaps he was having another male menopause moment, he decided, wondering if there really was such a thing. Women could talk about this stuff so easily. Men would run a mile from it. But physically he was changing, he knew it, his muscle tone, his fitness, even though he worked on them. He was beginning to have aches in his knees. Was it because his testosterone levels were lower? He didn't have the same unassailable energy of his forties and early fifties. Even his golf swing wasn't as powerful, he thought, sighing, as he expertly fastened Charlotte's diaper and pulled her little trousers up over her plump, dimply thighs.

She smiled infectiously at him and Austen's heart melted, and his crankiness drifted away. "Ah, sure you're my best girl, aren't you, pet?" he said, nudging his head into her tummy the way she loved, and chuckling at her delighted gales of laughter.

First-world problems, he knew; he should be thankful for all he had. There were many who would like to be in his shoes. "Let's go to the park," he said, putting Spain, and the golf course, and the vision of a glass of beer under the orange blossoms at the table for two by the sea, to the far reaches of his mind.

Chapter Thirty-Six

AUGUST

Austen / Anna

"How are you feeling?" Austen asked, always his first question now when he was away from Anna.

"Ah, not a bother. I'm behaving myself, but I'm definitely having a drink or two when I have lunch with the girls."

"Go easy. You don't want another trip to the ER," he warned.

"I will." Anna made a face. "I'll run Tara and James to the airport. They're flying Ryanair, and at least it won't be at the crack of dawn." She wriggled out of her high heels, plopping her hot, tired feet onto the arm of the sofa where she was sprawled talking to Austen, who was sitting on the balcony in La Joya, enjoying a pre-dinner beer.

"Great stuff. Text me the flight number and I'll pick them up."

"Sure," she agreed. "Is it hot out there?"

"Roasting. You'd hate it."

"I know," she agreed. "It's hot enough here too today, and no breeze until about an hour ago. It's perfect now. Any news?"

"Wait until I give you a laugh," Austen said, and she wished he were home beside her, on the sofa, telling her the latest gossip. "You know the English chap who owns the penthouse in block three?"

"Yeah."

"Well, seemingly he and *El Presidente* had a big row."

"Really? About what?"

"The parrot—what else?" Austen laughed.

"Oh, that parrot is a hoot," chuckled Anna, who had grown quite fond of the cantankerous old bird, who used to squawk loudly and indignantly from his perch on his owner's balcony.

There had been some complaints about the noise, but Anna and Austen had just laughed when they heard the raucous cacophony echoing around the grounds.

"Anyway, De La Fuente stops your man down at the bar, and the bird is on his shoulder, and he says in his most authoritative voice, 'That parrot has to go.' And the other lad says, 'I'll get rid of my parrot when you get rid of that yappy little bitch of yours, and I'm talking about your dog, not your wife—'"

"*OMG!*" laughed Anna.

"And then the *parrot* told De La Fuente to 'fuck off, *hijo de puta*—'"

"The bird said, 'Fuck off, you son of a bitch'?"

"He certainly did. Our beloved *El Presidente* went purple in the face and looked as if he was going to have a heart attack. It was hilarious. Everyone was trying to pretend they hadn't heard, but they were all snorting into their drinks. I wish you'd been there."

"I wish I'd been there too, Austen. I'd have enjoyed that." She smiled. "But it won't be long until October—"

"*October?*" Austen's voice rose an octave. "What about September?"

"Michael's starting play school, don't forget. He might have to be dropped off some mornings if Tara is on the early shift," Anna said lightly, and heard her husband's sharp intake of breath.

"I thought they were getting another au pair," he said sharply.

"They are, Austen; she's just coming later than planned. Now, don't get in a bad humor about it, and don't harass them about it when they come over—"

"I'm not going to harass anybody," he snapped. "And stop telling me what to do and what not to do as if I were a seven-year-old."

"Right, back at ya! Good night," she retorted, and hung up.

Anna glared at the phone and marched irately into the kitchen. There they were, bickering again, and always about the same thing, minding the grandchildren. The contentment of their romantic anniversary getaway seemed like a dream.

Anna opened the fridge and poured herself a glass of chilled chardonnay. To hell with her dodgy gall bladder. If he could sit on the balcony guzzling beer, she could sit on the deck and knock back at least one glass of vino, she thought crossly, shaking a few green olives out of a jar into a dish and adding a few slices of chorizo, Serrano ham, and a slice of melon. "I can have my own tapas evening, matey, without having to listen to you grousing," she muttered, walking through the open French doors to sit at her patio table.

In the distance she could hear the church bell ringing for six o'clock, but the sun was still high in the sky and she raised her face to its munificent rays, far less harsh and intense than the Spanish sun.

She'd holidayed in La Joya in August the first year they'd bought the apartment, and that had been enough for her. She'd spent most of her days inside in the air-conditioning, seeking respite from the oppressive, sweltering heat, emerging only in the evening when the sun was slipping away to the west, and sitting in a shaded spot on the balcony, still baked in 95 degrees. Austen tolerated heat far better than she did, and he'd flown over for the two weeks in August that she was working, to attend the AGM and to play some golf. Tara and James were flying out for a couple of days and she would be minding her grandson for one night.

Anna took a sip of her wine and closed her eyes, trying to regain her earlier equilibrium. The birds were chirruping in the apple trees and a bee droned lazily in the cushiony pink blooms of the hydrangeas. The aromatic scents of her herb garden— mint, rosemary, thyme, sage, marjoram, dill, and fennel—wafted around on the light breeze, and she tried to concentrate on the sights, sounds, and scents of nature to counteract the tension and irritation her conversation with Austen had induced.

As long as their daughters were financially constrained and having problems with their child care, there was always going to be friction between herself and her husband, she thought glumly. She yawned. She was tired. While she still enjoyed dipping her toe back into the workforce, having to get up at a certain time and having to be in a certain place and having to commute was more tiring than she remembered . . . or else she was getting old. She grimaced, taking a slug of wine. And Austen needn't think she'd be sending a makeup text, either; he'd been bloody rude, taking the nose off her. He could go and stick a hot poker up his ass for all she cared, because she was *sick* of his attitude.

Anna finished her wine, stripped down to her underwear, and lay down on the lounger. The garden was completely private, her haven, and she slid the straps of her bra down and settled herself comfortably and closed her eyes, enjoying the warmth of the sun on her body before falling asleep, snoring lightly, so that not even the Enterprise from Belfast to Connolly, thundering past in the distance, whistle blowing in a long low howl, could wake her.

◆

Bloody women, Austen thought grumpily, draining his San Miguel. His stomach rumbled; it was almost half seven and he was hungry. He went in to the kitchen and foraged in the fridge for a steak and a couple of eggs. He poured some oil into the pan, seasoned it and, when it was sizzling, slapped the steak onto it, turning it over after a minute or two to seal in the juices. He buttered a ciabatta roll, and when his steak was almost cooked he cracked the eggs into the pan, fried them and placed them on the bread, sliced his steak thinly and added them to the bread and eggs, cracked open another beer, and meandered back out to the balcony with his feast.

Anna could stay in her snit. She'd hung up on him. She could make the first move in this row, he fumed, and bit into his dinner.

◆

"When you're coming home on Sunday, don't forget to get some Nexium and Elocon cream in the chemist, and get a couple of Seretide inhalers for Chloe," Anna reminded her husband. They were being polite to each other but not overly lovey-dovey.

"OK. Anything else? I'm bringing Tara and James to La Canada this evening if you think of anything."

"Not that I can think of. If anything comes to mind, I'll text you. Don't go mad in Leroy Merlin's. Remember your excess baggage charge the last time."

"OK, I'll give you a buzz tomorrow night; I'm bringing James for a game of golf in the afternoon while Tara goes to have a facial and massage. Enjoy your lunch with the girls tomorrow."

"I will. I'm looking forward to it."

"And you can give out about me," he teased, and she smiled and relaxed.

"We discuss *important* topics when we get together," she retorted, and laughed.

"Bye, Anna, talk tomorrow. Take care of yourself."

"You too. See you, Austen. Enjoy your game with James."

"I will. Be good," he said as he always did.

"You too."

"Sure I'm a saint," her husband joked, and hung up.

Anna exhaled and put her phone back on the shelf beside the bath. She was luxuriating in an Epsom salts bath in Tara and

James's house, with half an ear open in case her grandson stirred. She was having an early night, because she knew Michael would be climbing into her bed for a story at seven a.m. if not earlier.

At least there was a thaw between her and Austen. She knew that once she saw him at the airport and he hugged her and kissed her, their latest coolness would slide away and their reunion would be warm and loving and they would stay on an even keel for another while.

Her grandson was staying with his other grandparents for the weekend, giving Anna a chance to go back home and shop and tidy for her husband's return. She, Mary, Breda, and Yvonne had decided to have a much-needed catch-up lunch. She was looking forward to it. They hadn't got together for a while. It would be good to laugh and chat and have a vent.

They more than anyone would understand her difficult position trying to balance the needs of her husband and the needs of her daughters.

"Don't think about it," Anna muttered, feeling tension flare up as it always did now when she contemplated her current dilemma.

She yawned again and topped up the hot water and picked up *Hello!*, flicking through the pages to see how the other half lived.

◆

"I'm celiac now!"

"Celia?"

"*CELIAC!*"

"Did you change your name? I thought your name was Amy!"

"Turn on your hearing aid!"

"What?"

"Turn on your HEARING AID!"

"That will be us in a few years time," Yvonne murmured sotto voce as Anna, Mary, and Breda snorted into their napkins, overhearing the conversation of four elderly ladies at a table opposite.

They'd finished their mains and were sharing a pavlova and a banoffee slice, Anna just taking a small taste of each. "Pity we weren't in the restaurant beside La Joya; they'd be coming over to us with the double Baileys, on the house," Breda remarked.

"We'll have to try and get there again, sooner rather than later." Mary licked cream off her spoon.

"You can see how stuck I am, though." Anna made a face. "Girls, make the most of your freedom, because when the grandchildren arrive, forget it. I swear to God, Austen and I have never argued as much in all our marriage as we have about the time spent looking after them. I'm pulled one way, I'm pulled another. If they're not all careful, I'll do a runner."

"Ah yeah, with that dodgy knee of yours you'd get far," kidded Mary affectionately.

"Will we get a double shot of Baileys anyway, just for old times' sake?" Yvonne suggested with a glint in her eye.

"We came in a taxi; we might as well be poured out of one going home," Breda joked, trying to catch a waiter's attention.

"Yeah, to hell with housework. I'll change the bed in the morning; I don't have to pick Austen up from the airport until the afternoon. I *deserve* a double Baileys," Anna giggled, feeling lighthearted and giddy after her girls' lunch and looking forward, despite their niggling problems, to seeing her darling husband.

◆

"I think it's going to be a birdie, James." Austen couldn't hide his delight as he shaded his eyes from the sun, having followed the glorious arc of his golf ball over the wide emerald sward below him, with the iridescent sea in the background. A superb swing. A rare and perfect moment. "Wait until I tell Anna tonight," he said proudly, knowing she would be delighted for him.

The light was so strong and it seemed to be getting brighter, but, strangely, it stopped hurting his eyes, and there was no need to shade them from the glare any longer.

"*Oh!*" gasped Austen, surprised at the sudden sharp jolt of pain before he crumpled in a heap at the younger man's feet.

Chapter Thirty-Seven

Anna

"It's amazing how practiced waiters are at the art of looking over your head without seeing you when you try and catch their attention." Mary frowned, swiveling her head to try and nail the young man who was doing a superb job of ignoring her as he looked into the far distance with his head in the air.

In the din of chat and laughter and the sound of silverware against crockery, Yvonne heard her text message notification and looked down at her phone and saw with surprise that it was from Tara. Why would Anna's daughter be texting her? Something made her keep her mouth shut as she scrolled down to read it.

Yv can you ring me without Mum knowing. It's URGENT.
Tara

"Excuse me a sec, girls, I need to make a quick call," she said lightly, standing up from the table. Her heart was thumping but she kept her expression neutral. Something was clearly wrong if Tara was sending *urgent* texts.

She made her way through the tables to the foyer and pressed the call number. "What's wrong, Tara love?" she asked anxiously when the younger woman answered.

"Yvonne, Dad's had a massive heart attack—well, they think that's what it was. He's dead." Tara's voice wobbled and then she was sobbing her heart out.

"Oh, good Jesus, Mary, and Joseph!" Yvonne felt faint with shock.

"I don't want Mum to be on her own when she hears the news. I know she was having lunch with you. Are you still in the restaurant?"

"Yes, we are, but I'll make some excuse to get us home, and I'll text you when we arrive if you want to ring then, OK?" she managed, her throat constricted so that it was painful to talk.

"OK."

"I don't know what to say, Tara. What happened?"

"Dad and James were playing golf and he'd hit a great shot and was so pleased with himself, and then James said he just said, 'Oh,' sort of in surprise, and then he collapsed."

"That's terrible, Tara. At least you and James are there and he wasn't on his own." Yvonne's lip trembled and tears filled her eyes. She couldn't believe that Austen, always so vibrant and full of life, was dead. "Look, I better get your mother home. I'll text you ASAP," she said, struggling to compose herself.

Oh, God, help me do this right, she prayed, swallowing hard and wiping her tears on her sleeve. She took a deep breath and went back into the restaurant hoping the waiter hadn't taken the order for the Baileys. Fortunately he hadn't and she said in as normal a tone as she could muster, "Girls, I'm really sorry, I've got to go. Dad's locked himself out—"

"Aw, no," groaned Anna.

"And, Anna, I've got to call in to your house because I left my tote in the kitchen and brought my wallet and phone in my jacket pocket. I'm really sorry," she fibbed.

"Ah, no bother, we were meant not to have that Baileys," Anna said cheerfully. "I just need to go for a pee before we go. Get the bill and be stingy with the tip for that little scut who kept ignoring us."

"I'll give him a tip, not to go out in the rain without his umbrella," Yvonne quipped, and her heart ached when Anna laughed.

"I need to go too." Breda pushed away her chair. "My excuse not to have to do the sums," she said, and winked, following Anna to the ladies'.

"Mary, my dad's not locked out. We need to get Anna home. I got a text from Tara to call her urgently," Yvonne said breathlessly, sitting down beside her friend. "Austen's had a massive heart attack. He's dead."

"Oh, good God!" Mary's hand flew to her mouth and she stared at Yvonne in horror. "Lord Almighty, it can't . . . I . . . I . . ." Her face crumpled and she started to cry.

"It's true. Tara wants to phone Anna and she doesn't want her to be on her own when she hears, naturally."

"Thank God we're with her. Oh, Yvonne, this is horrendous," Mary exclaimed, trying to control her tears.

"Stop, don't cry any more or I'll start. We *have* to pretend everything's normal until we get her home," Yvonne urged. "Call that bloody waiter, pay the bill, and tell him to order us a taxi quick, and let's get out of here."

"OK," sniffled Mary, rummaging for a tissue to blow her nose.

They'd paid the bill and ordered a taxi by the time Breda and Anna arrived back at the table. "The deaf old lady was in the loo and she couldn't open the lock. I thought Breda was going to have to give me a leg up and I was going to have to shimmy over the cubicle to get in and open it," Anna said, grinning. "Could you not hear us screeching to PULL IT THE OTHER WAY?"

"Thankfully, no," Yvonne said with admirable sangfroid. "That could have been taken to have a rather different meaning than intended."

"*Yvonne!*" exclaimed Breda, and Anna chuckled.

"You are incorrigible—"

"Glad I don't have to spell *that*," Yvonne riposted, scanning to see if there was any sign of the taxi. "Here we go," she said with relief, seeing a cab pull up outside, her heart breaking for her dear and much-loved friend, knowing that these lighthearted moments were the last ones Anna would have for a long time to come. It was unbelievably surreal to think that she was now a widow.

Because Breda was unaware of the tragedy, she was able to converse with Anna with ease, and the taxi ride home was, for the two of them at least, perfectly normal.

"Go in and put the kettle on, Anna, and you get your bag, Yvonne," Mary ordered briskly. "I'll sort the taxi driver and tell him to wait for you." She gave Yvonne the tiniest wink.

"OK, bossy-boots," Anna retorted, scrabbling in her bag for her house keys.

"You should have looked for them when we left the restaurant." Breda stood with her arms folded, used to her friend's scattered ways as she explored the depths of her handbag.

Yvonne texted Tara discreetly:

We are at the house. Would you like me to tell Anna or is it something you'd rather do yourself?

Oh WOULD you Yvonne? I can't bear to say those words to Mum.

Of course pet. She'll be ringing you shortly then. XXX

Sick to her stomach, Yvonne murmured to Mary, "Tara wants me to tell her," as they walked up the path behind Anna and Breda.

"I think that's a better idea than hearing it on the phone out of the blue." Mary patted her friend on the back. "At least we're all here and you don't have to do it on your own."

"Don't keep that taxi waiting too long, Yvonne, if it's on the clock. There's your bag under the table," Anna said when they walked into the kitchen.

"Erm, actually Anna, my dad didn't lock himself out. I just needed to get you home. Sit down, love, I . . . I've something to tell you."

"You're not pregnant, are you?" Anna kidded, but seeing the expression on her friend's face she felt a sudden uneasy fear. Breda stared at Yvonne, concerned.

"No, not likely." Yvonne managed a smile, sitting down on the chair beside Anna and taking her hand.

"What is it? What's going on? Is it the baby?" Panic rose in Anna and her voice shook.

"Anna, Anna." Yvonne swallowed. "Tara rang me—"

"Tara! Is it Austen?" Anna asked fearfully, her hand going to her mouth.

"Yes, lovie, I'm afraid it is. They think it was a heart attack—"

"Oh thank God, that can be sorted. I'll fly out immediately." Anna jumped up.

"No, Anna, it was a massive one. I'm sorry, love, he's . . . he's gone," Yvonne gulped, unable to say the word "dead," white-faced with shock and grief. Breda gasped and looked at Mary, who nodded.

"Gone? Gone where?" Anna asked, uncomprehending.

"He's . . . he's . . ." Yvonne hesitated.

"Anna, Austen's dead," Mary said gently but firmly so that there was no mistake.

"He *couldn't* be. Austen couldn't be *dead*!" Anna shook her head, bemused. "He's coming home tomorrow. I'm cooking his favorite Sunday lunch, roast lamb and mushy peas," she said, almost to herself.

"Darling, Tara's waiting for you to phone her. She sent me a text asking me to phone her urgently when we were in the restaurant, and when I did, she told me," Yvonne explained.

Anna looked at her blankly. "But he's playing golf with James, and she's having a facial."

"Ring Tara. Here, use my phone," Yvonne offered, pressing the call-back key and handing it to her.

Stunned, Anna took the phone and the foreign dial tone only rang for a moment before Tara answered.

"Oh, Mum, Mum," she wept.

"Tara, where's Dad? Is he in the hospital? Are they working on him?" Anna asked frantically, terrified when she heard her daughter's sobs.

"No, Mum, didn't Yvonne tell you? He's dead. He died on the golf course. It was too late to work on him when the ambulance came. It was instant, they said."

"Oh, God! Oh, God! Oh, God!" Anna muttered, the color draining from her face. "I'll get a flight over, even if I have to go via the UK."

"No, Mum, don't put yourself through that ordeal. James is really brilliant; he's got everything under control. He's got consular assistance and Aer Lingus have been terrific. Once they have the postmortem done we can leave with . . . with . . . Dad's body," she managed, before breaking down again.

"Oh, but I want to be there, I want to see him. I want to be with him." Anna started to cry, great heartrending sobs that tore at her friends' heartstrings until they too were all sobbing.

"Please, Mum, please don't come out. I'd be so worried about you coming over. Please be waiting for us when we get back. And besides, you have to organize the funeral at your end. You need to go to Massey's and let them take it from here," Tara urged. "And you've got to tell Chloe."

"Oh, heavens, I forgot about Chloe. She'll go to pieces," Anna wept. "But tell me, was Austen ill at all when you arrived? Was there any indication that he wasn't feeling the best?" Anna was desperate to know every detail.

"No, not at all, we had a great time with him. And James said he was really enjoying his game. He thought he'd scored a birdie. He said to James that you'd be delighted. They were his . . . his last words." She broke into a fresh paroxysm of sobs.

"Oh, Tara, Tara." Anna wept with her daughter, unable to grasp the enormity of what she was hearing. Was she in some sort of nightmare from which she would awake with a thumping heart but great relief that none of this was real?

"Mum, I have to go; James is calling me. I'll ring you as soon as I have anything more to tell you," Tara said. "I love you, Mum, and Dad loved you," she added before hanging up.

At these words, Anna bowed her head and sobbed uncontrollably while Yvonne held her. Breda made the tea, and Mary, ever practical, looked up the undertaker's number to have it ready for when Anna felt composed enough to make the call.

◆

When Anna looked back on those unbearable days, what struck her most was how bizarre it all seemed. Much of it was a blur, with only flashes of coherent memory that stayed in her consciousness. Chloe's screaming hysterics until Mary told her sternly that Austen wouldn't approve of her losing it in such a fashion. Ringing family to tell them the inconceivable news but unable to bring herself to say "Austen's *dead*." Saying instead that he'd "passed away." It seemed somehow less harsh. Less final. Having to repeat the story time after time.

Her father's distress. "But he's a young man," he kept saying. "I can't believe I'm still here and Austen isn't. I wish with all my heart it was the other way around, pet."

The calming, authoritative tones of the undertaker, who took the whole burden of the arrangements off her shoulders in such a professional but most kind manner. The sense of utter disbelief and numbing shock at having to choose a coffin and select what clothing she wished for Austen to be waked in.

The hordes of people coming and going, offering stunned condolences, while her steadfast friends made copious pots of tea and platters of sandwiches, staying in the background but always there, like a safety net for her. Even the arrival of her husband's body and the short service in the airport chapel seemed unreal. Tara and James's stalwart comportment despite the traumatic few days they'd endured was a credit to them, she'd the wherewithal to say. But mostly she felt that she was an observer in someone else's drama. It didn't really have *anything* to do with her. Austen was out in Spain playing golf and would be home soon, filling the house with his welcome presence.

It was only when the undertakers brought Austen home and placed his coffin in the candlelit, flower-decorated study, looking out onto the back garden—his favorite room in the house—and when the lid was lifted that reality hit Anna and she trembled with devastation and the most overwhelming, heart-piercing, gut-wrenching sense of loss and grief to see her beloved husband lying as though he were asleep, with a hint of a smile playing around his lips, as though inviting her to share a private joke.

"Austen," she said in disbelief. "Austen, why have you left me? How could you leave me all alone?"

She stayed beside his coffin all that night, alternately telling him of her love for him and raging at what she perceived as his ultimate act of betrayal and abandonment. As she followed his coffin out of the house and watched the undertakers place it in the hearse to take it to chapel the following morning, Anna knew that her life had changed irrevocably. Changed to "before" and "after" and a future that stretched ahead of her, dark and forbidding. A very lonely vista that Anna did not know if she'd the strength to face.

PART IV

Time to Say Good-Bye

Chapter Thirty-Eight

Jutta / Eduardo / Anna / Sally-Ann

"Hello, Anna, how are you?" Jutta asked when she saw the Irish-woman's name come up on her phone. Her heart sank. It was hard to know what to say to a bereaved person if you didn't know them very well. She tactfully refrained from wishing Anna a Happy New Year.

"Hello, Jutta. I'm putting one foot in front of the other; it's all I can do," her client said flatly. "I had keyhole surgery to have my gall bladder removed in November, so that's helped a lot. Listen, I want you to put the penthouse up for sale for me, please. If you can get what we paid for it, I'll take it. All the better, of course, if you can get more for it."

"I'm glad to hear you had the surgery but very sorry to hear you're selling up," Jutta said sympathetically. Although at one level she was excited to have a penthouse to sell, she was sorry to lose Anna as a client. The MacDonalds had always paid their fees on time and had left their penthouse in good condition when they went back home after a stay, unlike some clients who left their apartments like pigsties.

"I couldn't bear to set foot in it again, to be honest," Anna confessed sadly.

"That's understandable, I suppose," Jutta said slowly, "but don't they say you shouldn't make big decisions in the first year of bereavement?"

"Perhaps, but I *really* won't ever step inside that penthouse again. We never had luck from the day we bought it and I don't want to be reminded that Austen spent his last days there without me. I don't feel the same about the place. It's hard enough every day here in the house."

"I understand. So presumably you want to sell it furnished? What about your personal effects?"

"The girls said they'd go over in the spring for a couple of days to clear out, unless of course you get a quick sale," Anna said forlornly.

"And of course you'll have to come over when there is a sale agreed, whenever that may be. We use a notary in Marbella. You can always stay in a hotel there if you wish. We'll sort all that when the time comes."

"OK. Just keep in touch and let me know what's happening, will you?"

"I will, of course, Anna. Take care," Jutta said kindly.

"Thanks, Jutta. You were always very good to us."

"*De nada*, Anna. Again, my sympathies for your loss," she murmured before hanging up.

What a terrible tragedy had fallen upon the MacDonald family. In the blink of an eye, life had changed for them. Life was so arbitrary, it could happen to anyone at any time. There was her elderly father, rejuvenated after his hip replacement, and a man she would have presumed to be fitter and healthier than Oskar was under the clay!

She remembered the time she'd had dinner with Austen in the

restaurant beside La Joya. He'd looked terrific for a man of his age. To tell the truth, she'd found him quite attractive, and if he'd made a move on her she might have followed it up, because she'd been quite drunk, as she remembered. But Anna had been Austen's love. That was quite obvious when he spoke about her, and about how much he was missing her and wishing she were there with him.

And now Anna was selling up. Five other Irish owners in La Joya were also selling, unable to afford their mortgages and the maintenance fees as the EU was brought to its knees by recession.

If Felipe's business wasn't hanging by a thread, and they were still in boom times, she would have considered buying Anna's penthouse herself. To own a property like that, in a complex such as La Joya, would be all she could wish for. Jutta sighed. But now she was the main breadwinner, and she'd a young child to think of, and au pair fees, and bills, bills, bills. Her chance to buy a home as opposed to renting one would probably never come about in Spain again, she thought glumly.

And it was all Felipe's fault.

This thought, as it often did, came unbidden, and she sighed deeply. Would her marriage end up as rock solid as Anna and Austen's had been when she and Felipe were their age? Right now she didn't think so. She was angry with her husband, *extremely* angry and frustrated. He'd dived headfirst, despite her urging caution, into borrowing to buy development land in Spain's south-eastern Costa Blanca. He'd wanted to get as many units per acre built as he could, while she'd advised to build fewer units but at a higher spec, and with bigger gardens to ensure privacy. In some of the so-called villas that she'd seen there was not one room in the house which was not overlooked. The vista from the roof terraces filled her with horror. Every hill in the area covered in miles and miles of whitewashed, orange-roofed houses with their ubiquitous satellite dishes as far as the eye could see, and not even a pine tree in sight to add a splash of color. The sea was a faint blue blur on the horizon.

"Felipe, why don't you buy in unspoiled, uncrowded areas and build classy apartments? They'll sell as quick and for a higher price," she'd suggested. "These little egg boxes are hideous!"

"Because I couldn't care less about who buys; I want the money to pay off the loan as quickly as possible, so I can make a good profit and move on to the next deal," her husband declared. "Your business is different. You're a service provider; you have to keep your clients sweet. I just buy, build, and run. You're a snob, Jutta. Why shouldn't people be allowed to have their little bit of heaven in a Mediterranean country even if they're halfway up a mountain and surrounded by units. Why should owning a place in Spain be the privilege of the wealthy types you service? The common man has his place in the world too," he'd sneered, eyes watery and red, speech slurred from the bottle of rioja he'd drunk on his own one evening when she'd come in from work, tired and annoyed, to find the apartment a mess and a dirty diaper in a ball on the bathroom floor.

There was no point in arguing with Felipe when he was drinking, and when she'd pointed out the following morning that it wasn't very responsible to be drinking and in charge of their baby on the au pair's night off, he'd apologized.

The discussion on his property deals had resurfaced later in the week and she'd reiterated wearily, "Just finish one development, and have all your units sold before you start on another, so you won't be compromised financially." But her husband hadn't listened and now he was stuck with an apartment block and villas that he was struggling to sell. He was resentful of her thriving agency and even recently made a snide remark about her "making her money cleaning other people's dirt." *That* had stung, and she was being very cool with him.

Just as well she *was* able to run a business properly, even if a portion of it *was* cleaning other people's dirt, Jutta thought crossly while she sat in traffic, idling at traffic lights, on the outskirts of San Antonio del Mar. Her husband had some nerve. At least she was responsible in the way she ran her business and not feckless like he was. Felipe's exuberant, go-for-it-no-matter-what approach that had so appealed to her when she'd first met him now exasperated her hugely. Her husband never considered the consequences of his ill-thought-out actions. She, on the other hand, was never happy to take on a new venture until she'd satisfied herself that it had a good chance of succeeding.

Her "cleaning" business had expanded to selling property, and it was taking off slowly but steadily. Considering how the Costa had been ravaged by the downturn, that was quite an achievement, Jutta thought proudly, noticing how quiet it was in the town she was driving through. Normally the restaurants would be bustling with ex-pats spending the winter in Spain. At least four businesses along the strip had their shutters down and *Se Vende* signs up. In all her years in Spain she'd never seen the coast so deserted. At this time of the year her long-let rentals should be keeping her busy, but at least half remained empty this winter.

Pulling up into a guest parking space in La Joya, she noticed the cleaners carrying their mops and buckets to clean the reception area. *They* were cleaners, Jutta thought snootily, tempted to take a photo and send it to Felipe; it wasn't as if *she* was doing the cleaning *personally* in her apartments. She *employed* a team of cleaners, so what was Felipe's problem? Her increasing success and his continuing failure, she supposed. It wasn't a contest between them. They were supposed to be a team.

Concentrate on what you have to do, she chided herself, sliding out of the car with her usual long-limbed elegance.

How timely to get Anna's phone call. She was doing her weekly checks in the complex; she could begin taking photographs of the penthouse and do some of the inventory and get it typed up in the afternoon, and put a For Sale post online.

She'd start on the kitchen. That would take the longest. January was a good time to put a property on the market. Nordic buyers especially always started looking at sunny destinations in the winter and liked to have their properties bought by the summer. She couldn't imagine that the MacDonalds wouldn't have all their taxes and utilities paid up. Most of their bills were paid by direct debit. She would organize the necessary checks and have everything just right so there would be no delays. Jutta had always liked to have everything organized to the nth degree, and she was glad of that trait in her personality. Selling or buying a property in Spain could be very tricky if all the *t*'s weren't crossed and all the *i*'s dotted.

"*¿Qué tal?*" Jutta greeted Constanza, who walked around the corner, heading towards her office.

"*Ah*, Jutta! *Hola! Asi asi.*" The older woman gave a resigned shrug and made a face.

"Only so-so? Aww. Is *El Presidente* in situ, then?" Jutta made a face.

"*El bastardo* is, as we speak, sending an email to all the owners, telling them that pets are definitely going to be allowed now that the trial period is over. He has his own dog up in his apartment. He's rubbing my nose in it, Jutta, because I wouldn't allow him to have that mongrel here before. It's in the constitution of the complex. '*No pets!*' " she fumed.

"Has he been here long?"

"He and his wife and aunt have been here since the first of January. What a start to the New Year. I may go mad, *completamente loco.*" She gave a wan smile, inserting her key in the door to her office. "He summoned me up to his apartment like the little dictator that he is to tell me *this* news."

"Not good," frowned Jutta. "Barking dogs cause rows. Dog shit causes rows. And animals in rental apartments are a big no-no! Landlords don't like them."

"Also there is to be *no* topless bathing at the pool." Constanza flung her keys on her desk and poured water from a bottle into a kettle and switched it on. "Coffee?"

"No *gracias*, Constanza. I'd love to but I have to go and take an itinerary. Anna MacDonald is selling her penthouse. I want to put it on the boards ASAP."

"Ah, no. How sad that Austen died. Shocking. Shocking." Constanza shook her head. The concierge had aged in the past few months, Jutta noted. The lines around her amber eyes and coral-slashed mouth had deepened and she had an air of despondency that was most unlike her.

"Good luck with the topless rule: I can't see anyone taking any notice of that. I suppose the old crones from Madrid who've been kicking up about the 'nude' women are behind that."

"He probably is too. He's a prissy little *monja*," Constanza spat.

"He is a bit of a nun all right," Jutta laughed. "Well, hopefully he's not a pigeon fancier. The president in another complex I have apartments in decided out of the blue to install a pigeon loft without a by-your-leave from anyone and announced that the concierge would look after it. It caused *uproar*. Pigeon shit everywhere. And the noise! Power goes to their heads when they get elected—"

"*Especially* the Spanish ones," Constanza said grimly. "But this too shall pass, as my mother used to say."

"Bear up, he'll be gone back to Madrid soon."

"Next week. He's here for another week."

"*Ah, Madre de Dios! Adiós,* Constanza. If you hear on the grapevine of anyone who is looking for a penthouse to buy, let me know."

"*Adiós,* Jutta, I will." The concierge gave her a smile before turning her attention to a slew of emails from Pablo Moralez, incensed that *El Presidente*—or "*ese idiota, De La Fuente,*" as he generally labeled him—had given the gardeners instructions to remove a host of flowering shrubs in favor of hardy annuals in the borders.

"This is not his own personal garden, his private fiefdom," the irate owner had raged down the phone at her, until she told him crisply to put his complaint in writing. He'd taken her at her word, she noted unenthusiastically, as she counted six separate emails on her computer screen.

Jutta completed all her vacant apartment checks before heading to Anna's penthouse. The sun was shining after several cloudy days, and the wind had died down, although it was chilly. She turned right to walk along a shrub-lined path towards the entrance to Anna's block and saw, coming towards her, Constanza's bête noire. *El Presidente* was linking arms with his elderly aunt, and Jutta surmised they had gone for a walk on the boardwalk that ran along the beach adjacent to the grounds. "*Buenos días,*" she greeted them politely.

"Ah, Ms. Sauer, is it not?" The notary looked her up and down.

"Señor." She nodded, looking *him* up and down.

"I propose to cc you, and the other agents, into any emails that I send to the owners you and they represent. I wish to have the names of all the agents who work here. I would be obliged if you would forward me your contact details so I can add them to my database."

"Hmmm," she said coolly. "My contract is with my clients. I'll ask if they are happy for me to be cc'd into their emails from you."

"Why would it be a problem?" he said haughtily.

"For example, if any of my clients were in arrears, or in a dispute with you, they might not like me to know that. And, to be perfectly frank, I am a busy woman. My time is valuable. My PA has a lot of emails to deal with already. I'm not sure she nor I need extraneous work—"

The elderly lady leaning on her stick gave a little moan and grabbed Eduardo's arm.

"What is it, Beatriz?" He looked at her in alarm.

She tried to speak but her eyes rolled in her head and she blacked out, collapsing against him to his shock as he caught her.

"Can you carry her?" Jutta asked. "It's too cold to place her on the ground; your apartment is too far away. I have the key to an apartment here."

"Thank you, yes." Eduardo had no problem lifting his frail aunt into his arms as Jutta hurriedly opened the entrance door, praying that the lift was on the ground floor. It was, and she followed Eduardo into it and pressed the penthouse button. "Beatriz, Beatriz, wake up, *querida*," Eduardo urged, and his aunt's eyelids fluttered open.

"Eduardo . . ." she murmured weakly.

"Hush now, we will get you lying down in bed to make you more comfortable and then we will call an ambulance," he soothed, and she closed her eyes and rested her head against his shoulder.

The lift came to a smooth halt, and Jutta hurried to open Anna's front door.

"In here," she said, indicating the master bedroom along the hall, and Eduardo carried his aunt inside and laid her on the king-sized bed.

Jutta pulled back the pale lemon drapes and looped the egg-shell-blue tieback into the hook before hurrying to get a glass of water for the stricken woman.

Eduardo was on his phone issuing brisk instructions to the cardiac ambulance call center, all the while tenderly rubbing his aunt's hand. "All will be well," he said reassuringly, taking the glass of water Jutta proffered and holding it gently to her lips. Jutta placed a Tommy Hilfiger throw that was on the end of the bed over the elderly woman to keep her warm.

"Her breathing is quite labored," she murmured.

"Yes, she has a history of heart problems," Eduardo said worriedly, observing his aunt's gray pallor.

"Eduardo?"

"I'm here, *Tía*, what is it?" he asked, and Jutta would never have expected such tender concern from the pompous *madrileño*.

"I think you need to contact Isabella," she said feebly.

"Let's see how you get on at the hospital," he soothed.

"I would like to see my sister," she whispered.

"Very well," he agreed. "I'll get in touch with her."

"*Gracias*," Beatriz said, and closed her eyes again.

It would be such a tragic irony, thought Jutta, hearing the wail of a siren getting nearer, if the old lady died of a heart attack in Anna's apartment. She resolved if this was the case not to mention it to the grieving owner, and would tell Eduardo to do likewise.

The EMTs, when they arrived, radiated reassurance and consideration as they placed an oxygen mask over Beatriz's nose and mouth and gently opened her clothes to take an ECG.

"She's having an event," one of them murmured to Eduardo as he studied the readout a little while later. "Does one of you wish to accompany her in the ambulance?" He looked from Eduardo to Jutta.

"Oh, I'm not related," Jutta said hastily.

"I'll go; this is my aunt," Eduardo replied calmly.

"*Muchas gracias,*" Beatriz managed to say to Jutta as she was lifted into the chair.

"*De nada.* I'll say a prayer for you." Jutta bent down to her so that Beatriz could hear what she was saying, and saw a faint smile flicker across her face.

"*Muchas gracias* for your enormous assistance. May I give you my card?" Eduardo said at the door.

"Of course, Señor, I would like to know how your aunt does. I'll text you and you may text me back." Jutta dismissed their earlier froideur. She understood only too well the trials and tribulations that went with having the responsibility of an elderly relative.

"*Ciertamente,*" he agreed, passing an elegant business card to her before taking the stairs to be with his aunt as quickly as possible.

What a day, thought Jutta, listening to the wail of the ambulance siren disappear into the distance as she poured water into the kettle to make herself a strong cup of coffee before beginning the inventory of the contents of Anna's kitchen and utility room.

She'd just finished itemizing the saucepan press when her

phone rang again and she saw Sally-Ann Connolly Cooper's name appear. She could let it go to her voice mail, which would direct Sally-Ann to Jutta's office, but the American woman rarely called, so she decided to answer it.

"Sally-Ann, how are you?" she answered crisply.

"Good, Jutta, good. And you?"

"Fine, thank you. How can I help you?" They did the polite social dance around each other. Jutta didn't particularly like Sally-Ann—she was too brash and too opinionated—but she was a valuable client, and her husband, Cal, owned property in Alicante with Felipe. She needed to keep the Americans sweet.

"I want to book the penthouse for all of August, and I was wondering, would you have any other apartment, preferably in the same block, to rent to me?"

"I need to check our calendar, Sally-Ann. I just have one other apartment for rent in your block, but I have a couple more in the other ones. I'll get back to you ASAP." She could have opened up her booking calendar, but she was conscious the other woman was ringing from the US, and she preferred to take her time taking bookings. She'd never double-booked and she wasn't going to start now. Why the other woman couldn't have emailed her query she didn't know, she thought crossly.

"Thanks, y'all," Sally-Ann replied in her distinctive American accent, which had taken Jutta a while to get used to.

Jutta sat down at the table and took her iPad out of her bag and logged in. She studied the spreadsheet of bookings for La Joya and saw that the apartment two floors below was available for the last two weeks of August but not the first two. She'd availability for all of August in block 2. She pressed the callback button and heard Sally-Ann's voice as clear as a bell. Jutta gave her the information.

"I suppose I could book block two for the first fortnight and change over to my one for the last two weeks," she said.

"There might be one other option," Jutta said thoughtfully. "Anna MacDonald is selling the penthouse next door to you—"

"Aw, is she selling? What a shame," exclaimed Sally-Ann. "Mind, I'm not surprised. She said she couldn't bear to come over to stay the last time I spoke to her, before Christmas."

"I wonder, would she rent it to you if it wasn't sold by then? I know you're friendly. Shall I ask her?"

"That would be *perfect*!" Sally-Ann enthused. "It would suit me down to the ground, actually."

"Let me get back to you," Jutta said. "But, just in case, I'll provisionally book the two apartments for you."

"Thanks, Jutta. Appreciate it."

Why hadn't she suggested going down the rental route to Anna? It made sense. She might as well have an income from it while it was empty and awaiting a buyer, Jutta mused, as the phone dialed the Irishwoman's number.

"Hello, Jutta. Have you a buyer already?" Anna made an attempt at humor.

"No, Anna, but I've a proposal for you. Your neighbor, Sally-Ann, is looking for an apartment to rent in your block, along with her own penthouse. There's only one available for two weeks, and she wants it for the month of August. I was wondering, would you be interested in renting while you're waiting for a buyer? I can get my girls to bag up all your personal items and prepare it for letting if you'd care to. It would be a source of income until you sold it," she added.

"Oh! I see. I certainly wouldn't mind Sally-Ann having it, but I'm not sure about renting it out. Can I think about it? I'll let you know by the end of the week."

"Of course. And don't feel any pressure. I'm taking an inventory now. I would hope to have it on the market by the weekend."

"Good," said Anna wearily. "Talk soon. Bye."

◆

"So she said she wouldn't mind you having it either way if it hasn't sold," Jutta reported to Sally-Ann.

"But if it's sold, I could lose the other apartments. I really do need to be sure I have a second apartment for August in La Joya. Perhaps I'd better take what you've offered me," Sally-Ann said regretfully.

"OK, if that's what you prefer, no problem," Jutta agreed. "I'll send you the confirmation email."

A busy but satisfying day, she concluded several hours later, having logged details of all the fixtures and fittings in the penthouse. She was hungry; she might go and eat in the restaurant below, she decided. Her daughter, Alicia, was recovering from a kidney infection and was cranky. She would demand attention as soon as Jutta walked in the door.

She would eat in peace and then go home to her sickly child. After all, what was the point in employing an au pair who was well paid and enjoyed good conditions if she couldn't even have a meal in tranquillity? Jutta reasoned, closing the curtains in the penthouse before locking up. She loved her daughter, but she loved herself too. Too many mothers made martyrs of themselves. That was not her way. In fairness to Felipe, he was an excellent father, Jutta conceded. He adored their daughter and had endless patience with her. Much more than she did. Alicia's paternal grandparents treated her like a little princess, and Jutta had to guard against them spoiling her. Felipe had texted her to say he was in the Don Carlos at a business meeting that was almost over; if she waited awhile he would be home before her and could put Alicia to bed. She deserved this time to herself: she was looking forward to a white wine spritzer and a plate of mussels.

She wondered how Eduardo's aunt was. Would he text her to let her know of Beatriz's condition? She'd seen another side to *El Presidente* today. Dr. Jekyll and Mr. Hyde, Jutta thought in amusement as she clickity-clacked her way along the shrub-lined pathway in her Bionda Castana lilac pumps, which were the *exact* shade of her cashmere jumper.

She'd seen the Spaniard looking her up and down and known with confidence that she presented an impeccable businesslike image in her tailored navy trouser suit, accessorized by her Chanel bag and sunglasses and discreet gold earrings.

An *excellent* businesswoman, and wife, and an *adequate* mother and daughter, Jutta admitted, not shying away from what would be, for some, an uncomfortable truth. She settled back into her chair in the warm restaurant, looking forward to her solitary meal.

Chapter Thirty-Nine

Anna

"Don't do that, pet," Anna said to her grandson, who was scribbling on one of her magazines.

"I'm drawin' you a picture," he said indignantly.

"Oh . . . oh, thank you. Why don't I get you some pages, then?" Anna sighed. She'd a thumping headache and would have liked nothing more than to crawl into bed and stay there, but Michael had been home from play school early because of a burst pipe due to freezing conditions, and she'd had to go and collect him.

It had been a nerve-racking drive. She'd always hated driving on snow and ice, and envied Austen's calmness and knowledge of when to apply brakes and when not to and knowing about rear-wheel and front-wheel drive and the like.

Anna couldn't believe that as the days increased since her husband's death, so too exponentially had her grief. She could not credit, either, how physically painful that grief was. Her heart literally *ached*. Sometimes she felt it was being cut to ribbons with razor blades. Christmas had been an absolute agony, although she'd spent it with Tara—who was pregnant again—and James and Michael.

She couldn't face being in her own home without Austen. She hadn't decorated, not even a holly wreath on the front door, and hadn't done any festive baking; so that when she came back home on the second of January, it was as though the season had never happened.

Why? That was her constant question to Austen, to God, or whatever energy had created them. Just *Why?*

She was very angry. And, Anna conceded, she was becoming dour and sharp. She knew she had to make an effort, especially for the family, but they expected *so* much from her. She was the glue that held them together. She was the focal point now for the family, but she didn't want to be. She didn't want to have to comfort and sustain her children; she wanted *them* to comfort and sustain *her*!

And she was angry with her daughters. It was because of their child-minding requirements that she and Austen had had disagreements. His words about her putting their daughters' needs before his came back to haunt her often. She was riddled with guilt remembering the way she'd hung up on him a few days before he died, after their argument about when she was coming out to Spain with him.

Had their arguments contributed to his heart attack? They must have, she reasoned. Although Tara maintained it was the stress and worry caused by the loss of their savings. No doubt that had contributed too. And easier for Tara to think that it was financial worry that had caused her father's sudden death, rather than her and Chloe's child-care impositions.

She would never, of course, verbalize her resentments to her daughters, Anna thought crossly, much as she'd like to vent. She wouldn't burden them with that particular guilt trip. But it was hard to keep silent sometimes, and her restraint added to her resentfully carried burdens.

She lay down on the sofa and closed her eyes to shut out the thin, wintery sunlight. Michael was engrossed in his drawing, her granddaughter was having her nap, and she'd have a little one too, Anna decided.

It seemed as though she'd only closed her eyes when she heard a cry on the baby monitor. Anna's eyes flew open. *Ah, no, child,* she thought irritably as the whimpers turned into a full-blown wail. She hauled herself off the sofa and went upstairs to where Charlotte's cot now reposed in Chloe's old bedroom.

"What are you doing awake? Go back asleep," she said firmly, to no avail. Her granddaughter, tousle-haired and red-cheeked, stood up and held out her arms when she saw Anna appear at the door.

Anna picked her up and felt a brief moment of unexpected happiness as the toddler nuzzled into her neck, thumb in her mouth.

"Come on, then, Anna, one foot in front of the other," she muttered, remembering her words to Jutta earlier. She was very glad she'd made that phone call, Anna reflected, walking slowly down the stairs with her granddaughter in her arms.

Tara and Chloe had urged her not to act too hastily in selling up when she'd discussed it with them at Christmas. "Will and I could go out for a week on our own, and then you could mind the baby and fly out a week later and we'd all be together," Chloe suggested.

You mean you'd have a cheap babysitter, thought Anna sourly, knowing what way her daughter's mind worked. And how selfish of her to think it was OK for Anna to have to deal with an infant on a flight to Málaga on her own, having had responsibility for her for the previous week while Chloe had a week "off" in the penthouse. Her daughter's sense of entitlement was incredible. According to her, she "needed" and "deserved" a week off after all she'd been through since her father's death.

What about me? Anna wanted to shout. *WHAT ABOUT ME?* She could hardly believe, either, that her youngest daughter had even thought that far ahead. It was all she could do to get by, day by day, so overwhelmed was she by grief, loneliness, unutterable sadness, and always the underlying anger and resentment.

Anna didn't want to go back to the penthouse. She couldn't imagine being in La Joya without Austen. So what was the point in paying out the huge expenses incurred by having a property abroad? She'd enough to do to pay her taxes at home; she wasn't interested in paying Spanish taxes and the increased maintenance fees for La Joya if she wasn't going to use it. Deciding to sell up had not been a hard decision, and at least she'd done one positive thing today.

Anna sighed from the depths of her being. It was almost five months since Austen had died and she hadn't even selected his memorial card, let alone posted them out. It was a chore she was dreading, but it had to be done to honor his memory and show appreciation to all who had come to his funeral and shown her and the family such kindness. Tears blurred Anna's eyes at the memory of Austen's funeral and how she had stood beside his casket in the open hearse, greeting the throngs of mourners who had come to support them.

"Are you very sad, Nannie?" Two anxious blue eyes stared at her from the bottom of the stairs, where her grandson stood with his picture held out to her.

"Yes, darling, I am," she admitted, struggling to swallow the lump that constricted her throat.

"Don't be sad, Nannie. Granddad isn't gone away. I was playin' jumping with him last night."

"Were you, sweetheart?" she exclaimed.

"Yep. I had to ask him to stop playing 'cause I was getting tired. He got a new heart 'cause the old one was broken," the little boy explained earnestly, patting her arm kindly.

"Did he?" She managed a smile.

"Yep. He comes to play every night when I go asleep."

God bless your innocence, Anna thought. But their conversation lifted her. Who was to say that Austen and Michael didn't play together in the dream world? Michael believed firmly that his grandfather came to him; she would try to believe it too, Anna decided as her granddaughter planted a sweet little kiss on her cheek.

Chapter Forty

Eduardo / Sally-Ann / Cal / Jutta / Anna

"So tomorrow you will be well enough to go home to Madrid and spend a few days in a nursing home there to recover. Consuela will go with you in the ambulance and I'll follow behind. Is that not good news?" Eduardo asked his aunt, who was sitting propped up against a bank of pillows, reading her paper. She looked so much better than the whitewashed ghost who had arrived at the hospital a week previously. Her cheeks had some color and there was a hint of a sparkle back in her eyes.

"It will be nice to be home, Eduardo," she agreed. "This time I did not think I would see Madrid again. I felt I could have gone."

"Beatriz, you would never go down here in the south," he teased. "'They don't do things *properly* down here'—isn't that what you say?"

She laughed. "They minded me well enough here. I can't complain, but, yes, when I go I would prefer to pass in my beloved Madrid."

"That won't be for a long time yet," he assured her. "Consuela will be in to see you tonight. I must go now and fulfill some of my presidential duties," he said, bending down to kiss his aunt's cheek.

"*Gracias mi hijo,*" she said as he walked out the door. His aunt called him "her boy" only in moments when she was deeply touched. Eduardo liked it when she did. It was a validation of sorts for all the care he gave her.

It had been a busy week. He'd commuted twice to Madrid by train to oversee that the office was running smoothly—which, of course, thanks to his extremely high standards, it was. The train journeys had been, strangely, a blessing in disguise. They had given him time to formulate a new plan that would claw back even more rental arrears in La Joya. His proposal to rent out the apartments and claim the rent until the amounts outstanding were paid had met with approval from the board and the owners.

Tough negotiations would be necessary with the errant owners—something Eduardo secretly relished, especially when he was in a position of power. He'd also rewritten the duties of the concierge and proposed that the community hire a second one. He'd exactly the person in mind. Someone who would report *everything* to him. Eduardo's nostrils flared as he remembered his last encounter with Constanza Torres. "I am paid to be the manager of the complex, not your secretary or gofer," she'd practically spat at him. And had refused point-blank to come up to his apartment at his request, telling *him* to come to *her office* instead. That woman needed to learn her place. He would put his proposal to the board and see how they took it. If they agreed, that Torres woman would have her hours cut and her wings very much clipped.

The complex was very quiet even though it was now the third week in January. At night, some blocks had only a smattering of lights to show that apartments were occupied. Eduardo liked it when it was peaceful. August was always very busy, the shouts and cries of children in the pool vaguely irritating. Spring and autumn were his favorite times to holiday in this glorious piece of paradise.

As was his wont, he perused the noticeboard and saw to his surprise that the MacDonalds' penthouse was up for sale. Eduardo had been shocked to hear of the death of the Irishman, who had been popular with the other owners for his genial and helpful manner. Eduardo hadn't cared for the wife so much. She'd been somewhat indifferent to his concerns and requests that first year when she was on the management committee.

It was a beautiful penthouse with magnificent views. He couldn't help but notice how stylish and elegant the décor was the day the letting agent had been so kind as to allow him to bring Beatriz in after her collapse.

The sky had been so blue that day, he'd almost felt he could reach across and touch the Rock, and the outline of the High Atlas had been etched so clearly against the sky. The sea view from his own apartment was from the side, and Anna MacDonald's block obstructed his view somewhat. Nothing obstructed the stunning vista from the penthouse.

Eduardo felt an uncharacteristic tremor of excitement. In view of the economic climate, Anna MacDonald would hardly be selling it at an outrageous price. Nothing was selling for crazy money like the sales that had taken place in the good years. The penthouse would have fetched €600K-plus then. She would be lucky to get anything like that now, although she would still make a profit or at least break even, he mused.

Should he, for once, take a chance and do something spontaneous and out of character? Eduardo mused. He'd an excellent pension, shares, no mortgages, and a very good income from his legal business. He deserved to treat himself for once in his life. It was time to throw caution to the winds. He would put in an offer. He read the notice again and saw that it was Jutta Sauer who was the selling agent. That was possibly a good thing. He remembered guiltily that he hadn't contacted her to tell her how his aunt had got on. That had been remiss of him. Consuela had chided him about it.

"You really should ring that woman. She showed you a kindness," she'd said.

"I will, I will," he'd said irritably. "Up until now I never really liked her. She's quite arrogant."

"You don't like anyone," retorted his wife before going to sit in the guest bedroom to do her "meditation," as she called it.

He would do his paperwork and ring Ms. Sauer this evening and steer the conversation around to the sale of the penthouse. He'd find out what the asking price was.

With a spring in his step, Eduardo strode through the grounds and heard his little dog barking a welcome from his balcony.

◆

"Can y'all meet me for coffee, Cal?" Sally-Ann left a message on her ex-husband's cell. She smiled as she clicked off. She and Cal were getting on better since their divorce than they had in years. Strange, really. She would never have thought she'd get over the bitterness and anger that had been her unwelcome companions for so long.

When she'd told him she was truly adamant about getting the divorce, he'd argued vehemently against it, trying to get her to change her mind.

"We're getting on well enough. You and the girls have accepted Jake in a way I could only dream about. Lenora and I are over. We don't need a divorce, Sally-Ann," he pointed out.

"*I* do, Cal. This isn't about *you* anymore, or the girls. It's about *me*. It's about finally putting myself first. And getting a divorce allows me to do that once and for all," she'd stated with an intensity that focused him finally on the fact that she was totally serious. Unbelievable as it was for him to acknowledge that she no longer saw them as husband and wife, despite their travails, he had, much to his dismay, reluctantly agreed.

After her passionate declaration, he'd put no obstacle in her way. They had sat down together and thrashed it out between them. There were two options available to them, they knew. Texas, being both a fault and a no-fault divorce state, cited seven grounds on which to base a divorce. To speed it up, as Sally-Ann was anxious to do, she simply had to state that their marriage had become "insupportable." This was the no-fault ground under Texas law that shortened the amount of time it took to get divorced, provided that they both agreed to the terms set forth.

The fault-based grounds included cruelty, adultery, felony conviction, abandonment, or insanity. Her lawyer advised her to file for reasons of adultery so that she would get a higher alimony settlement and she did point this out to Cal.

"I can't argue with you about that, and Jake's the proof of it." He'd held his palms up. "Look, Sally-Ann, I don't want this to be a fight; the girls don't need to be in the middle of a battlefield. I don't want it. You don't want it. The only ones that do are the lawyers. Let's work out our settlement, just you and me, until we're happy with it and move on from there."

"That suits me just fine, Cal, just fine," Sally-Ann had agreed, and that was what they had done.

She'd filed her petition, it had been served on Cal, they had waited the sixty-one days required before the hearing could be held, and she'd had her divorce decree in just under three months.

She and Cal had kept it all very low-key and not said anything to the girls when the decree came through. They had adapted to the separation once they had realized that Cal was in their life as much as he ever was and they still did a lot of family stuff together. Sally-Ann and Cal decided to let them adjust even more to the family's new circumstances before telling them that their parents were actually divorced.

They had been so excited to hear that Cal was moving to a house close by with the baby. And best of all, Madison confided, they wouldn't have to see Lenora anymore. The other big bonus was that they were going to have their own rooms in the new house and Cal had said they could decorate them whatever way they wished.

Their father had involved them in every step of the purchasing of the new abode, less than a mile from where they lived.

Sally-Ann had persuaded Cal to buy a house nearby rather than continue to rent the condo when Lenora had left. "Jake will have a yard to play out back in when he grows older and neither you nor I will have to endure heavy traffic when the girls are to-ing and fro-ing," she'd pointed out.

"Good advice; I hadn't thought of that," he'd agreed.

Savannah and Madison had thoroughly enjoyed choosing paint colors and soft furnishings, curtains and bedroom furniture. The only thing they weren't too happy about was sharing a bathroom.

"Are you two gals for real?" Sally-Ann rebuked them sternly on hearing them whine about having to share. "Don't y'all realize how privileged y'all are? There are kids in this world that don't even have enough food in their bellies to stop them from starvin' to death. I'm disgusted to hear the both of you behave like this. Y'all can just forgo your pocket money this week and put it in the charity box, and shame on you both."

That had given them something to think about, and Madison, always the softie, had apologized and offered to fill a bag with clothes, toys, and books to bring to the thrift shop.

Sally-Ann was very anxious that her daughters grew up realizing just how extremely fortunate they were. She was most anxious too that they were not, as they anticipated, going to be hanging around the mall every summer.

Sally-Ann had heard disturbing news from one of the other mothers. One of the teens that the girls palled around with, Luanne Gaynor, had been posting nude pictures of herself to Jackson Bushman, a classmate, because Jackson was emotionally blackmailing Luanne. He was telling her he'd cut himself if she didn't do as he asked, and binding her to an oath of secrecy. Jackson had quite the collection of nude photos of his high school classmates, Darlene Regan informed Sally-Ann in a whisper as they stood in line to buy a coffee to go. "And her mom is so enamored with her new boy toy, she has no clue what's going on in Luanne's life."

"She should be told!" Sally-Ann was aghast.

"Who's gonna do the tellin'? That's not news any momma wants to hear. And you know what a sharp tongue she has. I'm staying out of it." Darlene paid for her coffee and waved good-bye to a horrified Sally-Ann. Darlene had teenagers herself; wouldn't *she* want to know if one of her children was in trouble?

She'd gone back to her office, closed the door, and rung Luanne Gaynor's mother. "Nell? Hi, it's Sally-Ann. Are y'all free to talk for a moment?"

"Sure, sure, honey, what's up?" Nell said gaily; she'd probably just got out of bed with the boy toy, Sally-Ann thought, a tad enviously. The sooner she got to Spain, the better!

"Nell, this is not a call I want to make and I'm sorry to be the one to tell you, but you should be aware of this, as I would want to be if it were one of my daughters. I heard that Jackson Bushman is emotionally blackmailing Luanne to send him nude photos of herself by threatening to self-harm if she doesn't, and has sworn her to secrecy. Y'all need to deal with it."

"Who told you this?" Nell demanded.

"I heard it on the grapevine today from another mother, who didn't have the decency to ring you herself, Nell. It's been goin' on a while seemingly. As soon as I heard about it, I decided to call you. It's too serious not to."

"Well, if it's true, I appreciate it," Nell said tightly.

"And I would appreciate if you didn't say it was me that told you. I don't want my girls blackballed by their classmates for being snitches, especially as they haven't said a word to me about it."

"I get it," Nell agreed. "Bye."

One mother's day ruined, Sally-Ann thought ruefully, wishing she hadn't met Darlene in the coffee line.

Sally-Ann had casually asked the twins for their phones and iPads to do her "inspection," as she called it, and, grumbling, they had surrendered them. But they knew the score: no inspection, no phone or iPad. She and Cal had been very firm about that once the twins had been allowed phones and to go on social media. She'd gone through them with a fine-tooth comb and seen nothing untoward, although she was slightly appalled at the inanities and self-absorption that filled their lives. Those Kardashians had so much to answer for; she needed to get her daughters to Europe to broaden their minds and expand their horizons.

She'd taken the girls to lunch at Tacos a Go-Go, and while they sat in one of the bright orange booths tucking into *barbacoa*, fries, and soda, she'd said casually, "What's this I hear about Luanne Gaynor sending nude photos to Jackson Bushman?"

"Mom, how did you know *that*?" Savannah demanded. "Maddy, did you tell Mom that?"

"No, I *didn't*," her sister spluttered indignantly.

"I heard," Sally-Ann said coolly. "Were either of you ever asked to send nude photos to any boy?"

Savannah averted her gaze and concentrated on drinking her soda.

"Savannah?"

"Yeah, I was asked, but I didn't," she retorted.

"Well done, darlin'." Sally-Ann felt a wave of relief mixed with apprehension wash over her. Savannah used her phone and iPad a lot more than Maddy, who was much more into sport. "Who asked you?"

"I can't tell you, 'cause you'll only go and let them have it. And Luanne only did it 'cause she was scared that Jackson would commit suicide. That's what he said he was going to do. She didn't *really* want to do it, Mom. Although Deena Layton *loves* showing off her ta tas. She wants to be a model. She even posted her Brazilian!" Savannah crammed a forkful of fries into her mouth.

Sally-Ann was horrified though not surprised at Deena Layton, who was a precocious little madam whose skirts were always up to her butt cheeks and whose tops were practically open to her navel. How her parents let her dress in such a revealing fashion was beyond comprehension.

"Savannah, don't stuff your mouth full," she remonstrated mildly, not letting them see how taken aback she was. "Look, girls, when something like this happens, you really need to tell an adult. It's not ratting out—"

"We can't be snitches, Mom." Savannah rolled her eyes.

"When someone is threatening to commit suicide, Savannah, snitching doesn't come into it. OK?" Sally-Ann said sternly.

"OK," her daughter agreed reluctantly, shrugging her shoulders.

Rearing teenagers who lived their lives on social media was nerve-racking. After that particular conversation, Sally-Ann was even more determined that the twins would not be spending long summer holidays hanging out with their peers.

"I want to bring them to Europe, Cal. I want them to experience other cultures; I want them out of Houston for the summer. You should see the things that preoccupy them. Lord above, at least we lived our lives outdoors and didn't know what a damned selfie was or who or what a Kardashian was; we just had Madonna baring her ass and her boobs and defiling crucifixes—"

"Which she's still doing, although she's beginning to look like Joan Crawford now," Cal said, grinning; he had paid twenty dollars to get a look at the rock star's "dirty book" behind the Wainwrights' barn.

"And if you asked me what a Kardashian was, I'd have said aliens on *Deep Space Nine*." He was sitting with his ex-wife under a green sun umbrella outside Agora, drinking Americanos. It was a blue-skied late-January day and the temperature had hit almost seventy.

"Be serious," chided Sally-Ann, laughing. "And they were Cardassians, as I recall. Actually, Gul Dukat was quite sexy," she added, grinning.

"Going to Europe's a bit drastic, though," Cal hedged. "We can't protect them from real life, Sally-Ann."

"I know that, Cal, but when we were growing up, we didn't

have all that social media pressure. And I want them to be curious about other civilizations, other traditions, different arts and philosophies. The years are flying by. They'll be going to college before we know it and that's it, they'll have flown the Connolly Cooper coop," she punned.

"OK," he agreed reluctantly. "If you feel that strongly, go for it. But how will you manage about work?" He eyed her over the rim of his cup.

Sally-Ann smiled. How typical of her workaholic ex. "Now that I have alimony, I can take longer holidays," she teased.

"Ha ha," he said drily. "You're a hoot an' a half, Sally-Ann."

"I know. But, seriously, I've been thinking about it. I want to spend time with the girls; they're growing up fast. So I'm gonna make Viola a director. She's managed that office and held the fort for me so often, she deserves it."

"Swell, good thinkin'. How long do you plan on going to Europe for?"

"Well, we do have custody arrangements in place, Cal. That depends on you," she said. "If you're not happy with the idea, it's nixed."

"You know I'm not gonna make an issue out of it," he said, a little irritable that she would think he would.

"It's only manners to ask, darlin'."

"Appreciate it. Jake will miss them as much as I will. I expect you'll be gone at least a month; not much point otherwise."

Sally-Ann took a deep breath, trying to contain her excitement. Since she'd had the brain wave at sunrise, it was all she could think about. She would burst if she didn't say it to him soon. "Yeah, well, here's the thing, Cal. I was hoping you'd be OK with it. I thought I'd bring them to France for two weeks and then Spain for a month, so I rang Jutta to book the penthouse and I took a chance and provisionally booked a second apartment in the hopes that perhaps you and Jake and the au pair might come for a couple of weeks. It's no big deal to cancel, because it's only January and

I've booked for August. We could have some real good family time if you wanted to."

"Hey, that's somethin' to think about. I *like* it," he approved, relieved that she'd considered him in her plans. "It could be fun."

"That's what I was thinkin'. And listen to this and don't faint." Her eyes were sparkling. "I told y'all that poor Austen who owns the penthouse next to ours died last year; well, Jutta told me that Anna's put it up for sale, and I was thinkin' I might just put in an offer. It would be good to have a place of my own. It would be an investment, and it would mean our extended family could spend time out there together if you wanted to."

"I really do like your thinkin', woman. Where will I be sleepin'?" He grinned.

"In your own penthouse," she said firmly.

"Now that we're divorced and we're reasonably good friends, couldn't we be good friends with benefits?" He studied her intently.

"You could have had all the benefits y'all wanted when we were married before you . . . eh . . . ya know."

"OK, just checking; didn't mean to offend you. You're still a hot woman, and that's a compliment."

"Cut it out, Cal," she laughed. "It ain't gonna happen."

"I miss you."

"Well, I don't miss you," she said lightly, determined not to go down that path.

"So you're thinkin' of becoming a woman of more property? Will you take out a mortgage or buy it outright?" He stretched his long be-jeaned legs out in front of him and raised his face to the sun. All he needed was a Stetson and his spurs and he'd look like a cowboy, she thought in amusement. And a sexy one at that. She wasn't going to close the door on bedding him again, but it would be at a time of *her* choosing, not his.

"I don't know yet. I want to have a chat with my accountant."

"Put in your offer either way, that's a damn fine penthouse on a top-class site. It won't stay on the market for long, economic downturn notwithstanding," Cal advised. "The vultures are hovering all over Europe, snapping up bargains."

"And there are bargains to be had," she agreed. "By the way, Cal, just so y'all know. I would have put in an offer for the penthouse even if we hadn't been divorced. I won't have to touch my alimony. I made sure I became a woman of independent means, with my own business, when things went wrong for us." She stood up and took a bill out of her wallet and put it under her empty cup. "Coffee's on me. See y'all. Bring Jake over soon; I haven't seen him in a while."

"OK, boss!" Cal raised his hand in salute and smiled at her.

Sally-Ann blew him a kiss and headed to the parking lot. She felt strangely lighthearted. Divorcing Cal had been a liberation for her. She was her own woman. She knew where she stood personally, financially, and professionally. The girls were doing OK. And she and Cal were on an even keel and made a strong team as parents. It was a good place to be.

◆

Cal watched Sally-Ann walk away with that graceful, long-legged stride of hers, and couldn't but admire his ex-wife. She was a great mother, he acknowledged. To his shame, he'd never really appreciated that when the children were young. He sighed and signaled for the bill. She'd stood firm in her desire to divorce him, much to his dismay. He'd hoped to persuade her to stay as they were and try and woo his way back to having a proper marriage, but she wasn't having it. He'd never seen her so determined.

Perhaps the summer in Europe might be the time to renew his efforts, because they *were* good together, and their family— including Jake, and that was a big thanks to Sally-Ann—was solid. In the meantime he'd keep having coffee-morning dates with her. He really looked forward to them. He picked up his phone and dialed Eva, Jake's au pair. "Everything OK, Eva?"

"He's sleeping, he's eating, and he's pooping," Eva laughed.

"How do you fancy traveling to Europe in the summer? Just letting you know it's on the cards, if you decide to stay longer than the six months you'd planned."

"Oooooh, I like it, Cal. Perhaps I'll stay for a year instead."

"Sally-Ann and the girls will be with us, so you'll be able to have some good free time."

"It sounds better and better," his au pair replied gaily.

And so it does, thought Cal, *and so it does.*

◆

"Please eat your mashed banana, *Liebling,*" Jutta urged, pressing a spoonful against Alicia's pursed lips.

"No, no, Momma." The toddler waved the spoon away and the mashed fruit spattered across Jutta's blouse. "*Scheisse,*" she cursed, wiping it away with a tissue, but there was a stain right on the boob. She'd have to change. She had a meet and greet in three-quarters of an hour, at Mi Capricho. She'd need to get her skates on. Her phone rang and she saw Eduardo De La Fuente's name come up on the screen. There was no point in even taking the call. Alicia was starting to wail. She wouldn't be able to converse with him. She'd ring him later.

"Felipe, will you try and get this into her? I'll have to change and I'll have to leave soon," she asked her husband, who was slouched on the sofa, watching a football match.

"Sure," he agreed, taking the dish and spoon she handed him. He sat down at the table beside Alicia's high chair and waved the spoon at his daughter before dipping it into the mash. "Open up for the choo-choo train," he said in a funny voice. Alicia giggled and opened her mouth wide as the spoon got nearer.

"Num, num," said Felipe, spooning the mash in.

"Num, num," echoed Alicia, eating it.

"Simple," her husband raised an eyebrow. "At least I'm good at something. Maybe I should have opened a day care instead of going into the development business."

"Oh, don't start," she snapped, putting her phone in her bag.

She wasn't in the humor to listen to him beating his breast about his failing business. She went into their bedroom and unfastened her blouse and threw it in the laundry basket. Two clients had failed to renew their contracts this week; that was six lost this year so far and it was only January. She could understand why. Money was tight. Maintenance fees were going up. Municipal taxes were going up. Owners were looking to make cutbacks. All along the coast, businesses like hers were suffering.

She opened a drawer and selected a pale lemon V-neck jumper from the neat pile. It looked good with her tailored black trousers. She'd stay well away from Alicia.

Her phone pinged with a message. It was her clients to say they had just landed. She'd better get on the road. She touched up her makeup, brushed her hair, and went to the balcony that ran the length of their apartment and looked out. The sun was dipping low towards Africa and, to the east, banks of rain clouds loomed ominously along the coast. The clients she was meeting would not have good weather for the next few days, and it was chilly too, now that the sun was setting.

Her phone rang again and she half expected it to be Eduardo, but Sally-Ann Connolly Cooper's name appeared and she answered it.

"Sally-Ann, how can I help?" Jutta put on her most business-like voice.

"Hey, Jutta, this is not out of curiosity but a genuine query. How much is Anna looking for for the penthouse? I'm interested in putting in an offer." Jutta's jaw dropped. She could hardly believe her ears. Anna's penthouse was hardly up on the boards and she was getting an offer. Win-win situation. If Sally-Ann bought it, hopefully she would retain Jutta for management and cleaning services and—icing on the cake—she would get her seller's fee, and a good one at that.

"That's great news, Sally-Ann. You've seen it, and the high standard of décor. The sale will include all fixtures and fittings.

I'm just on my way to meet some clients who are arriving. Can I call you back in five minutes, when I'm in the car, and I'll give you all the details then?"

"Perfect," Sally-Ann agreed. "Talk to y'all in five."

Jutta almost did a little dance in the bedroom but restrained herself. She knew of apartments that were still on the market two years down the line because of the property crash, their owners not willing to make a loss. And she was selling a penthouse in less than twenty-four hours of it going up for sale. That would encourage other sellers to come to her, although she doubted she'd ever be so lucky again.

She was just about to rush into the lounge to tell Felipe the great news, when she stopped short. She'd better not say anything, Jutta thought regretfully. Her husband would think she was rubbing his nose in it. Her business was doing fine; his wasn't. She should take cognizance of his masculine sensibilities, she thought ruefully. But if it were the other way around, that wouldn't even be a consideration, and he wouldn't think twice about telling her his good news. So much for equality in marriage. Why should she hide her light under a bushel? Because it was the easiest thing to do, Jutta admitted, slipping her phone back into her bag. "See you in a while," she said, blowing a kiss at Alicia, who was pulling Felipe's ears and chuckling happily as he pretended it hurt.

"*Adiós.*" Felipe didn't even look in her direction, he was so busy entertaining their daughter.

Jutta took the lift to the foyer. She was the breadwinner in the family; she'd better go and earn a tasty loaf, she decided, anxious to get back to Sally-Ann and secure the deal as soon as possible.

◆

"I'm sorry I missed your call yesterday evening, Señor De La Fuente—"

"Eduardo, please."

"Thank you, Eduardo. I'm Jutta. How is your aunt doing?"

"Quite well, Jutta. We are back in Madrid today and she will be in convalescence for another while. I would like to thank you very much for your great kindness to her when she took ill."

"Not at all, Eduardo. I have an elderly parent myself. I know the worry of taking care of aged relatives."

"Indeed."

"Well, thank you for letting me know," Jutta said politely. "I'm glad to hear the good news."

"*De nada, muchas gracias* once again, Jutta. Um . . . just before you go . . . I might be interested in buying the MacDonald penthouse. I saw on the board in Reception that it's up for sale."

"Oh!" exclaimed Jutta, completely thrown by this new development.

"Yes, it's rather spectacular. The views are magnificent. Could you tell me what price Señora MacDonald is looking for?"

"Well, actually, I have a buyer. It's off the market," Jutta informed him proudly.

"Oh! So soon. Is it someone in La Joya?" Eduardo asked, and she knew by his tone that he was quite miffed.

"As you, more than anyone, can appreciate, Eduardo, I have to be mindful of confidentiality regarding my clients," Jutta said diplomatically.

"Of course. Of course," Eduardo exclaimed hastily. "I should not have asked."

"If anything goes awry and the sale doesn't go through, I'll get back to you straightaway if you would like me to," Jutta promised.

"That would be excellent. *Adios*."

"*Adiós*, Eduardo." Jutta hung up, delighted with herself. It was a big if, because Sally-Ann was gung-ho to buy the penthouse, but if the American's deal didn't go through, now Jutta had a safety net to fall back on. The gods were smiling on her for sure. And if another penthouse came up, she had a potential buyer already. What more could she ask for?

◆

"Are you sure y'all don't mind me buying it, Anna? Please say straight out if you do," Sally-Ann urged.

"I couldn't think of anyone I'd prefer to have it—honestly, Sally-Ann. And are you OK with the price?" Anna asked hesitantly.

"Yup, I sure am. It's a fabulous penthouse in a fabulous location, I can't wait to get the girls over, and Cal and Jake are coming too. A real family holiday. I'm glad for the girls. They don't even know we're divorced. We never said it to 'em." Sally-Ann laughed.

"That's a terrific idea. The less they have to worry about at that age, the better."

"And listen, y'all, if you and the ladies ever want to come over, because it will be empty a lot—I'm not going to rent it out—feel free, Anna, won't you?" Sally-Ann urged.

"That's kind of you, love, but I don't think I could ever go back again. Too many memories. It's hard enough here at home."

"I can't imagine," Sally-Ann said sympathetically. "Well, if y'all and the girls ever feel like coming to Texas, I'd love to have ya."

"Well, I might do that sometime," Anna laughed. "I better go, I hear Charlotte waking up from her nap. There's a nappy—you call them diapers, don't you?—waiting to be changed."

"I'm doing a bit of diaper changing myself. And I still have the knack of it," Sally-Ann boasted. "Take care, Anna darlin'."

"And you too," Anna returned, cheered by the call from her friend.

She couldn't believe she had an offer for the penthouse already. And from Sally-Ann at that. Austen was looking out for her, she thought sadly, walking up the stairs to her granddaughter. It was kind of Sally-Ann to invite her to use the penthouse, but that chapter in her life was closed.

She glanced out the bedroom window when she opened the blinds. The rain was pelting down, the wind blowing the skeletal trees mercilessly. How lovely it would have been to relax in Spain with her husband. And, oh, how she missed him. Grief overwhelmed her, as it always did when she thought about him. Her mother had an old country saying: "You never miss the shelter of the bush until it's gone." How she missed the shelter of Austen's love and care. His stalwart presence had given her a strength she'd never really acknowledged until it was gone. She felt like one of those trees out there, battered in the wind. Would it ever end? she wondered. This indescribable sorrow that had her wrapped so tightly in its unrelenting grip that sometimes she almost felt she could not breathe.

Chapter Forty-One

MAY

Eduardo / Jutta

Should he tell Consuela that he was meeting Jutta Sauer for coffee? Eduardo wondered as he took out his phone to call his wife. But then she would want to know why, and he didn't want her to know that he was interested in buying another penthouse that had come up for sale in La Joya. Best to say nothing for the time being. There would be nothing worse than telling Consuela about it and then having it fall through.

He was excited, Eduardo admitted. The particular penthouse that was for sale had a better aspect than the MacDonald one. The roof terrace would give him views over the whole complex, as well as across the Mediterranean. He would be the king of all he surveyed in his well-appointed aerie. There was only one problem. He did not get on well with the current owner. In fact they loathed each other. Eduardo had sent stern letters to him demanding an *immediate* settlement of his maintenance arrears or face imminent legal action.

The owner had knocked on his apartment door and told him in no uncertain terms to "fuck off and stop annoying me; you'll get the arrears when I sell up," while his revolting parrot had hurled obscenities from his perch. Eduardo had told the owner the previous year that he must get rid of that pesky bird, and again he'd been treated to a tirade from both the owner and his obnoxious pet. The Englishman had been intimidatingly threatening, and even Eduardo's imperious authority had quailed under the aggressive response.

Eduardo felt certain that because of the bad feeling between them he would be the *last* person the owner would want to sell to. Hence his coffee meeting with Jutta. He'd a strategy to deal with the problem if she was willing.

"*Hola,*" he said, hearing his wife's voice at the other end of the phone. "How are things?"

"*Muy bien,*" Consuela said in her usual calm tones. "I'm just home from my classes. I dropped in to Beatriz and had lunch with her and she was in good form, and afterwards I pushed her along the riverbank in her wheelchair and we sat and read our books in the sun. It's a beautiful day in Madrid."

"It's beautiful down here too. May is *such* a pleasant month," Eduardo said, relieved that Consuela was in one of her serene moods. "It was kind of you to take Beatriz for a walk."

"She loves the *río*, and it was relaxing to sit under the shade of the trees and watch the world go by. How did your meeting go?"

"It's all about finances, really; the coastal erosion is getting worse, and we need protection, but we are one of many urbanizations along the coast with the same problem. We spoke with the engineers and they are going to compile a report, and I can bring it up at the AGM so that owners are aware that there *is* a problem. All in all it went fine, so I'll take the eight-oh-five tonight and get a taxi from the station."

"OK, text me when you're in the taxi. I'll have a light supper waiting for you."

"*Muchas gracias, querida,*" he said gratefully. "*Adiós.*"

"*Adiós,* safe journey," his wife said, and he exhaled as he hung up. He never quite knew what to expect with Consuela these days, but today they were friendly and there had been no arguments, and that was a plus.

He sat in the shade of a sun umbrella in a quiet corner of the terrace of the hotel where he'd arranged to meet Jutta. This was not his first coffee with the German woman. He'd bumped into her by chance in Marbella in March and they had stopped to exchange greetings. He'd been early for a meeting at a lawyer's office—in his capacity as *Presidente*—to discuss the ongoing problem of maintenance arrears. He was just about to sit at one of the coffee shops in Orange Square when she stopped at the table to say *hola*, and he heard himself ask if she would like to join him for coffee. He'd surprised himself as much as her, but they had sat and had a most enjoyable conversation, about the economy, the problems he was experiencing as *El Presidente*, the problems her husband was experiencing in the downturn, and suchlike, and he was astonished when he looked at his watch and saw that thirty minutes had passed in what seemed like five, and he was rather looking forward to their coffee and conversation now.

He admired the German woman's work ethic; it was similar to his own. Eduardo had been impressed in spite of himself that she would not break her client's trust by revealing to him who was buying the MacDonald penthouse.

They had a lot in common, Eduardo decided after their conversation. Both of them found the *mañana* culture, so prevalent in the south, decidedly irritating. Both of them thought the under-the-counter payments and the tax evasion that was so prevalent in Spanish society less than admirable. They had a discussion about the trial of the Infanta Cristina—sixth in line to the Spanish throne—and her husband on corruption charges, and Jutta told Eduardo that she'd been most impressed when King Juan Carlos had declared that "justice is the same for everyone," and wondered if it was a sign that things were changing, and if the monarchy would last.

He liked her clipped, efficient style. She wasn't a fan of small talk; neither was he. She was opinionated. Normally, opinionated women irked him, but her arguments were well reasoned and surprisingly similar to his own. What topics would their discussions cover today? he wondered, putting his phone on silent.

He spotted Jutta crossing the square, shoulders back, head straight, eyes looking confidently ahead. Excellent deportment; he approved. How chic she looked in her tailored cream suit trimmed with navy. Consuela always looked smart but never chic. She didn't have the height or the figure.

What on earth was he thinking, comparing his wife to this tall, elegant woman who was striding confidently towards him? Eduardo chided himself. He almost felt disloyal. He stood politely and felt unaccountably nervous.

"*Buenas tardes. ¿Cómo está usted?*" He used the more formal greeting.

"*Bien gracias, ¿y usted?*" She was equally formal in her response. He liked that. She had a reserve that appealed to him.

"*Bien gracias,*" Eduardo smiled, indicating for her to sit. "Coffee? Iced tea?"

"I think *café sin leche, por favor.*" She settled herself gracefully in the chair opposite him.

"The almond cake here is rather special, if you'd care for some . . . or any accompaniment you might like," he added hastily, not wanting her to think he was too mean to buy her something more expensive.

"I do love the almond cake, Eduardo. It's one of my favorites, but disastrous for my waistline," Jutta confessed, laying her bag on the empty chair beside her and sitting with her usual poise.

"Just this once, then." He clicked his fingers authoritatively and gave their order to a waiter who appeared at his side almost instantly.

"So, Eduardo, I'm intrigued by your phone call." Jutta flicked her long blond hair back over her shoulders and looked at him expectantly.

Eduardo cleared his throat. "As you know, I'm interested in buying a penthouse, and I see number five has gone up for sale. Now, the unfortunate thing is that the owner has issues with me because I've been trying to get him to pay his arrears, and he has taken grave umbrage." He stared right back at her, admiring her clear green eyes, which met his so confidently.

"That's unfortunate."

"Indeed."

"What do you propose?"

Their coffee and cake arrived and they busied themselves with sugaring the steaming drink and Jutta took a forkful of the cake. "Delicious," she pronounced. "You were saying?" She arched an eyebrow at him.

"What I propose is this, Jutta, if you are in agreement." He raised a dark eyebrow and studied her intently. "I give you power of attorney to buy the apartment for me in your name. The seller won't know that I'm the buyer and it also means I don't have to be at the closing with the notary. You can do that in my stead. Then you and I'll meet with the notary to transfer the deed of ownership."

Jutta clapped her hands and laughed. "Of course! Masterful," she exclaimed. "And may I say that I'm honored to be considered for your power of attorney."

"So you will do it?" he asked eagerly.

"*Ciertamente*," Jutta agreed.

"*Excelente*, Jutta, *excelente*. I could not be more pleased." He was almost boyishly excited, his brown eyes glittering almost black as he smiled at her.

"I am always pleased when my clients are pleased, Eduardo," Jutta said, raising her cup to him. "We will be the perfect team."

Later that night, as the AVE flashed through the dusky dark

countryside, heading north to Madrid, Eduardo remembered her words. "We will be the perfect team." It was the most affirming thing anyone had said to him in a long time. She was a very singular lady, this Jutta Sauer. He looked forward to their next encounter. They'd arranged to formalize their agreement the following week in the office of a notary colleague of his who practiced in Marbella. Perhaps Jutta might even have lunch with him that day, Eduardo hoped. There would be several more meetings before the penthouse was finally his.

He was glad he was keeping his purchase secret. That meant he didn't have to tell Consuela about Jutta's participation in the deal. He supposed it was quite an underhand thing to do to the owner. Consuela might not approve of his sleight of hand. That was his reason for keeping quiet about his interactions with the German woman. No other. He closed his eyes as the train sped along the tracks, and revisited every moment of his afternoon meeting with Jutta.

◆

Jutta cleansed the makeup from her face, then toned and moisturized it before wrapping a light robe around her. Felipe was overnighting in Murcia, and Alicia was asleep in her room: she could hear her daughter's even breathing on the monitor. She was tired but exhilarated. She was more used to selling property than buying. And to act as Eduardo De La Fuente's buyer and have power of attorney was quite the feather in her cap.

She poured herself a glass of red wine and took it to her lounger on the balcony. It was a balmy night. A full moon cast silver streamers across the sea and the cicadas chirruped in the gardens below as a light breeze wafted the scents of jasmine and orange blossom on the night air. Jutta took a sip of the fruity rioja and lay back against the cushions. It had been a long but interesting day. Eduardo must be tired too. He was presently on a train, racing to the capital, very pleased with his undoubtedly foolproof plan to buy the penthouse of his dreams. Once she too had dreamed of buying a penthouse in La Joya. That dream had vanished like vapor in the wind.

To give her power of attorney was a seal of approval she would never have expected from the haughty *madrileño*—and a testament to her own high standards, she acknowledged with a hint of pride. Eduardo too ran his business professionally and ethically. They had many similarities in their work ethics, Jutta reflected.

He was an interesting man. His self-important bearing hid his inner shyness. He was intelligent, well read, very *au fait* with current affairs. Their conversation had been stimulating. He was an attractive man too, in that fine-boned, aristocratic way of high-bred Spaniards. He reminded her of Adolfo, Duke of Suárez, the revered prime minister who had steered the country to democracy and bravely faced a military coup, standing courageously as gunmen fired while his parliamentary colleagues dived to the floor to take cover. Eduardo had similar amber eyes and a raven-haired widow's peak, the long straight nose and firm mouth, but not the charm and easy manner of the dashing duke.

He was sexy in an untouchable sort of way. What would he be like in bed? Or would he ever be able to let go of his inhibitions? Jutta had seen his wife down by the pool several times. Small, curvy, with dark feathered hair that framed her oval face, she was an attractive woman, but quiet and restrained and not very vibrant, unlike so many Spanish women. A woman who knew her place, Jutta guessed. Perhaps, then, she and Eduardo were very well suited.

What would Constanza Torres think if Jutta confessed that she actually considered Eduardo De La Fuente a little sexy? Constanza hated his guts, and with good cause, Jutta thought in amusement.

What would Felipe think if he knew that she was fantasizing about other men when once all she could think about and lust after was her husband? There was no lust in their marriage now; for her at any rate the sex was mediocre. A habit. This was what their marriage had come to. She felt Felipe had let her down. He'd failed in his business because of recklessness. Once she'd admired her husband's go-getting attitude, comparing it to her own cautious, restrained approach. She was exceedingly glad now that she'd listened to her instincts.

She yawned. She needed to go to bed. She would be up early with Alicia. Her au pair had to go to the dentist. A toddler in the morning was not for the fainthearted. Draining her glass in a long gulp, Jutta locked the balcony door, switched off the lights, and slid into her bed, pleased to have it to herself. One thing she was determined about: Eduardo De La Fuente would never work with a more professional businesswoman than Jutta Sauer, she vowed, listening to the lullaby of the moon-kissed sea.

◆

If she didn't know better, Consuela would have said her husband was slightly drunk, she thought, lying beside him in the dark, listening to his deep, regular breathing as he slept soundly.

He'd arrived home from La Joya in unusually good form, regaling her with every detail of his meeting with the engineers and council personnel. Telling her bits and pieces of gossip about the owners—the Gilots and the Van der Valks had had a row about the Gilots' wisteria trailing over the dividing wall, culminating with Japp Van der Valk taking shears to it and dumping what was on his side back over onto the Gilots' balcony—confiding that he was exceptionally pleased that his planting regime was beginning to look extremely pretty in the red and yellow colors of the Spanish flag, despite the constant whines of some that the flower beds were now too regimented, and that they preferred the profusion of shrubs that had been there before he made his highhanded decision to clear them.

And then, when they had got into bed together, he'd turned and taken her in his arms and kissed her, telling her that he loved her. He'd made love to her with a passion that she'd not experienced in years. Fortunately, Consuela smiled in the dark, his passion had coincided with one of her menopausal estrogen surges and she hadn't had to fake her orgasm, as she very often did. The goddess within had had a most enjoyable time.

The power of the presidency was suiting her husband. He was clearly reveling in his duties. She should make the most of it, she thought. The AGM in August might see him deposed, and Eduardo, and life, would return to normal. Tomorrow might be a good day to tell him that she and Catalina were planning a weekend in Paris to walk the labyrinth in Chartres Cathedral and follow the mysteries of the Magdalene.

Chapter Forty-Two

JUNE

Eduardo / Jutta

"Here is the printout of the agenda for the AGM for your inspection; let me know if you are happy for me to email it out to the owners," Constanza said in her snootiest voice, handing Eduardo a slim file.

"*Gracias*," he replied, equally curt. He would go through it with a fine-tooth comb.

"I see you have inserted a clause that you intend to employ your *friend* Facundo Gonzales as a full-time concierge and reduce my hours."

"Señora, may I immediately point out that Facundo Gonzales is not a friend as you suggest but a mere acquaintance who came highly recommended, and I refute your inference. I think two full-time concierges at shorter hours would be better for the community than the present situation of one full-time and one part-time. The work would be divided more evenly and get done more efficiently."

Constanza bristled and her eyes flashed contempt. "Señor De La Fuente, my work record is impeccable. But let me tell you one thing here and now: *If* by employing that little lazy lump Facundo full-time you think you are going to edge me out, take note that—just like a concierge up in Jasmine Gardens who was sacked because she was not on good terms with the president—I shall take you to court for unfair dismissal. As did that woman, who, I may point out, won her case and a large settlement that cost the Jasmine Gardens community a lot of money. *And*, may I add, the new concierge who took over from her was so busy running his own business while he was supposed to be managing the complex that he couldn't see what was going on under his nose. Apartments were being let to drug dealers and other undesirables, and the owners were most unhappy. He had to be sacked, and the president was voted out at the next AGM." She stalked away with her head in the air, leaving Eduardo fuming.

That woman was a thorn in his side. His plan indeed had been to, as she termed it, "edge her out" and put his own man in, but Constanza was no fool. She could see his strategy. He'd heard about the carry-on in Jasmine Gardens. He certainly wouldn't want an unfair dismissal case on *his* watch, he thought irascibly. It looked like he just might have to put up with the Gorgon, as he privately called the outspoken concierge who did not know her place.

Eduardo glanced at his watch; he needed to hurry. He was meeting Jutta for a quick coffee, and to give her the check with the deposit for the penthouse, in Fuengirola train station before taking the commuter train to María Zambrano to catch the AVE to Madrid. It was all about travel today. His mother was flying into Madrid-Barajas and he wouldn't have time to go into the office, collect his car, and drive to the airport. As he was traveling on the AVE, he was entitled to a free train ticket to Madrid Airport. A small consolation, he thought, feeling tired at the thought of all he had to do.

He knew why he was stressed—apart from that Torres woman's antics. His mother was coming back to Spain, and Isabella's arrival always brought up emotions he preferred to keep suppressed. Was it abnormal not to want to see your mother? Eduardo wondered, packing his briefcase and overnight case before locking up the apartment and phoning for a taxi.

When Beatriz had taken ill at the beginning of the year, she'd asked to see her sister, thinking that she was going to die. Fortunately his aunt's health had improved and she was quite stable, thanks to *la warfarina* drugs that she took daily. Eduardo had suggested that Isabella wait until the summer to visit, and Beatriz and her sister had agreed that she would come in June. Now the time had come, and his mother would be staying with him and Consuela for a fortnight initially, after which she would travel to Barcelona to stay with friends and then travel south to join him, Consuela, and Beatriz for a week in La Joya.

His phone rang. It was Jutta and he answered it eagerly. "*¿Hola?*"

"Eduardo?" she said in her brisk accented voice.

"*Sí.* Jutta, is everything all right?" She sounded stressed.

"I'm so sorry. I have to cancel. My daughter has fallen and is on her way to hospital. The au pair just phoned. I have to meet them there."

"Oh, dear. Well, don't worry; I can lodge the deposit directly into your account if you send me the account number and IBAN. I was looking forward to our coffee and catching up."

"Me too," Jutta sighed. "Typical, when Felipe isn't here and I have to cancel. It's frustrating, Eduardo."

"I'm sure it is," he said sympathetically. "Look, I'm back down for a board meeting at the weekend. Perhaps we could schedule something in—only if it suits you, of course."

"Great, Eduardo. It would be good to catch up, and I can bring the keys and you can have another look around the penthouse if you like," she suggested.

"I'd like that very much indeed," Eduardo agreed.

"OK, I better fly. *Adiós,* Eduardo."

"*Adiós,* Jutta. I hope all will be OK with your daughter."

"*Gracias,*" she said, and hung up.

The one highlight in his day, and it wasn't going to happen, Eduardo thought disappointedly as the taxi took the slip road into the bustling city where they had been due to meet.

Chapter Forty-Three

Eduardo / Jutta

It's the first time she's looked old, Eduardo thought, slightly shocked when he saw his mother pushing a trolley loaded with luggage through the Arrivals doors. "*Madre,*" he greeted her formally, kissing both her cheeks. "Let me take this."

"Eduardo." Isabella's eyes lit up. "You look so well, so handsome. It's good to see you." She hugged him and he tried not to be uncomfortable in her embrace.

"You look well also," he returned, pushing the trolley towards the exit. His mother looked very fashionable in her black trousers and red linen jacket with a Hermès scarf looped in an elegant fashion around her neck. Her hair, still chestnut—he was sure it was dyed—was cut in a stylish bob and she was the epitome of an affluent, stylish, well-traveled older woman. She was in her mid-seventies by now.

"Eduardo, wait," she said as he led them to the taxi rank. "We need to talk, privately, before I meet Beatriz. I've taken the liberty of booking us a room for a couple of hours in one of the airport hotels. We can have dinner if you wish—"

"But Consuela will have a meal prepared. What is it you wish to talk about?" He tried not to be irritable.

"Eduardo, there's a shuttle; let's take it and you can listen to what I have to say, *then* we will go home to Consuela," his mother said firmly. "I *do* need to talk to you. This is the hotel." She showed him the name on her phone.

"I know it," he said. "Can we not talk in one of the lounges here?"

"No, it has to be a private place. Please humor me. You'll understand shortly."

"Very well," he agreed, somewhat unnerved at his mother's strange request, reversing his direction to head to the shuttle buses. "Is something wrong? Are you not well?" he asked, concerned at this turn of events.

"I'm fine," she said firmly.

"And the family? Your husband?"

"All well. Now tell me, how are Beatriz and Consuela, and what are you up to? Do you like the apartment in Andalucía?" she asked gaily, but he knew she was putting on a façade. A knot of anxiety twisted in his gut. Had Isabella got some terminal illness or some such? He sincerely hoped not. The hotel was a couple of kilometers from the airport and he sat beside his mother, unsure of whether to talk or to leave her to look out the window at the tree-lined street that led to the hotel. "It's nice to be home," she murmured. "Tell me, how is Beatriz?"

"Indomitable." Eduardo permitted himself a smile.

"She always was," Isabella laughed as the bus pulled up outside the hotel.

"Shall I order coffee?" Eduardo asked when Isabella had checked in.

"A drink for me, I think. A gin and tonic. And, please, Eduardo, it would be good if you joined me, seeing as you aren't driving. "

"Very well. I'll tell them to send the drinks to the room." He was becoming more rattled by the minute, despite his outward composure.

The room was clean, white, and soulless, and he sat in the white faux-leather bucket chair gazing unseeingly out the window at the pine trees opposite while his mother freshened up in the bathroom. A knock at the door announced the arrival of their drinks and he tipped the room service boy and carried them to the table.

Isabella slipped off her jacket and sank gratefully into the chair opposite Eduardo's. "Cheers, *mi querido*." She raised her glass to him and took a swig of the sparkling white drink. "That's so good," she sighed. He could see the weariness in her eyes, and her hand that held the glass shook slightly.

He took a sip of his dry sherry. "What is it you have to tell me so privately, *Madre*?" he asked bluntly.

"Eduardo, when I see Beatriz, she will beg me to promise not to say anything. It's always the same when we are all together. But I can no longer live this lie. It's unfair to me and to you, and it always has been, but she has been adamant that I say nothing. Now she and I are old and . . . shall we say . . . in the departure lounge to the life beyond. I . . . I . . ."

"What? What is it? Tell me, for the love of *Dios*." He tried to keep the impatience out of his voice.

"Eduardo, I am not your mother. Beatriz is," Isabella said flatly before taking another sip of her drink.

Eduardo stared at her, uncomprehending. Had Isabella just said that Beatriz was his *mother*?

"Beatriz is my mother?" he repeated frowning.

"Yes, *querido*," Isabella said gently. "Soon after Santiago and I married, Beatriz became pregnant by a young man, and of course at the time it was a scandalous thing, so she was sent to a convent that took care of unmarried mothers. When you were born, she came with you to live with us in Valencia, where Santiago was doing an internship. When Santiago transferred back to Madrid, she and our parents begged us to pretend that you were our child. You were still only a baby, ten months old. They couldn't bear the shame, the disgrace, of having an unmarried daughter with a baby. We agreed."

Eduardo swallowed hard. "Who was my father?"

"He was the son of a lawyer, an ambitious, impatient young man, but very handsome and charming. Your . . . Beatriz adored him and was brokenhearted when he abandoned her. She never got over it, really. She never allowed herself to fall in love again, and she punished herself so harshly, becoming rigid and cold and embittered. It *must* have been a dagger to the heart every time you called me Mama." Isabella had tears in her eyes.

"This is *outrageous!*" Eduardo stood up and clenched his fists in fury. "Why wasn't I told this before now? Why have I been kept in the dark about a truth that is rightfully mine to know—"

"Beatriz didn't want—"

"I had a *right* to know!" he roared. "I had a right to know who my mother was and who my father was instead of living this . . . this charade . . . this unholy *lie!*"

"Eduardo, please, be calm," urged Isabella, weeping quietly.

"Don't you dare tell me to be calm. Have you *any* idea how I suffered? Have you any idea how unloved I felt when you went to America and left me behind with *her*! And then you had Victoria and I felt so abandoned, so utterly and completely abandoned." To his horror, tears filled his eyes and a strangled sob erupted from him.

"Oh, Eduardo, Eduardo." Isabella jumped to her feet and went to embrace him but he brushed her roughly aside and went to stand with his back to her, staring out the window.

"I hate the two of you. Between you you've made my life a misery. I was a lost, lonely, isolated little boy always trying to fit in, and all you and the rest of my godforsaken family cared about was what people would *think*. Did no one ever stop to think about me and how *I* would feel?" He turned around and glared at her, wiping his eyes on his sleeve.

"I wanted so badly to bring you to America. It was a great

opportunity for Santiago, and I had to get away from my parents, from Beatriz, who was always trying to control everything. *Please* understand, Eduardo. I loved you. From the minute I held you in my arms I adored you. You were the most *beautiful* baby, and a gorgeous little boy. You had the biggest eyes and the longest blackest lashes. People were always stopping us in the street to admire you. Eduardo, it broke my heart that Beatriz wouldn't allow you to stay with us. I understood, of course. She loved you too. You were *her* child, *her* son. How could she let you go? You were her life. Her reason for living. It is such a tragedy that you felt unloved, for you truly were a *most* loved child." She rummaged in her bag for a tissue to wipe her eyes. "I knew you resented me—hated me, even—because you thought I had abandoned you.

"Eduardo, leaving you here in Madrid was the hardest thing I have ever done in my life, and enduring your bitterness down the years, which of course I understand, has been a heavy cross to bear. I wanted you to know that I didn't abandon you. I wanted you to know that I loved you very much, and I still do. To me, you are my son as much as you are hers. It would probably be best if I stay in a hotel while I'm here. I'm sure you cannot bear to have me in your home after this. Now you can see why I wanted us to be somewhere private?" She took another sip of her drink and slumped back down in her chair.

He saw how pale she'd become, how weary, and his anger drained away and he composed himself.

"I'm sorry I shouted, Isabella," he said stiffly. "It was the shock."

"The only one who heard was me; better than in an airport lounge, yes?" She managed a faint smile.

"Yes, you were thoughtful in your choice of location for the grand reveal. What was my father's name?" He sat back down opposite her and finished his sherry in one gulp.

"Rafael Navarro," Isabella sighed.

"It should be easy enough to find out more about him," Eduardo said grimly.

"Don't bother, *querido*, I can tell you what you need to know. As I said to you, Rafael was wealthy, ambitious, impatient, and, to be honest with you, he was a spoiled young man. He drove a very fast sports car, and he was partying in Seville a few years after you were born, and you know how narrow the streets are in Seville? He crashed his car. He was in a coma for seven months before he passed away."

"Did he know about me?" Eduardo loosened his tie and ran his fingers through his hair.

"Yes, he did. He paid Beatriz a lump sum if she undertook never to name him as the father. She used every cent of that money to raise and educate you. Try not to think too harshly of her, no matter what you think of me."

"I don't think harshly of you," he muttered. "I just have to adjust to all of this. It's like the rug has been pulled from underneath me, and all I thought I was is just a chimera."

"You are who you are, a very fine, good, and successful man. That comes from within, Eduardo. Not from Beatriz or Rafael. It is who you are. You should be proud of yourself."

"Shall we have another drink?" he asked quietly. "There is much I would like to know."

"Why not? But perhaps you could tell Consuela a little fib and text her and say my flight was delayed. We don't want to be rude and leave her wondering where we are."

"Of course. I'll do it straightaway. Just one drink and then I'll take you home. I'm sure you're exhausted."

"Yes, I am," she admitted, "but very relieved, Eduardo, that finally you know the truth and will come to realize how greatly loved you were—and still are."

"Thank you," said Eduardo bleakly. "I hope that you're right."

◆

"*Mi Isabella.*" Beatriz held out her arms to embrace the sister she loved with all her heart.

"*Beatriz, querida.*" Isabella hugged her back. "It's so good to see you. So good to see everyone, Eduardo, Consuela. They've made me feel so welcome."

"I would expect no less," Beatriz said firmly. "Consuela, *por favor*, bring in the iced tea and sandwiches. Eduardo, lower the awning, we shall take lunch on the balcony." Beatriz issued her orders.

"*Sí, Tía Beatriz,*" he said automatically and caught Isabella's knowing gaze. Yes, he remembered how she'd called her sister controlling. She issued her orders and they all jumped to obey. Everything was as it always was, but nothing was the same. He hadn't promised Isabella that he wouldn't confront Beatriz. That was a prerogative he would retain, but finally he knew the truth about his past. It was a secret no longer.

◆

"Is anything wrong, Eduardo? Do you have any concerns about purchasing the penthouse?" Jutta asked, perturbed by the Spaniard's somber mien. He'd been uncharacteristically subdued while they inspected the penthouse that would soon be his. Dusk had fallen, and the lights of Ceuta and Morocco twinkled across the Strait of Gibraltar. They had decided that this was the best time for him to view the property. Eduardo was well known in the community. He didn't want anyone to know that he was the potential purchaser.

"Forgive me. I've had a very tough week, Jutta," Eduardo confided, opening kitchen presses to inspect the contents.

"I know the feeling," Jutta sighed. "I felt I was being picked upon personally by whatever deity is supposedly up there."

Eduardo laughed mirthlessly. "Try finding out that the woman you thought was your aunt was really your mother and the woman you thought was your mother was really your aunt."

"*Guter Gott!*" she exclaimed, so shocked at his news—and that he would reveal it to her—that she spoke in her native tongue.

"Good God, indeed," Eduardo repeated. He opened the last press and saw a selection of wine and spirits on the bottom shelf.

"Would you like a drink, Jutta?" he asked impulsively. "I can offer you . . . eh . . . let's see, whiskey, gin, rum, red wine. The parrot's owner keeps quite a bar."

"Well, why not? I could do with a drink. Felipe, my husband, informed me he has laid off four people who worked for him. My daughter has a fractured wrist. My au pair is handing in a month's notice. I'll have a drink with you for sure. Red wine for me, *por favor*."

"*Excelente*. We will share our sad stories." He waved the bottle of wine at her. After all, he was the son of a reckless man, so he would behave in a reckless fashion, he decided bitterly. Eduardo poured a velvety ruby Faustino into two balloon glasses, which he first wiped with a paper towel, and handed one to her.

"Let's open the balcony doors to air the place and sit in the lounge," Jutta suggested, leading the way into the huge room with the panoramic vista. A soft cream leather couch faced out to sea and she opened the doors and felt the cooling evening breeze whisper in. Three round candles sat on a silver platter, and impulsively she lit them. "Isn't it pretty?" she said, admiring the flickering flame, which threw the faintest of glows around them.

"Could you imagine if Lord Muck from Essex knew I was sitting in his penthouse, drinking his wine, how he would react?" Eduardo laughed derisively.

"Wait until he finds out you've bought the apartment."

"He was such a snob, you know? He wanted separate outdoor lavatories down in the bar, for the penthouse owners." Eduardo sneered, taking a long draft of the fruity red. "I couldn't understand how he'd own such a common bird as a parrot, especially a parrot who used such vulgar language. But then again *his* language was most crude. He was nouveau riche, I think. They're always the worst, in any society."

"Really? He must be in a bad way financially, in that case; he keeps pushing to have the sale completed." Jutta took a glug of wine.

"A lot of the British have had to leave the Costa now that there's almost parity between the euro and sterling. Did we ever think we'd see the day?" Eduardo commented.

"No harm to see some of them go," Jutta remarked, not having much time for the old enemy.

"Were you loved as a child?" Eduardo asked abruptly, taking another swig of his drink.

"Um . . . well, I was the youngest. My siblings would say I was the pet of the family. I might disagree." She made a face. "I know I'm my father's favorite now, though."

"I thought I was the son of a successful, divorced, retired New York cardiologist. It seems I am the scion of some reckless-type playboy who crashed his sports car into a church wall and died young," Eduardo declared bitterly. "I'm not allowed to tell my wife. I'm not allowed to confront my aunt, who is really my mother. What kind of a life is that for a successful man in his fifties? These women have me trussed up and trapped and I'm sick of it, Jutta. Do you understand that?" he asked with a wild glint in his eyes as the alcohol took hold.

"That's terrible; to think your past and who you are was authentic, and then to find out it was all a lie must be very difficult indeed, Eduardo."

"It is, Jutta. Very hard. I feel bereft. I feel alone. I feel unsure of who I am. What if I've inherited my real father's characteristics?" He turned to her and stared at her.

"I would imagine," she said carefully, "that they might have revealed themselves to you before now. To me you are a most conscientious, high-achieving, ethical person. That doesn't sound like someone who's reckless to me."

"You are kind," he sighed, pouring more wine into their glasses. "I rarely drink wine," he confessed. "It must be my father's traits emerging." He gave a bitter little laugh.

"Don't say that," Jutta said, impulsively reaching out to take his hand. Their eyes met.

"I'd like to kiss you," he murmured, his eyes slightly glazed.

"I'd like you to kiss me." Jutta stared back at him. In the candlelight, with his tie loosened and his hair faintly disheveled, he looked almost rakishly swarthy, reminding her of Felipe when she'd first known him.

"Will we be reckless for just this once?" he said, smiling, his eyes, heavy-lidded, glittering with desire, and she felt a welcome moist heat between her legs. He had strong, white, even teeth, she thought; would his tongue be firm and probing? Closing her eyes, Jutta leaned over and her lips met Eduardo's.

It was as though she'd released a passion in him that he'd kept suppressed for years. Their sex was hungry, animalistic almost, as he stripped her naked while she did the same to him, unbuckling his belt and unzipping his trousers to release him to her. He pulled her astride him on the sofa and groaned with pent-up desire as he thrust hard into her.

"Oh, yes! Yes, Eduardo, don't stop!" Jutta gripped his shoulders, grinding into him as they writhed in unison, their moans and grunts of pleasure adding to their uninhibited coupling. They came in a frenzied, urgent wave of pleasure that left them limp and spent, covered in a sweaty sheen.

"Eduardo," she murmured as he buried his face in her neck. She felt dampness and his tears trickled down to her breast.

"Why do you cry?" she asked, smugly pleased that her lovemaking had brought this proud man to tears of joy.

He raised his face to hers and she saw the sadness in his bleary, reddened eyes.

"I cry because I have betrayed my wife," Eduardo said, "and because now I truly am my father's son."

Chapter Forty-Four

Anna / Sally-Ann / Jutta / Eduardo

"Anna, meet me in your lobby in ten minutes with the girls. Have I got news for y'all!"

"OK. Is it good or bad?" Anna asked warily.

"Mind-blowing," teased Sally-Ann.

"Ah, tell me," Anna was intrigued.

"Nope. Get the girls together and order a *big* pot of coffee, and I'll have one of those almond croissants. I'll be over to you in ten. Byeeee."

Anna smiled at her American friend's exuberance. She was very pleased that Sally-Ann was buying the penthouse and that it wasn't going to a stranger. Today was closing day, and she'd flown to Spain for a long weekend with her beloved girlfriends. They were staying in a smart boutique hotel, in the old part of San Antonio del Mar, less than ten minutes from La Joya. Anna had not been able to bring herself to visit the penthouse for the last time.

She'd driven them along the motorway, eyes straight ahead, trying hard not to remember how excited she and Austen used to get as they whizzed past Fuengirola, La Cala, Calahonda, the Don Carlos, bypassing Marbella and Puerto Banús and taking the slip road off the A-7, with the sea glittering below them, until the elegant whitewashed sign and the granite block, flecked with white and veined with yellow marble, with the name San Antonio del Mar etched on it in gold, appeared just beyond a curve in the road.

In the distance she could see the Moorish minarets of La Joya and she gasped involuntarily, caught by the now familiar physical ache of grief.

"You OK?" Mary asked supportively, knowing how difficult the whole journey was for her friend.

"Painful," Anna confessed, switching on her satnav and calling out the name of the street they were heading for.

"Please repeat," said the irritating saccharine voice.

"*Calle friggin' San José,*" she said irately. Mary patted her on the shoulder.

"Stay calm, dear. It's not St. Joseph's fault. It's the first turn on the right."

"How do you know?"

"Remember that little square we had coffee in? Calle San José is on the far side of it. I remember because of the beautiful Church of St. Joseph, where I lit a few candles."

"A few," scoffed Yvonne from the backseat. "I'd call it a conflagration. I thought that we were going to have to call the fire brigade."

"Ha ha, spell that, you, with your big words," retorted Mary, pointing out the turn to Anna.

"Oh, yeah, I know where we are now. Well remembered, Mary." Anna swung the hire car into the square.

"Well, I *am* the youngest and my marbles are still intact. I'll say no more," Mary said smugly.

Having her friends with her made everything that little bit easier. She could laugh with them and not feel guilty, and she could withdraw and be silent when she needed to be, knowing they were a hugely comforting presence and all they wanted was to help her in any way they could. She'd even laughed out loud a few times—a first. It was strange how guilty it had made her feel. How could she possibly laugh when Austen was so tragically deceased? She'd actually mentally apologized to him once and then called herself the biggest eejit going.

The hotel had been a good choice, perched on a steep cliffside overlooking a cove with its own private beach, reached by steps at the end of the flower-filled terrace. It was small but luxurious and her room overlooked the sea. Cypress trees lent an Italian air, and because she'd never been there with Austen, there were no memories. That helped enormously.

Sally-Ann completely understood that she didn't want to be anywhere near La Joya, and she'd joined Anna and the girls for dinner on the night of their arrival and regaled them with tales of the new baby and the divorce, and Lenora's abysmal efforts at motherhood. "I'm not bein' superior, y'all, but when Cal told me she arrived with a Lego Duplo Batman set for Jake, who puts everything he possibly can into his mouth, I thought, *You need to think things out, gal.*"

"Charlotte is still doing that," Anna said, and the discussion turned to babies and her grandchildren, and how much she loved and resented them at the same time.

"I feel so guilty that I didn't listen to what Austen wanted. I was too wrapped up in the grandkids," she'd admitted to Yvonne one day at the start of the summer when they were having coffee after a walk around the Botanic Gardens.

"Don't do that to yourself, Anna. You did what you had to do, and stop beating yourself up. Austen wouldn't want you to," her friend remonstrated. "And if it was the other way around, you wouldn't want Austen making himself miserable, would you?"

"No, thank you, you're *absolutely* right." Anna had decided there and then to try and fight her way through the dark miasma she was trapped in. Impulsively she'd invited her friends to join her for a long weekend in Spain instead of the overnighter she'd planned for the closing of the sale. They'd agreed with alacrity.

It was a start, Anna thought ruefully, ringing their rooms to tell them to meet up in the foyer.

"And Sally-Ann didn't say anything other than that she'd news?" Breda sank into one of the squishy sofas in the bright, airy lobby overlooking the sea.

"Except that it was mind-boggling and to order a big pot of coffee and almond croissants," Anna replied, sitting on a sofa opposite her.

"I think I'd fancy one of them, even though it's only two hours since we ate breakfast."

"It's the sea air," Mary declared as Anna ordered the pot of coffee and a plate full of the sinful croissants.

"I suppose it's a bit early for prosecco?" Breda asked hopefully.

"You suppose correct." Yvonne grinned at her friend. "Anyway, here's Sally-Ann; let's get the goss," she said as the American ran up the steps to the entrance and hurried across to join them. "Well, what's going on? Spill," she demanded, and Sally-Ann laughed.

"Let me get a coffee into me first," she begged. "But it's *goooood*," she teased.

When the coffee had been poured and they were feasting on the almond croissants, and after Sally-Ann had taken a couple of hits of her coffee, her four companions stared at her expectantly.

"You'll never, *evah* in a million years guess who I saw—what's the way you put it, Anna?" She glanced over at Anna and grinned. " 'Having a rugged ride'?"

" 'Riding someone ragged,' " Anna corrected her, laughing.

"Oh, yeah. Guess who I saw riding each other ragged?" She sat up straight, eyes shining with mischief.

"Who?" came four voices in unison.

"Guess?"

"Who? Stop teasing us," groaned Yvonne.

"Facundo Gonzales and Constanza," Mary ventured.

"No," scorned Sally-Ann. "They hate each other."

"Love can be akin to hate," Anna pointed out. "Bert Dwight

and that little plump, tarty blonde in the first block who prances around in her thong?"

"Eeewwww." Sally-Ann made a face. "Listen up, y'all, this isn't a word of a lie. I saw *Jutta* riding the ass off *El Presidente—*"

"*What!*"

"*No way, you must be mistaken!*"

"*Are you kidding?*"

"*OMG!*"

The four women stared at Sally-Ann, gobsmacked.

"I swear to God," Sally-Ann declared, eyes dancing. "They were butt naked together! I *know* what I saw."

"Where?"

"How?"

"Are you sure you don't need new eye glasses?" joked Yvonne.

Sally-Ann took another drink of coffee and regaled them with her astounding news: "It was around sunset, I was out on my rooftop terrace, and you know that big penthouse owned by that English guy who fancies himself as Brad Pitt? Well, they were in the lounge and the door was open and candles were lit and the drapes weren't pulled. I could see the reflection in the big plate-glass door, because they had it open and the angle it was at, whatever way it was, I could see them because that building is at right angles to ours. They were sitting on the sofa *tearing* the clothes off each other and she was on top, starkers, flinging her blond hair around and, as Anna would put it, riding Eduardo De La Fuente ragged."

"Well, the little divil, I didn't think he had it in him," Yvonne observed humorously, and they all fell about laughing, chortling until tears ran down their faces.

"Oh, God, she's going to be at the notary's with us this afternoon, Sally-Ann." Anna wiped her eyes with her napkin.

"I know. I won't know where to look."

"Don't forget to ask her was *El Presidente* a good ride." Yvonne grinned.

"Poor Consuela," Anna said. "I wonder who seduced whom?

I always got the impression he was so prissy and chaste, banning topless sunbathing and the like."

"And Jutta's always so superior and self-righteous and so disparaging about the Spanish, even though she's married to a Spaniard," Sally-Ann remarked. "I remember when Cal and I had dinner with her and her husband when we bought our penthouse, she was quite scathing about their business practices."

"She's very chic," Breda added her tuppenceworth.

"Yeah, she's got a lot of style," Anna agreed. "And she's extremely efficient, isn't she, Sally-Ann? The sale couldn't have gone more smoothly."

"She is, although for all her talk about the way business is conducted down south, she still went for cash over tax declaration," Sally-Ann pointed out.

"Really?" exclaimed Mary. "I would have expected more from her."

"As we speak, I have eleven thousand euros cash in my handbag to pay the various agencies *and* Jutta. I had to collect it from my bank this morning. None of them will be paying tax. No wonder the country is in the state it's in. The cash will all be dished out in brown envelopes by our German seductress."

"Cripes, don't get mugged." Mary made a face. "I'd be petrified carrying that amount of money around."

"I know, but that's what Jutta *ordered* me to do," Anna said. "I think it's because her husband's business is in trouble. Perhaps Eduardo likes that cool, bossy German superciliousness, him being a bit cool and bossy himself."

"There was nothing cool about what I saw. I thought I was watching a porn movie." Sally-Ann tucked into a croissant.

"Was he . . . er . . . how shall I put it . . . *impressive*?" Yvonne cocked her head.

"*Yvonne!*" snorted Anna.

"Just curious," said her irrepressible friend.

"I couldn't really see if he was well hung or not. I mean, it was only a reflection I saw in the window, but she was bouncin' up and down on him for sure and he was grabbing on to her booty for all he was worth." Sally-Ann laughed.

"OMG, I hope I don't bump into him," Anna exclaimed, wishing with all her heart she could share this juicy piece of gossip with Austen.

"I'll burst out laughing if I do." Yvonne licked the sugar from her fingers, eyes creased in mirth.

"I hope I'm not with you." Mary stood up. "Now, I don't know about you lot, but there's a lounger out on the terrace, by the pool, with my name on it. Let's continue with this riveting discussion outside."

"Yes, riveting, that's what it is. Jutta and *El Presidente*—who would have thought? It's better than the soaps at home," Sally-Ann declared, delighted with the effect of her bombshell.

◆

Several hours later, Sally-Ann and Anna sat together in the cool marble foyer of a notary's office in Marbella. It was a busy, bustling place with clients standing or sitting in little groups until they were called to one of the anterooms where the notary joined them for whatever business he was called upon to do.

With one minute to spare, Jutta marched in, back straight as a poker, blond hair swept up in a chignon, wearing one of her tailored trouser suits, looking the very epitome of the successful businesswoman. There was nothing about her to suggest she'd had a night of raw passion with a married man. She was as cool, calm, and collected as ever. She was accompanied by her accountant and tax expert, who had run all the checks, made sure all Anna's utility bills and taxes were paid up to date, and had chased the documentation necessary for the legal process to proceed. He would also be the recipient of a brown envelope full of euros.

They made small talk, but Anna's mind was elsewhere, remembering the day she and Austen had signed for their penthouse with such carefree optimism.

"You OK, sweetie? It will be over soon, or do you want to change your mind? If y'all do, it's no problem," her American friend said earnestly.

"No, Sally-Ann, I'm doing the right thing; I don't want to keep it. I'm glad you're buying it for the family. You'll have very happy days in it."

"Well, if you're sure. I don't want you to feel railroaded," Sally-Ann murmured as they were ushered into a room with a large, burnished mahogany table. Anticipation heightened as they awaited the notary, who arrived moments later. An expectant hush fell among the gathering as he laid his files on the table in a slow, deliberate manner before lowering his bifocals and looking out over the tops of them to welcome them.

"I don't feel at all railroaded, honest," Anna whispered to Sally-Ann. "It's time for me to say good-bye to La Joya de Andalucía."

◆

She couldn't be more pleased with the way the MacDonald apartment had sold. Swiftly, efficiently, with not even a minor hiccup, as was seldom the case in property sales. Jutta stood in the queue in the bank, waiting to lodge the firm, crisp pile of fifty-euro notes in her handbag. She'd opened a separate account from the one she shared with her husband a couple of years ago, where all her earnings from work now went. It gave her great comfort knowing that it was there. Right now she could foresee a time when Felipe would drive her to the edge of splitting with him with one of his schemes for a get-rich-quick project, which were now very thin on the ground.

He'd decided on the spur of the moment to fly out to Northern Cyprus. A friend of his had told him there were good business opportunities to be had and that tourism was booming.

His timing for leaving her had been most inconvenient as always, and resentment towards her husband had played a big part in what had happened the previous evening with Eduardo. Jutta gave a deep sigh. It had been a satisfying interlude for her, both physically and emotionally, until he had raised his tearstained face to hers and ruined the moment with his uncalled-for declarations of guilt.

It was unfortunate. She'd enjoyed the physical experience very much. She would have liked to continue their intrigue at least until she'd secured the penthouse for him. Now she would have to be brisk and businesslike with him and pretend that it had never happened. *That* annoyed her. She didn't feel one bit guilty. Felipe was no longer satisfying her sexually. He was completely obsessed with his business problems. If he couldn't see that he was driving her into the arms of another man, he wasn't worth being married to, Jutta thought crossly as a bank teller became free.

Perhaps it was time to step away from her marriage for a while. It was certainly time to take stock, and that was what Jutta intended to do, she decided, lodging a satisfyingly large amount of euros into her secret German bank account.

◆

Eduardo still had a pounding headache, thanks to the amount of red wine he'd quaffed the previous evening. What had possessed him? he wondered, lying sprawled on his sofa with a cold facecloth on his forehead. He couldn't deny that he'd enjoyed the physical experience enormously. Jutta's ardor, her sexual hunger, had been a revelation to him, and extremely arousing. It had added enormously to his pleasure to know that he was giving her as much satisfaction as he himself was experiencing. But when it was over, he'd been overwhelmed with guilt and feelings of self-disgust. He who had always prided himself on his self-control had exhibited none, just when he needed it most.

They might have their difficulties but Consuela had been a true and loyal wife, and this was how he'd repaid her. He was sick to his stomach with remorse and self-hatred.

Now he had to go back to Madrid and pretend that everything was normal, as well as to cope with his bitter rage at the revelations about his birth mother. That wine had tasted good last night;

he was tempted to go and buy another bottle. Eduardo grimaced as the pain behind his eyes deepened. He would have to be reserved and distant with Jutta for the remainder of their dealings with each other.

Once the penthouse was his, he would end contact, he decided. He wondered if he should apologize to her for the previous evening. After all, she was a married woman and he'd made the first move, saying in a most juvenile fashion that he would like to kiss her. Eduardo blushed with shame at his gaucheness.

"Oh, what a mess," he groaned, dipping the facecloth into iced water and replacing it on his throbbing forehead.

◆

"What a delightful afternoon it's been, Beatriz. I enjoyed it. *Gracias*."

"As did I, *mi querida*." Beatriz smiled at her sister companionably. They had spent the early evening, after siesta, sitting in the shaded courtyard of Beatriz's apartment block sipping iced tea and looking through old photos.

"It seems like a dream sometimes that I ever lived in Spain." Isabella tidied up a selection of faded sepia photos of their parents and grandparents. "Oh, look," she exclaimed at a photo that fell out of one of the albums. "Wasn't he an adorable child?" They gazed at the image of a very young Eduardo. His raven-black hair, curly then, framed his square face, with the straight nose and determined chin. Two enormous brown eyes fringed by silky black lashes stared out from the photo, a hint of a smile curving around his mouth.

"He was beautiful," sighed Beatriz.

Isabella took her hand. "*Mi querida*, we are both getting on in years now," she said gently. "I in my seventies, you in your eighties. Did you ever think we would be this elderly?"

"*Never*," said her sister emphatically.

"Do you think it's time perhaps to tell Eduardo the truth about who his mother is?" Isabella probed.

Beatriz held up her hands, palm out. "No, not now, not ever. Even when I'm gone. Promise me you will never tell Eduardo when I pass away."

"I promise," Isabella said, assuaging her conscience that it was not a lie. She could not tell Eduardo something he already knew. "May I ask why, Beatriz? Wouldn't you like him to know you are his *madre*?"

Beatriz's lower lip trembled. "Of course I would, more than anything; but if I told him now, it would be such a waste and he would want to know why I had kept it from him for so long," she said brokenly.

"But why did you?" Isabella handed her a tissue.

"Because I did not want him to be ashamed of me," she cried. "I did not want him to think that I was an easy girl and he was *un bastardo!*"

"But people don't think like that now, Beatriz. Nowadays they have the babies first and the wedding afterwards," Isabella said with an attempt at humor.

"It wasn't like that then and all my life I have been ashamed. I won't have *him* feel shamed," Beatriz said firmly. "So not a word!"

"OK," agreed her sister as a wave of guilt enveloped her. Perhaps she should have said nothing and let sleeping dogs lie. Now it was too late. Eduardo knew the truth; Isabella could only hope that he would never confront his real mother with it.

◆

Sally-Ann walked into her new penthouse. She'd been in it anytime her holidays coincided with Anna's, so she knew what it was like. Nothing personal remained of Anna's and Austen's. Anna had treated her daughters and their families to a week's holiday at Easter and they had packed up all the personal items that Anna had requested and brought them home.

Jutta's cleaning team had been in. Every surface gleamed in the sunlight dappling through the snowy-white curtains. It wouldn't be too long now until she was back with the twins. She was looking forward to seeing her daughters' reaction to this new holiday home. She was looking forward, too, to spending time together with Cal and Jake. He was such a good little boy. You couldn't but fall in love with him. Sally-Ann would never forget the heart-stopping moment when Jake had held his arms up to her to be lifted for the first time, and he'd snuggled in against her content-edly and she'd loved him as though he were her own child. The girls adored him. Instead of dividing them as she'd expected, his birth had brought healing to their family for sure, she reflected. Life was funny the way things worked out sometimes.

She would be saying *adiós* to her Spanish lover this trip. He'd told her he was getting married in the autumn. It was time to say good-bye. She would make sure it was a long farewell, Sally-Ann thought, smiling to herself, looking forward to the lusty encounter that was to come later that evening. She and her tall, sexy banker would give Jutta and Eduardo a run for their money, but she'd make damn sure the drapes were closed. *She* didn't want to cause a scandal in La Joya de Andalucía now that she was the new owner of Penthouse *Ático, Portal* 1.

◆

"But that's the day of the AGM, Jutta. I won't be able to attend," Eduardo exclaimed when she told him the date of closing for the purchase of his penthouse.

"But you wouldn't have been attending anyway," she pointed out crisply. "I'll be there in your stead with power of attorney."

"Of course, of course. What am I thinking?" he said distract-edly.

"Don't worry about it; we all have things on our minds. It's a busy time of year. The vendor has confirmed his attendance. At least you won't have to have contact with him, either," Jutta added.

"Good. The less I see of him, the better. He has sent an email to Señora Torres to say that his arrears will be deducted from the sale of the penthouse and forwarded to the community account." Eduardo stared out between the slatted blinds of his office window as he spoke to Jutta on the phone and tried not to think of her pert breasts, which fitted just nicely into each hand when he'd been having sex with her.

"So I'll email you over some documents to sign and scan?" he heard her say, and reluctantly turned his attention back to the conversation.

"Of course."

"Fine. I'll give them to my accountant. Everything is up-to-date. We have fulfilled all our requirements. Hopefully on the day the vendor will have fulfilled all of his and it will go smoothly. Clearly the owner has no idea that you are the buyer, and if and when he does, it will be too late." Jutta stifled a yawn. She felt terribly tired. The season was getting into full swing, and with her new venture into apartment sales there was a lot more work to be done.

"Hopefully yes," he agreed in a serious tone, and Jutta wondered yet again why he just could not react like she did to their night of sex, because that was all it was now. His dour self-flagellation and awkwardness each time she phoned him about the purchase of the penthouse was such a turnoff.

"It was sex, and good sex too; now grow up and forget about it like most men would," she wanted to snap, but of course she couldn't, so she endured the sighs, and short, clipped sentences, and the attempted formality as best she could, at least until she had the purchase secured and their business complete. Then she could wash her hair of him or seduce him again; Jutta couldn't quite decide.

"So, Eduardo, I'll be in contact nearer the date, unless there are any problems. On the day itself, I can meet you in La Joya with the keys after your AGM. If you would lodge the remainder of the purchase price into my client account, as you did with the deposit, that would be excellent. There's no need for you to do that until a couple of days before we close. I'll present you with my bill, which we have already agreed upon, once I hand over the keys. And then you and I will complete the signing over at the notary's office. Is that satisfactory?"

"Indeed, and thank you for your hard work, Jutta," he said awkwardly.

"*De nada, Eduardo, adiós,*" she said before hanging up as though it were a run-of-the-mill business call and nothing existed between them.

It dismayed Eduardo that she seemed to have dismissed their tryst so easily. Jutta had shown no embarrassment when she'd phoned him a few days after their encounter. His life was one falsehood after another, it seemed. He was subsumed in a mire of secrecy, his infidelity with her another deception to add to the list. He couldn't but admire her cool detachment. It was something he aspired to, but all he could think of was the wild feeling of abandon and freedom he'd experienced when they had coupled so passionately, so earthily, so uninhibitedly. He wished it had never happened and he wished he could stop brooding over that night of shame.

Tonight he had to pretend to be lighthearted and carefree. He was taking the three women in his life to dinner. Consuela, Beatriz, and Isabella had all booked appointments at the hairdressers "to go out on a special date with their special man," Isabella had announced. He wondered if they would think he was so special if they knew that he'd royally shagged a married woman in La Joya de Andalucía.

◆

"And Jeananne and Sneery Hole's son got married last month and we weren't even invited." Yvonne lay on her lounger sipping a piña colada. "I was devastated," she said, grinning.

"I was invited, but that's only because they were at Chloe's, and, needless to say, I didn't go." Anna lay under the shade of her umbrella feeling more relaxed than at any time since her husband's death. "It was a very grand occasion in the Four Seasons, I believe."

"Don't I have the photos to prove it." Yvonne hunted for her phone in her beach bag.

"I thought you were going to unfollow Jeananne on Twitter or Instagram or whatever she's on," Anna said, pulling down her sunglasses to look over at Yvonne, who was scrolling madly.

"I keep saying I will, but it's sort of addictive. She has no boundaries. She shares every minute detail, or rather *boasts* about every minute detail of her life. I mean, look at this." She passed the phone to Anna.

"It's a photo of a pair of shoes. Why would she put that up? They're a bit blingy. All those glittery bits will fall off. Can't see her getting much wear out of them," she remarked.

"They're the 'Mother-of-the-Bridegroom Shoes,' as she captioned it." Yvonne handed the phone over to Breda.

"Don't you know a designer shoe when you see it, Anna? You're hopeless. They're Oscar de la Renta!" Breda pointed out. "So Jeananne was having a boasty moment."

"Ah, I see!" Anna grinned. "What's new about that?"

"I wonder, are they in the villa in Antibes?" Breda passed the phone over to Mary.

"Well, I tell you one thing, girls, if I had feet the size of a yeti, I wouldn't be showing off pictures of *my* shoes. Look at the size of them. Jabba the Hutt could wear *them*," Mary quipped.

Anna started to laugh; she laughed so hard her sides ached. It came from the depths of her, great belly laughs that went on and on. They were all guffawing, tears streaming down their cheeks.

"Clench, Anna, keep those legs crossed; we don't want any little accidents," Yvonne advised, and that set them off again, great hooting chortles they hadn't enjoyed together for such a long time.

"Oh my God, I'm not the better for that," Anna wheezed.

"We possibly need another drink," Mary suggested.

"I think we possibly do." Yvonne jumped up with alacrity, being the fittest of the quartet. "Where's the kitty purse?"

"Right here, sista, right here." Mary waved it at her and gave her the thumbs-up, so happy that their much-loved friend had had a thoroughly enjoyable moment of forgetting.

◆

"You know, you should stay on for a while and rest after all you've been through, Anna," Mary suggested casually as the four of them enjoyed a Baileys after dinner that night, their last in Andalucía for the foreseeable future. "It's so peaceful here. So restful."

"Dead right," said Yvonne. "If I had the chance, I'd down tools and stay put."

"But what about minding the grandkids?" Anna exclaimed.

"Not your problem, Anna. Your priority is minding *you*, and as a dear friend I just want to say, you're minding the family and have been for the last ten months. No one is minding *you*!" Mary said firmly.

"Mary's right," Breda agreed. "Now it's time for *you*. Why don't you stay until the anniversary? You intend coming over for that anyway—"

"But that's two months away," Anna exclaimed.

"And? Or, as the kids say, So?"

"Stay in a hotel for two months! Ah, no! That's way too expensive," she protested.

"No more expensive than the maintenance fees were on the penthouse. And not being too personal about your affairs, but was a large lump sum not lodged into your account from the sale? Could a teeny few little bob out of that not go for a little bit of luxury for our friend Anna?" Mary cajoled. "You paid for the girls to come out for a week—"

"That was to empty out the apartment of our personal stuff," Anna interjected quickly.

"It was still a week in España, missus! At your expense. And that's fine, but what I'm saying is, if you can spend it on the girls and the children, can you not spend some on yourself?"

"It sounds lovely," Anna agreed wistfully. "But I'd feel guilty spending that amount of money on myself—"

"What would Austen say?" Breda said quietly. "Don't answer, because I know he'd be all for it."

"He would, yeah," she said sadly. "And I love the hotel. It helps that I have no memories of him here, so there aren't constant reminders of things we did together. I've stayed well away from La Joya. I don't have to go near it. Maybe I might go home with you all as planned tomorrow and give the girls two weeks to make other arrangements, and then come back." She took another sip of Baileys and said decisively, "You know, I think I'll do it, girls. Great suggestion. I *do* deserve some time for myself."

"Good woman," applauded Yvonne. "You'll have time to absorb all that's happened—time to grieve—because you haven't given yourself *any* time. You've just thrown yourself into minding everyone, trying to run away from it."

"I know," Anna agreed. "That's *exactly* what I did."

"You can never run away from grief. It always catches up with you until you deal with it," Breda commented sagely.

"Well, thank you, girls. I wouldn't have even considered staying on longer without your encouragement. Hopefully I can book a room. It's a bit late in the season to be booking, do you not think?"

"Do it now," Breda ordered, "and then we'll buy a bottle of bubbly and raise a glass to you."

"Will I? Chloe and Tara won't be impressed." Anna made a face.

"They'll have to suck it up and deal with it. Come on, I'll go with you just to make sure you do it." Yvonne stood up and pointed the way to Reception. "Breda, order that champagne."

Anna laughed. "Bossy-boots," she said fondly, but she followed her friend out the door.

◆

The following afternoon Anna sat at a window seat and watched Málaga Airport disappear as the Airbus thundered down the runway and launched itself into the bright blue void above it. She'd said good-bye to La Joya de Andalucía when she'd given it a quick glance as they drove to the airport and felt the familiar barb of sadness assail her.

It was a closed chapter now. She would come back to stay in the peaceful little hotel in San Antonio, and on the day of Austen's first anniversary she and her daughters would place a rose at the spot where he'd died. The first year of mourning would be complete. Perhaps the second one might not be as horrendous, she thought wistfully. There had been milestones in the last few days and she'd laughed again with those true and stalwart friends of hers. She was surviving, Anna reflected. She'd come this far by putting one foot in front of the other every day, no matter how she felt. Bereavement was something that came to all and had to be endured. Why should she be any different?

Austen, Austen, Austen! she cried out to her beloved, silently. And as the plane banked over Málaga harbor to head north across the High Sierras, the sunlight caught the silver wing tip and sent a prism of rainbow light right to where she sat. A benevolent peace seemed to envelop her, and Anna was strangely comforted, as though her husband's loving presence was all around her.

Chapter Forty-Five

Sally-Ann / Lenora / Cal

Sally-Ann tried not to show her amusement as, out of the corner of her eye, she watched Savannah preening in front of a long wall mirror that reflected the big floor-to-ceiling windows facing the sea. Her daughter was wearing an orange and white floral-print bikini that had caused Cal's eyebrows to shoot skywards when he'd seen it. She was deciding which way to tie a floaty matching sarong, undulating this way and that, tying it at the waist, then around the neck, then over one shoulder. On her head sat perched the "to-die-for" Gucci sunglasses that were "seriously trendy" and that Sally-Ann had made her pay half for because, as Sally-Ann had put it, they were "seriously *expensive*."

"I never heard of anyone having to pay half for their birthday present," Savannah had sulked, but Sally-Ann had insisted she take the money out of her savings and, while she was at it, put a twenty in the charity box for spending such an outrageous sum on sunglasses when she could have bought a pair for twenty dollars in the mall.

One of the reasons for the preening and posturing sat poolside with a rippling six-pack, long legs with hard, muscular thighs, a tanned, handsome face hidden beneath a peaked Nike cap, and dark glasses.

The lifeguard was "seriously sexy," Sally-Ann had overheard Savannah say to Madison, who was already in the pool in her black one-piece swimsuit with the hot pink side panels, which was much more suited to the serious swimming she liked to do than prancing around in a bikini.

Several other gangly teenage reasons sat sprawled on white chairs, drinking sodas under the coconut roof of the coffee bar, watching the girls go by. Savannah had actually told her mother that this was "by far, beyond the best holiday" she'd ever had. Much to Sally-Ann's relief, because, Lord knows, her daughter had whined enough about it once she'd heard her parents' plan for the summer.

From the balcony, Sally-Ann could see Jake's little red hat as he splashed up and down in the baby pool with the au pair.

"Bye, Mom." Savannah finally decided to go with her first choice of sarong tied at her waist for maximum exposure of her pert little boobs. She had the long, tanned, coltish legs Sally-Ann had had as a teen, and she was almost the same height as Sally-Ann. Savannah and her sister were growing into beautiful young women, their mother thought proudly.

"Enjoy, sweetie," Sally-Ann called, but she was speaking to thin air. Savannah was already in the lift, admiring herself in the mirror as it descended.

She cleared the breakfast dishes and stacked the dishwasher before having her shower. Cal had gone for his daily five-kilometer walk along the boardwalk, stopping to have a coffee and a read of the paper on his way back. She'd lie on her lounger reading under the awning and let the breeze whisper across her body. Later she was meeting up with Anna in San Antonio to go to the AGM.

"There's no reason for me to go; I'm not an owner anymore," Anna had protested when she'd suggested it.

"Aw, come on, Anna, I don't want to go on my own. Cal's not

going, and besides, it would be nice for you to see some of your friends there. A lot of people have asked me about you."

"I suppose I should have called in and said hello. I just couldn't bear the thought of it."

"I understand that, darlin', of course I do, and that's why it might be easier to meet them in the hotel." Sally-Ann had been ever so pleased when Anna had agreed. It would be good for her to catch up with her friends, most of whom didn't realize that she was staying in a hotel only ten minutes up the road.

She luxuriated under the large round air-powered showerhead as the hot water sluiced over her shoulders and she scrubbed her skin with exfoliant cream until it was glowing. Wrapping a terry robe around herself, she strolled out onto the balcony and toweled her hair dry. She could see Savannah in the baby pool with Jake and her heart lifted at the sight.

Lenora had tried to throw a wrench in the works there, but Sally-Ann had called her on it. Her face darkened, remembering Cal telling her that his ex-girlfriend wasn't happy with the idea of Jake being out of the States and so far away from her for a month. What kind of a nerve did she have? She hardly ever saw Jake now, being too busy leading the high life, trying to find a wealthy new lover, having been ditched by Boyd Garland. He'd announced his engagement to one of the McClellan gals, who had a southern pedigree Lenora Colton would never have.

"Let me deal with it, mother to mother," she'd said to Cal, who was reluctant to involve her. "Honestly, I'll sort it," she'd insisted.

"You see, Lenora, it's like this. Cal has two daughters, as you know, and we want to spend time together with them. We'd like Jake to be part of that holiday," she'd said sweetly, having finally arranged a date to meet for coffee in the Granduca, because Lenora was "way busy." She'd swanned into the hotel in head-to-toe Ralph Lauren, looking like a million dollars.

"I'm not happy to let him out of the country that long," Lenora said snootily.

"OK, how about Cal lets the au pair take two weeks off, and I rent an apartment for you, and you come over for two weeks?"

"And you'd pay for me to fly to Europe and stay for two weeks?" Lenora looked at her quizzically. "Why?"

"Because I think it's important to be together as a family, and Jake is family," she said coolly. "OK, it won't be all holiday for you. I mean, you'll be minding him and bringing him to the pool with all the other toddlers. That can be a bit wearing after a while, and there won't be much socializing at night because the au pair will be on holiday," Sally-Ann said, rubbing it in a little, "but you'll have the time with your son that you crave and so will Cal."

"If I didn't go, would you be prepared to pay me what you would have spent on the holiday?" Lenora eyeballed her.

"So let me cut to the chase and get this straight, Lenora. You're not really *that* interested in spending time with Jake, and you're prepared to accept the money in lieu of two weeks you could spend with us so we can have Jake stay for the month."

"You got it in one, Sally-Ann." The younger woman was brittle and unemotional.

"Some people might call that blackmail," Sally-Ann remarked sweetly.

"Some people might. I prefer to call it a practical solution to our dilemma."

"Let me take a day or two to think about it." Sally-Ann picked up her bag and walked out of the hotel. She drove straight to her lawyer and handed him her phone on which she'd taped the conversation.

"Perfect," he said. "Let me get y'all a coffee while my secretary types this up. I'll have it couriered to Ms. Lenora as soon as it's done. Good work, Sally-Ann."

"Thanks for the suggestion!" Sally-Ann grinned.

Lenora had caved, begging Sally-Ann not to tell Cal.

"It will be our little secret . . . for now . . ." Sally-Ann drawled, with the implied threat that if she caused trouble, there would be a reckoning that Lenora wouldn't want.

"You're quite the bitch, aren't you, in spite of your goody-goody perfect momma façade," Lenora spat down the phone.

"I fight for my kids, and I consider Jake as much my child as our daughters now. I get that you aren't a maternal woman, Lenora. That's OK, but let me tell ya, seeing as we're being frank here, your behavior stinks. You're nothing but a gold digger behind all the finery. Don't talk to me about façades; you're as fake as your tan. And I know you trapped Cal by getting pregnant. The oldest trick in the book, honey."

"Well, at least I gave him a son. You gave him two little she-devils, and they don't lick it off the ground," Lenora raged.

"Coming from you I take that as a compliment. Grow up, make something of yourself, and be a mother Jake can be proud of," Sally-Ann advised before the younger woman hung up the phone with a furious expletive.

She had sincerely meant that, thought Sally-Ann, laughing when she saw Jake throw his beach ball at Madison, who had climbed into the baby pool to play with him. Lenora was Jake's mother and she had no idea what a gift that was.

"What are you laughing at?" asked Cal, who had emerged onto the adjoining balcony on what had once been Anna's penthouse. He too had showered and was drying his hair vigorously.

"Oh, hi." Sally-Ann smiled. "I was looking at our children playing down in the pool."

"Great, isn't it?" he said, smiling back. "Fancy a coffee?"

"My place or yours?" she teased. In two swift movements he'd vaulted over the dividing planter filled with lavender at the edge of their respective balconies. "I couldn't be bothered going out and knocking on the door," he remarked nonchalantly.

"God, be careful, you could fall!" Sally-Ann gasped. "If *El Presidente* sees you doing that, you'll be hauled up," she reproved, following him into the lounge. Cal made the coffee and she put some chocolate biscuits onto a plate and they went back out to the balcony. They sat on the cane sofa chatting companionably about their plans for the rest of the week and she was laughing at something he'd said when he leaned across suddenly and kissed her full on the mouth.

"Cal," she murmured against his lips. "Don't."

"We're on holiday as a family, a family who love one another. People who love each other kiss each other," he murmured, sliding his hand into the top of her robe.

"God Almighty, Cal, don't do that out here!" she exclaimed.

"No one can see us," he assured her. "But if you want to go inside, I'd love to."

Sally-Ann looked at her ex-husband. She'd always known this moment would come. Why would she deny herself the pleasure that she knew awaited if she led him into the bedroom? They had grown close again and he'd grown up.

"Come on, then," she agreed, taking his hand. "A holiday romance."

Later, deeply, sensuously satisfied, she lay in her ex-husband's arms. She had it all now, Sally-Ann thought. Great kids. Her business. Her independence *and* her divorce. And the pleasure of being with Cal, no strings attached. Life couldn't get any better.

◆

Cal lay with his limbs entwined with Sally-Ann's. He was where he wanted to be at last. Home! He would woo her until she married him again, and judging by this morning's lovemaking that day wasn't too far away, he thought smugly. And this time he'd never fool around with anyone . . . ever! Sally-Ann was his gal, and she'd be adding the Cooper name right back alongside her own.

Chapter Forty-Six

AUGUST

The AGM

Jutta was unaccountably nervous as she drove under the iconic white arch into Marbella. She'd made this journey hundreds of times and she could never remember feeling so tense. It hadn't helped that Eduardo had phoned three times in as many days telling her that one could never be quite sure how such meetings could go. An incorrect parking space number, or apartment number on the title deeds, one missing tax payment—the *smallest* detail—could derail a closure, and until the notary had actually handed over the check, she must not count her chickens, and she must let him know the *instant* the meeting was over and she had the deeds in her hands.

"I will, Eduardo, be assured of it," she said with a calmness she did not feel.

So much depended on this morning's business going right. Far more than she'd anticipated when she'd taken on *El Presidente* as a client. It was very fortunate for her that the AGM for La Joya was taking place today. Eduardo was preoccupied preparing his annual report and she could sense that he was distracted, which suited Jutta down to the ground. She didn't need extra pressure from him; she was under enough with her own problems.

She was so stressed and so exhausted, she could sleep for a week. Felipe had returned home from Cyprus and she'd flown to Germany at the weekend to spend time with her father, who hadn't traveled south to stay with them for his annual summer holiday because of a continuing problem with gout. A blessing in disguise for her; a big irritation for her sisters.

"Three days isn't a very long visit, daughter," Oskar had moaned when she told him that was as long as she could stay.

"I know, Papa, but it's my busiest time, and I can't leave Alicia for too long. We might visit in the autumn for longer," she'd said, trying to pacify him but beset by guilt.

Don't think about it, she told herself as she drove into the multistory car park in Marbella. *Just concentrate on what you have to do.* A knot of anxiety formed in her stomach, adding to the faint queasiness she'd felt all week. There was a tummy virus going around Alicia's playgroup, and a bug was the last thing she needed.

This was one day she'd be glad to see the back of, Jutta sighed, giving her hair a comb and tracing some nude lipstick over her lips.

◆

"Relax, Eduardo. You have given the community your very best; you have ensured that you would follow up on your election promise to reduce the maintenance fee arrears. You can do no more. If you are not voted in, so be it. It's an enormous amount of work for you, *mi esposo.* I thought you bought this apartment to take a rest from work, not take on more." Consuela poured her husband a second cup of coffee, which he always permitted himself to have with his breakfast while on holidays.

"Thank you, *mi querida,*" he responded gravely, touched by her loyalty and kindness. "I really don't deserve you."

"What a nice thing to say, Eduardo. You never said that to me before." Consuela smiled at him, and he felt like the biggest cad in the world.

"It's true," he said, reaching across the table to squeeze her hand.

"Beatriz and I'll be there to support you, and so will Gabriel," Consuela assured him.

"Yes, it's good to have a wingman." Eduardo smiled. His cousin had informed him only the previous night that most of the *madrileños* would be voting for him again, and quite a few of the other owners who were pleased at the firm stance he'd taken on arrears. There were of course his many detractors, encouraged, he was sure, by Constanza Torres, but after her warning to him he'd decided that prudence was the best path to follow in her particular case. He would certainly look for Facundo Gonzales to become a full-time concierge, but his plan to finally get Constanza replaced would be put on hold.

It wasn't only the AGM that was making Eduardo edgy. Later this evening, when it was over, he'd arranged to meet Jutta in the Don Carlos to get the keys and title deeds of his new penthouse. He'd asked her to buy two bottles of champagne and put them in the fridge, and a selection of savory snacks so that he could invite his wife, aunt, and mother—or real mother and real aunt, he thought wryly—and his cousin and his wife to a little celebratory gathering. Jutta had assured him, in his phone call to her about the matter the previous day, that she would indeed do as he asked.

She was such a competent woman. A woman you could trust to do a job very well indeed. All her clients spoke highly of her. He intended to ask her to take on the management of his old apartment, which he would use for rental purposes to pay off his new mortgage. It would be difficult seeing her in the flesh, so to speak. They had only spoken on the phone since their torrid encounter two months ago. He was as nervous as a schoolboy at the thought of being in her company again.

Idiota, Eduardo cursed himself mentally, buttering another slice of toast. If he didn't develop an ulcer after this day, he would never suffer from one. He hadn't felt this anxious since he'd taken his law exams all those years ago.

◆

"... And crucially, this year under my guardianship, the arrears to the community have been halved, the planting has been upgraded, measures are under way to protect our grounds from coastal erosion, and a painting scheme to freshen up the outside paintwork will commence once the main holiday season is over. If you care to honor me again by electing me to be your president, I'll do my best to further enhance our community. Thank you for your attention and cooperation." Eduardo graciously acknowledged the acceptable smattering of applause that greeted his speech before striding down to join Beatriz and Consuela in the front row.

"*Excelente.* Well done, very good speech," Beatriz approved, her eyes glittering with pride.

"You should be well pleased; you were very impressive, Eduardo." Consuela smiled at him, and he felt warmed by her praise. Whether he was elected or not, he'd done his best; he could do no more. As had happened at all the previous AGMs, the vote was taken by a show of hands, and the results added to the proxies. A Scandinavian owner, and his old enemy and countryman Pablo Moralez, were up against him. He would like to win against Moralez in particular, but it was now in the hands of the owners.

Discreetly, not wishing to appear rude to Beatriz and Consuela, he glanced at his phone and saw the message he'd been waiting for.

All is well. The deal is closed. Would it inconvenience you terribly if we met at La Joya instead of the Don Carlos? I have to deliver a prearrival shop, as my staff member who was supposed to do it has phoned in sick. I'll let you know when I'm at the apartment. J.

PS good luck at the AGM.

In a way it suited him better to meet in La Joya, Eduardo decided as he swiftly texted back.

That's great news. Yes we can meet here. Thank you for your good wishes.

He hesitated a second and wondered should he end it with *E* but decided against it. Too intimate. From now on their dealings would be strictly businesslike and professional. He pressed "send" and slid the phone back into his pocket. Whatever happened, he was now the proud owner of the best penthouse in the complex. He couldn't be more pleased.

◆

Anna was surrounded by well-wishers as the meeting broke up for a tea break. She was touched by the generosity and the warmth of their welcome; many who stopped to chat she'd only known to say hello to.

There were a lot of new faces too, and familiar ones missing—couples who had sold up because of the downturn, she remarked to Sally-Ann, who was glowing and tanned and so healthy looking she could have been a model, Anna complimented her.

"Thanks, darlin'," she whispered. "Maybe it's because I'm back in the saddle. Cal's been riding me ragged," she confided.

"Ah, Sally-Ann, I'm delighted for you." Anna hugged her. "I always hoped you two would get back together."

"Don't y'all worry now, I won't be waltzing down the aisle; this is strictly friends with benefits. I'm a divorcée now and I intend staying that way. No man's gonna put a ring on my finger again and hog-tie me."

"Somehow I doubt you'll *ever* be hog-tied," Anna laughed, and turned as someone tapped her gently on the shoulder. "Oh, Señora De La Fuente, how are you?" she asked politely.

"Señora MacDonald, I just wanted to offer you my condolences. I was very sorry to hear about the loss of your husband," the attractive Spanish woman said with earnest sincerity.

"Why, thank you very much," Anna responded warmly. "I came with Sally-Ann today. Have you met?"

"How do you do, Señora." Sally-Ann held out her hand. "Very nice to meet you," she said, smiling.

"And you too," the other woman said, smiling back.

"As you may know, Sally-Ann bought our penthouse, about which I am delighted," Anna explained. "She persuaded me to come today and it was nice to catch up with old friends and acquaintances. I couldn't bring myself to go back to La Joya."

"How very understandable," the other woman said kindly. Her English was good. Anna couldn't help but think how much more genuine and sincerely warm Consuela was compared to Jutta's hard, cool personality.

Anna had met Jutta in the square in San Antonio the previous week, and the German woman had barely stopped to speak to her, she was in such a hurry. Clearly, now that Anna was no longer a client, Jutta didn't have time to waste talking to her. Eduardo De La Fuente was a fool to risk his marriage to a lovely woman like Consuela for the likes of Jutta.

"The anniversary is soon, is it not?" Consuela asked.

"How thoughtful of you to remember. Yes, it's next week. My daughters are flying over. My son is in Canada, so he won't be here. We'll attend Mass. And after that, I may not come back to Spain for a long while," she said sadly. The closer she got to the date of the anniversary, the harder to bear she was finding it.

"France is very beautiful. You should go there. I've been visiting with my cousin. We are following the trail of Mary Magdalene. It is so *very* interesting." Consuela took a sip of tea.

"How lovely. Yes, I've been to France a few times with my girlfriends—only for long weekends, though, so I didn't get to see as much as I'd like to."

"Have you been to the Languedoc?"

"No, it was Provence and the Côte d'Azur we were in."

"The Languedoc is very magical and mystical and *so* beautiful. I have the names of some nice hotels that we've stayed in— family-run. We were made very welcome. I could email them to you if you'd like, should you ever decide to go," Consuela offered as the secretary announced that the AGM would resume.

"How very kind of you. Here, let me find a pen and paper and write down my email for you," Anna said.

"Don't worry, it's on my husband's computer, I'm sure, in the *La Joya* file; I'll ask him for it. Take very good care of yourself." She patted Anna's arm.

"And you too," Anna said, touched by her compassion.

"I hope she never finds out what a shit that husband of hers is," Sally-Ann murmured as they walked back into the event room. "He doesn't deserve her. I wonder if he'll get reelected."

"Let's go see," Anna said lightly. If not for Sally-Ann, she would have slipped out of the room and gone back to her hotel and cried. Meeting everyone again had been overwhelming and she wanted to be alone.

"With the highest vote, once the proxies were counted, and by a margin of five votes, I am pleased to announce that Eduardo De La Fuente has been reelected president."

A beam of pleasure broke across the Spaniard's handsome features and Anna saw him look down at his wife and realized with a jolt that there was love in his gaze. What would possess a man to turn to someone like Jutta Sauer if he loved his wife? Had Austen ever cheated on her? She hoped not. She felt he hadn't, but men looked at infidelity differently to women, and Eduardo, at this moment, certainly looked as though his wife was the most important woman in his life. For Consuela's sake, she hoped so.

"Sally-Ann, would you mind if I went back to the hotel? I'm a bit low today," she whispered.

"Of course not, darlin'. Shall I go with you? I shouldn't have made you come," the other woman said contritely.

"I'm glad you did, actually. I feel now I've really said my good-byes and cut my ties with Spain. Once the anniversary is over, I won't come back. It's time for pastures new." She leaned over and kissed her friend on the cheek. "Go back to Cal and be happy with him the way that suits *you*," she said firmly. "Happy riding!"

Sally-Ann laughed. "I'll call y'all tomorrow, but if you need me, if you're upset, ring me, won't you?"

"I'll be fine," Anna said. "See y'all."

Walking along the narrow meandering cobbled streets back to her own hotel, Anna's heart was lacerated with grief. This was the way of it, she'd come to realize. Some days she would think she was doing really well—the couple of days with the girls had been a tonic, and she'd felt a bit like her old self again—and then out of the blue the tidal wave would sweep right back in and she'd be back at square one. Someone had said to her at Austen's funeral that grief was like a tsunami at first, but gradually the waves would weaken and lessen until they only lapped around the edges of your heart now and again.

Her heart was being battered today, but perhaps tomorrow it would be easier. She would go and sit on the peaceful terrace and look out over the narrow cove and watch the town's evening lights grow bright against the velvet sky, and sit with her sorrow and hope that it would ease away.

◆

Eduardo glanced at his watch. It was almost nine p.m. and there was no sign of Jutta. And her phone was going to voicemail. Something must have cropped up. Something to do with her daughter? he pondered. But it would have been good manners, *and* professional, to let him know that she was being delayed. All around him people were drinking and celebrating at one of the barbecue nights held in La Joya to promote friendship and good-neighborliness. Even Beatriz had joined the party and was seated, chatting to Gabriel's wife and sipping a dry sherry. Consuela was in intense conversation with some Dutch woman who was into the esoteric stuff she filled her head with. Eduardo, while he waited for Jutta, was being as charming as he could manage, especially to the owners who had voted him back for another year. It was part of the duties of a *presidente* to mix with the proprietors and be convivial on nights such as this.

Out of the corner of his eye, he noticed a light come on up in "his" penthouse. Had Jutta thought to meet him up there? He felt a flicker of nervous anticipation.

He moved away from the pool area with its twinkling party lights and scented incense sticks and flickering candles and hurried across the lawn towards the entrance to the block. He and Constanza held master keys to all the entrance halls, and he slipped inside and saw that the lift was stopped on the *Ático* floor.

She must be waiting for him there, he thought, slightly stunned at her brazenness as he pressed the button to call the lift. She must realize there could be no repeat of their previous encounter, especially on a night such as this with his wife and Beatriz down at the pool. He straightened his hair and wiped his damp palms on his trousers and took a steadying breath before knocking on the door.

Eduardo couldn't have been more shocked to see the Englishman from whom he'd bought the penthouse standing there. "Why are you here?" he asked, perplexed.

"I still own the place, De La Fuente. I'm entitled to be here."

"But I thought you were selling up and paying us your arrears—"

"Don't bloody start; you'll get your money. You were supposed to be getting it today, but the bloody bitch that was buying it never showed up. I wasted money I don't have flying over, and I wasted four hours sitting in that fucking notary's office in Marbella. A wasted fuckin' journey. Now leave me in peace. I've not had a good day. And now I've to go and find another buyer. Bloody hell!"

The door was slammed shut in Eduardo's face. He made his

way into the lift and leaned against the wall when the door closed, his heart pounding so fast he thought he was going to faint.

"The bloody bitch who was buying it never showed up!"—that was what the Englishman had said. But there must be some mistake. Jutta had texted to say that everything was fine and the deal was closed.

He pressed the redial number again when he reached the ground floor and yet again it went to voicemail, but this time the tinny voice said that the mailbox was full and he could not leave a message. A cold sweat broke out on Eduardo's forehead and he half walked, half ran along the footpath to his own block. Five minutes later he was sitting at his computer, checking his bank account. There was no mistake. Four hundred and fifty thousand euros had been debited from his account and credited to the client account of Ms. Jutta Sauer. What was going on?

He went to the bathroom and splashed cold water on his face. There must be some logical explanation. He must stay calm.

He went back to the party and excused himself to the woman who was in conversation with Consuela. "*Querida*, I have a migraine coming on. Would you excuse me if I left and went to bed? Beatriz is enjoying the evening; it would be a shame to spoil it for her, so I won't bid her good night."

"It's probably after all the worry and stress of today, Eduardo. You must not take it all so seriously," remonstrated his wife gently. "I'll be very quiet when I go to bed and try not to wake you."

"Thank you, Consuela, I'll see you in the morning," he said, bending to kiss her cheek. He walked back to his apartment in a daze. This had to be some sort of nightmare. He couldn't think the unthinkable. Jutta was a conscientious woman with high business ethics, if not morals.

Tomorrow all would be sorted and his fears would come to naught, he was sure of it, Eduardo reassured himself as he undressed in the dark and got into bed—then lay wide-eyed and fearful, all kinds of scenarios going through his head.

Chapter Forty-Seven

Jutta / Felipe / Eduardo

At least Alicia was asleep, in the window seat, curled up catlike in a ball, her thumb in her mouth. The aisle seat in their three-seat row was empty and Jutta could leave her travel bag on it, free to take out whatever child-care items she needed on the flight to Istanbul. They were flying economy on the Boeing 737, and she longed to stretch her legs. Being tall had its disadvantages on long flights. She glanced at her watch; they had being flying east for over two and a half hours. They should be over the Tyrrhenian Sea, heading for Italy. Still in European airspace. In another couple of hours they would be landing in Ataturk Airport in Istanbul, where Felipe would be waiting to meet them. It would not be a joyful reunion.

Anyone looking at her would think she was calm, composed, a seasoned traveler. They wouldn't believe that she was actually a thief, and a fugitive, and an accomplished liar. Jutta could hardly believe it herself. The last ten days had been the most surreal of her life—from the moment a chunky, muscular bearded man in his fifties, wearing an ill-fitting blue suit that hardly seemed to contain his barrel chest, had walked through her office door and introduced himself as Fedor Orlov, a friend of her husband's. Jutta couldn't remember Felipe mentioning anyone of that name to her. She'd pasted on a polite smile and asked how she could help him.

"I may engage your services in the future. I hear you run an excellent business here on the Costa, I was passing, and I just wanted to drop my card in to you. Do give Felipe my best wishes. We must all have dinner sometime," he said in his broken English. His eyes were watchful, flitting around the office, taking everything in. Jutta felt uncomfortable and took an instant dislike to him.

"I'm sure my husband can arrange that," she said politely. "Thank you for dropping in, but I'm afraid I have clients to meet and greet at one of my apartments, so I must leave now."

"But of course, drive carefully in that big old Mercedes of yours." He smiled, but the smile didn't reach his eyes, which were hard and watchful. How did he know that she drove a Merc? she wondered, watching him leave and nod politely at her secretary. Perhaps Felipe had mentioned it.

"Fedor Orlov came to your *office*!" The horror in her husband's voice when she phoned him as she drove along the A-7 shocked her.

"Why? What's wrong with that?"

"*Jesucristo*, Jutta, this isn't good. Tell me *exactly* what he said."

". . . And then he told me to drive carefully in that old Mercedes of mine. How did he know I drove an old Merc, Felipe? What's going on?" she demanded, driving onto the slip road to get to the apartment block.

"This isn't good . . . this isn't good at all," muttered her husband. "Where are you now?"

"I'm doing a meet and greet in Jasmine Gardens. Why? What's the problem, Felipe? Tell me."

"I'll meet you in the Don Carlos at twelve, OK? I've things to do. I'll see you then." He hung up abruptly and she shook her head. He was driving her mad lately. He was distracted, moody, irritable, and when she asked him how work was going, he'd clam up and say he was dealing with it.

He was sitting on one of the big orange sofas in the foyer, waiting for her, but the hotel was busy, with people milling around, and he stood up and said, "We need to talk somewhere private. Let's go outside to the terrace."

"It's August in the Costa del Sol. You're not going to get anywhere private here," she'd said crossly, annoyed that she had to factor in this meeting when she could ill afford the time.

A couple were just standing up from a table under the shade of a massive palm tree. "Sit there. I'll get us coffee," he ordered, and only then did she notice how utterly stressed he looked, a gray hue overtaking his sallow complexion. Jutta felt a knot in her stomach. He was probably going to tell her he was bankrupt or something. She wouldn't be surprised. She'd been half expecting it, she thought morosely. Thank God she had her own business and it was totally separate from his. It looked like she'd be paying the bills for the foreseeable future.

"Tell me what's going on right now, Felipe," she demanded when he arrived back with two coffees and a large tuna-and-salad roll cut in half. He gave her one half and started eating the other.

"It's like this," her husband said, wiping tuna flakes from his mouth before swallowing a slug of coffee. "I got involved with some Russians over a land deal and I can't pay them back at the moment—"

"Russians!" She couldn't believe her ears. "You got involved with *Russians*. You fucking *Arschloch*, Felipe. You know what they're like. They're hoodlums if you get on the wrong side of them."

"I know. We have to get the hell away from Spain, Jutta. If they don't get the money from me, they'll come looking for it from you. That's why that thug Orlov visited you today. He was just letting me know that they'll get their money one way or another."

"How much?" Jutta demanded, sick to her stomach.

"Two hundred thousand euros," he muttered.

"I don't have two hundred thousand. *Jesu*, are you mad?"

"Jutta, I'm telling you now we have to get out of here—"

"*You* have to get out of here," she said angrily, her voice raised.

"Shush," he hissed. "Don't draw attention to us. Even if I go, they'll come after you. That's what that visit was about this morning."

"But *I* don't have any dealings with them," she protested heatedly.

"That doesn't matter to them. You're my wife, you run a business, you have money, and they want theirs. It's that simple."

"Well, fuck you, Felipe, for bringing this threat to me. How could you?" she raged.

"Look, it's done now and we have to deal with it. Remember when I went to Cyprus a while back?"

"What about it?" she said, in turmoil. All around her, tourists were laughing and chatting and lazing in the sun, and her life was collapsing around her ears.

"I've had a look around Famagusta and Kyrenia, the tourist cities in the north; it's a nice place. We could start afresh. I have a plan," he said.

"I've had enough of your plans," she said bitterly.

"Well, if you don't want the Russians knocking on your door, and they *will* keep knocking and they'll start making threats," he said grimly, "you'd better listen."

"I won't do it, Felipe," she said, outraged when he outlined his proposal.

"That's up to you, Jutta. I'm getting out. I have my bags packed; they're in the boot of my car. I'm taking a room in the Ibis, at the airport, and I'm flying to Istanbul tomorrow, and then on to Cyprus."

"You're leaving . . . just like that? What about Alicia?" She was stunned.

"If I stay here, I'm in trouble and in danger. Those guys don't mess around. I *have* to go, Jutta, and *you* have to come with me. I'll go and rent us a place to live and we'll take it from there. Just do exactly what I tell you and we can make a fresh start. There's no extradition north of the Green Line."

A fresh start, Jutta thought bitterly as the plane bumped across Italy. She could never look herself in the eye again. Eduardo's hard-earned money, which had been sitting in her client account, had gone to pay off the Russians, and the rest was in a bank account in Germany, opened when she'd visited her father and ready to be transferred to a bank account in Cyprus as soon as she set it up. Every fiber in her being hated what she'd done to the Spaniard.

How ashamed her father and mother would be of her; how ashamed she was of herself.

Poor Eduardo, had he discovered yet that she'd skipped the country? No doubt he was phoning her to see where she was. He could phone all he liked. The SIM card was cut in pieces and floating somewhere in the sewage pipes at Málaga Airport, where she'd flushed them down the toilet before checking in.

Jutta sat exhausted, listening to the thrum of the engines. There was yet another ordeal she had to endure before she landed in Istanbul. She pressed her call button and when the stewardess came she said calmly, "Could you keep an eye on my daughter, please? I need to use the restroom."

"Of course, madame," the young woman said.

Jutta made her way up the aisle and let herself into the narrow cubicle. She opened her handbag and took out the pregnancy test kit she'd bought that morning before leaving for the airport.

She unzipped her trousers and pulled her clothes down and squatted and peed over the stick and placed it beside the sink while she adjusted her clothing and washed her hands. She really didn't need the test to know she was pregnant. It had hit her like a ton of bricks when she'd been sitting in her office two days previously, wondering why she was so extraordinarily weary.

Not since she'd been pregnant with Alicia had she ever felt so exhausted, she thought idly, and then she knew! She and Felipe had talked about having another child so that Alicia would have a sibling. She'd stopped using contraception but wasn't particularly interested in calculating her fertile times. If it happened, it happened. Why now, just when she needed a pregnancy like a hole in the head? A thought struck her and an image floated into her consciousness as she watched two faint blue lines appear and grow brighter.

"*Oh mein Gott!*" she exclaimed in dismay. With all that was going on in her life, she'd given it no thought. With uncharacteristic recklessness and lack of foresight, she'd used no protection on the night of her torrid sexual encounter with Eduardo. Was this child his?

Could this nightmare get any worse? Jutta deliberated, making her way back to her seat just as they hit turbulence and Alicia woke up and started to howl. She managed to soothe her with the help of a lollipop and eventually the toddler fell asleep again, leaving Jutta to her thoughts.

"No extradition north of the Green Line"—Felipe's words came to mind. She was now a fugitive. No doubt they would be reported to the police and Interpol would be informed. She had two passports, German and Spanish. Which should she use?

Silent tears slid down Jutta's cheeks. She suddenly longed to be in Dornburg and feel the comfort and security of home. Longed to be with Oskar now that she knew she couldn't. Would she ever have security again? She didn't think so. There was no fresh start in Cyprus. She would be trapped on the island, living with the husband she'd lost all respect for, and everything she'd ever dreamed off was now well and truly beyond her reach.

◆

"She's not answering her phone. There's been no word from her. Her husband isn't answering his phone, either, Señor De La Fuente," Jutta's secretary said, trying to maintain an air of unruffled composure. "If I hear anything, I'll get back to you immediately."

"Please do, it's of the *utmost* importance," he barked, and she glared at the phone as he hung up.

"Join the queue," she muttered. The phone hadn't stopped ringing all morning. Clients had arrived at their holiday apartments and hadn't been met by Jutta with the keys. The office of the notary in Marbella had been on the phone yet again, having made several calls the previous day asking for her whereabouts.

Jutta's au pair had phoned, having come back to the apartment after Jutta had given her an unexpected day off, to find no trace of her employers and their toddler. The wardrobes were mostly empty, she reported, mystified.

"I think Jutta's gone for good," Christine confided to the office manager.

"Don't say that! We haven't been paid this month," the other woman exclaimed, tapping swiftly on her keyboard.

"*Madre de Dios,*" she muttered. "You're right! The client account is empty, closed. Jutta's done a disappearing act and left us to deal with it. Print off her client list right now. Don't answer the phone. You and I'll have to relocate, but we can keep up the cleaning and maintenance end and set up on our own if we play our cards right," Olga said grimly. She'd always thought Jutta's professional integrity was too good to be true. And now she'd been proved right. The German woman was clearly a thief, for all her sanctimonious pontifications about the underhanded Spanish that Olga had been forced to listen to over the years. But still, it was hard to believe that only the day before yesterday she'd been making out the roster for the cleaners and today Jutta Sauer Perez had vanished, leaving chaos in her wake.

◆

It seemed the unthinkable had happened, Eduardo thought bleakly, staring at his phone. He'd once again phoned Jutta's office, and they had no idea where she was. But Eduardo knew in his gut that the German woman had absconded with his money. It seemed yet another woman had grievously betrayed him. His plan to buy the penthouse had been the most impulsive decision of his life, and now his imprudent behavior would cost him dearly.

He'd been so sure that he could trust Jutta. Now his lack of judgment—something he'd always prided himself on—would haunt him for the rest of his life.

He took a deep breath and walked back along the boardwalk to La Joya. He'd taken the walk to make his phone calls in private, and to walk his dog. The apartment was no place for the conversations he was having, with Consuela and Beatriz within hearing distance.

He glanced at his watch; in another hour or so he'd be taking Isabella to Málaga Airport for her flight to New York. He would have the return journey to make more calls and absorb the enormity of his loss, financial and other. His eyes darkened, remembering his encounter with Jutta. Had that been a ploy to lull him into a false sense of security? Had she been that calculating? What a fool he was. An absolute and complete fool. There were probably more of his father's genes in him than he cared to know.

"What's wrong with you, Eduardo?" Isabella asked quietly as he drove them along the motorway east towards Málaga two hours later.

"Why do you ask me that?" he answered, surprised by her perception.

"I know when someone is putting on a front. I did it long enough when my marriage to Santiago was breaking down." She turned and smiled at him. "You're here physically, but mentally you're elsewhere, and wherever you are it's a dark place."

"*Madre . . .*" He used the word out of habit, but to his surprise he realized that, despite all that had been revealed to him, he still considered Isabella to be his mother. "*Madre . . .*" he repeated slowly. "*Mama*, can I tell you things that I can never tell anyone else and that I wish no one else to know?"

"Of course, *mi querido*, I would be honored to be your confidante," Isabella said warmly.

And so, between Calahonda and Málaga Airport, Eduardo broke the habit of a lifetime and revealed his innermost secrets to the woman he called mother. Isabella listened quietly, interjecting a pertinent comment here and there, and when he'd finished the whole sorry saga, she said, "A secret shared is no longer a secret, so let it go and don't dwell on it. Move forward and deal with your financial losses." She reached across and stroked his arm. "Tell Consuela about the penthouse," Isabella advised. "Share that with her, because she will only worry, knowing that you are worried about something. Consuela loves you, Eduardo. She's a very special person. Share your life and your joys and your fears with her. Forget about that other woman. We all make foolish mistakes at some time in our lives. Even you," she teased gently, and he laughed and felt unbelievably unburdened.

"*Gracias*," he said, "for listening and understanding and for not judging me."

"That's what mothers do, Eduardo. You will always be my beloved son. That will never change for me."

"Thank you, *Mama*," he said with heartfelt gratitude as the knots of bitterness he'd carried all his life at her perceived desertion of him untangled and drifted away, leaving Eduardo experiencing an unexpected sense of liberation, feeling more loved than he'd ever felt in his entire life, despite the unholy mess he was now mired in.

Epilogue

Anna closed her eyes and listened to the priest perform the anniversary Mass for Austen, in the little peaceful church of San José. The scents of polish, candle wax, and jasmine intermingled and the rays of the sun diffused into prisms of golds, reds, blues, and greens through the stained-glass window. The day she'd dreaded for so long was finally here. Strange though it was, in the previous year she'd been able to think, *Austen and I were doing such and such on this date or the other,* and she would draw those memories to herself and relive them. It had been a comfort of sorts. That last link was gone now. She'd spent a year without her beloved husband. There would be no more "this time last year." It was time to move on.

She glanced at her daughters beside her, each lost in their own world as they stared ahead in the dim, cool light. She would return to Ireland with them the following day and begin this new chapter of her life. And she would make sure to take time for herself and not make the mistake she'd made of giving all of herself to them and her grandchildren as she had in the past.

She'd been touched to see Sally-Ann and Cal in the pew behind them, and Consuela in a seat opposite and Constanza Torres behind her. People were kind, she reflected gratefully, as the priest raised his hand in a final blessing.

Sally-Ann and Cal had left after Communion, as Cal had a business meeting he'd had to attend in Marbella. Constanza pressed a Mass card and a candle in her hand. "You are in my prayers, Anna," she said simply, and kissed her cheek.

"Thank you, Constanza. So kind of you to come," Anna murmured, squeezing her hand. Several other neighbors and acquaintances came to pay their condolences and eventually they drifted away and the church grew still.

Anna sat in the peaceful silence, letting thoughts drift past as Chloe and Tara lit candles for Austen.

"Señora MacDonald, I just wanted to wish you every blessing in your life," Consuela De La Fuente said softly, stepping into the pew to greet her.

"Oh, please call me Anna," she urged. "And thank you *so* much for coming today, I'm very touched by your kindness."

"*Gracias*, Anna. You must call me Consuela. I just wanted you to know that I have sent you an email with the names of the hotels in France. I feel the Languedoc is a place you would find healing," she said earnestly.

"Thank you. I think I'll take your advice, Consuela. The memories in Spain are too sad now. It's time to find somewhere new."

"Yes, life is a journey with many twists and turns. May your new path be peaceful, Anna. I'll keep you in my prayers."

That evening, after she'd dined with her daughters, Anna had gone for a walk alone on the beach and sat on a wooden bench and gazed unseeingly out over the little cove where she'd found a measure of peace in the last few weeks.

Her phone rang, breaking the silence, and she saw Sally-Ann's name. Sally-Ann was insisting upon driving them to the airport the following morning and wouldn't take no for an answer. Perhaps there was a problem. "Hi," she answered, walking down to the water's edge.

"Y'all will *never* guess what's happened!" Sally-Ann said breathlessly.

"What?" Anna laughed, amused at her friend's sense of drama.

"Jutta and the husband have ripped off a load of folks, including some of us in La Joya! And it looks like they've gone on the lam. She cleaned out her client account and left her staff high and dry without being paid, and *he* owes money all over the place. Cal's lost about fifty thou! That's why he had to go to the meeting today. Can y'all believe it?" Sally-Ann was still gobsmacked.

"You're joking me? I don't *believe* it. *Jutta!* Miss High and Mighty herself?" Anna was astounded.

"Believe it, then. All the people in La Joya, including *moi*, that have paid our yearly fees to her have been dang well *defrauded* by Miss Holier-Than-Thou! Some folk even had their tax monies taken as well as their fees, because doing tax returns, and paying them for clients, was one of the services she provided."

"She is the *last* person in the world I would have expected to do something like that. You never know, do you!" said Anna in disbelief.

"Imagine if they all knew what I'd seen her up to with *El Presidente*," Sally-Ann exclaimed. "Behind that cool exterior there's one wild gal!"

"Poor Consuela. I hope she never finds out about *that*," Anna murmured.

"Well, she won't hear it from these lips. So unless anyone else saw them, and I really wouldn't think so, their sordid little secret is safe with me. I'll see y'all around nine-thirty tomorrow morning."

"Thanks, Sally-Ann, you're a pal," Anna said gratefully.

"And so are you," said the Texan before hanging up.

Her friendship with Sally-Ann was one of the gifts she would take from her time in Spain, Anna thought as she packed her clothes in the big blue suitcase she used to share with Austen. The familiar stabbing ache battered her heart but she carried on until everything was neatly stashed away, apart from her nightie, her toilet bag, and what she was wearing the following day.

She recalled Consuela's words about the twists and turns on the path of life and remembered that the Spanish woman had sent her an email. She picked up her iPad and went and sat out on the deck chair on her balcony.

She read the descriptions of the hotels in Carcassonne, and Lourdes, and Montségur, and the Midi that Consuela had so thoughtfully provided, and followed some of the links that gave a history of the Cathar country. It was fascinating. She *would* go to France for her next holiday, Anna decided. That was where her journey would lead next.

I have taken the liberty of choosing a card for you from my Mary Magdalene pack. I asked her that you be given the message you need right now and this is what came for you from the Magdalene's own card. I hope you don't mind, Consuela had added at the end of her email.

"How thoughtful," Anna murmured, intrigued. What would be her message? She scrolled down along the email and read:

Magdalene
Go forth and be true to yourself
Dare to be different
To make mistakes
Create, for it is in creation that you exist
In a world full of dreams that stem from your heart
In oneness, love and hatred
Wonder and awe, softness and pain, joy and light.
In the stillness the unknown awaits
A void wanting to be filled
Step into it with courage and strength
Like a budding rose reaching for the light
Love will lead you to greener pastures
Keep your pockets full of dreams

For life is a test of faith.
Allow your light to shine
There is no beginning or end,
There is only love!

Tears came to Anna's eyes and she wept for all that she'd lost. And yet she knew that Austen would never truly leave her. He was all around her in every sweet memory that she held dear in her heart. Memories she would keep as long as she lived, and for all eternity.

◆

"It's nice to have the apartment to ourselves again," Consuela remarked, handing her husband a glass of dry sherry and settling down with her glass of red wine. They were sitting on their sofa with the balcony doors open, listening to the rain hammer down on the ground outside. Growls of thunder rumbled out to sea and lightning zigzagged on the horizon. Consuela was grateful for the turn in the weather. The thunderstorms would cool and clear the clammy air. She was waiting for their chicken casserole to finish cooking and had suggested a pre-dinner drink.

"It *is* nice, but Beatriz enjoyed herself and so did my mother," Eduardo said. It was a week since the AGM; he'd taken Beatriz home on the AVE and had come back to spend the final few days of his holidays with his wife.

"That year went by very fast," Consuela observed, enjoying the tangy red.

"Yes, this time *two* years ago we were having a tiff and you were staying with Catalina," he reminded her with a smile.

"Ah, yes, the start of my pause from men," Consuela said with a twinkle. "I've settled down more lately, have I not?"

"You have," he agreed, "and as always you're very kind to me and most hospitable to my family. I very much appreciate it," he said gravely.

"Eduardo, *mi esposo*, you are troubled these last few days; I know by you and by the way you're behaving," she said calmly. "Is it something that you can tell me about?"

"Am I so easy to read?" he asked, remembering his conversation with Isabella and how she'd known that he was preoccupied.

"When you live with someone, you get to know their humors and ways very well. I always know when you're troubled. I'm your wife," she added. "I hear you tossing and turning at night as you've done all this week."

"You won't like what I have to tell you," he said slowly. "I've been very foolish."

"Tell me," she invited, moving to sit closer to him.

He took her hand in his. "I wanted it to be a surprise for you and Beatriz," he began. "An even bigger surprise than this apartment was."

"And what happened?" Consuela looked at him, her brown eyes shaded with concern. Eduardo took a deep breath and for the second time he told one of the women in his life of a mistake he'd made. He only told of the one; the other, the night of shame with Jutta, Consuela would never know about. He wouldn't hurt the woman who loved him and whom he'd taken so much for granted.

"*Dios,*" Consuela exclaimed, stunned. She stared at her husband, wondering how *he*, of all people, could have behaved so recklessly. So much of their savings lost, and a mortgage to pay at this stage of their lives.

"*Lo siento,*" he muttered, turning away from his wife, who stood up, aghast, trying to absorb what he'd just told her.

Sorry, thought Consuela furiously. Was that the best he could do? What good was "sorry"?

"Why?" she demanded, bewildered. "Why?"

"I wanted to surprise you," he said simply.

"Oh, you have, Eduardo," she retorted bitterly. "A *great* surprise. I need to be by myself for a while." She walked out of the lounge to Beatriz's bedroom and sat on the bed. Why was this happening? She shook her head. Of course she knew. She hadn't spent the past two years delving deep into metaphysics not to know that this was a life lesson, a spiritual growth opportunity for her husband and herself.

Why did his lessons have to impact so greatly on her? she thought petulantly, listening to the great roars of thunder rending the skies. Couldn't he have his own "growth" opportunities and leave her out of them? She'd enough of her own to cope with.

Consuela gave a wry smile. It didn't work like that, she knew. She was being disingenuous. It was now, in this time of upheaval, that her greatest test would be. Had she absorbed any of the knowledge she'd learned? Now was the time to truly put it into practice. She could sink into old ways and old patterns of thought and behavior . . . or not. The choice was hers.

But all that hard-earned money *scammed* because Eduardo wanted to *surprise* her! Consuela knew better than that. Eduardo hadn't been completely honest. She knew her husband well. He'd wanted to own a penthouse so he could lord it around La Joya and quietly boast about it in Madrid. And he wanted to impress Beatriz. It was all about his complicated relationship with his aunt. Who was the teacher and who was the pupil in *their* complex waltz?

Consuela took a deep breath and stood up. Eduardo was where she'd left him, slumped despondently on the sofa, his face gray, and creased with anxiety.

"You know," she said, sitting down beside him, "I have learned much on this journey of discovery that I've begun, and one of the things I've come to know is that experiences such as this happen for a reason. There are lessons we've come back to learn and sometimes what can seem the *worst* thing to happen to us can actually turn out to be the best. This is a turning point for you, Eduardo. You've been brought to your knees because the universe is trying to get your attention. *Listen* to what life is telling you."

"That I'm a fool and I don't deserve a wife like you, is it?" he said dejectedly.

"Don't say that. In time you'll know what this is all about. We can sell this apartment to help pay off the debt, or we can cash in some investments or shares," she suggested. "We have options, fortunately. Strange, I never liked that Jutta woman. She was always so sure of herself. Arrogant, even. She's on her journey too. There can be no happiness for her, stealing from people. I pity her."

"Really! *Pity*? I *hate* her!" exploded Eduardo.

"Don't hate, it only comes back to you, and damages *you*, not the person it's directed at. At the end of the day we're *all* from the one Source no matter who we are, sinner or saint," Consuela sighed, getting up to go out to the kitchen to take their meal out of the oven.

He'd expected anger, shock—tears, even—not this calm, almost fatalistic acceptance of their new predicament. He could see Consuela moving around the kitchen, surprisingly composed after her initial outburst.

Isabella and now Consuela had surprised him by their reactions to his tales of woe. Did women know something that men did not? Eduardo pondered. Was this the Divine Feminine Energy that Consuela and Catalina were always talking about together? It was a balm to torment if so. Perhaps he should read some of those books his wife read and expand his outlook somewhat. It was certainly working for Consuela.

Eduardo felt weary in every bone, but at least his secrets were no longer secrets, as Isabella had pointed out earlier. He would sleep better tonight than he had for the past week, having made part confession to his wife. For the first time since Jutta had betrayed him, he felt like eating. The casserole that Consuela was dishing out smelled delicious. He refilled her glass and hesitated before filling his own sherry glass up. He didn't want to turn into a drinker, but he'd been through a lot this week. One extra glass of sherry wouldn't kill him or turn him into an alcoholic.

How lucky he was that his wife had not abandoned him to

deal with his catastrophe alone. He'd made one exceptionally good decision in his life and that was marrying Consuela. Although he'd never realized it until now, he had three remarkable women in his life. That had to count for something.

◆

Consuela flavored the casserole with just the amount of salt and pepper that her husband liked. Now that he'd unburdened himself to her, he might be able to enjoy his meal instead of picking at his food as he had for the past week. She was relieved that she knew what was at the root of his agitation. She wouldn't have to drag it out of him and endure his moody silences.

Eduardo had chosen a hard lesson to learn. He would come to realize that money was merely energy to be used for good or bad, and that material possessions didn't matter in the long run. He'd started to change, although he didn't realize it, she reflected, ladling pieces of tender chicken on his plate. The old Eduardo would never have told her what had happened, and the old Eduardo would certainly never have said, "I'm a fool and I don't deserve a wife like you." The learning of humility was never easy, and that was his first lesson. Others would come thick and fast. In the words of that famous old Doris Day song that she'd come to hold as her mantra, "Que Sera, Sera." What will be, will be. She wouldn't abandon her husband in his hour of need, but neither would she give up her own voyage of discovery, wherever it would lead her, Consuela promised herself. Who knew if they would stay together or go their separate ways; that was a decision for the future. *Que será, será* indeed.

She placed her husband's supper on the table. "Eat well, Eduardo. As the old adage says, 'This too shall pass.' But for now we'll forget our worries and concerns and make the most of the last few days of our holidays. We'll be back to the grindstone soon enough."

"*Gracias*, Consuela. You are a most forgiving and reassuring woman," he said gratefully.

"I am," she agreed, and laughed at the expression on his face, offering him some crusty bread to soak up his gravy.

"And I'm a very lucky man," Eduardo said ruefully, raising his glass to her.

"You are," she agreed again, and they smiled at each other and began to eat as the thunder grumbled away towards Africa.

◆

Constanza Torres studied two posters advertising cleaning and maintenance services that had been handed in to her to display. Word had got around that some owners might be interested in employing a new company to look after their apartments now that Jutta Sauer was no longer in business.

Be Clean and Atlantis Property Management and Cleaning Services were very professional. She knew Emma and Brendan, and Jason and Luis, the couples who ran the companies, and regarded them highly. She would permit the posters to hang on the noticeboard in Reception. Constanza always made sure anything on "her" noticeboard came with her imprimatur.

She logged out of her computer and glanced around her office to make sure that everything was in its place. Satisfied that this was so, she picked up the photographs given to her by Dora Sheldon from *Portal* 3. Dora, one of Constanza's spies in the camp, had photographed "Little Fat Facundo," as she liked to call him, loading busy Lizzie plants into the back of his car from a consignment delivered to La Joya to be planted in the grounds. Dora had dated the photograph. She'd also, on a different date, observed and snapped the new full-time concierge chucking a large packet of toilet rolls and a couple of bottles of cleaning spray into that self-same boot.

"Semtex wouldn't move that lazy lump, normally, but when De La Fuente's here, Little Fat Facundo is bustling around, all business and full of his own self-importance," sniffed Dora, who lived in La Joya all year round and knew everything that was going on.

"*Gracias*, Dora, this may prove *most* helpful." Constanza took the photos from the elderly lady, who gave her a wink and a thumbs-up.

So *El Presidente*'s new concierge was nothing more than a common thief, Constanza thought. Just like that Jutta Sauer.

That news had shocked Constanza to her core. She'd always thought Jutta was a lady and a trustworthy businesswoman. She'd got that wrong for sure. One thing about life in La Joya, it was *never* boring.

The news of De La Fuente's reelection had not stressed Constanza as much as it had previously. She had the measure of him now. That would make life easier. So, she'd had to reluctantly admit, did having another concierge to share the burden of work. Having shorter working hours was proving to be extremely pleasant indeed, Constanza conceded, switching out the lights and locking her office door. She would keep her ammunition close to her chest if she needed it, but for now she was still managing La Joya de Andalucía, a little piece of paradise on earth.

Acknowledgments

As always, my first acknowledgment is to my Spiritual Team led by Jesus, Mary, St. Joseph, the Divine Feminine Energy of Mary Magdalene, Saints Michael and Anthony (the stalwarts), and all my Angels, Saints, and Guides. My books would never be written without your Divine Inspiration.

Thanks to my dear and precious dad, for all your prayers, for the fun, laughs, and fascinating chats we had, and for setting a fine example to me of how to handle life's difficulties. I will miss you more than I can say. You were an outstanding father.

To my sister, Mary, who is always there to share the highs and lows and without whom I would never get my books written.

To Yvonne and Breda (and Mary), my Besties, for inspiring some of the scenes in this book. It was such fun writing them and I love our jaunts away and our "girls' nights"!

To my family, especially my nieces, who keep me au fait with trends, makeup, and slang, for my younger characters.

To Helen Gleed, my fantastic publicity manager and a dear friend. What would I do without you?

To my much loved "Tribe" and Soul Family: Aidan, Murtagh, Joe, Pam, and Simon for true friendship and constant, kind encouragement and sound advice for the Field project, and to Dr. Mary Helen Hensley, and Mrs. Helen Hensley (Mama H.) likewise, and huge gratitude also for your sound advice on all things southern, Texan, and American, for the character of Sally-Ann and her family. ("We's just folks!")

To Geraldine Tynan and Marian Lawlor, the most loyal friends I could wish for.

To Sarah Lutyens, my rock and wonderful agent, and to Felicity, Jane, Daisy, Juliet, Susannah, and Francesca at Lutyens & Rubinstein (and Gillian, who is also striding up the publishing ladder). Thanks, my dears, for all the hard work you do on behalf of me and all your authors.

I have a wonderful team behind me at S&S UK, USA, Australia, India, and worldwide. A huge thanks to Jo Dickinson, my steadfast and very dear editor. It is a joy to work with you. And to Carla Josephson, Sally Partington, and all in editorial. To Dawn, SJ, Rich, and all my Schusters in the various departments, a massive "thank you."

To Judith Curr in Atria Books, and my American editor, Jhanteigh Kupihea, thank you and all my US Schusters for your enthusiasm and continued support.

To my Schusters in Australia and in India, far away but much appreciated for the great work you do on my behalf.

To all my translators, foreign publishers, and subagents: it is such a thrill to see my books in other languages.

I have the best publishers' agents *ever*. To Simon, Dec, Eamonn, Nigel, and of course Helen at Gill Hess & Co, there aren't enough thanks.

◆

There are some very special people I'd like to thank who have helped me and my family in ways that there aren't enough words to say thanks.

To all my extended family, especially our great cousins, and to Betty Halligan, the administrator of St. Aidan's cemetery, Kilrane.

To Fr. Brendan Quinlan, our friend and pastor and our rock in times of trouble. Thank you for your great kindness to my late mother and father.

Thanks also to Fr. Joe and Fr. Harry, Noel Horgan, the bereavement group, and the choir in Our Mother of Divine Grace Parish, Ballygall.

To Dr. Fiona Dennehy, Nurse Maria, Mary, Noreen, Doreen, and all the staff of the Cremore Clinic for your great care and kindness to my parents over the years. We are very grateful to you all.

To Mr. Hannan Mullet, Grainne Roche, and Finn and Orla, and Mr. Denis Collins and Sheena Murtagh, I am in your debt and am so grateful for all you've done for me. And to all the staff in the SSC for terrific care when I had my hip op.

To Professor Joe Duggan, Dr. Denise Sadlier, Laura, Tara, Sara, Karen, Joe, Paula, and all the nurses and carers on St. Benedict's ward, and to Professor J. Egan, Siobhan Ryan, Jackie, Linda, and all the very kind kitchen staff, who gave me and the family many cups of welcome tea, and to all in the Mater Private Hospital: your kindness and care are greatly appreciated. Thanks also to Fr. Kieran, hospital chaplain, for his very kind care of Dad.

A very special thanks also to Kamila, Dave, and all the staff of Oakwood, and to Beneavin House for your immense kindness.

And our most grateful thanks to Keith Massey and his team at Masseys Funerals for taking care of our dad and us, as he did for our late mother. You are exceptional and kind beyond words.

A very special thanks also to Toni Carmine Salerno, gifted artist and bestselling author, who generously permitted me to quote from his beautiful Magdalene Oracle Cards.

Thanks also to Mary Mitchell of Green Angel Skincare for your very generous contributions to our Facebook competitions.

And finally, and most importantly, a huge thanks to all in the book trade worldwide who have supported each and every one of my books. And to my dear and ever-loyal readers and Facebook followers, you are the ones that make the writing of my novels such a rewarding and gratifying endeavor. The pleasure I get from your enjoyment of my writing means so much. Thank you, m'dears. XXX